Alexandra Jones·was born in 1943 in India of British parents in the Colonial Service. She has won prizes for her short stories, and was for a long time the secretary of her local writing circle. She now lives in Kent, and is married with three sons. SAMSARA is her second novel to be published.

Also by Alexandra Jones from Futura

MANDALAY

ALEXANDRA JONES

SAMSARA

Futura

A Futura Book

ISBN 0 7088 4204 6

Reproduced, printed and bound in Great Britain by
Hazell Watson & Viney Limited
Member of BPCC Limited
Aylesbury, Bucks, England

Futura Publications
A Division of
Macdonald & Co (Publishers) Ltd
66–73 Shoe Lane
London EC4P 4AB
A member of Maxwell Pergamon Publishing Corporation plc

To Dennis

L. Balkash

L. Ozero

'RUSSIA'

S I N

Samarakand

TADZHIKISTAN

Khotan

AFGHANISTAN

Hunza
Baltit
Karakoram Mts.

Ladakh
Leh

KASHMIR
Rudok

Demchok
Thok Jalung

Indus River

Gartok
(Tsu)

Simla
Mensar
Manasarowar
Lake

Dehra Dun
Nagari
Hills
L H A S A

Delhi

I N D I A

.... Frontiers
------ Sonya's journey from
Samarakand to Lhasa

0   500 km

MONGOLIA

KIANG

CHINA
(With suzerainty over Tibet)

Amdo Province

TIBET

CHANG TANG
(Plateau of Tibet)

Thok Daurakpa
(16,000 ft)

Kham Province

Nam Tso

Drepung • Lhasa

Po Yul Province

Tsang Province

Shigatse   Brahmaputra River

Lhatse Gyantse   Turquoise
Tuna Thug Tso   Lake

SIKKIM BHUTAN

North East
Frontier
Agency

Yunnan

BURMA

Author's Note

Origins of 'The Great Game' between Russia and Great Britain were due to Russian expansion of her boundaries at the rate of fifty miles per day during the latter half of the 19th century. Ili 1854 (later returned to China), Tashkent 1865, Samarakand 1868, Bokhara 1869, Khiva 1873, Khokand 1876, Turkmenistan 1881, Merv 1884, Penjdeh 1885, Pamirs 1895.

Thupten Gyatso, 13th Dalai Lama, became of age and assumed power from his Regent in 1895. In flight from Tibet 1904. Exile in India until 1910. Returns to Tibet 1913. Reigns until his death in 1933.

The rare Blue Poppy was discovered by Frank Kingdon Ward in his travels through Tibet, 1908-1912. (See *Land of the Blue Poppy* by Frank Kingdon Ward.)

Acknowledgement

My grateful thanks to Michael Bailey MA (Newcastle University) for his help and cooperation during my research for Samsâra.

ABJ

Unknowable is the beginning of that long pilgrimage of beings enveloped in ignorance and who, spurred on by desire, carry on the round of rebirths and of lives renewed without ceasing.

From the *Samyutta Nikaya*

Like visions seen in a dream, so must we regard all things.

From the *Prajñâpâramitâ*

Unknowable is the beginning of things... beings veiled in ignorance who... counted on by desire, carry on the round of rebirths and of lives renewed without ceasing.

From the Samyutta-Nikaya

Like visions seen in a dream, so must we regard all things.
From the Prajñaparamita

PROLOGUE
Lhasa: Winter 1895.

Through the dark muddy alleys at the foot of the Potala, the beggars, maimed, blind and mute, slunk with the lepers and the *ro-gyapas*, butchers of corpses. They came like the dispossessed dogs that fouled the refuse-laden streets, as from the stone hovels of their misery they clawed a path to the feet of the Dalai Lama.

It was the time of the New Year Festivities, with processions and bands, pageants and religious dramas; a time to drive out the King of Impurity into the barren grasslands beyond the shimmering snow-capped hills of the city. He would take with him poverty, sickness and all the sins and misfortunes that had burdened the inhabitants of Lhasa over the past year, leaving behind only *yangku* – health, wealth and prosperity.

A servant-monk to a High Lama of the Yellow Hat sect burrowed his way to the forefront of the crowd. The humble Geyok and his master were as eager as the rest to obtain a good view of the God-King – perhaps, too, the touch of the Dalai Lama's holy staff of ribbons. Spare and bent, dressed in the brown robe of an ascetic, the Geyok's face and body were thick and smelly with smearings of yak-butter to protect his skin from icy blisters. He clutched his trident and prodded the backs of the unobservant. Immediately the Geyok and the Yellow Hat were ushered forward by the mêlée of unwashed bodies, for the holy men and

11

their revolving prayer-wheels offered a powerful protection to everyone during the Samye Ceremony.

'*Om mani padme hum! Om mani padme hum!*' Reciting the Mantra as effortlessly as breathing, the Geyok lifted reverent eyes to the rock-hill of the magnificent Potala. Dazzling tongues of ice-fire reflected gloriously from the golden roofs and myriad windows of the thirteen storey fortress; but a man could be eaten alive by scorpions in the dungeons below the Potala – the old monk knew it. He blinked nervously, prayed more loudly, turned his prayer-wheel more vigorously and hoped fervently the evil spirits would remain in the *bardo* of emptiness where the dead go.

To the melancholy wail and throb of hautboys and drums, the Dalai Lama's entourage descended the Potala Hill. Bodyguards came first, riding from the West Gate, the God-King hidden from view in a forest of ten-foot lances. An enthusiastic roar of religious fervour, a tidal wave of people, the Geyok and his master were swept along to witness the scourging of the scapegoat. Flags and banners caught by the wintry wind, the youthful Dalai Lama also shivered in the teasing chill blowing across the roof of the world. Although he had recently attained his majority and was no longer under the dominance of the Regent, fear still rode him, an oppressive cloak of uncertainty that weighed him down. Why, only last night his very own cup-bearer had died of poison! History lessons had taught him about the deaths of four of his predecessors who had died before they had begun to rule in their own right. He had, therefore, elicited the help of a *siddha*, a man of extraordinary perception, to use his magical powers upon any would-be assassin. In the *siddha*'s vision there emerged a plot by foreign devils; a foregone conclusion, for no Tibetan would ever dream of destroying a god incarnate – let alone attempting it. But the assassin had not been found before the vision faded.

Handsome and smooth-chinned, the reincarnation of Chenrezig the first Dalai Lama, Thupten Gyatso leaned forward from his gold and silver chased saddle and patted the neck of his black, well-groomed mule. Only in the company of dumb animals did he feel truly safe. His pale oblique eyes cast about warily, searching the faces in the crowd. His Court hemmed him in: ecclesiastical lords in their *shamtabs* of red, yellow, blue and gold; noble dignitaries in brocade and silk robes; burghers in Mongolian hats and expensive furs from Russia. Suddenly it all became too much. He desired to be free of such useless pomp and ceremony, and only wanted to be with his guileless people. Breaking away from the sea of lavish umbrellas, he touched his staff of ribbons to the forehead of a blind child, then another, and another, then a cripple, a beggar, a consumptive, a leper . . .

Held in the awed responses of his loyal subjects, Thupten Gyatso, smiling now, continued healing the sick. His staff of ribbons of the five sacred colours – red, blue, green, yellow and white – in silken waterfalls, touching, touching, touching the briefly animated faces of the unfortunate – until the King of Impurity stood before him. Painted half-black, half-white, the King of Impurity held a plaited black yak-tail to flay the demons, another yak-tail bound his head. Magnificent white goat-fur robes adorned him, bought on taxes of tsampa-flour and butter from the poor, and silver *trankas* from the more wealthy, who could afford to purchase a greater *yangku* on the glorious Lotus Mountain.

The Dalai Lama swayed, almost falling from his mule. Dizzily his world spun away. With an effort he collected himself, opened his eyes and stared into the wild eyes of the King of Impurity. He willed himself to touch the demonic face with his beribboned staff and murmured, '*om mani padme hum!*' The scapegoat's body contorted. Slowly he began his deadly dance with the demons that had plagued Lhasa for the past year. He gyrated to the rhythm of the chanting crowd and watchmen's whips. He grinned grotesquely. Perspiration poured from him, showering the pressing crowd in neat droplets of a salty baptism. He spun around, faster and faster. Faster and faster he revolved on his own axis in a heady whirlwind of sensation. He flirted with the spirits from the *bardo* of emptiness where the dead go. In an ecstatic posturing of demon-possession he absorbed the sins of the world. Delirious, blinded by his own potency in bartering his soul, the throbbing vibrations of the devil-dance surged crazily through him . . . Then his eyes dilated in another kind of agony, this time a soft stealthy seepage of life, his heart pierced by a cunning stiletto. His clawing hands gripped the air convulsively, and a heavy weight seemed to press him relentlessly to the ground. In a fomentation of blood-blacked lips and chin, the scapegoat's eyes glazed, rolled in their sockets, upward, to meet the eyes of Chenrezig.

The God-King, frozen in fear and the fleeting space of eye and time, could only stare down at the twitching body lying at his feet. His very own sin-eater stabbed by a treacherous hand, white goat-fur cloak stained red with blood, the demons were free again. The thirteenth Dalai Lama prayed this was not a bad omen for his future reign.

Not even the city watchmen with their plaited whips of yak-hair could find the Geyok who had cleared a path for his master, or the mysterious master himself, a High Lama of the Yellow Hat sect. Like yak-butter in a cooking pan, both had melted into the cheated crowd.

PART ONE

The Russians

Chapter One

ENGLAND
Summer 1895

Moonlight silvered the velvet-headed reed mace standing like poker-backed sentinels of the river. Water plants rustled in the dark, breathing to the agitated movements of the sooty moorhens and their chicks disturbed by the ripples from the punting-pole. White-billed coots skidded out from between the osiers and bulrushes, circles of bright water illuminating their hasty departure.

But, when Lodden lilies are tarnished by glottal stops, Lewis remembered as he punted energetically round Fiddler's Elbow, it's time to go home. After all, one can't have everything in life, he told himself sternly. All right then, an inner voice argued, maybe he was being overly fussy. Since there was no such thing as perfection, then either go home, or stop talking to himself and make the most of what he'd got.

He found an isolated rural mooring between Sandford Lock and the Radley boathouse and only wished the girl would keep her mouth shut. She giggled a lot, too, and disturbed the water birds with her fallen 'aitches and glottal stops.

'The jay makes answer as the magpie chatters, and all the air is filled with pleasant noise of waters,' Lewis said, disentangling the pole from waterweeds. He secured the punt to a willow tree trailing its supple branches in the river.

'Pardon me?'

Oh God, he groaned inwardly, wondering why he was wasting his breath on her. 'Wordsworth, actually. A quotation from *Resolution and Independence.*'

'You don't say!'

He wondered how he could have got his brains so boiled without realising it. He decided that in the morning he ought to tell Gerald his taste in women was . . . well . . . definitely gingerbread off the pantry shelf!

In the early hours she deserted him for greener pastures, and his only reason for being dismayed was the loss of such an obliging diversion. Her shoes in her hand, she scrambled up the bank and disappeared. He didn't even know her name.

The summer dawn chorus trumped the last star and Sunday morning drifted past his satiated senses. Mid-afternoon the punt began to drift downstream, its gentle yet insistent tugging on the frayed mooring-rope finally severing it from the willow. The river took her, daintily at first. Then, caught in a swift weir current, the punt gathered energy and performed a passable arabesque across the bows of a steam boat.

Lewis remained unconscious of the danger until raucous voices sounding like jackdaws in his dreams, clamoured, '*La, la, Monsieur! Oh, bon Dieu . . . qu'est-ce que cet imbecile fait dans sa bateau? Monsieur, attention, s'il vous plaît!*' Reluctantly Lewis surfaced from the bottom of the punt, wishing he had gone to sleep on the less public Cherwell. Dizzily he became aware of the danger he was in, the looming bows of the large vessel threatening to make two halves of himself and someone else's punt. He panicked head-first into the river, vaguely aware of a girl in a white lace dress doing the same – only she had done it backwards from the deck of *The Belle Dame Sans Merci*. Before Thames water numbed him completely, he wondered if he had dreamt the name.

'Oh, oh, Monsieur, I can't swim . . . !'

Lewis fought the girl, the weir currents and his own inadequacy. She refused to let go. Clinging like a limpet

18

round his neck she dragged him under time after time. Tenacious underwater weeds like an army of octopuses wanted to tether him to the bottom of the river, while above him, from the safety of the deck, the jackdaws of the boat-party were ready with all kinds of advice on life-saving techniques. But not one jumped in to help, infuriating him even more. A sudden angry upsurge of adrenalin gave him the final push he needed. Lewis caught hold of the girl's flailing arms, held her on her back with one hand under her chin and the other he used to dog-paddle his way to the river-bank. Choking out polluted water, Lewis collapsed beside the terrified girl.

She lay on her back, her eyes closed, heavy lids blue-veined. Harsh wheezing sounds gurgled from her chest. Then an ominous silence ensued. He raised his head to look at her. She wasn't breathing and was beginning to turn navy blue. Her eyes, wide open now, stared at the sky. Without a second thought Lewis whipped her onto her stomach and began artificial respiration. Trembling with river-chill, delayed reaction and pent-up agitation, he prayed the girl wasn't about to die on him.

In difficulties because the gang-plank wouldn't reach the bank, the boat-party began to get on his nerves with their puerile comments and unhelpful suggestions. It made him angrily aware of what kind of fools they were. The crisis was over by the time he received help.

The girl spewed riverwater over his cuffs and gurgled. 'Don't be so heavy-handed, you're hurting . . . '

Lewis drew a shuddering breath and stopped pumping. 'It was meant to hurt.' His voice gruff with relief, he added, 'It'll teach you not to go running around the decks of boats without a lifesaver on. Who on earth was that idiot at the wheel?'

She rolled on her back to stare up at him with grey soulful eyes. Her wet dress tautly transparent over small, scarcely developed hard breasts, he imagined she was about thirteen or fourteen, while her saucy retort gave him the distinct impression she was either putting on the agony to gain attention, or he had stupidly over-reacted to the whole situation.

19

'Who are you to tell me what to do? You're not my father.' She spoke remarkably good English but with an accent he recognised immediately as Russian. Russian nobility sometimes spoke French among themselves, and Lewis guessed that was why he had been warned off by those on deck in a language that would come to them almost instinctively.

'You certainly recover fast, young lady, and, were I your father, I'd have left you at home,' Lewis scolded. Getting over his fright, he only wished to let the whole boatload have a piece of his mind. 'You and your lot are a menace to Sunday civilisation. This river is far too narrow for a battleship like that . . . that thing over there trying to run itself aground. And who on earth was that other idiot chasing you along the decks?'

'Kirsten, he's my brother. And I think you're too young to be my father.'

'Really?' He cocked a dark eyebrow and regarded her as he knelt in the grass with one foot beside her head. Her long chestnut-brown hair like a bedraggled mermaid's, at least she was regaining a little colour in her cheeks. Now that she was out of danger he began to take stock of himself. His evening trousers were hopelessly grass-stained, while the jacket he had rolled up as a pillow in the punt, was definitely over the Abingdon Weir by now. He couldn't, however, be angry with a girl who could give a good imitation of a dying donkey, only with her short-sighted companions. Lewis turned to the sharp tap of high heels on the boat's gangplank which had, at long last, been manoeuvered into position by unskilled hands.

'Petrouska . . . mama is here now! Oh, you poor darling, it's a miracle you're still alive! This naughty man here . . . ' Lewis was vanquished with a chilling look, 'gave us all the most terrible fright! I shall never forgive him.' Long gloved arms, in a paroxysm of maternal joy, were wrapped around the girl's drenched body, squeezing the life out of her. She was kissed frenetically, over and over again.

Lewis stood up, embarrassed by the display of affection – or affectation – he didn't know which, by the woman who spoke in superlatives. Dressed in a figure-hugging navy-blue sailor costume that emphasised her pretty petiteness, a white, wide-brimmed, fruit and flower bedecked hat sitting on her head like a plate on a pyramid of warm chestnuts, icy blue eyes vanquished him yet again with another petrifying glare when he managed to shake water over her like a dog after a bath.

'Mama, don't hold me so tightly, I'm not a baby,' the girl protested, wriggling out of her mother's arms to peer self-consciously up at Lewis. Then another voice intruded, this time from the protection of *The Belle Dame Sans Merci*.

'Marya, Sonya is perfectly all right now, so don't smother her after she's been saved from drowning. Young man, you're a careless and vapid dreamer who ought to know better than to go to sleep on a busy river! You might have caused a nasty accident,' said an aging lady on deck in a canvas chair, gnarled, veined hands held one above the other on her walking stick, regarding him autocratically.

Lewis, on one foot among the celandines and wayside grasses, wrung out his socks, aware that his every action was being censored by someone aboard the boat with the unfortunate name. A dapper middle-aged gentleman regarded Lewis stonily from beside the old lady's deck chair. Then he unclamped his teeth, took his cigar from between the thin hard line of his lips, and held it in a manner that flaunted his status and wealth in Lewis's face. On the back of his left hand was a strange sickle-shaped red mark that did not escape notice.

'Who are you, young man!' he suddenly exploded. Dressed in nautical outfit, navy-blue blazer, white ducks and sea-going Captain's cap complete with anchor – or was it a Russian bear? Lewis was unable to tell at the distance – aquiline features and pale cold eyes beneath contrasting black brows and high domed forehead, scowled at Lewis in an attitude of owning the river. Lewis took an immediate dislike to him.

A younger man with a glossy brown moustache groomed to perfection, dressed like all the rest of them, pushed past Lewis making him wonder how many more Russian sailors were aboard *The Belle Dame Sans Merci*.

'Young man, I asked you who are you and where you come from?' bellowed the Russian.

'Lewis Joyden. I've come from the city,' Lewis, tight-lipped, flung back.

'Are you then at one of the Colleges?'

'I was. Not any more.' Lewis stooped to extract water-weed entangled with his shoelaces. He enjoyed the Russian bear's momentary frustration.

'Then, if I can't speak to your Dean, I'll at least speak to your father – I take it you have a father?' The question conveyed the insult well enough.

'My father would be delighted to receive you, sir. Who shall I say will be calling?'

'Count Mikail Vremya, Russian Envoy to Her Majesty Queen Victoria's Court of St James.'

Weary of the Vremyas – the fellow wasn't even an Ambassador – Lewis turned his back on them. The young man who had pushed past him so rudely turned out to be the girl's brother Kirsten. He carried his sister aboard while the mother teetered behind him in her high heels and spiked herself into the wood at each tread. The gang-plank was hauled up.

'Lewis Joyden, where does your father live?' demanded Count Vremya, behaving like a bull with a red rag.

'He's the Rector of St Anne's, not far from here. Just by Nuneham in fact,' Lewis curtly told the aggressive Count.

'I will inform him that you placed all our lives in jeopardy, and are responsible for practically drowning my daughter whose state of health is weak enough without the fear of pneumonia. If she suffers for this, I'll hold you personally responsible. And neither is my mother-in-law, the dowager Lizaveta Woodman, strong enough or young enough, to stand the strain of a broken limb – which she could easily have sustained when you tossed her out of her chair.'

'Did I?' Lewis looked astonished.

'You most certainly did – we had to slam the boat into reverse in order to save my daughter's life. It is only because I know how to handle a boat, you yourself are alive now.'

22

'Thank you, sir.'

'Hrrumph!' Count Vremya thrust his cigar back into his mouth and angrily returned to his wheelhouse.

'Mr Joyden,' said Kirsten Vremya leaning on the iron boat-rail while he lazily smoked a cigarette. 'I, too, am at Oxford . . . Radley actually, from where I think you must have pinched one of our skiffs, which alas, is no more, as my father appears to have made short work of it. My grandmother lives at Abingdon . . . perhaps you two have met each other at some time?'

'No, I don't think so. Abingdon's a big place.'

'Kirsten, don't be such a fool, of course I haven't set eyes on such a vapid young man before! If I had, I'd have remembered. Anyone who did what he did when an ocean liner is bearing down on him deserves recognition. I think it must have been a good party last night, eh, Lewis Joyden, to make you go to sleep like that?'

'Yes, Madam,' said Lewis absently, not at all amused by the discovery of having lost a friend's revered bow-tie in the pocket of his evening jacket together with his own wallet, 'very good party . . . until the Count ran me down.'

'As I thought. All the undergraduates, they are the same year after year! On the nights of their Commemoration Balls they turn this river into a boulevard in Montmartre. Have you ever been to Montmartre, Mr Joyden?'

'No, Madam.'

'Just as well. There are a lot of loose women in Montmartre. I hope your boat didn't cost you much money, otherwise you'll have to gather the pieces to sell as matchsticks.' She turned to her grandson: 'Your father is taking his time moving, Kirsten, what's the matter with the engine?'

'Nothing grandma. They're trying to get Sonya to breathe properly. Mama doesn't want the boat to move until Sonya is more physically stable in case it upsets the rhythm of her heart again.'

'It's not Sonya who's unstable but your mother – my daughter Marya, Mr Joyden. Marya is neurotic and keeps a doctor in attendance at all times – although today Anatole Pratikayit's not with us – he's gone to London on an errand. He maintains that Sonya's ills are due to the pollen of the English countryside – Sonya's only used to the pollen of the big cities, *nyet*, Kirsten?'

Grandmother Woodman gave a loud disdainful sniff and flicked a derisive hand in the air, Pratikayit obviously not to her liking. 'I live at Fairmaster Manor, Mr Joyden. It's only a short distance from the Parish of St Anne's – as the crow flies, that is, otherwise it's inclined to be all up-hill and down-dale. Come and see me tomorrow when we shall be able to talk in more comfortable surroundings. Go home now before you catch your death – we're preoccupied with that kind of nonsense in our family.'

The Belle Dame Sans Merci began to pull away into the mainstream of the river. Aboard, Madam Lizaveta Woodman, her dark Slavic eyes fixed upon Lewis still hopping about among celandines while he wrung out his clothes, directed her walking stick at her grandson's elbow to shift him from her line of vision and, leaning forward from her canvas chair, called shrilly; 'You might like to tell your father I've heard of his reputation though I'm not one of his parishioners. I'm Russian Orthodox and never renounced my faith even for my English husband. He's dead now, so we'll leave him in peace. To get to the point, I believe the Rectory garden is unique. Tell your father its fame has spread so much, I'd like to visit it, one day.'

Lewis smiled. 'Yes, he spends a great deal of time on it. He'd be delighted to show you around.'

'By the way, Mr Joyden, Mikail's bite is very much worse than his bark, and he'd see you in Siberia for what you did to Sonya. Don't forget to get out of those wet things as soon as possible, but preferably not here!'

Shaking his head in bemusement Lewis wondered what he had done to Sonya Vremya apart from saving her life – for which he had received precious little thanks. The strange Russian woman waved to him energetically; an overdressed marionette in black, her teeth like yellowed tombstones set in the dark cavity of her mouth and against the stark whiteness of her over-powdered complexion.

Five hours after his ducking Lewis, on his bicycle, pedalled furiously from his lodgings opposite his old College in St Aldate's over Folly's Bridge and past Christchurch Meadow. He took the tow-path to St Anne's. Panting hard, but at least dry and presentable once more, he propped his bone-shaker against the smooth mellow walls of his father's Rectory, and took several deep breaths.

Evening shadows stretched langorously to the lych-gate. Birdsong, sweetly muted, hung on the scarcely hushed notes of the church organ while the house in which he had been born and brought up unfailingly distilled its haunting sadness like a stab wound through the heart. Whenever he returned to St Anne's, nostalgia hindered the rational workings of his mind, a kind of perpetual frustration overcame him, and he was pulled in two directions at once. Swamped in the gloom of St Anne's ancient yew trees, the headstones in the churchyard warning him of the futility of it all, he knew for certain he would never again feel 'comfortable' in the home of his childhood – and yet he longed to be. Guilt was the dividing factor, it always had been: guilt because he and his father did not get on anymore; guilt because he did not want to try anymore; guilt because he did not visit 'the old man' nearly often enough when home on leave and did not want to; guilt for a whole host of complex reasons. And betrayal of course; there was always betrayal. Betrayal when he stayed in the pokey rooms of friends from undergraduate days instead of with the parent who had sustained him – and sustained him well enough right up to that final betrayal. Betrayal that made him shy away from those ghostly memories of mother and sister hauntingly buried, so to speak, in the back garden. And so he dreaded seeing his father again; a dread that grew worse with each returning visit.

Lewis found his father seated alone at his enormous tooled-leather desk, as usual the top of it hidden beneath mountains of clutter – the pater was a notoriously untidy man. He sat in an upright armchair of Jacobean dimensions known as 'The Throne' to Jenny and himself when children. From there, the Rector had always written his sermons. Still wearing the same shabby maroon cardigan as in previous years; still with the third button missing, still with one hand hovering on a small glass of sherry, the other on the time-glass of his sermons, his patched elbows still on *Goddard's Horticultural Seed Catalogue* – only that the year had progressed to 1895.

Raising tired eyes to the unaccustomed intrusion on this, a Sunday evening, his father said in surprise; 'Lewis m'boy! How nice to see you again – and so soon! I know, you've come to tell me your liver's healed, the jaundice has disappeared, and you're off back to India sooner than expected. No, don't tell me, you're living with the Duchess of Argyll while intending to marry a Hottentot belly-dancer. Am I right, or am I not?' Lewis opened his mouth to reply but his father had the advantage. 'Please don't interrupt for at least half a minute, dear boy, I'm timing next week's sermon. If I don't settle to it while the last one's still fresh in my mind, I'll have to think of something new to say and that gets awfully tedious at my age – frightful waste of time when nobody listens anyway.'

The Rector turned over the sand-glass. White eyebrows like untidy tufts of carded cotton drawn together, brown eyes quizzed Lewis. Uncomfortable under that penetrating scrutiny, Lewis suddenly resented his father's eyes burrowing through the subterranean passages of his secret being. He could almost hear the cogs of his father's brain revolving in accusation: Yes, Lewis, frittering your life away in idle pursuits that will get you nowhere. Can't even remember what her name was, can you? (there it was again, guilt about last night). All right, no I can't remember, father. She wasn't your kind of girl anyway. All I can remember is her cheap perfume, grubby petticoats, and my wallet getting lost somewhere between Abingdon and St Anne's. If I want to fritter my life away, that's my business. Yes, I know the female-sex isn't a menu-card on the table of God's Hotel, you've told me often enough. But I prefer à la carte to table d'hôte. At least I can pick and choose my fare rather than be tied down to one dish at one price.

'There's whisky if you want it, though it'll rot the liver

faster if you're prone to that sort of thing,' the Rector said when his son, wearing the vacant expression that so annoyed him, maintained a hostile silence. He found it very difficult to get through to Lewis. Clearing his throat awkwardly, the Rector said rather too boisterously, 'Sunday night's m'bath night. I find my best ideas come when I'm lying soaking in the steam. I'm deep into the subject of ask and it shall be given, seek and ye shall find, knock and the door will open – so why are you really here, as I can't believe God's answered my prayers so promptly?' Reverend Joyden gave his sand-glass a little flip for good measure, took off his reading glasses, rubbed the bony bridge of his nose in a weary gesture, then leaned back in The Throne and sighed. 'Lewis, dear boy, I'm glad to see you, truly I am. Maud's gone home, but there's a pigeon pie in the meatbox if you're hungry.'

'Don't worry about me, father, I've already eaten. I had supper with Gerald . . . I er, can't stop long . . . '

'Didn't think for one moment you could.'

'I'm sorry.'

'Don't be,' said the Rector with a sudden swift lightening of his expression, as if he, too, had remembered and was guilty for making Lewis feel bad. 'Solitude works wonders for the digestive system. I'll never have an ulcer, y'know. Unlike you.'

Lewis forced a little grin. Immensely relieved by his father's change of heart, he seated himself, but not comfortably. He always felt he had to perch on the edge of his seat in his father's presence, while the Rector himself saw his son only as a rare winged species about to take off at the slightest bang. 'Father, you're right – I've, come to say goodbye. I'm returning to India the day after tomorrow.'

'Thought so, thought so.' Thin parchment fingers formed a pyramid of regret above *Goddard's Seed Catalogue*. 'Nothing of course to keep a young man in St Anne's. Much more life going on elsewhere. Don't blame you m'boy, for wanting to get away – only wish I were thirty years younger.' Sad eyes sought the corners of the cobwebby ceiling, blackmailing Lewis.

27

Before his father went off more deeply into one of his reveries concerning the passage of time and the distance of continents, Lewis chipped in with a forced exuberance; 'By the way, you might get a visit from a rather obnoxious fellow by the name of Count Mikail Vremya – a Russian. But that's not the real reason for my being here . . . as I said, I've, er, come to say goodbye.'

Getting himself into an awful coil, Lewis felt the need of some moral support after all. He got up, went to a small table beside the sooty, ash-laden fireplace Maud obviously didn't know existed, and helped himself to a double brandy. Taking a deep gulp that burned all the way down, but certainly made him feel a lot better, Lewis began again while he toyed absently with the bulbous glass. 'Father, I just wanted you to know that if, by chance, something should happen to me while I'm abroad . . . '

'Good heavens, is that the time?' The Rector scraped back his chair abruptly, and charged full pelt through the open French doors, calling for Lewis to follow. 'Come along. Let me show you how well my new pergola's doing before it gets too dark to see anything.'

In his shabby slippers, holes in the heels of his socks, the Rector strode purposefully along thyme-carpeted flagstones to his precious pergola. Lewis followed reluctantly, the subject of gardening farthest from his mind. The sighs of frustration were all there when his father launched into a horticultural discussion on the merits of aphid spraying. 'The *Eccremocarpas Scaber* is doing infinitely better than the *Jasminium Officinal* which hasn't as yet received a soap and water spray. The latter has a far sweeter scent. I don't want to unsettle nature's fine balance by putting an end to that scent – especially now it's summer. The perfume of honeysuckle drifting through one's open bedroom window at night is quite intoxicating – much better than my bed-time glass of sherry. The clematis is doing awully well, too, but the roses are rotten. Now then, m'boy, what've you been up to with the Cossacks?' The Rector's eyes twinkled. 'I know – you've seduced one of their Grand Duchesses and landed yourself in hot water!'

'Cold actually,' Lewis murmured.

28

'The geographical magazine you ordered is piling up here like Everest, so you might like to relieve me of a few copies. Interesting stuff in it, most informative.' Pipe in one hand, the Rector fumbled in the sagging pocket of his shabby cardigan and took out his tobacco-pouch.

The hang-dog expression back in his father's eyes, Lewis knew exactly what he was thinking; Oh dear, Lewis, I know you only come home when the mood takes you, or when you have bad news for me, or when you're in need of moral support. Yes, son, I do miss you. Why must you live on the other side of the world? You do owe me something, you know, dear boy. And so Lewis pretended to a few finer emotions because he sensed his father's despondency and his great disappointment in him. 'Father, I'm sorry,' he said, feeling he was apologizing rather a lot tonight. 'Honestly, I'd stay if I could, but two days is all I have left.'

'Spare me the tears, Lewis.' The Rector turned to examine his honeysuckle. Fidgety with his fine hands, he tugged at some wayward yellow-pink fingers of bloom, his gesture abstract, almost angry, as though he would put an end to the sweet-smelling vagaries of life. 'So tell me what you think of it. Hewson put it up for me so that I could train the honeysuckle and clematis over it. A shady place for me to sit and mull over my sermons on a hot summer's day, eh what?' He drew thoughtfully on his pipe. 'This Russian fellow about to descend so unceremoniously on me – what've you done to cause a breach of the peace?'

'A storm in a teacup,' Lewis murmured, not meeting his father's eyes but keeping his own downcast. He swirled the amber liquid round and round the bottom of the brandy glass he had absentmindedly borne outdoors, his thoughts far away. 'They were cruising on the river – hundreds of them.' He raised his eyes then, a half-grin on his face as he tried to make light of it. 'I happened to cut across their path in a punt. The daughter tumbled off the deck of their boat and almost drowned. The family went a little berserk over the whole affair – quite out of proportion to the danger anyone was in.'

The Rector, with a sympathetic smile, did not know what

29

to make of Lewis's stilted version of what he could only see as quite an amusing little incident. With one breath he was saying the girl had almost drowned, in the next stating there was no danger. 'Did you rescue her?' he asked, visibly brightening.

'I had no choice, she almost drowned me as well.'

'Foreigners are like that, m'boy, get all steamed up about nothing. Gains them the attention usually given to we Brits of a more modest make-up . . . there's a little bit of alliteration there for your next poem. The girl, was she pretty?'

A gleam in his eye, Lewis knew exactly what his father was driving at. 'No, in fact, she was pretty ugly.' Before his father could pursue the theme closest to his heart these days, Lewis added quickly, 'And she wasn't a day over fourteen. Father, please listen, there's a box deposited with my bank . . . it contains all my papers. Otherwise Gerald Knollys with whom I'm lodging . . . '

'Yes, yes, yes,' said the Rector impatiently. 'Gerald is your alter ego, Gerald is this that and the other to you. Gerald knows what to do in the event of your premature death through jaundice, yellow fever, rabies, cholera and general boredom. Dear Lewis, I know the song off by heart, and it's the same tune every time you return to Dehra-Dun. If it's any consolation to you, in my job I've discovered only the good die young – and then it's a question of whether or not the gods consider you to be good-looking. When it's time for you to go, dear boy, you'll go, so don't wish it upon yourself before you've scarcely lived. Nothing is going to happen to you, though sometimes I wish it would – like getting married to a decent girl and giving me grandchildren before it's too late. I don't like you hob-nobbing with the scarlet women you seem to prefer.'

It was hopeless. Lewis sighed in silent exasperation. His father was becoming increasingly senile over the subject of family ties when life was so much simpler without the trappings of responsibility. 'Father, I must be off,' he said, sad because so many things remained unresolved between them. 'I'll call in on my way to the railway station the day after tomorrow.'

30

'Thank you Lewis. I'd offer to accompany you to Tilbury, but I know how that kind of elaborate gesture always embarrasses you. You might like to take the pigeon pie with you. It'll only go off in the meatbox.'

Chapter Two

The following afternoon, his trunks and bags packed and taken to the railway station on the carrier's cart, Lewis cycled through Abingdon's water meadows and eventually found the back entrance of Fairmaster Manor. The shady lane was thick with honeysuckle and dog roses, reminding him of his father's pergola. He hadn't shown much interest last evening, or praised the pater's green fingers, and he wished now he had.

A little hill on his left, a leafy copse, gently rolling meadows sloping to the banks of the Thames, he found the ugly Gothic house in its superb setting. Built of red brick, its architecture gave the impression someone had more money than taste. Heavy, over-ornate, rambling and high, its gabled roofs and forest of pseudo-Elizabethan chimneys made him shudder – the Rectory appeared remarkably aesthetic in comparison. He wondered what the dowager-lady Woodman's husband had done for a living – railways, iron, coal, gold, or gun-running? It had to be one of those, surely, if not the lot, since a man of wealth must have his foibles! Lewis propped his bicycle against a hawthorn hedge. Trying to get it to stand, he heard the hard phut-phut of tennis balls being thrashed on the other side. Over the top, he saw a young man and woman playing with more energy than skill. He ducked as a ball came whizzing over. Having hoped to creep past the courts without being observed while trying to find his way to the front door of the mansion, he was caught in the act of removing his bicycle clips by Sonya Vremya's brother who found him in a very undignified position.

'Hello, it is Mr Joyden, isn't it?' Kirsten asked in amusement. 'I hope I didn't injure you by thwacking that ball over the hedge.' He peered down at Lewis doubled over. 'I say, you're not in pain, are you? I didn't get you in a strategic part of the anatomy, did I?'

'No, I'm er, trying to unfasten my cycle clips . . . ' Lewis stood up, red-faced. 'The ball missed me by a yard. I hope I'm not intruding, but I wanted to find out how your sister is before I leave for India.' He took his handkerchief from his pocket and mopped his brow, promising himself never again to try and beat any cycling records on a hot day.

'You're off to India? How lucky for you,' Kirsten Vremya remarked. 'I envy you very much. I've always wanted to visit that country – but I don't think I'd be very welcome there.'

'Oh, why not?' Lewis with raised brows enquired politely.

'Being Russian and all that . . . ' Kirsten Vremya turned aside and began to hunt for the lost tennis ball. Spying it under the hedge, he retrieved it and tossed it from hand to hand while eyeing Lewis up and down with a lazy curiosity. His eyes were grey like his sister's, his hair and handsome moustache of the same glossy chestnut depths as his sister's lustrous hair. 'Do you play tennis, Mr Joyden?' he asked, changing the subject.

'I do, but I prefer polo.'

'Yes, I suppose in India you would. We have a croquet-lawn if you're interested in a less strenuous pastime. My mother enjoys the game, but since Sonya has a weak heart and is forbidden any exercise whatsoever, I'm the one usually roped in to oblige.'

Lewis's time was short, and he was anxious to pay his respects to the old woman of the house, and be gone. Kirsten Vremya however appeared to be in a talkative frame of mind.

'I must say, it's all pretty boring though. I'm becoming a little tired of England and its erratic weather. This morning's thunderstorm put paid to tennis, and now, though it's stopped raining and the sun is shining, it's too humid to want to do anything except sleep . . . with a beautiful woman of course.' Kirsten Vremya winked archly.

'Of course,' Lewis murmured.

'It's interesting, this work you do in India?' Kirsten asked, not taking his eyes off the tennis ball he was tossing about.

'Not really,' Lewis murmured again, almost apologetically, so that Kirsten Vremya got the impression that here was a very weak and tepid individual. 'In fact, it's pretty boring stuff. I'm with the Survey of India – as it's called. I spend my life tracing contours of unprepossessing hills and mountains, not to mention the odd bridge and railway line.'

'Yes, I can see that must be very boring. Excuse me please, my partner is shouting for me – and the ball of course.' Kirsten Vremya smiled in friendly dismissal. 'Go on up to the house and ask for my grandmother. It's her house, we're only here for a few days. Afterwards I return to Radley, my father and mother to London, and only poor Sonya is left to the mercy of my grandmother and Pratikayit – he's our doctor by the way. But my sister likes the country and doesn't mind it here. I find it very boring. Which college did you say you were at?'

'I didn't.' Lewis could not help but smile at the theatrical Kirsten who, while his speech was spiced with a certain amount of pomposity, was also a man of charm. He returned the amity by saying; 'I graduated from Christ Church – as did my father, and his father before him, and his father before him, *ad infinitum*. A family tradition one supposes, though they didn't all end up as vicars.'

'I find family traditions very boring. I think I shall be happy to return to St Petersburg after this family tradition of a summer holiday is over. It is in the air that my father is being recalled to Russia, in which case I shall go, too. If not, I shall perhaps try Cambridge for a little while as I am tired of Radley. Well, do go on up to the house and pay your respects to my grandmother. I doubt we shall meet again, Mr Joyden, but *bon voyage* anyway.'

'Thanks,' said Lewis, shaking hands, unsure of what to make of Kirsten Vremya and his acute boredom which

34

surely could only be sophistry he practised in order to impress. Lewis felt he would not have been so rash as to call at all upon the formidable Vremyas, were it not for a question of duty — he simply had to make certain everything was all right with the young lady so recently at death's door.

Somewhere in the background, dogs barked vociferously, making his presence known to all and sundry while he searched for the front door. Lewis knocked loudly on the impressive oak door, the brass knocker gleaming brightly above the stone heads of two lions rampant — or were they bears? He was none too sure. A pert young maid answered the door. She dropped him a curtsey and the kind of saucy wink he enjoyed returning. 'Af'ernoon, sir. Can I 'elp you?'

'Mrs Lizaveta Woodman, please.'

''Alf a mo', sir, she's right 'ere.' The maid turned to address someone over her shoulder. 'Ma'am, there's a gen'lemum 'ere without a calling card.'

'Show him in, Cecile. Gentlemen without calling cards are usually quite harmless, they can't afford to be anything else. Good afternoon, Mr Joyden, I saw you skulking in the bushes, do come inside.' The dowager-lady Woodman displayed broken yellow teeth before turning on her heel, the silver ferrule of her walking-stick tap-tapping on the black and white chequered floor tiles. 'I don't know where everyone's got to this afternoon, but the storm this morning upset the dogs. Sonya's allergic to dogs, and so is Marya, my daughter. Very tiresome, as I can't keep them inside the house when the family are staying with me. So nice of you to call, I hadn't really expected you to, you know. But now you're here, you will stay and take tea with me, won't you?'

Behind her, he apologized speedily. 'I'm awfully sorry, but I really can't stop . . . I only called to see if Miss Vremya has recovered after . . . '

'Nonsense!' She brushed aside his protests with an airy flick of her faded yellow hand. 'Cecile, fetch the samovar into the drawing-room — the silver one.'

He had no choice but to oblige.

'You mustn't rush away so rudely when you've only just arrived to pay your respects, it won't do, Mr Joyden. Now

35

then, be seated . . . no, not in that chair, it has a foot missing. The sofa if you please, where I can see you.'

It was a rather depressing room, overstocked with heavy dark furniture. Gloomy portraits and silver-gilt photographs of past and present Vremyas turned the room into a kind of family shrine. Sadly too, on such a hot day, the windows were closed and the heavy brocade curtains in a dingy fawn colour were partly drawn, shutting off the view of a pleasant garden sloping to the river. What a pity, Lewis reflected morosely, the house and its occupants were so much less inspiring than the gardens.

'So, you're here to ask after Sonya. I'll speak the truth and hope it won't put you off your tea. She has only been able to breathe with the aid of a steam kettle. Anatole Pratikayit has diagnosed bronchial-pneumonia . . . thanks to you, Lewis Joyden.' The old Russian woman stared at him vindictively.

'I'm sorry.'

'So you should be.' She tut-tutted, and he wasn't sure whether she was serious or not. 'It was entirely your fault. There was nothing we could do about avoiding you except slam on our brakes – if that is what one does in a boat.'

Mercifully tea arrived then, and she devoted her attention to pouring. 'Sugar?' Silver tongs hovered expectantly. 'Dear, dear, Mr Joyden, four lumps are not good for your blood – it makes it very sweet, according to Pratikayit.'

Lewis had a dreadful urge to ask after vampires with a sweet tooth as he had the feeling this doctor Pratikayit might be one. But he buttoned his tongue and let the old dowager do the talking.

'Pratikayit tells us it's something to do with Sonya's valves – everyone has them in the heart I believe, although I had previously supposed only trumpets had them to make the sound they do. He's half-Russian, half-French and half no good in my opinion, but Marya – she's my daughter – won't hear anything against him. Marya is a very nervous creature. It's all to do with the loss of six children before the age of five, and that's why Marya clings so to Kirsten and Sonya, the only survivors from a floundering marriage.'

36

'I'm sorry . . . ' Lewis, balancing the fragile cup and saucer precariously on his knees, hoped he would not do anything else clumsy, like spilling Darjeeling tea in his lap, as well as having tipped the young grand-daughter into the Thames. He took the proffered ginger-snap.

'We never did finish our little excursion up-river, Mr Joyden.'

'I'm sorry,' he murmured idiotically again, as he did not know what else to say.

'We circled Rose Isle six times. I must admit Mikail's boat is rather big for English waters, which aren't at all like the Neva around which St Petersburg is built – our little Venice of the Baltic, Mr Joyden.'

'So I believe.'

'However, you mustn't take to heart anything that happened yesterday. We're all very highly strung to start with, but quieten down in time – you'll soon get to know our little ways, Mr Joyden.' She smiled her repelling smile.

He did not think he would ever get used to the Vremyas, and certainly did not know what to make of her last remark.

The dowager Lizaveta Woodman continued pedantically; 'I don't think Marya's much in love with Mikail because a woman, if she's in love, doesn't imagine she has every illness known to man and many more that aren't. Would you care for more tea, Mr Joyden?'

'No, thank you, Mrs Woodman, I must be pushing off . . . '

'No, you mustn't. How old are you, Mr Joyden? I'm allowed to ask such an impertinent question as I believe I'm older than you.'

'Twenty-five.'

'Tush! Not even in the prime of your life, a mere chicken in time. Dear boy, a man is not a man until he's thirty-three and crucified like Christ. I'm seventy-seven and have been crucified many times. So come along, take another cup of tea with a decrepit old woman for whom romance is only a memory.' She beckoned imperiously for his over-sugared cup.

Blackmail again. Lewis surrendered his cup and allowed

37

his glance to dip towards a well-thumbed pile of magazines beside him on the sofa. 'Someone I see, is a keen reader of the *Geographical*. I mention it because I, too, am a fellow of the R.G.S.'

'Oh, then you must talk to Mikail . . . he belongs to the Russian Geographical Society, not the Royal, as I believe it is in England. What kind of work do you do, Mr Joyden?'

'Me? Oh, nothing exciting. I draw maps, look for mountains to stick on them and generally re-route any lines that get in the way.'

'My husband was also in the railways. He owned a great amount of rolling stock from the east to the west coast of America as well as Canada. We spent our honeymoon in a place called Niagara Falls – have you heard of it? It was very wet and we couldn't see a thing because of the spray, and we got hopelessly lost. The map we had to go by must have been drawn by the North American Indians with one of their totem poles – definitely not one of your maps, Mr Joyden, as I think you're a conscientious young man by what I've seen of you.' She sighed, adjusted the bombazine folds of her skirts and added sadly; 'I wish Kirsten was. As much as I adore my handsome grandson – he's an Officer in the Imperial Guard you know. I wish he wouldn't be quite so irresponsible. Kirsten never sticks at anything, or stays long enough in one place to be of use. He does tend to view life as one big joyride . . . Oh, do forgive the pun, Mr Joyden, it was quite unintentional!'

'Please don't worry, I get it all the time,' he said reassuringly.

'Kirsten gambles a lot. Unknown to his father and mother he comes to me for vast sums of money – which I don't mind giving him, if only he wouldn't keep promising to pay me back; he never does. Then, I suppose, it's all part of his charm. I'm mentioning all this, not out of disloyalty but love for my family who are a mixture of Russian and English temperaments . . . my husband was English, I believe I did mention it. However, I want to warn you about Kirsten. If he ever approaches you for money, refuse him at once. Many a friendship has been ruined by not paying heed to that old proverb, never a borrower or lender be. Are you married, Mr Joyden?'

'No, Mrs Woodman.'

'Are you engaged then?'

'No, Mrs Woodman.'

'Courting?'

'No.'

'Anyone at all in the offing?'

He shook his head.

'Are you by any chance a homosexual?'

'No, Mrs Woodman,' he said vigorously, feeling it was about time he took his leave. He set down the priceless Höchst teacup and saucer on an Oriental brass table of incredibly ugly design, and made polite noises of departure.

'Oh don't be offended,' said Lizaveta Woodman smirking wickedly. 'I only ask because all we've been subjected to lately is the practices of that poor man, Oscar Wilde, who is presently occupied in breaking stones for our pavements because he sent a few flowers to his boyfriend. I maintain that God made us the way we are, and it isn't up to a man in a wig to argue the facts of life. I believe in keeping an open mind. Now then, young man, I fear I've begun to prattle, so I'll allow you to return to India. I appreciate your gesture in calling upon us when you're obviously very hard-pressed for time, and I'm sorry Marya and Mikhail aren't here this afternoon to entertain you rather than an old woman like me. Cecile will show you the way out,' she said, hobbling over to the bell-pull by the fireplace.

In the end, Cecile did not show him out but the dowager-lady herself. Her walking stick tapping angrily on the hall tiles, Lizaveta Woodman snorted contemptuously. 'Servants are more of a liability than an asset these days. In my day, the girl would have been horse-whipped for not answering a bell.'

'I'm sorry . . . I ought to have made my own way out,' Lewis said uncomfortably, noticing how she was limping.

'Nonsense. You took the trouble of calling, so we must take the trouble of seeing you out . . . I'm not cross with you, Lewis Joyden, only that girl who's a wanton little hussy at the best of times, and at the worst, I dread to think. The reason why Marya and Mikail aren't here to meet you,' she said, going off at a tangent, 'is because they've been called to London by the Ambassador.'

'Not bad news, I hope,' Lewis said solicitously, pausing on the threshold.

'Oh no, merely a banquet in honour of some Chinese Ambans from Lhasa who are visiting London. The Russian Ambassador, I believe, is doing his own little bit to foster good relations with the Tibetans. But between you, me and the gatepost, Mr Joyden, our new Tsar Nicholas is making the most of this Chinese-Japanese war. Since the Manchu dynasty is about to topple, he's trying to get a foot in the Tibetan backdoor. I'm too old to be involved in politics, but Mikail lets a few things drop now and then to Marya. He's being recalled to St Petersburg.'

'Oh, I am sorry.' Lewis frowned at the lions – most definitely not Russian bears.

'Goodbye, Mr Joyden, safe journey to India. If you're on leave again in Abingdon before I die, come and take tea with me, otherwise I'll be greatly offended. I've enjoyed our little chat. I'm a Russian woman at heart and adore a good gossip.' She smiled expansively.

His former opinion of the old gargoyle definitely mellowed by tea from a silver samovar, Lewis found himself actually liking the dowager Lizaveta Woodman. 'Delighted,' he found himself murmuring.

She leaned towards him confidentially and whispered, 'Even though I married an Englishman and have lived here for forty years, I'm Russian. Marya my daughter,' she repeated, as though she had to keep reminding herself who Marya was, 'is cosmopolitan; born in England from a Russian mother and English father, educated in Paris and Switzerland, married to a Russian and now living in Russia. But our little Sonya is Russian through and through. She does, however, speak English and French beautifully.'

His head was spinning by the time he found himself on the gravel walkway that circled the great house. The heavy oak door closed firmly and finally by the hand of the indomitable dowager, Lewis imagined her tap-tapping on the tail of the saucy Cecile. He followed his nose to where he had left his bicycle, but was prevented from going very far.

'Psst!'

He revolved full circle on his heels, wondering from which clump of rhododendrons the urgent whisper had come.

'Psst, up here!'

He raised his eyes to the ugly chimney-pots. A tousled head and wide slate-grey eyes peered down at him from an upstairs window high under the eaves. The skinny creature he had rescued from the river the day before was now in imminent danger of landing on her head in the herbaceous border. Purple bunches of wisteria clinging to the eaves above her, gave him the distinct impression he was gazing at the label of a wine bottle displaying the chestnut-ringleted head of Bacchus. 'I thought you had pneumonia,' he said accusingly.

She ignored the assumption, and asked boldly; 'Are you here to see grandmama or me?'

'Your grandmother. What are you doing out of bed?'

'Mr Joyden,' she sighed like an old woman, 'Russians have very vivid imaginations. I'm perfectly fit and healthy, though they would have it otherwise. I sometimes suspect mama's doctor, Prat the Rat, of wishing to line his own pocket at papa's expense. I hope you didn't catch a chill after yesterday's swim?'

'No, indeed, thank you for your concern. I took the precaution of indulging in a glass of cognac to ward off the evil eye.'

'Very wise of you. I don't care for brandy very much, I prefer port. I drink vast quantities of it, you know. Prat says it's good for the blood. We're all very preoccupied with life and death in our household, which means one's state of health. Kirsten was caught in the rainstorm this morning and had to take a mustard bath. It's the same in St Petersburg, fuss, fuss, fuss, the day long!' Again she sighed heavily, as though all the troubles of the world were upon her young shoulders. 'You must come and visit us sometime in St Petersburg.'

A piece of paper fluttered to his feet. He picked it up.

41

'Are you left-handed, Mr Joyden?'

'Yes, why?' He looked up at her with a smile.

'All clever men are left-handed.'

'How do you know?'

'I read a lot – I've nothing else to do when I'm sick . . . and I'm sick quite often. It's boredom.'

A perennial Vremya disease, he couldn't help feeling.

'How tall are you?' She challenged him again.

'Oh, about ten foot.'

'Please be serious, Mr Joyden. I am, utterly!'

'Then I'm five foot eleven and eleven-twelfths of an inch.'

'Is that with or without your shoes?'

'Most definitely in my bare feet.'

'Then I'll mark it down as six foot.' She stopped sucking a pencil for the moment. 'What colour are your eyes?'

'A muddy jaundice I believe.'

'Hazel, I think. That's a nice mixture of woodland colours; green, brown and yellow. I know that, because I happened to notice their colour in the river. Your hair is jet black, I know that, too. It's a very nice combination. Grandmama says you're passably attractive, but I prefer the term interesting. Tall dark handsome men do nothing for me unless they're also intelligent.'

He was beginning to feel acutely embarrassed by the young lady's probing questions, and wondered how he could bring the interview to a gentlemanly end when she continued unashamedly; 'I copied out our address for you so that you'd have somewhere to stay when you come to St Petersburg. Sometimes I get the feeling certain things are meant to happen – like the ducking yesterday, and you calling upon us today. This morning, after the storm, the rainbow shone and seven trees on that little hill over there were each a different colour, like a row of soldiers in national uniforms. Kirsten said I'd seen the end of the rainbow and that was very lucky. So you see, Mr Joyden, I shan't die of pneumonia or anything else – not just yet anyway. Nor will you, because I believe there's a purpose to our lives . . . that's why you're here now.'

Astounded by the grand philosophy of one so young, he

42

wanted to say, oh do you, Miss! And how have you worked all that out? Instead, he smiled indulgently at the young creature who was all hair, eyes and teeth, like the panda in captivity he had once seen on his travels in China, and said, 'Miss Vremya, I should forget all about your ailments and get out there to retrieve your pot of gold without further delay.'

She returned his warm whimsical smile. Her smooth featureless face at once animated by mischievous dimples, she said; 'Please may I call you Lewis? You can call me Sonya if you like – but never Countess! It's too fairytale-ish and I prefer normal things. When you come to St Petersburg, I'll offer you tea out of a silver samovar just like grandmama does to anyone who takes her fancy.'

43

Chapter Three

RUSSIA
Winter 1897

Underneath the golden cross of Peter-and-Paul Cathedral, a hanging angel on a chain moved with the wind. Only now, the flying angel hung motionless on the frozen air, icicles weighing her down. Everything was iron-hard and grey. The river Neva was frozen solid, the Baltic fleet now in warmer waters, so the harbour was used as an elaborate skating-rink across which the inhabitants of St Petersburg glided bridge to bridge from November to April.

Close by the Kirov Bridge on Kirovsky-Prospekt with its fine view of Vasilevsky Island, the Vremyas lived in their mansion. From her bedroom windows Sonya could see the great gilt towers of Peter-and-Paul Fortress, the prison in which a Tsar's son, on his father's orders, had been tortured to a grisly end. Something about that place always brought Kirsten to mind. A brutal picture would disturb her; Kirsten, her beloved brother, imprisoned in the Petropavloskaya on account of some foolhardy escapade. She imagined the agony of it all – and told herself not to be neurotic, Kirsten was old enough to take care of himself. But she did so hate St Petersburg in the winter, its grim image of the frozen angel and the frozen prison on its frozen island in the frozen river. She longed then for the white nights of spring to return, when the silver birches surrounding her father's hunting lodge near Novgorod would whisper in the warm breeze, so that lying in bed at night was like hearing an age-old story in a language left long unpractised, or a piece of music from the past, hauntingly unfinished. But best of all she loved her summers in England with grandmama Lizaveta . . .

The ornate clock of Peter-and-Paul Cathedral coldly chimed the quarter hour; a quarter past four on a depressing afternoon. Sonya could hear her mother still weeping bitterly behind her locked door. She had intended to ask her something important, but now she hesitated. The Countess's distress was usually contagious.

They had been quarrelling again of course – her mother and father never at peace with each other. This morning's row, however, had been especially acrimonious. Her father had accused her mother of some very tawdry things, details of which had been bandied around the house to finally settle in the salon. The servants, naturally, had been all agog. The Countess had been accused of being unfaithful with Prat the doctor, Sasha her handsome cousin and, above all, seeking an unnatural relationship with her own son, Kirsten . . .

Sonya could not believe the things she was hearing, and considered her father to be quite mad.

'You were seen, both of you, whispering and canoodling in your opera-box!' The Count's harsh voice had risen to a crescendo of wrath behind the closed doors of the salon, which did not prevent people in the street hearing him. Sonya could not make out from the third-floor landing whether he was referring then to Sasha or to Kirsten . . . or even Prat the Rat, although Prat seldom went to the opera.

Her mother, weeping hysterically, had denied everything. 'No, no, no, Mikail, how could you! It isn't as you think. Sasha came to me because his step-mother is ill. And Kirsten! How could you be so despicable! It isn't true that I'm hearing this from you . . . you his father, to think such things of me, his *mother*!' Here the Countess Marya's voice had also risen shrilly as she tried to vindicate herself.

45

'Then *don't embrace him in public!*'

'But Mikail, he is my cousin, a relation with whom I've shared childhood tea-parties.'

'I'm talking about Kirsten.'

'But Mikail, Kirsten's my *son*, my darling boy!'

'Precisely, dear woman, so *don't treat him as though he were your lover* . . . '

'You are jealous and . . . and quite insane!'

'It is not I, Countess, who is insane, but you! You and your preoccupation with death, disease and . . . and dissipation. Ever since that business with . . . '

'Yes, go on, say it now!' Her mother had interrupted her father furiously, unusual, Sonya thought then, because no one, least of all her mother, ever interrupted the Count when he was in full swing. 'It is that which separates us now, Mikail, and it always will.'

'And that's another thing, Madam, the holding of yourself from my bed.'

'Can you wonder at it, Mikail when, when . . . after what I've had to endure in the way of . . . of shame, disgrace and humiliation?'

'Yes,' stormed the Count, 'Yes, I wonder at it, and I'm equally dismayed . . . dismayed and disgusted that my wife prefers her son to her husband.'

At this juncture, a fiendish cry from her mother put an end to any further acrimony between her parents. Sonya gathered her mother had fallen in a faint at her father's feet – her usual mode of escape when she had had enough. Anna, her mother's personal maid, and the housekeeper, had both been summoned then by the Count to remove his wife to her bed. He had left straightaway for his club on Nevsky-Prospekt.

Her father still out of the house, Sonya now bit her fingernails outside her mother's bedroom door, wondering whether or not to disturb her when she was in so much distress. Perhaps it would help her to think about something else . . . Sonya knocked timidly. She began to feel a familiar tightness in her chest, and hoped she would not have need of the steam kettle tonight, the camphor-fumes of which made her eyes and throat sting mercilessly.

Sonya knocked again, louder this time. 'Mama, it is I, Sonya.'

'Sonya, not now, please, petroushka, I have such a head-ache.'

'But mama, it's important.'

After a little while, Anna, who always slept like a faithful hound at the foot of her mother's bed, drew back the bolts that hopefully would prevent the Count's forceful entry, opened the door a fraction, stuck out her head and hissed in Sonya's face; 'Don't stay long. And *don't* mention your brother's name because she will die if you do. She is vastly fed up with your father, your brother, your second-cousin and her whole life. She's married to a fool and I told her so over twenty years ago – now it's too late. Come on in if you're coming!'

Sonya squeezed breathlessly past Anna who then re-bolted the bedroom door, top and bottom, as well as turning the key in the lock. The old peasant woman settled herself back on her narrow iron cot close to the floor, her sharp black eyes following every move Sonya made.

'Mama,' Sonya whispered, settling herself close to her mother on the vast bed, 'please don't cry anymore.' The Countess dissolved into greater floods of tears, her hand-kerchief wet and useless. Sonya fetched another from the drawer. The heavily draped room was dark and filled with an over-powering scent of incense and soap. Candles burned steadily before the icons in a corner of the bedroom, not a breath of air stirred the flames, the windows closed and shuttered. It was as if her mother and Anna feared the Count would climb up the facade of the house, five storeys high, to attack them. Two ornate reading-lamps with pink glass shades above the bed-head made a warm rosy oasis behind the bed-curtains, the only intrusion coming from the slowly hissing gas, like someone blowing between their teeth.

'Mama, I wouldn't have disturbed you for any other reason but this, why must I eat raw liver sandwiches?'

'Monsieur Pratikayit thinks it's necessary, petroushka. Now that you're sixteen and a woman, it's to replace your blood loss each month.'

'But mama, the sandwiches are revolting! I would rather have no blood at all in my veins than eat such disgusting food.'

'It is necessary . . . ' her mother sniffed, 'and I hope, too, you're remembering to drink up all your port-wine after supper as Monsieur Pratikayit prescribed.'

'And that's another silly thing, mama! Aren't you afraid I might end up a dipsomaniac like him?'

Her mother sighed wearily and asked Anna to renew the cold compresses on her aching head. 'Sonya, Sonya,' said the Countess passionately, 'why must you ask so many difficult questions the whole time? Why can't you accept that adults know best?'

'Do they mama! Sometimes I don't think so. Besides, how else will I be educated when I'm not allowed to ask questions or go to school?'

She realized there were two more questions there, to which her mother's feeble reply was; 'You'll only pick up diseases from other children. Isn't a governess, a maid, a dancing-master and a music-teacher enough company for you, petroushka?'

'No, I hate them. I'm alone all day long with no one to talk to.'

'Dear child,' said the Countess impatiently, making it obvious she found talking to her daughter very tedious, 'I think you're becoming restless. It's time we found you a husband so that you have other things to think of.'

'I don't want a husband, and I've plenty to think of. I want someone to talk to. I want to know why I must eat raw-liver sandwiches that are too despicable to look at, let alone stomach.'

'Sonya, you must learn now, a woman has to put up with many heavy burdens in life, the heaviest being that she's a woman. We cannot argue with our life, we have to make the best of it – like eating raw liver sandwiches to prevent you from getting anaemia.'

'Why is it bad to be a woman?' Sonya asked stubbornly.

'It is when one is married to a man like your father.'

'Then why did you marry him if neither of you love each other?'

'It was necessary,' the Countess sighed.

'Why?'

'My family wished it.'

'Why?'

'Wealth and position.'

'Whose wealth and position?'

'Oh, mine of course, petroushka.'

'Then that was a very foolish thing to have done.'

'Yes, it was. But you know your grandmother Lizaveta cannot be argued with. My mother sought a title for me, and my English father was rich enough to buy it. It was unfortunate his eye happened to alight on Mikail at the time. I was not in love with him, but with another, a gentleman who was too poor for my family. Don't listen to those who tell you love grows during a marriage, it doesn't. When you marry, petroushka, it must be to a gentleman . . . your father is not a gentleman for all his grand title.' The Countess sniffed again, rather pathetically to Sonya's mind. If she did not like her life, then why didn't she change it, Sonya thought. 'I don't know why I'm talking to you like this, it can't be right,' the Countess continued. 'Just pretend to yourself I love your father – which doesn't mean I like him. Anna, fetch the *sal volatile* from my drawer, it's hot in here and I feel a little faint.'

While Anna scrabbled in all sorts of drawers looking for the smelling salts, Sonya asked the question she had been meaning to for a long time; 'Mama, what do married people do in bed that's so important? I asked Kirsten but he told me to mind my own business.'

Sonya was suddenly aware of Anna's dark scolding eyes on her for having mentioned Kirsten's name. Toothless gums worked together convulsively in a wrinkled face as leathery as a piece of salted meat left to dry too long in the sun. With knotty joints like walnuts growing from her shrivelled brown fingers, she tugged her headscarf forward as it had slipped back on her balding scalp peppered with velvety brown grave-spots. Sonya had always felt intimidated by Anna, not at all the cowering hard-worked stencil of serfdom the revolutionary organizations for the liberation of mankind shouted about for propaganda purposes – organizations led by that man, Vladimir Lenin, her father had such a grudge against and always talked about angrily. Sonya avoided the piercing black eyes and turned her attention back to her mother who suddenly appeared as rosy-cheeked as the lamps above her, when just now she had been as pale as an oyster.

'Sonya,' the Countess Marya said in exasperation, fidgeting with her cold compresses, 'your questions disturb me. It isn't becoming for a girl of your age to probe into the world of adults. When I was your age, I wouldn't have dreamt of approaching my mother with such brazen and unladylike questions. After you're married, you can ask such questions of your husband – if he doesn't provide you with the answers first. I think it's high time to launch you into society in the proper way so that you can meet a suitable young man of wealth and prestige. We must go to Nevsky-Prospekt tomorrow to have you fitted for some ballgowns from Madame Génève in Sadovaya Street – she is good, but not too expensive.' Her mother appeared to cheer up at the likelihood of a shopping expedition.

Sonya could imagine nothing worse. 'I don't think I wish to get married at all. Not when it seems such an unhappy business.'

'It's a fact of life,' the Countess agreed. 'Sonya, return to your room now, there's a good lamb. My head aches so badly . . . and petroushka, please wrap your nightgown closer to your chest. You don't want to catch phthisis in the draughts – besides, it's unseemly to be caught wandering in the corridors half-undressed. A healthy mind and body is a great asset to a woman . . and that's what your father has always held against me, that I'm not physically suited . . . ' the Countess Marya's lower lip began to tremble ominously. 'As if I, in my weak state, could prevent the loss of six children . . . when . . . when he's always so demanding . . . Petroushka . . . oh, how I wish I was dead!' Again the Countess dissolved into a bundle of weeping nerves. 'I wish I were cold in my grave . . . the only warming thing would be to know your father's tears above me were hot with grief and remorse.' All of a sudden she lifted her tear-stained face and listened. 'Is that Sasha's troika returning?'

Sonya got off the bed with an unhappy sigh, and peeping through one of the ill-fitting shutters saw the dark curly head and handsome figure of her mother's cousin getting out of his old-fashioned sleigh. Having no wish to meet Sasha the bold, she made her excuses. Her mother, in any case, wasn't listening. Animated by Sasha's unexpected return, the Countess was ordering Anna about, right left and centre, to fetch her her new blue satin nightgown, her silver hairbrush, a bowl of cold water in which to bathe her swollen face, to draw aside the curtains and to open the shutters to let in some fresh air!

Sonya, another undisguised sigh escaping, returned to her room, the question of raw liver sandwiches remaining unresolved.

ii

Kirsten Vremya, unlike Ivan Ivansky, had not held a good hand all evening. Ivan had accumulated a tidy little nest-egg which would have paid off Kirsten's debts quite nicely. His grey eyes crinkled against the blue fug of cigar smoke, his glossy moustache vying with Ivan's ginger one, Kirsten waited patiently for Ivan's luck to run out. Soon, soon, he promised himself smugly, he was certain Ivan's luck could not hold out much longer. Ivan had shown off stupidly and had overplayed his hand by starting the game with too high a bet against the pot. Kirsten could not help reflecting that the last round of yablon, where Ivan had claimed the jackpot, had rather gone to his head. And now the silly fool was going for it again.

'Lady-luck doesn't smile twice with the same lips, Ivan!'

'You watch your luck, Vremya, I'll watch mine.'

The others around Prince Nikolay Dubrovka's gaming table, in his grace and favour apartment overlooking the Winter Palace in the Dvortsovaya Ploshad, were aware of the sparks of animosity between Ivansky and Vremya tonight, unusual because they had always been on the best of terms. They awaited the outcome with interest.

Ivan was dealt two cards, face down. He picked them up. Keeping them close to his chest he examined them. His face

51

betrayed nothing as he replaced them on the green baize. Taking his time, Ivan placed his bet, ten thousand roubles, with a smile at Kirsten.

Seated on Kirsten's right, Prince Nikolay (Kolya to the chosen few) gave Ivan the top card off the pack as he was dealer and responsible for all bets. He turned it face up on the table in front of Ivan.

'A knave if ever I saw one, Ivan,' said Kirsten grinning broadly.

'An agent provocateur if ever I heard one, Count, so shut up, please!' said the Prince testily. 'What's the matter with you two tonight? for heaven's sake!'

With a shrug and a quirk of a ginger eyebrow, Ivan turned up his two cards, three and ten.

'Lost, Ivan,' Kirsten said with relish, taking another cigar from the box Kolya's servant, Grigory, held towards him. He clipped his cigar and watched ten thousand more roubles being tossed into the pot.

'Don't gloat too soon, Vremya,' said Ivan, 'no sure-win hand in this game.'

'And you'd teach your grandmother to suck eggs, wouldn't you, Ivan?' said Kolya gathering in the cards.

The game then ante-ed round the table. Dealer played his hand. Kolya, too, lost to the pot, drawing a five against his deuce and four. Again play moved round the table, the jackpot having no takers. Kirsten became dealer. To his left sat Philip Chulkovo, then Yuri Lubertsky, then Philip's twin, Peter, on Ivan's right and finally back to Kolya. The cards were shuffled by Yuri, and cut twice by the Chulkovo twins. Kirsten dealt each player two cards, one at a time, face down. Then he dealt himself two cards, face down. Philip began play to his left, placed his bet and lost. The game moved round the table, each player losing his bet and increasing the jackpot at every turn. By the time it was Kirsten's turn to play the pot contained fifty-thousand roubles. He broke out in a cold sweat – rather like Russian roulette Kirsten couldn't help feeling. No takers for the pot – was this where his own bad luck changed? Fifty-thousand roubles . . . he'd already lost a small fortune and couldn't afford any more losses. If he lost now, he'd never be able to pay up – not on his allowance. This bunch of gamblers here tonight didn't have Kopeck-pinching fathers who, with visible pain, counted out a miserly allowance each month.

'Come on, Vremya, Count! What's keeping you?' asked Kolya peevishly.

'The size of the jackpot.' Ivan's smirk conveyed far more – go on Vremya, you're shamming, you're morally unable to meet the pot so why don't you pass?

Fifty-thousand roubles . . . Kirsten swallowed, licked his dry lips. His hand reached automatically for his glass of vodka. He downed it in one without thinking. To give in or not to give in, that was the burning question – lady-luck smile on me, he pleaded silently while agonizing about whether to play or pass; enough money to pay all his debts and to live very comfortably for a very long time on what was left, or, lose, and be cashiered from the service because he was dishonourable, his father turning him out of the house because he would be unable to look the Tsar in the eye again, exile in Paris, no Irene anymore . . .

'Do get on with it, Count!' Kolya frowned, pulling at his lank grey hair falling over his forehead like hoary tassles draping a marble mantelpiece. The others, too, began to fidget uncomfortably.

'Play,' said Kirsten, putting down another promissory note – all or nothing this time – fifty in the pot. 'I raise the pot thirty-four,' and the only satisfaction came from seeing the smirk wiped off Ivansky's face.

Kirsten could hardly bear to keep his eyes open while he withdrew the top card off the pack.

The king of diamonds . . .

Ivan was watching him like a hawk. Kirsten felt the perspiration chill and damp under his tunic. He doubted he would be able to stand up if he tried.

'Well, come on then, Vremya, let's see what you've got.' Ivansky had already written him off. Kirsten could feel vibrations of triumph from the fellow, and puzzled on why Ivan, for some reason tonight, wanted to see him fall flat on his face.

Kirsten turned up his two cards.

53

'Ace-deuce!' said Lubertsky clapping his hands resound-
ingly.

'My God, he's won the jackpot!' said Peter Chulkovo
disbelievingly. 'You damn actor, Kirsten! For a moment
you had us all fooled.'

Kirsten managed to stand up after all. Grinning broadly,
his cigar in his mouth, he swept the jackpot towards him
while Kolya said to his man-servant Grigory; 'Go fetch the
Old Monk, eighty-eight, this is a cause for celebration . . . I
can now receive what you owe me, eh, Count Kirsten?'

Kirsten wasn't listening, he had saved himself thirty-
four thousand roubles and gained fifty. He was too preoccupied by what the money could do for him.

'Just a moment, Vremya.' Kirsten found his wrist locked
in Ivan's steely grip. Ivan thrust his face close to Kirsten's,
their moustaches almost touching. 'You're a bloody cheat!'
he hissed in Kirsten's face.

In the sudden heavy stillness of Kolya's under-furnished
and over-mirrored gaming room, the insult echoed and took
on a sinister dimension. Kirsten's face set into rigid lines.
'What?' he said, his colour changing from red to white. A
pulse began to throb in his temple as he glared at Ivan.

'You're a bloody cheat, Vremya.'

'I say, Ivan, that's a bit offensive to my chap,' said Kolya
warningly, the champagne forgotten as all eyes turned to
the protagonists.

'Lubertsky shuffled . . . the twins cut. You watched them
closely enough, damn it all, Ivan! I'm not defending myself
to you . . . ' Kirsten wrested his arm away from Ivan and
shrugged his tunic sleeve back into place. 'How dare you
make such an accusation!'

'Because it's true, Vremya. You're a cheat and a liar and
I'll prove it.' His face livid, Ivan turned to the others; 'We
all know how he keeps children amused at tea-parties with
his card tricks and sleight of hands, but there's no magic
about what he did here tonight by juggling his hand for the
jackpot.' Ivan was beside himself with rage.

'What on earth are you bumbling about, Ivan, Count?'
asked Kolya, peering shortsightedly up at Ivan's stalwart
bulk.

'Vremya's little tricks that don't become so amusing when he uses them to cheat . . . go on, take a look for yourselves. There are fifty-four cards in that pack, not fifty-two as he'd have us believe now that attention is focused on the jackpot and not the cards. My bet is you'll find five ace-deuces in the pack.'

'Do you know what you're saying, Count Ivansky!' Kolya screeched in temper. 'If you're instigating a *casus belli* against my Aide, I'll have you drummed out of your Regiment, I'll report you to the Tsar, I'll peel your nasty little hide off you! Lubertsky, gather up those cards, lay them out, face up every one. Now then, each of you fellows count the pack . . . I've never heard of anything so disgusting in all my years around the green baize. Ivansky, if you're wrong, God help you!' The Prince trembled in agitation as he observed, hawk-eyed, the cards being counted systematically.

'Forty-nine, fifty, fifty-one, fifty-two . . . '

'There you are Ivan! Apologize at once to Kirsten, otherwise I'll see you publicly disgraced for trying to create a scandal for a brother Officer,' Kolya declared triumphantly.

'I reiterate, Vremya's a cheat and a liar,' Ivan maintained stubbornly, 'I don't know how he did it, but he has another ace-deuce somewhere up his sleeve . . . yes, that's very likely where the two extra cards are, up his sleeve with his snotty little handkerchief.'

Kolya was disturbed. Count Ivansky was not used to making such wild and irrational statements – not without proof would he dare create a scandal for another Officer of the Palace Guard and member of the nobility, it would do him no good. Besides, he had always assumed Ivan and Kirsten to be friends. 'Come, come, Ivan, retract your accusations, apologize to Kirsten . . . '

'I'm damned if I will! Search him, I say!'

'No, no, no!' Kolya screeched again, stamping his foot. 'We cannot do it! I shan't let you insult my Aide on my premises. Kirsten . . . I implore you, in the face of Count Ivansky's accusations – and I hate myself for asking this – have you by chance miscounted the cards you dealt?' Kolya, very worked up, desirous only of restoring law, order and dignity to his little party, tripped over Lubertsky's sword lying on the floor. Picking it up he ordered him to buckle it on immediately. He did not trust Ivan in his present wild mood, the fellow looked capable of stabbing Kirsten in the back with it.

'Here is my answer, Prince Nikolay,' said Kirsten dramatically, and flung out his arms like a scarecrow. 'You may search me if you wish, but if you don't find anything on me, I challenge Ivansky to a duel for having insulted me.'

'No, no, no!' cried Kolya again. 'I won't allow it . . . the Tsar won't allow it. He has forbidden duelling.' Kolya wrung his hands in despair.

'Search him,' said Ivan, 'and you'll find the cards somewhere on his person, I bet on it – eighty-four thousand roubles.'

The Chulkovo twins and Yuri Lubertsky were acutely embarrassed by the whole affair. If word of this filtered across the square to the Tsar's attention, everyone of them would be in disgrace. Whatever was Ivansky dreaming of?

'Very well,' Ivan said, 'then I'll search him, if no one else is willing.' He took hold of Kirsten by the scruff of the neck, choking him and almost ripping his tunic collar. Kirsten, usually very easy-going and placid, on the rare occasions he did lose his temper, invariably precipitated far-reaching and frightening consequences. He lost his temper now and jabbed his elbow sharply into the pit of Ivan's stomach. Ivan let go immediately, doubling over with a gasp of pain as he looked at Kirsten in amazement. And because his chin was so accessible Kirsten let fly again, this time with his fist, catching Ivan squarely on the chin. Ivan crumpled to the floor while Grigory and Yuri Lubertsky rushed to the rescue.

'Idiots!' Kolya roared impotently. 'Idiots! Stop this brawling and shouting on my premises. Stand up, Ivan, Count, and be a man! You deserve what you got. Kirsten, apologize at once for striking Ivan. You've both had your say now and are quits, so we'll have no more of this nonsense. Kirsten did not cheat, Ivan did not call him names, Kirsten did not strike him, and they've both apologized to one another. If anyone contradicts me, I'll skin him alive. Now then, let's all go to Camilla's. I fancy her kind of folly more than this one. Come on, get your coats on, the evening's on me.'

Ivan got shakily to his feet. Nursing his sore chin, he clashed with Kirsten once again, determined to have his pound of flesh. He addressed the company, not the individual; 'Let him swear before the icon of the Holy Virgin Mary he is not a cheat and a liar, and I'll apologize.'

'How dare you, Ivan!' Kirsten cried in outrage. 'How dare you! You know full well I'd never blaspheme before a saint in order to salvage my reputation. If you can't accept a gentleman's word, then the only way to settle the matter is without the Holy Virgin being brought into it – I challenge you to a duel, Count Ivansky.'

'Done!' said Ivan, a gleam in his eye.

'Gentlemen, gentlemen,' Yuri Lubertsky pleaded, 'this is madness. . . . '

'Shut up, Yuri. Don't interfere,' Kirsten said, his face pale, nostrils pinched and quivering. The Chulkovo twins also tried to pour oil on troubled waters, realizing a matter of honour had gone a little too far. But Kirsten and Ivan were both now past reason and only wanted blood from each other. Kirsten had to be prevented from striking another blow to Ivan's chin, while Ivan deliberately provoked him further; 'Choose your seconds well, Vremya, because this will be the last night you'll be able to choose anything – including your marked cards.'

'Enough!' Kolya screamed in frenzy while Kirsten tried to shake off restraining arms; 'Stop this do . . . come on, let's all go to Camilla's.'

'You go, Prince Nikolay, I resign as your Aide.'

'Vremya, don't be a fool all your life,' Kolya scolded as he tried to put an end to all this nonsense.

'Sir, please don't call me a fool.'

'Vremya, Count, you are drunk! Ivansky is drunk! You are all drunk . . . pissed out of your tiddling little pockets, everyone of you! And that's why this affair is going no further than these four walls. Come along, let's go to the

57

OoLaLa on Nevsky . . . a woman all round will do everyone a world of good.'

Kolya was ignored. Count Ivansky said; 'Choose your
weapons, Vremya.'

'Roulette!'

'No, no, no!' Kolya, demented, clutched his head. 'No,
no, no! For God's sake, let's put an end to this madness.
The Tsar will put us all in the Petropavloskaya if he hears
of this. Roulette is strictly forbidden.'

'Tomorrow morning, Vremya,' said Ivan triumphantly.
'Since you have chosen the mode of despatch, I shall choose
the place. My man will bring word to you.' He asked
Grigory to fetch his coat. Shrugging himself into it, the
gleam in his blue eyes was more than simply calculating.
'Let's hope you can be as brave sober as you are drunk,
Vremya!' Turning on his heel, Count Ivansky strode out.
The others soon followed.

Kolya tipped the rest of the vodka from the bottle into
his glass and gulped it down sloppily as Kirsten scooped up
his winnings. 'Leave it,' Kolya said brusquely, scowling
over his shoulder at Kirsten whom he could see in the
mirrored panels. 'You shall have it tomorrow when
honour has been restored.'

Kirsten, his face set into a rigid mask, obeyed. He put on
his dark grey greatcoat, hat, scarf and, pulling on his
leather gloves, preceded Kolya into the wintry square.

'You didn't mean that about resigning as my Aide, did
you, you silly boy?' Kolya asked placatingly as he trotted
up behind Kirsten marching off.

'Yes, Sir.'

'Sometimes, Vremya, Count, you are like a spoilt child!'
Kolya said, shaking his head in exasperation. 'But I know
you don't mean what you say – because you're not so
stupid you don't know which side your bread is buttered –
or whose doing the buttering. You'll still be in my employ
this time tomorrow . . . provided of course you haven't
blown your brains out. Now, for God's sake, let's get into
the warmth of Camilla's.' Then he suddenly chuckled,
slapping his gloved hands together heartily. 'Tut-Tut! If
there's anything I despise more than cheating, it's a man

who accuses without proof . . . cab!' Waving his arms in the air like a windmill, Prince Nikolay attempted to draw himself to the attention of the driver of the horse-drawn cab. It clopped away around the corner. 'You're very inebriated, you know, Kirsten,' Kolya said gravely, 'so was Ivan. You're both young fools challenging each other to roulette. One of you is going to get himself killed.'

'That's the general idea, Sir. The only way honour will be restored . . . Ivansky is an upstart.'

'Let's not go into character assassination as well. You're a drunken little fool, and whether you did or did not cheat is irrelevant now . . .'

'I beg your pardon, Sir . . . Prince Nikolay . . . but I cannot serve a man who's under the impression I'm a drunken cheat!' Kirsten pulled out of Kolya's restraining grip on his arm, and began to weave his way in the opposite direction. 'Even if he is a man of benign seniority . . . and a Prince . . . *lèse-majesté* and all that to offend your honour. I'm only a Count . . . Count Good-for-Nothing . . . and if this is to be my last night on earth, I'll see it out with dignity. I'm not going to Camilla's but home to bed, alone!'

Behind him Kolya clapped heartily. 'Bravo, bravo! Let me introduce you to another protégé of mine, Madame Zavia, at the Pushkin Theatre. My young friend, she would take you as her leading man any day!' Then raising his voice sternly, Kolya called after Kirsten's receding figure: 'Come back at once! I don't know if you're still play-acting, Vremya, Count, but if you're not, neither can I stand a man who can't hold his liquor as soon as the cold air hits him. You're fast trying my patience tonight, Kirsten, as well as my good humour. In which case I can easily see you dismissed from a respectable post for drunken impudence and inciting another Officer to a dangerous and forbidden pastime.' Prince Nikolay, on spindly legs, his paunch preceding him, cut a very comical figure in a black Astrakan coat and hat, his grey hair sticking out in freezing spikes from beneath the hat. He caught up with Kirsten striding off into the darkness. He turned him round and pointed him back in the direction of Isaakiyevskaya Ploshad.

'And by the way, Vremya, Count,' Kolya added, puffing heavily and desirous only of getting into the lovely warmth of Camilla's bordello, 'had I thought you cheated at yablon, I'd allow you to shoot your brains out tonight instead of at dawn. The crime, dear boy, lies not in the crime itself, but in bringing it to everyone's attention. You're not a cheat, you're a wizard who succeeded in claiming the jackpot everyone else was panting after – including me, as rich as I am. That's enough for me to want to congratulate, not condemn you . . . cab!' He released Kirsten's sleeve and on spindly legs chased after the troika. 'Cabman . . . wait, wait I say! The devil! Do you see the way that madman drives?' Kolya jumped back in alarm.

The sledge, pulled by two handsome black horses, skidded to a stop twenty paces further along the street. Kolya, splashed with slush and suffering from fright, gave the sledgeman a piece of his mind: 'You are insane to drive like that in a narrow street! It's a wonder there're any runners left on that thing of yours. I shall report you to the Ministry of Public Outrages, sir!' Brandishing one fist, he held onto the rear wooden strut of the troika with the other.

The driver turned and waved; 'Kirsten . . . there you are! I've been looking all over St Petersburg for you.'

Kirsten, looking a little jaded, came up to the troika where Kolya stood with his mouth agape. 'Vremya, Count, do you know this enchanting creature? She seems to know you.'

'My sister . . . my God, Sonya, what're you doing? What're you wearing?' The vodka shifted very quickly from his head to his feet as, rooted in horror, Kirsten observed his sister holding in her ungloved hands the reins of two great black pawing horses snorting steam everywhere.

She looked down at herself, unsure of what she was wearing; 'Oh this . . . it's my nightdress . . . '

'I can see it's your nightdress!' Kirsten bellowed.

'Please don't shout at me, Kirsten! People have been angry all evening and I'm tired of being shouted at. I don't think I can stand much more aggression and told papa so.' She tossed back her chestnut curls with one hand, a gesture

Prince Nikolay found enchantingly seductive. 'I didn't have time to get dressed,' she explained.

'You didn't have time! My God, look at you Sonya, you'll catch your death half naked like that.'

'I am *not* naked!'

'You are. You look a sight!' Kirsten glared at some passers-by, late night party, opera or theatre goers, who had stopped to observe them with idle curiosity and much amusement.

Kolya stepped forward to stop any further friction between brother and sister. 'Kirsten, Count, you haven't introduced me to your charming sister.'

'Sonya, meet Prince Nikolay Dubrovka in the Imperial Service to the Tsar of all the Russias. I am but his humble Aide . . . Kolya, my wretched sister, Countess Sonya . . . will that do?' Kirsten bowed with a flourish, before leaping onto the pedestal of an equestrian statue of a Russian General. He hung there like a frozen flag at half mast.

'Kirsten, why are you showing off?' Sonya asked acidly while making it a point to ignore the Prince who had stepped forward to take her hand on introduction. She kept her hand to herself. When he solicitously offered his great-coat and scarf to shield her from the weather and the public eye, Sonya refused to grant him even that little pleasure.

'No, thank you, Prince Dubrovka, I'm warm enough.'

'Kolya, please call me Kolya, Countess Sonya.'

'I'd prefer to call you Prince Dubrovka as we don't know each other,' she said, putting him well and truly in his place so that Kirsten had to concede a sly grin. Sonya turned to her brother and wiped the grin off his face by saying, 'Today . . . tonight in fact, has been the last straw, Kirsten. I'm leaving home.'

'Why petroushka?' He presented her a sympathetically sober face.

'Papa has been more than usually intolerable and Prat the Rat has put me on a regime of raw liver sandwiches to restore my blood. I told him nothing about me needed restoring, but he could restore himself to Paris because he was nothing but a charlatan who was lining his own pocket at my expense . . . my health's expense to be exact. He's turning me into a neurotic like mama and I'm having no more of it . . . Kirsten, are you listening to me?'

'Of course, petroushka, I haven't gone anywhere.'

He still hung like a drunken lout on the Imperial statue. Sonya frowned at him severely. 'Come down off that statue and behave with some dignity. Prat got so angry with me, he reported me to papa for insolence. Then papa shouted at me, then at mama, then at Anna – all the usual scenes. Papa stormed out of the house to his Club and Prat to Paris – or so he made out. Then Sasha arrived and shortly afterwards papa returned. He caught Sasha in mama's bedroom and sacked Anna for not reporting such 'goings-on' as he called it. Anna packed her things to go home to her family at Novgorod, leaving mama having her usual nervous breakdown.'

'Slow down, petroushka,' Kirsten said laughing, 'you're giving me a nervous breakdown while you're running out of steam.'

'Please don't jest about such a serious matter, Kirsten.' Up till now she had avoided looking at the strange figure of Prince Nikolay Dubrovka with his rheumy red-rimmed eyes and frozen ears sticking out under his hat, everything about him grey, drab and watery. She did so now, conveying that she held him entirely responsible for her brother's condition. 'Kirsten,' sweeping her icy glance back to him, 'while Sasha and papa were squabbling about the meaning of immorality, I took Sasha's troika . . . this one here as you can see. I intend to drive to the estate at Novgorod with Anna and to stay there with her until everyone comes to their senses. But before leaving, I thought I'd better find you to put you in the picture. I've been looking everywhere for you. You must come home now and comfort mama because she's heartbroken over everything . . . you were supposed to dine with us tonight. Had you forgotten?'

Kirsten clapped a hand to his forehead, the other hanging onto the bronze horse's leg for safety's sake; 'Blast, I had forgotten . . . poor mama. But the Prince had a little party. Sorry.'

Again she dashed Prince Nikolay with a disdainful look, the chill edge of disapproval in her tone when she addressed him; 'Goodnight, Prince Dubrovka, I'm taking my brother home. Climb in, Kirsten. I'll drive, since you're incapable.'

'I'm not incapable . . . of anything!' And to prove it he dived headfirst off the statue into the bottom of cousin Sasha's old-fashioned troika. Kirsten settled himself into the warm fur rugs, a beatific grin on his face. 'Goodnight Prince . . . Sir . . . ' He waved an airy hand, 'Diana in her chariot is about to transport me to the land of sweet dreams . . . the only time I'm not in debt.'

'Lucky you,' said Kolya mournfully, once more stepping back with agility as Sonya got the horses moving, showering him with yet more snow and icy mud. He watched in admiration as she drove off fast and furiously along the street.

Concentrating on driving, Sonya said over her shoulder to Kirsten; 'Since you became that man's Aide, you've become even more irresponsible. What's the matter with you Kirsten that you wish to ruin your life and career by falling into such bad company?'

'Is he bad?' Kirsten mumbled sleepily.

'Why do you do it, Kirsten?'

'Maybe it's because I'm not happy. I have troubles. Kolya's the only one who will listen to them.'

'What troubles?'

'Oh, nothing to concern your pretty little head about.'

'Don't patronize me, Kirsten.'

He opened his eyes, propped himself on his elbows and said more coherently, 'Why, thou art a shrew in disguise, wherefore this new Sonya?' He sank back again with a heavy sigh. 'Petroushka, methinks you've grown up at last.'

'I don't know what you're talking about!'

'You managed to impress Kolya. Of that, little sister, I'm certain. I've never seen him with such a light in his eye – not even in Camilla's presence has he ever been so besotted by anyone.'

'And why are you so besotted with him?'

'Because he pays my debts and keeps me out of trouble.'

'Why would he want to do that? Kirsten, just tell me the truth. Why must you gamble and drink with him so that you lose all dignity and self-respect?'

'Why must you ask such damned awkward questions?'

'Don't swear in my presence, Kirsten. Prince Nikolay Dubrovka has a very unsavoury and disreputable reputation in St Petersburg,' she tartly rejoined.

'Has he? I didn't know that.' Kirsten yawned. 'He's very rich and very well connected, a member of the Imperial family, which must mean something.'

'It means nothing to me. It's where a person is going that matters, not where he comes from.'

'Oh dear, thou art a blue-stocking after all. I always feared it with Prat the Rat gnawing at your entrails the live-long day. Petroushka, it amazes me where you glean all your information from considering you never set foot out of the house – tonight being an exceptional revelation.' His words were slurred and Sonya thought her brother was pathetic. She kept her thoughts to herself and Kirsten added admiringly, 'Where did you learn to handle horses like Diana?'

'Novgorod, when papa had gone hunting for the day and couldn't object. And, if you must know, plenty of information arrives via willing gossipers every day through our front door, so I don't need to go outside for it.'

Presently, when Kirsten's gentle snores irritated her, she shouted above the iron ring of horses' hooves on the cobble-stones in Kirovsky Ploshad, 'Kirsten, we're home! Will you promise me something?' She drew to a halt by the iron railings in front of the house, praying her father had taken a trip to Siberia.

'What?' Kirsten mumbled, looking very dishevelled when he reluctantly emerged from under cousin Sasha's fur rugs.

'If papa isn't home – and I suspect he won't return again tonight after he's thrown everyone out of the house – please don't mention anything about my riding out in St Petersburg in my nightdress.'

Kirsten grinned lazily; 'I won't if you won't.' Then, upon further deliberation he sat up, yawned, stretched his arms to the frosty stars and drawled, 'Sonya darling, you wouldn't by any chance have eighty-four thousand roubles hidden in your mouldy liver sandwiches, would you?'

'Why?' she asked suspiciously.

'Because I'm a dead man if you haven't.'

Chapter Four

At four o'clock in the morning, having only just dropped off into an uneasy sleep, Sonya was wakened almost immediately by the squeak of floorboards outside her bedroom door. At once she was on the alert, sensing it must be Kirsten. She reached for her thin wrap at the foot of the bed and crept barefoot to the door.

She had left Kirsten with their mother who had poured out all her troubles on his shoulder so that by the time he had left her his epaulette was very wet. Their father had not returned all night, for which concession everyone was infinitely grateful. After flinging cousin Sasha into the snowy street where he had had to find alternative transport to get him back to his own house because his troika had gone missing, the Count had left Kirovsky Ploshad, and Anna reappeared. She had hidden herself in the Countess's great wardrobe, determined to stay at Kirovsky Ploshad despite its fierce master.

Sonya opened her bedroom door just a sliver. She saw no one. She tiptoed out onto the landing and peering over the banisters saw Kirsten in full dress uniform descending the marble staircase, his boots in one hand and his shako under his arm. His hair and moustache had been groomed to glossy perfection:

'You're looking very handsome this morning, Kirsten,' Sonya snorted with stifled laughter, her hand over her mouth so that the Countess might not hear.

With a start, Kirsten almost missed his footing. He turned on the stairs to glower up at his sister. 'What are you doing out of bed?' he hissed, his brilliant blue tunic with its breastful of gold braiding making him scintillate like a frosty Christmas tree, Sonya couldn't help another titter.

'What's so funny?' Kirsten demanded.

'You! You look the honest picture of bravery – if it weren't for your bare toes. Your socks need darning – you ought to give them to Anna. Anyway, where do you think you're going all dressed up like that?'

'To my barracks – if it's anything to do with you.'

'Why? Is there a war on?'

He sighed in exasperation. 'Sonya, why don't you be a good girl and go back to bed?'

'Why don't you stop patronizing me for a change?'

'Sonya,' he said getting angry, 'If you don't return to your room immediately, I'll . . . I'll tell papa about your little escapade last night.' He retraced his steps and came to stand just under the landing curve so that she looked down into his face.

Sonya smiled wickedly, her chestnut curls tumbling over her shoulders from where she leaned dangerously over the stair-well. 'And I'll tell him about you. I'll tell him you've gambled away your life for eighty-four thousand roubles. You cheated, and you can't vindicate yourself other than by calling for a duel. I'll tell him about fat Princess Irene who's your mistress and the wife of papa's best friend who happens to be Minister of the Interior. I'll tell him about Prince Nikolay Dubrovka who pays your mistress's bills and all your other debts, for some very sinister reason. Are you blackmailing him?'

'*Merde*!' said Kirsten, the French epithet coming easily, 'you're a minx!' He flung disparaging glances to the high ornate dome of the ceiling. 'What have I done to deserve a sister like you?'

'I'm only protecting both our interests, Kirsten,' she said sweetly.

'Well then, please be a good girl and go back to your bedroom before you catch your death.'

'Oh, I've already caught it.' She made an ugly grimace.

'Look at me, see my fangs? I'm the harbinger of death, a vampire fed on raw liver sandwiches and port wine. My blood is so rich they can drain it off to make iron-railings for the park. No one suspects how strong I really am after years of being fed on vampire food.'

He tried not to laugh. 'Petroushka, the joke's gone far enough. Wherever you heard that silly story about eighty-four thousand roubles, it just isn't true. I'm going.' He turned on the stairs.

'You told me, fibber. And do you know where you're supposed to be going?' she taunted. 'I do. Here . . . ' She opened her fist. 'A message from Count Ivan Ivansky, delivered by his servant a short while ago, if that's what you're waiting for. I know you're not going to the Kutuzov Barracks, because that's hardly the place to fight a duel when the Tsar has forbidden duelling. Russian roulette, too. Tut-tut, Kirsten!'

'Damn it all Sonya,' he began, but she cut him short.

'Did you challenge him, or he you?'

'It's nothing to do with you . . . give me that note . . . ' He leapt up the stairs.

'No!' She held it at arm's length above her head. 'If you're late for supper tonight, Kirsten, I'll tell mama you've been delayed because you've blown your brains out.' Then she dropped her tone of badinage. 'Kirsten Vremya, if you insist on going through with this thing, I'll have to attend a dual funeral because mama will surely blow out *her* brains! You know how she loves and dotes on you . . . as we all do. So don't be stupid. You're all we've got to stand up for us when papa gets angry with us. Send a message at once, please, to Count Ivansky calling this whole thing off.'

Kirsten groaned. 'You know nothing about a gentleman's honour, Sonya, so please mind your own business and return to your room. Were you my young brother instead of sister, I'd wallop you very thoroughly for your interference. Now give me that note.' He snatched it from her and his shako went tumbling down the stairs, reminding her of what his head would do if he insisted on playing Russian roulette.

'Very well, Kirsten,' she said. 'I shan't mourn for you, or

for Ivan Ivansky. I'm going back to bed while you fight it out between you. And don't worry, I shan't split on you to either mama or papa – not until it's all over and we're lighting candles over your beautiful dead body so thoughtfully washed and dressed in its hero's uniform. I think you're immensely selfish, and the glory you desire so much will always elude you – you're too stupid and too vain to know otherwise. Vassily's waiting outside in a carriage with your box of pistols!' she flung over her shoulder with a final shrug of indifference.

ii

From her bedroom window Sonya watched Kirsten climb into the waiting carriage, his shako and boots now in their proper places, his spurs catching the lamplight, for it was still very dark outside. She made haste to dress herself, putting on an assortment of thick underclothes and an ugly grey wool dress over which she donned a heavy winter cloak also in an indistinguishable grey. She pulled the hood over her head, wound a long scarf round her neck and lower half of her face, and tugging on her gloves slipped her hands into a grey wolf-muff. Sonya let herself out of the silent house. Outside on the frozen pavement she realized she still wore her thin indoor slippers. Not wishing to go back for her fur boots, she ignored her icy feet, every step feeling like a shard of glass through the thin soles of her slippers.

Icicles as thick as logs hung from the drainpipes and gutters of the imposing mansions along the river Neva. Kirsten's carriage had gone down Kirovsky-Prospekt and had turned right towards the Commercial Harbour. Though the carriage was nowhere in sight, Sonya knew exactly where it was heading; Ivan Ivansky's note had been only too explicit. He had mentioned the Rostralniye Columns, the lighthouses for ships that came in from the Baltic. Nearby, on the same stretch of high ground overlooking the harbour, waste common land overgrown with trees, was to be the venue for what, in Sonya's opinion, was nothing but a murder-ritual about to be enacted by some very disagreeable young men with nothing better to do than seek sensation.

Once through the parkland to the north of Vasilevsky Island and its fortress prison, the ground became harder going. Her breath hung like frosty lace on the air. Sonya realized of course they would have to choose somewhere isolated like this to play their silly games, as far away from the Winter Palace and the Kutuzov Barracks as was possible. Another twenty minutes and she saw three or four carriages parked on the edge of a copse, the leafless trees like skeletons in cottonwool shrouds. Sonya made her way carefully through the semi-light of dawn, her figure in its grey cloak merging with the landscape rimed with a thick hoar-frost. She found a spying-place behind the trunk of a stout pine tree. Within a ring of hurricane-lamps, two camp-tables had been placed together. On each was a box.

Her brother and Count Ivansky sat facing each other across the expanse of the tables. Sonya recognized all the Guardsmen present, some of them attached to the Tsar's General Staff as Kirsten was. Prince Nikolay Dubrovka she had met for the first time last night. Ivan's man-servant was beside his master, and Vassily danced attendance upon Kirsten. With a nasty shock Sonya saw Anatole Pratikayit also there, standing with a priest. Prat the Rat had not sneaked back to Paris after all, but was here to make more profit by attending upon his master's son's body were he to pick the fatal bullet. Traitor! Sonya breathed silently.

'Blindfold?' Philip Chulkovo asked Kirsten, voices carrying clearly on the still, frosty air.

'Of course. I don't wish to be accused of cheating again.'

Ivan stared Kirsten straight in the eye until the blindfolds were tied. Kolya took two identical revolvers, one from Ivan's box and one from Kirsten's. He inserted a single bullet in the chamber of each. He spun the chambers before handing over the two weapons to Kirsten and Ivan.

Sonya chewed her nails, wondering if Prince Nikolay had received the message she had sent via Anna to his rooms on Dvortsovaya Ploshad; wondering how he could substitute blanks for real bullets when everyone had been watching him so carefully; wondering, too, if he would do such a thing to save lives instead of honour just on her pleas alone. She had treated him so coldly last night in St Isaac's Cathe-

69

dral Square, almost running him down in Sasha's troika in a gesture of defiance which she now regretted. Wretched, wretched, Kirsten! She breathed again, almost chewing her fingernails to the cuticles.

'Do you retract your accusation, Count Ivansky?' Yuri Lubertsky asked Ivan as that man's second.

'I do not!'

'Count Vremya, do you wish to retract your challenge to Count Ivansky?' Philip Chulkovo asked Kirsten.

'No.'

'Count Ivansky, do you wish to make peace with Count Vremya?'

'No.'

'Do either of you have anything at all to say to each other before we start?'

'No,' they both replied in unison.

Then the priest came forward, gave them absolution and blessed them with the sign of the holy cross, while Sonya wondered what good that would do when both men had hardened their hearts against each other and were determined to see each other dead. Kolya had the final word. 'Well, let's get on with it then for God's sake. I have to make arrangements to get to Paris before the Tsar gets hold of me – I advise you all to disappear very quickly once one of these fools is dead at our feet. Go on then, Ivansky, Count!'

Ivan raised his revolver, and put it to his head. Sonya shut her eyes as Ivan's finger tightened on the trigger. She heard only a click on the empty air. Ivan was still in one piece. Kirsten's turn.

Her clothes were damp not only with the chill of the morning, but also because of terrible nervousness. The palms of her hands felt clammy and slippery inside her muff. Sonya could not bear to stand silently by, doing nothing, while her brother killed himself, perhaps at the first round. Neither could she trust to Prince Nikolay Dubrovka's sincerity – even supposing he had got her message. Kirsten raised the revolver to his head but even as he pulled back the trigger, Sonya darted from the cover of the trees, launched herself on him and they both went

70

crashing down with his camp stool, table and gun box. Before he could rip his blindfold away, on her knees, she had picked up his revolver. Holding it in both hands, Sonya pointed it at Ivan's heart.

By now, he, too, in the confusion had wonderingly torn aside his blindfold to stare at her in astonishment.

'Sonya . . . don't be a little fool,' Kirsten implored, helplessly observing her foolhardy action as he lay sprawled on the hard cold ground.

'I'm going to be the one to kill Count Ivan Ivansky if you don't stop this nonsense,' she informed the dumbstruck company of men.

Count Ivansky shrugged in acceptance. 'Countess, I didn't know you, too, bore me such a grudge. Vremya, it appears I now have a two-to-one chance of survival. Lady-luck is not smiling at me – as pretty as she looks this morning kneeling there with a gun at my heart. Yes, I will marry you, Countess,' and how he had the nerve to make light of the situation when he had started all this in the first place, Sonya never knew.

'Give me the gun, Sonya . . . Sonya don't . . . !' Kirsten pleaded.

She had moved the gun away from Ivan and pointed it at her own head instead. Breathing hard, she did not dare to pull the trigger – just in case. She looked then at Prince Nikolay who was as mesmerized by her actions as the others, all of them not knowing what to do in the circumstances. 'Thank you for acting on my message, Prince Dubrovka?' she said simply.

'What message, Countess?' He shifted uncomfortably from foot to foot.

'About putting an end to this before it started, about substituting a blank bullet in each gun . . . you did, didn't you, Prince Nikolay?'

'Damn it Sonya . . . you didn't ask him that, did you?' Kirsten got off the ground and lunged for the gun, but she forestalled him.

'Yes, I did, Kirsten! Don't come any nearer otherwise I'll pull the trigger . . . one never knows who to trust.'

'How dare you Sonya, how dare you interfere in men's

71

affairs,' he said in disgust, words failing him, 'give me that gun at once!'

'No!' she said sharply, pressing the barrel more ruthlessly to her temple. 'If Prince Dubrovka has gone along with all of you, then I'll play roulette, too – the way you and Ivan are playing it. Go on, Ivan, let's start again. Your turn, or is it ladies first?'

'Sonya, you idiot.' Kirsten did not know what to do or say, like the others afraid to push her too far, none of them sure of her potential.

'Don't worry, Vremya, Count.' Kolya came forward, holding out his hand. 'Give me the gun please, Countess, it will do nothing . . . see here . . . give it to me, please. All the chambers are empty.' He took the revolver calmly out of her hand and in rapid succession fired at the pine tree behind which she had been hiding. No bullet embedded itself in the trunk, whatever he had substituted for a bullet in the chamber of the revolver, utterly harmless.

Kirsten seemed to crumple, whether in relief or in disgust, nobody could tell because Ivan, behind everyone's back, as a further test of Kolya's scruples, took up his own gun next and shot himself, this time with a very real bullet.

iii

Sonya, tearful for a whole week, had been bombarded from all sides. The very worst had been Kirsten's silent censure for interfering in matters that did not concern her. He refused to forgive her for having placed Prince Nikolay in a very difficult situation by making him choose between brother and sister. Both revolvers had indeed been harmless, Prince Nikolay as good at juggling bullets as his protégé had been at cards. Having guessed as much, Ivan had taken up a pistol from his box while attention had been focused on Sonya. Knowing full well that that weapon was fully loaded, Ivan had deliberately aimed at his foot, thus salvaging his own reputation – at the same time annihilating the credibility of Kirsten and Kolya in everyone's eyes. While sympathy was being lavished on him in the hospital, he became the hero of the moment and Kirsten was once

72

more the villain of the piece. That Sonya had been the one to set the scene for Ivan Ivansky's vindication while disgracing not only her brother and herself, but also Prince Nikolay, was too much for Kirsten to take. He ignored her, the first time they had ever fallen out, and bitterly.

'It serves Ivan right if he is in a lot of pain,' Sonya told her mother savagely, 'he has really messed things up for all of us . . . especially Kirsten.'

Her mother wept and suffered with her. Not only was her beloved Kirsten in disgrace with the Tsar, but Count Vremya had refused to allow their daughter to be brought out into society until the scandal of her night-ride through the streets of St Petersburg had died down. Parties and new clothes for Sonya would not, after all, be providing the Countess with light relief, so she took to her bed, and stayed there. Even cousin Sasha wasn't permitted to the house anymore; life had indeed become intolerable at Kirovsky Ploshad.

'I cannot believe . . . no I cannot believe that you, a mere snippet of a girl, interfered in matters of honour between young gentlemen,' her father had ranted and raved at Sonya.

'But papa, Kirsten was going to kill himself . . . '

'Desist!' Her father had roared. 'It might not have been a bad thing . . . now look at the harm he's done all of us. And you! You of all people, in such fragile health, something your mother has had me believing for years, to go parading yourself on the wintry streets of St Petersburg wearing only your chemise . . . '

'Nightdress, papa.'

'Silence girl! You're a wanton hussy. I know now it wasn't your body that required as much attention all these years as your head. I've been wasting my money on you, your mother and that miserable Pratikayit wriggling around this house and my wallet like a worm in a glass bottle. Well, it's going to stop. Either you and your mother get well fast or you can both go into a sanatorium for the rest of your lives. Now then, have you given further thought to Prince Nikolay Dubrovka's proposal of marriage?'

'Yes father.'

His cold grey eyes gleamed. 'Good.'

'But I can't marry him.'

'Why not?'

'I only met him a week ago.'

'He has already made up his mind about you and his judgement must necessarily count for more than that of a mere snippet of a girl lacking in all things, including judgement. Anyway, he doesn't intend marrying you until your seventeenth birthday – another year. He has, nevertheless, agreed to settle a large sum of money on you if you agree to the engagement. Personally, I think he must be off his head to want to wed you after the way you've behaved, but since he has, you're going to take the best offer ever likely to come your way after what you've done to ruin your reputation.'

'No, father, I will not marry him . . . I can't . . .'

'And pray tell me why not?' Count Vremya stood stiffly before the fireplace in the salon, the flames leaping behind him as he stood warming his hands. Sonya said nothing, irritating him further. 'Stop plucking your skirts and answer me!'

'I don't love him,' she said, raising her tear-stained face beseechingly.

He snorted contemptuously. 'What kind of answer is that!'

'The truth, father.'

'A Prince from the House of Romonov offers you marriage and you turn your nose up at him because you do not love him! You're as silly as your mother, dear girl, with her idle dreams about love and marriage. I have provided the very best of everything for her all these years and she has provided me only with illness, dead children and unfaithfulness through a misguided notion that she's in love with someone else – someone, incidentally, who never offered her marriage! She has filled your head with the same kind of romantic rubbish, so I don't want you to use the word love to me, but something more solid on which to base your rejections of Kolya.'

'He's been married three times before.'

'So?' The Count's black brows disappeared into his hairline.* 'His wives are dead, he's not a bigamist if that's what worries you.'

'He has grandchildren my age.'

'Then you'll have company enough to entertain your lonely hours, won't you? You're always complaining about your lack of suitable companions, so at Dubrovka-Dvaryets you won't feel deprived, will you?'

'He's too old for me, father. I shall be seventeen, he's nearer seventy!'

He turned his back on her, reached for his gold and malachite snuff-box on the high marble mantlepiece and opening the lid pinched out the nuttish brown powder which he inserted into each nostril with a hearty sniff. He replaced the box before turning to her. 'He is a man in the prime of his life. A man of influence, experience, wisdom and wealth, quite apart from his birthright. A man thought very highly of by the Tsar and Tsarina. Can a younger man give you all that, eh, dear girl? A younger man like your precious brother, perhaps – God forbid – who will end up in a debtors' prison or worse? An irresponsible young fool who whiles away his time in sordid sport to leave you widowed and with child because he's decided to blow his brains out as the pressures of his easy-going existence are too unbearable to take anymore? *Zounds*, but what has your mother produced in the way of children! So, I think Prince Nikolay Dubrovka will make you a very suitable husband.'

'I will not marry him, father,' she said with quiet conviction, her damp handkerchief four square in her lap as she sat bolt upright on the sofa and wished only to get away from her father's domineering presence.

He regarded her piercingly from under his heavy black brows. 'Have you someone else in mind? I wouldn't put it past you, considering your shameless behaviour of late. Have you been having secret assignations with some young fool?'

'No, father. Where would I get the opportunity?'

'Don't be impertinent, young lady! Very well then, you will marry Kolya, and there's an end to this discussion. I will inform him directly of your change of heart.'

'No, I will not marry him. I'm grateful to him for offering me marriage, and for keeping Kirsten and his silly friends out of the Petropavlovskaya, and for smoothing things over with the Tsar, and for whatever else he's done for our family, but I shall not marry Prince Nikolay Dubrovka.' Sonya got up and headed for the double doors of the salon.

'Sonya, I'm warning you!' said her father, sounding as ominous as his daughter sounded determined. 'I'll give you one month in which to change your mind. If, after that time, you still insist on behaving in this stubborn, selfish and impudent manner to cause offence not only to me but also to Prince Nikolay, then you will be banished from St Petersburg. You will be sent to Novgorod to live in solitary confinement until such time as you do change your mind.'

'Very well, papa,' Sonya answered levelly. 'I'll live at Novgorod until I'm an old lady.' He would never wear her down, never! She was quite determined.

'*Zounds* girl!' he bellowed, so that the Countess upstairs in her boudoir heard and cringed for her daughter's sake. 'You deserve to be horsewhipped! Get out of my sight before it comes to that. *Ropa, Ropa! Zounds man*, where are you?' His man-servant came running. 'Ropa, fetch me my stick, and the newspapers, the carriage and my hat. And for God's sake rid me once and for all of this ungrateful family of mine! I shall go to my Club for lunch.'

iv

Ivan Ivansky, grinning broadly and looking positively perky despite a badly injured foot, comfortably relaxed without his crutch while helping himself to more vodka from a table beside him. He sprawled full length on a sofa, a fur rug covering him since he wore only a silken nightshirt and velveteen dressing gown in a deep magenta shade that clashed disastrously with his vivid auburn colouring. Ivan caressed his waxed moustache lovingly, raised his glass of vodka and winked at Yuri Lubertsky paying him a social visit in his rooms at General Staff Headquarters off the Winter Palace Square. 'Am I not a genius, Lubertsky?'

Yuri, buffing his nails with a jewelled silver buffer he always carried in his pocket, paused from his labours, sat straight in his chair, and looked at Ivan in admiration. 'A genius,' he agreed wholeheartedly.

'Not only have I killed several birds with one bullet,' Ivan chuckled in delight, 'but that immature Vremya will be off my back for several months . . . and of course darling rich Irene's, too.'

'Sheer genius,' Yuri murmured, gazing in apparent awe at the soft blue-velvet underside of his nail-buffer shaped like a Venetian gondola.

'When I first heard about my new assignment, I could have shot Vremya's old man himself for having arranged such a thing for me, while leaving his own son's name out of it. Smacks of nepotism in the Foreign Ministry if you ask me.'

'Entirely!' Yuri agreed emphatically. 'After all, Kirsten's Prince Nikolay's Aide, not you.'

'Precisely! Who in his right senses would wish to be posted to Tibet, anyway? I am not in my right senses as the Tsar has since realized. God, it's cold enough here in winter to freeze the balls off a brass monkey, let alone mine stranded on the Chang-Tang. And that's why Count Mikail put my name down for the Legation Escort, and not Kirsten's, his wonderful son and heir. Rather that Count Ivan Ivansky with several brothers attached to the family name perish in the middle of nowhere than the precious Vremya darling who scrounges for a living.'

'Nepotism,' Yuri murmured as he once more concentrated on his manicure.

Ivan spluttered into his glass of vodka, almost choking himself with mirth. 'I wish I could have been there to see the Vremyas' faces, father and son, when the Tsar ordered Kirsten to Lhasa in my place. Banished, in other words!' With his knuckles Ivan drummed a tattoo on his heavily bandaged foot. 'God, but I'm a genius. A real brave, wouldn't you say, Yuri?'

'Indeed, indeed,' Yuri murmured. 'But I doubt I'd have done what you did just to get out of escort duty, Ivan.'

'The joy of it all, Yuri, was in the manipulation of

77

Vremya! That Kirsten allowed himself to be manipulated by me so easily was damn laughable. But then, the fellow always can be led by the nose by anyone. Weak, that's Vremya, weak and hot-headed. I know he didn't cheat at yablon, that it was Lady-luck smiling on him with fifty thousand roubles worth of teeth which gave him the jackpot – he always was a lucky bastard! But because he let himself fall so easily into my trap, his luck's run out. Serves him right.' Ivan yelled then for his man-servant to fetch another bottle of vodka, he and Yuri having finished the other in half-an-hour of conversation.

'What's it all for, anyway?' Yuri asked as he languidly observed his glass being topped up by the servant.

Ivan asked for his box of cigars. Selecting one, he slowly stripped it of its tissue-paper wrapping. 'Barakov's Mission to Lhasa, you mean?' He concentrated on clipping the end of the cigar. 'Rasputin's idea, I believe. The Tsar and Tsarina fall for anything that smacks of the occult and they can't wait to colonize the Khang-Yul and its monks. They intend to send prettily embroidered clerical vestments done by the Grand Duchess's fair hands to that other reincarnated monk called the Dalai Lama in return for his country.' Ivan lit his cigar and almost singed his moustache. 'Dorjiev is organizing the whole show between Lhasa and St Petersburg.'

'I thought Barakov was,' Yuri said, glancing up for a moment.

'Barakov's leading the Legation, while Dorjiev is acting as go-between.'

'Then where does Prince Nikolay fit into it?'

'He, my dear Yuri, is to lead a surveying-party. Count Mikail, who incidentally is also a big noise in the Geographical Society, wants Kolya to gather as much information as he can on the interior of Tibet, an area nobody apart from a few Tibetans themselves know about. Something to do with beating the British to it, all that sort of imperialism. Count Mikail's anxiety over Kirsten's welfare and safety meant I was detailed to Kolya's Escort party instead of his own Aide, namely Kirsten Vremya. Subtle, but not subtle enough on Count Mikail's part.'

'So that's why you shot off your own foot,' Yuri remarked thoughtfully over his nail-buffer, 'to get out of going to Tibet and not to get at Kirsten for any particular reason?'

'Clever, ain't I?' Ivan smirked above his cigar.

'But how could you be so sure the Tsar would get angry enough with Kirsten to banish him to Tibet in your place, or that your plan concerning the duel would work?' Yuri asked.

'I wasn't. I could only guess he would be damned mad enough with Kirsten Vremya to want to pack him off to outer darkness with Kolya, who after all, is his mentor. Kolya might look an oaf, but underneath he's a shrewd and calculating old devil. I knew that he would play tricks with the guns, that he would never put real bullets in them so that one of us would be killed, because the scandal for him would be disastrous. He values his own good reputation with the Tsar far too much. That's why he was elected – by me – to oversee the formalities of the duel. Human nature is pretty predictable – even a Tsar's, and since duelling is forbidden, especially Russian roulette, I thought he was bound to be disgusted with the Vremyas and their disgraceful behaviour, since Kirsten challenged me in the first place, and not I him. You heard, I take it, about the daughter, too?' Ivan cocked an eyebrow at Yuri.

'Who hasn't,' Yuri replied laconically. 'The whole of St Petersburg is buzzing over what she did or didn't do in her nightdress. By Jove, Ivan, I think Kolya's off his chump to want to marry her after she's exposed herself to the whole world. Though, mind you, I suppose that kind of little stripper is just up his street.'

Ivan pulled a face. 'Too skinny for my liking. I admire her spunk, though, but not her brother's lack of it, or his sneaky ways with Princess Irene when my back's turned. I couldn't have him with his mouth still full of pap climbing into her bed while I was in Lhasa, winning favours and feathering his nest.'

Yuri looked up in exaggerated horror. 'You mangled up your own foot to get out of going to Lhasa for big fat Irene's sake?'

'Not entirely.' Ivan gritted his teeth as he shifted the position of his bandaged leg. 'At least I took a calculated risk by shooting off my big toe and not my head – even if the pain is pretty gruesome. But you see, my dear Yuri, that all has been contrived, and my strategy has worked out marvellously well for me – I think I might even make Field-Marshal one day. Now then, are you staying to supper, I'm feeling vastly peckish?'

'What have you on offer?' Yuri asked, pocketing the nail-buffer to stare vaguely round the room.

'Not much,' Ivan confessed. 'Half a rissole brought with me on discharge from the hospital yesterday. But I can send Hubert out for caviare and pancakes.'

'Thank you Ivan, that will do me nicely.' His pearly nails gleaming, Yuri put an effete hand over his mouth to stifle a yawn. 'Ivan, I always thought Kirsten and you were the best of friends, so why didn't you just ask him outright to take your place to Lhasa, instead of going to such elaborate lengths in staging a fake duel, thereby risking everyone's livelihood and reputation?'

'A good question, Yuri. I did ask him, and the swine merely laughed in my face while quoting the brass monkey joke he'd learned in England. So I thought I'd teach the braggart a lesson. But I've nothing really against Kirsten, it was all good fun – except perhaps for eighty-four thousand roubles the Tsar insisted went into the orphans and widows fund.'

Chapter Five

Tucked away on the edge of her father's hunting estate outside Novgorod was a gloomy family chapel. Sonya, her dark hair prettily covered by a lace scarf grandmother Lizaveta had crocheted and sent from England for her name-day, lit a candle before an Icon of the Virgin Mary.

'I will not marry him, I will not!' she muttered darkly to the Icon, and the priest in the shadows shook his head sadly at the tremulous voice whose prayers were definitely not in accordance with God's wishes. 'After all,' Sonya flung defiantly at the Virgin Mary, 'you're closer to the throne of God than the Tsar, who tells me I must obey my parents. But I can't obey them, I can't! Not when I know they are wrong about Prince Nikolay and me. It will be a disastrous marriage, so please intercede on my behalf and I promise I'll dedicate my life to good deeds, as I have no wish to marry anyone – not ever!' Fiercely Sonya crossed herself before getting up from her knees. Without a backward glance, she left the chapel.

Even grandmother Lizaveta had turned traitor. Her letters were full of glee that Sonya's hand had been asked for in marriage by a Prince from the house of Romonov! 'It's not my hand I'm worried about,' Sonya had written stubbornly and angrily to grandmother Lizaveta, 'but the rest of me!'

'Dear child,' came a swift reply, 'if the question of

having an old man's children bothers you, don't let it. Close your eyes and think of our Holy Russian Empire. You do not want to end up on the shelf as one of womanhood's failures, so stop all this nonsense about not wanting to get married to Prince Nikolay Dubrovka and do as your family know best. It's late as I write this letter, petroushka, and if you are reading my advice to you at the end of your day, then tuck my prayers and God's blessings under your pillow this night and wake to a new day with the resolution that you will make us all very happy by marrying Kolya. Your loving grandmother, Lizaveta.'

But the only thing to lie under Sonya's pillow that night and for many nights to come was a sodden handkerchief.

Six months after banishment to her father's country estate, he came to see her. He brought gifts from the rest of the family, who were not allowed to visit her – even on this special occasion, her seventeenth birthday. The summer was rampant, the air balmy, the sky azure blue and the lake in the grounds thickly covered with waterlilies. Sonya had taken a long walk early that morning to the village of Gorodishche, closer to the family estate than the town of Novgorod, which Gorodishche had formerly been a part of. On her return to the hunting-lodge she was most surprised to see the courtyard teeming with her father's retainers. Her surprise quickly gave way to dismay when she realized the Count was visiting alone, with no Kirsten in attendance eager to make it up with her father after the horrible Ivansky affair.

'Good afternoon, papa.' Flushed and disturbed, Sonya dutifully kissed him on the cheek before taking her place at luncheon where Count Mikail was already seated at the head of the table, waiting for her. It was only when she took up her serviette that Sonya realized she was so flustered at seeing her father, she had forgotten to wash her hands before the meal and her fingernails were black. She kept her hands in her lap and her eyes downcast, not a bit hungry now, whereas an hour ago she had been starving. Around her plate, small presents had been arranged by a loving hand, and Sonya wondered if the housekeeper Lala, her daughter Grechen, or her father himself had arranged the gifts for her. She realized soon enough it could not have been he when, without preamble, he launched into the purpose of his visit, not extending good wishes for her birthday but intent, it seemed, to torture her still further on the subject of Kolya.

'Prince Nikolay and your brother are setting off to Lhasa in six weeks time. The Tsar's order regarding Kirsten accompanying the Legation still stands, and I can do no more – as your mother has forced me to do in such an embarrassing fashion. However, I will not be humbling myself anymore in front of the Emperor, and Kirsten has got what he deserves for being so irresponsible. Your brother wished to speak with you before his departure, but I forbade it – you are still in solitary confinement. But, if you should wish to change your mind regarding your marriage to Kolya, then you will be restored into the bosom of the family and Kirsten may see you.'

He paused expectantly, but Sonya remained silent. Count Mikail sighed deeply, picked up his knife and fork and attacked the meat on his plate. 'Your mother sends her regards and good wishes.'

'Thank you. I will write to her . . . '

'No! I haven't given you permission to write to anyone or to receive letters here at the Lodge. I hope the servants haven't been disobeying my orders?' Black brows scowling, he looked across at her, his pale eyes pebble-hard.

'No, father.' Sonya kept her eyes on the food she was unable to eat. It would be more than her life was worth to confess to collecting her own letters from Gorodishche before they had a chance to fall into any servant's hand. Even grandmother Lizaveta was a life-line to sanity.

'Sonya,' Count Mikail said, slicing into his beefsteak, red with blood as he enjoyed his meat almost raw, 'Kolya has again asked me to intercede on his behalf. He still wants to marry you – though don't ask me why after your shameless behaviour where he's concerned. He has increased his settlement with this his latest and his last request of marriage. You'll never want for another thing throughout life if you consent to marry him, so don't continue to be so stubborn and foolish. Let me return to St Petersburg with your answer in the affirmative.'

'No, father.'

He frowned, but his concentration did not waver from his plateful of food. He helped himself to more asparagus, heaping it onto his sideplate. Munching noisily, butter from the asparagus slipping down his chin, the Count dabbed his mouth with the serviette and said slyly; 'Dear girl, you are making a very stupid mistake. Kolya is shortly off to Lhasa and who knows what might happen to him there; Tibet is a hostile land. You will have Dubrovka-Dvaryets to yourself, a vast fortune at your disposal and no husband to watch where you spend it. Any girl of your age would not think twice about such a proposal.'

'But I am not any girl, father. I am me, Sonya Vremya!'

He slapped his hand so hard on the table the crystal and silver jumped together, his serviette and the table-cloth splashed with the juices from his various plates. Sonya, bunching her fists around the serviette in her lap, looked down in misery at what her life had become – just an untidy mess like the table linen. 'Damn you, girl! You are nothing but a stubborn wench who deserves to be horsewhipped for disobedience, insolence and . . . and wantonness!'

Sonya, two bright spots of colour highlighting her cheek-bones, looked up then, her grey eyes icily defiant. She refused to be mastered by such an unfeeling parent. 'Father, why does Prince Nikolay wish to marry me when he's going off on an expedition that will keep him away for at least two years? Is he hoping to make me a widow swift on the heels of making me a bride? And if so, then please tell me what his motives are?'

Her father's sigh was deep and regretful, sounding most disappointed that months of solitary confinement and social deprivation had left her unperturbed, unchastened, and as wilful as ever. 'Sonya, Sonya . . . ' He laid aside his knife and fork and reached for the *vin claret*. Shaking his head in bemusement he said; 'Is it not enough that Kolya loves you?'

'He doesn't know me, father, and so he can't possibly love me.' Sonya steeled herself for another outburst from him, fearing that his hand would either slap down again on the table or worse, that he might use it upon her. Instead, his reaction was totally unexpected. After several moments of pondering silence over his glass of wine, he set it down and then reached out for her hand, the red sickle-shaped birthmark on the back of his left hand very noticeable against the clammy pallor of his skin.

'Dearest girl,' he murmured thickly, 'let's put an end to this silly business and be friends again. I have no wish to quarrel with you, so please make your old papa a happy man today and say yes to Kolya's proposal of marriage. You will make us both so proud and happy, and I know Kolya will give you everything your heart desires. Say yes, darling girl, for all our sakes, hum?'

What was the use! Sonya felt even more of a helpless victim. A pleading fawning father was not one she was used to, and she did not think she liked this new side to him any better than the old. She withdrew her hand from under his, trapped where it lay on the table between them. 'Please excuse me, father, I feel a little faint in this heat. I went the long way round to Gorodishche Church this morning, not by boat across the river, so I'm a little tired.' Having made her excuses, she fled his over-powering presence.

Sonya did not emerge from her bedroom for the rest of the day, not even when the servants called her for tea. The old peasant woman, Lala, who kept house with Grechen, her mute daughter, poked her head inside Sonya's room to find out what was wrong, but was sent packing swiftly by the one person in the world she never imagined possessed such a waspish nature. 'Very well, Miss, I'll buzz off and settle elsewhere. And here's all the gratitude I get for minding the child I wet-nursed to seventeen! Happy birthday, Countess!' Lala slammed the door on Sonya's headache.

Only when she heard the iron-ring of horses' hooves on cobblestones did Sonya become aware of time slipping by and her father returning from hunting in the nearby forests. The stable-clock chimed the hour of eight. Again Sonya slipped into an uneasy doze.

Her nerves only jumped to alertness hours later when she

heard heavy footsteps on the polished wooden stairs. Her father was going to bed at last! By the bedside clock Sonya could see it was past two o'clock in the morning, her father having stayed up to drink with either his hunting friends, or, hopefully, less drunkenly, with Ropa, his servant, as he sometimes did when the others had departed. The stars shone out of a midnight-blue sky and the silver birches, ghostly in the moonlight, rustled in the warm breeze that came through the open window. The trees sounded as if they were whispering together, telling each other secrets, and Sonya smiled contentedly to herself. But then the smile faded as her unlocked bedroom door was rudely flung open by a discourteous hand, and her father came inside the bedroom with his arms laden with her unopened presents.

'Sonya . . . petroushka, are you awake?' he whispered much too loudly to be sober and Sonya quickly pretended to be asleep. But he still came beside her, dropped the packages on her feet and turned up the oil lamp by the bed before placing himself heavily on the side of the bed.

Behind her closed lids Sonya was aware her father was staring hard at her, the fumes on his heavy breath full in her face. 'Petroushka . . . darling . . . you're so pretty when you're asleep . . . ' He reached out and took up her hand lying on the coverlet and put it to his lips. 'Poor thing,' he murmured fondly, 'you're cold. Shall I shut the window, darling?'

Sonya's eyes flew open. 'No! Please don't, I can't breathe when the windows are closed.'

'As you wish, dear girl.' Then he tried again. Caressing back her thick hair from her wide smooth forehead, his hand hot and sweaty, he smiled. 'It hasn't been much of an anniversary for you, eh, love?'

'It has been enough for me, father.'

'Do you dislike me so much, my child, you cannot bring yourself to call me papa anymore?'

Sonya bit her lip, she felt dangerously close to tears.

'Or is it that my child, my dear little girl, is suddenly a woman and doesn't need her old papa anymore, eh, petroushka?' He chucked her under the chin, forcing her to look at him. 'Why do you make me so unhappy, my child?'

'That was not my intention . . . papa.'

'Come then,' he said, beaming at her, his face marred by thread-veins almost purplish by the light of the oil lamp shining upon them, 'let's open your birthday presents together, shall we? There is one here from Kolya – a diamond and sapphire engagement ring, I think,' he chuckled agreeably as he took it out of its plush little box and held it to the light where it danced and winked enticingly.

Sonya turned her head away, tears spilling from her eyes. 'You're making me unhappy, papa. How can I ever be happy with a man I don't love? By forcing me to marry Prince Nikolay Dubrovka, you will be ruining my whole life, isn't that enough to make me unhappy?' Sonya dashed away her tears, stupid to show weakness in front of her father; a woman's tears enough to put him into a bad mood at once.

But he wasn't angry with her, only loving and gentle as he wiped away the tears, his touch, for a change, almost fatherly. 'Understand, petroushka, as I do, you are a woman now and therefore given to displays of nerves and tantrums. You wouldn't be a woman otherwise. I understand your behaviour and have made allowances for it. You have been in the process of changing from girlhood to womanhood and that is a great time of unrest for you. When you were offered marriage at the tender age of sixteen, it was too much for you to comprehend and to come to terms with all at once. But now a year has passed since your sixteenth birthday, and six months since Kolya's first proposal of marriage, so I think it's time enough for us to stop playing silly games with each other and to start behaving like adults. We will forget about Kolya for a little while, eh darling?' Again he chucked her under the chin and for a wild moment Sonya's heart leapt in relief as she watched him put away the ring in its box. She felt as if a burden had been lifted from her shoulders, a burden that had threatened to bow her down to the ground these past six months. But now her father had seen the sense of it at last, given up the struggle where Prince Nikolay Dubrovka was concerned, and Sonya, swallowing the lump in her throat, gave a feeble smile, her face brighter than it had been for months.

'The country air has worked wonders for you, eh, my little petroushka? You have filled out and blossomed nicely. Been going for long walks by yourself every day?'

She nodded. Then she looked away as his fingers brushed her cheek. He was definitely not sober, nor was he drunk, but a strange introspective mood was upon him, one she did not understand. 'So soft . . . so pure,' he murmured more to himself. 'Kolya is a lucky man . . . you are so much like your mother was at your age . . . she had such lovely shining hair and wide eyes containing her soul . . . just like you, Sonya.' His voice was cracking with emotion. Then he gave way, crumbled and trembling in an agony of conflict and desire, he clutched her to his breast. Sonya, unable to breathe, he held her to him so tightly, was at first bewildered then afraid. She was unable to cry out in protest, and her father said with his lips buried in her hair, 'Sonya . . . oh, my little Sonya, what an entrancing woman you have become. Too good for any man, too good even for a prince . . . darling girl, look at me . . . ' Then he was drawing her head back to make her look at him, his pebble-eyes wildly shining, devouring, like some predatory animal.

'*Papa!*'

'Yes . . . yes, my child . . . you are wonderful . . . wonderful!'

His mouth on her throat, his hands searching beneath her nightdress, exploring her breasts, her waist, the promise of her maturing body, he swept across her in waves of ardour. Count Mikail's impatient hands flung aside the bed covers and lifted Sonya's nightdress above her thighs, his weight pressing on her so that she screamed frantically; 'Papa . . . don't . . . oh don't . . . please let me go, please . . . '

'Petroushka, petroushka darling . . . ' His mouth, wet and slippery, repulsed her. She struggled for air, and, in desperation, clutched at his thinning hair and with a terrified strength managed to pull him off her. Bewildered, humiliated and frightened, she could only sob, 'Don't, oh please don't do this, it's horrible. I will marry Prince

Nikolay, I will, I will, I'll do whatever you want of me, I promise, only please go away and leave me alone.'

All at once he seemed to recollect himself. Jerking away, he stood up. In a hasty yet abstract gesture that was both absurd and pathetic, Count Mikail pulled down his daughter's nightdress. Then, clutching his head, he looked at her as if he wasn't certain who she was or what he was doing there. With a sob of fright, he left the room.

The following morning he was gone from Novgorod.

Lala informed Sonya that 'the master' had been recalled urgently to St Petersburg and would not, after all, be spending a few days in the country. 'God be praised, for he's a difficult man to please,' sniffed Lala deprecatingly over the pies she was making in the kitchen.

Sonya went to the tiny dark chapel she and Kirsten had firmly believed was haunted in the days when innocence was golden-pure as the summer sun on a ripening cornfield, and life stretched ahead as untarnished as the silver moon in Novgorod's midnight sky. Now everything had suddenly darkened, like a storm coming out of the blue. Stony-faced and stiff-backed, she knelt, staring into space, not moving for hours and hours until the priest in the shadows began to get worried.

'My child,' he whispered to the girl he had baptized at this very same font of life, 'would you care to talk about it, tell me what's troubling you?'

She seemed to come from a long way away. Regarding him steadfastly, Sonya said with perfect composure; 'No Father, I have no wish to talk about anything to anyone.'

She got up, genuflexed before the Virgin icon and walked sedately out of the chapel.

No, she had no wish to talk about it, not now, not ever.

ii

Grandmother Lizaveta Woodman came to Russia for the wedding of her grand-daughter Sonya, to Prince Nikolay Dubrovka, a minor Prince of the great Romanov family. The ceremony was a splendidly regal affair held in the Peter-and-Paul Cathedral with its imperial tombs, gilded eagles and hanging angel beneath a golden cross. The Tsar and Tsarina's wedding gift to the fortunate but ill-suited couple was a solid gold Easter-egg encrusted in diamonds, rubies and sapphires, its design and workmanship by the renowned hand of the jeweller, Fabergé. Afterwards, the newly weds left by train for a brief honeymoon at Prince Nikolay's country estate at Tula. The honeymoon had to be brief, for Prince Nikolay was due to accompany the Russian Legation to Lhasa.

On her wedding night (three days after the wedding as Sonya and Kolya had been stranded at a country railway-station on account of revolutionaries causing disruptions in and around Moscow) Sonya was unprepared for Kolya's assault on her body. If her father's behaviour had been anything to go by, then everything she had learned in whispered conversations by those more knowledgeable from behind a shield of hands and fans was even more horrible than she had previously imagined. Kolya's cold slimy tongue, bad breath, his hands like her father's groping the intimate places of her body, made her writhe in disgust not pleasure. But, she told herself sternly, that mysterious act of procreation begun for her at the altar of Peter-and-Paul Cathedral, had also been endured by her mother and if she, poor, sickly and frightened creature, had been able to bear it, then so could her daughter! Sonya gritted her teeth and waited for Kolya to get on with it − whatever that mysterious 'it' was meant to be.

Kolya's grunting, gasping and sweating antics while he poked, probed and apologized, only made her more and more exasperated. Sonya wanted suddenly to laugh as he wriggled all over her, his nightgown entangling with hers to rope them together like a couple of Chinamen's queues. Her breathing hampered by his weight, her movements restricted by an octopus assortment of limbs − and she marvelled how two arms and legs had suddenly multiplied in all directions − he, in the end, with his nightcap askew on his damp bedraggled hair plastered to his head like a skull-cap, grunted the plea, 'Sonya, I can't do it if you keep your legs shut tight as a bank vault.'

'Do what, Kolya?' she asked in all innocence.

'Oh, goodness me . . . do please assist me in gaining an entry.'

'Where to, Kolya?'

'Child, child! Did your mother tell you nothing?'

'Only that my husband would teach me all I wanted to know.'

'What do you wish to know, Sonya?'

'What you're trying to do.'

'I'm trying not to be flaccid – it's bad for my dignity. I've never been let down by it before. In fact, it has always functioned very well. But now I think it's not used to virgins after so long. Excuse me please, Sonya, I have a letter to write before I leave for Lhasa.'

He slithered off her like a snake and that was the last she saw of her husband in her bedroom before Tibet claimed him.

Only grandmother Lizaveta got to hear the story (with some reservations). Seeing the funny side of it, the old lady could not stop laughing and became quite breathless. Sonya thrust a tumbler of water into her grandmother's hands and wished she had not said anything at all; it only made her feel more of a failure, and a very embarrassed one at that! She had returned to St Petersburg to see her husband and brother off on the first stage of their journey to Tibet, after which it was grandmother Lizaveta's turn to depart Russia. She was sailing to England via the Gulf of Finland and Sonya saw her safely aboard *The Baltic Star*, as her parents were engaged elsewhere and could not do the honours. It was while the sailing was delayed by fog that the facts concerning Sonya's disastrous honeymoon had reluctantly emerged after a comment from her grandmother concerning the imminent likelihood of becoming a great-grandmother to a host of princes and princesses – hopes Sonya dashed with asperity; 'Not when my husband has two feet in the grave, grandmama.' And then the truth emerged.

'Oh, oh, petroushka.' Grandmother Lizaveta had exlaimed in delight, You've quite enlivened my day! Poor Kolya! And you, too, poor child, still "intact", despite being a married woman for the past month, *nyet*?'

91

'I suppose so,' said Sonya foolishly. Tugging on her new white-kid gloves, she turned aside to stare beyond the stateroom porthole so that her blushes would not be too apparent to her inquisitive grandmother.

Grandmother Lizaveta leaned forward in her high-backed gilt and plush chair to pat Sonya's arm. 'Never mind, petroushka, impotence in a man like Kolya is to be expected; it's his age. Perhaps it is a fortunate thing for you, especially as he does have a certain, er . . . decadent "air" about him.' She chuckled wickedly. 'But he has, I see, despite the non-consummation of your marriage, bought you a fine sable coat.' She fingered Sonya's sleeve appreciatively. 'So – here's my advice to you, dear girl.'

Sonya turned to look down unhappily at the regal figure of her grandmother. 'With all due respect, grandmama, I've listened to everyone's advice against my own better judgement, so now I'd rather work out my own salvation if you don't mind.'

'Sonya, listen to me anyway. Your husband has gone for goodness knows how long, but as long as you're wise – and discreet – you can still have your cake and eat it – you follow my reasoning, eh, child?' Purple-dark eyes and grey brows were interrogative beneath the large black tulle and befeathered hat shading the old lady's face. She gave Sonya a sly wink, her yellowed smile and chuckles full of mischief despite her wrinkles and the dignity of her years. 'But don't tell your mother I've had this conversation with you, she'll have a heart attack. Marya, you know, is after all, very strait-laced.'

'Mother and I have nothing to say to each other these days – I'm afraid I've yet to forgive her for siding with father – and you, grandmama – in the matter of Kolya. I'd never have married him if all of you hadn't emotionally blackmailed me into it. I shall never set foot in Kirovsky Ploshad for as long as I live.'

'Tut-tut!' said grandmother Lizaveta disapprovingly. 'That's a very immature statement to make – of course you will! Meanwhile, take my advice and enjoy your freedom. You've done what your father and mother wanted of you,

you've salvaged the family reputation – and finances – gained yourself a fortune, and lost nothing, not even your virginity! So since you belong to your absent prince, your parents can ask nothing more from you, eh, Princess Dubrovka?'

'I'd rather have remained plain Sonya Vremya.'

'Nonsense! No girl can refuse a title. You have the world at your feet, so make the most of it. The pity of it all is that Kolya is not more of a man and less of a freak – but nobody can have everything in this life, not even a princess. Let's not talk about him anymore. Do you remember that attractive young man who rescued you from drowning in the River Thames several summers ago?'

'No.'

'Yes, you do, petroushka. Well now, he writes to me regularly from India. His father and I are also the best of friends, we share a common interest – several common interests in fact, one being gardening.'

'That's nice for you, grandmama.'

'Yes, isn't it! I hadn't realized how much of an English-woman I've become during these past forty years, living in my husband's country. Russia, petroushka, is incredibly old-fashioned. It's finished for the likes of us, I fear.' The old lady sighed, her knobbed hands on top of her walking-stick tensing for a moment. 'Somehow I feel this will be the last time I will ever see the old country of my birth.'

'Don't be silly, grandmama, of course you'll come to Russia again.'

'Only in a wooden box, petroushka. But let's not become maudlin. I was talking about Lewis Joyden. Not only have I a lively relationship with his father as we exchange seeds, bulbs and gardeners, but I have quite a nice collection of Indian stamps from him. I had once supposed that Lewis Joyden was a very insipid and boring young man, but he's nothing of the sort. He's well educated, well travelled and his letters make very pleasant reading. I look forward to them tremendously.'

'Grandmama,' said Sonya impatiently, 'please get to the point. The boat will be sailing any moment and I have to

93

get off it first.' She was fully aware her grandmother was up to one of her tricks.

'Well dear, in our correspondence over the years, I've told him all about you and Kirsten. He has always shown such a lively interest in our family – ever since that day he bumped into us accidentally on the River Thames. He's such a polite and courteous boy, you know, and need not have bothered to call on us the following day when he was about to set off for India. I only wish Kirsten were more like him.'

Again the pretentious sigh, and Sonya, had she not known grandmother Lizaveta better, would have taken it at its face value. She decided to give her grandmother a taste of her own medicine: 'Oh grandmama, I'm so happy for you. I know that you're trying to tell me you and the Rector of St Anne's have so much in common you've decided to get married. Congratulations!' She stooped to kiss the wrinkled cheek smelling of verbena, but grandmother Lizaveta gave a contemptuous snort and pushed Sonya away.

'Don't be ludicrous! I'm not concerned with the father but the son. You ought to write to Lewis Joyden at Dehra-Dun, Sonya. It will take you out of yourself. I know he'll be pleased to hear from you, as I'm sure there can't be much to enrich his life stuck away as he is in the hills of a savage land.'

'Grandmama, grandmama!' Sonya said despairingly. 'I will do no such thing. How will it look if I start corresponding with a strange man the moment my husband's back is turned?'

'You have more of your mother in you than I had supposed,' grandmother Lizaveta replied tartly. 'And he's hardly a stranger. He saved your life once, remember?'

'Yes, I remember. But now I'm a married woman and for all I know he might be a married man with a very acid wife tucked away among the hills of Dehra-Dun.'

'No, he isn't – married I mean. He would have written and told me so. No, I'm absolutely certain Lewis Joyden is not married because his father mentioned to me one day how he'd like grandchildren.'

'Grandmother Lizaveta, if you don't stop this nonsense at once, I'm leaving right now!'

'No, don't go yet petroushka.' She caught hold of Sonya's sleeve. 'My ! Marriage to Kolya has certainly made you very nervy, darling. You mustn't become like your mother, you know – as fond as I am of her. But you are a child of mine, petroushka, one after my own heart, and I want to see you happy.'

'Then why did you side with father and mother in the matter of my marriage to Kolya?'

'Sonya, the gods, you know, don't dish out golden opportunities to everyone. Your father, mother and I could see what you were denying yourself and we wished only to steer you in the right direction. Now that you're there, it's up to you to use your golden opportunities for your own benefit. You've got status, a title, a fortune, beauty and brains, a loving family and friends you can take or leave as the mood suits. Yes, I know that is not enough for you. You are seeking that most vital thing to anyone's existence, real love between a man and woman.'

'And you think I'll find it by writing to a man many years older than me? Thank you grandmama, I've had enough of old men!'

'It was only a suggestion, my child, so don't get so angry.'

'You're not very subtle, grandmama.'

'If you're shy about taking the first step in writing to him, then I'll give him a diplomatic push in the right direction.'

'You'll do nothing of the sort to embarrass either of us, I forbid it!'

'I'm sure he's never written letters to a real princess before and anything must be better than drawing squiggly lines all over maps and . . . '

'Grandmother Lizaveta,' Sonya said warningly, 'if you embarrass Lewis Joyden and me, I'll never write you another letter. And, if I do receive a letter from him – through you – I shall not reply. Besides, a pen-friendship between us can lead nowhere. We're worlds apart not only in our private lives but in continents and cultures too, so what possible use could our correpondence be to each other?'

'Who knows?' murmured the old lady with a secret smile as a blast from the funnel of *The Baltic Star* warned non-passengers to disembark. 'Who knows, petroushka?'

Chapter Six

Dubrovka-Dvaryets, Kolya's ancestral home, was situated at Peterhof twenty miles from St Petersburg. Although she was now far enough removed from her parents' home, Sonya liked her new surroundings even less. Through the vast echoing chambers of such a palatial residence, an army of servants crept about on slippered feet and addressed her in hushed voices, afraid, it appeared, of disturbing the sacred silences of long dead little gods. The accusing blank stares of marble statues destined to stand forever in the loggias offered only critical assessment – who did she think she was, this Sonya Vremya, in her out-moded clothes and worn shoes, with impoverished relatives always seeking favours from someone better off; who did she think she was, wandering beneath such sacred portals, where once the Tsars of Russia had trodden? And Sonya would think defiantly, I am now Princess Nikolay Dubrovka, châtelaine of this kingdom! And from what small beginnings do the heartaches grow; she was married to its master, who she did not love, because one night she happened to ride out in a troika wearing only her nightdress . . .

Sonya, overwhelmed by her new lifestyle, especially the numerous offspring and relatives through Kolya's previous marriages, avoided them as much as possible and earned the reputation of being an eccentric. She had insisted from the very beginning on having her apartments in a wing off the main living quarters, where she could remain out of reach of screaming tots and the senile chatter of dowager-duchesses, yet now she sighed moodily in the isolation she had created for herself. Her elbows pensively poised on a pretty little French escritoire Kolya, as a parting gift, had bought her, Sonya stared vacantly beyond her windows to the formal gardens and deer park surrounding Dubrovka-Dvaryets, way beyond to the misty Gulf of Finland. There would be no pleasure in taking a walk anywhere today, it was far too cold and miserable. She turned to a letter awaiting an answer. Strange to write such a date, she mused as she bit the end of the pen before dipping the nib into the silver inkwell: 2nd February, 1900! The twentieth century had begun, and she was only just beginning to keep pace with it. What more could be discovered in the next decade? What more could be invented. The magnetic tape-recorder, the motor-car, the teleprinter and now talk of men flying in machines as light as birds on the wing! And while Röntgen had discovered X-rays and Marie Curie radium, she, Sonya Dubrovka, had discovered only solitude in all her nineteen years.

She re-read Lewis Joyden's letter. If she felt out of touch with reality, her princess's dream life not dreamlike at all but sometimes tremendously irksome, then here was one person in the world who could be relied upon to keep her feet firmly on the ground. She smiled as she read again of the antics of 'a very snooty Collector's wife who goes around the countryside covering up erotic Indian images with the Union Jack', and the Raja who kept a lethal pet cobra he would take for walks at the end of a jewelled leash every day, and use the snake to poison anyone who annoyed him! Then Lewis went on to describe the torments of prickly heat-rash (for which there was no cure) and how the mosquitoes plagued the ladies of leisure (and pleasure) among the hills of Dehra-Dun and Simla. 'They wear army boots and stockings soaked in paraffin under evening dresses to prevent their legs from being devoured by mosquitoes – everything in this country designed to devour one. Yesterday I had to ride our elephant-mascot at a gymkana; he is a one-eyed, one-eared veteran of the Indian Mutiny called Lucknow.'

'How can you possibly imagine your life to be routine and dull? Rather, my own life here at Dubrovka-Dvaryets is unedifying in the extreme,' she wrote to him.

'How can that be when you're a princess of all the Russias?' he replied a month later, to which letter Sonya penned an abrasive answer; 'Please do not make fun of me, Mr Joyden. I cannot help my station in life!'

'No, indeed!' he had written again, the tone of that letter Sonya suspected very much tongue in cheek, 'and I beg your pardon, ma'am. I'm only a common artless philistine (as you must have gathered by now), not quite accustomed yet to writing letters to real princesses – even though this one I fished out of the Thames, with no conception at the time of what her future noble rank would be! Princess Dubrovka, I cannot imagine why you should want to waste your time in corresponding with a mere commoner and witless oaf like myself, so forgive me. Neither would I blame you if you wished to terminate our pen-friendship on the grounds of insulting behaviour.'

She did nothing of the sort. Thanks to grandmother Lizaveta, she had a friend more precious to her than all Kolya's wealth, prestige and rank. How much was revealed of a person's character through mere letters, she pondered. She felt she knew everything there was to know about Lewis Joyden, his work and office routine at Dehra-Dun, his temperament, tastes and personality, his humour, hobbies and lifestyle, and even his romantic streak evident in the poems he recommended her to read, as well as his favourite books. At the same time, when replying to his letters, she hoped she wasn't giving away too much of herself. She usually tried to keep the tone of her letters away from the personal and concentrated more on what was happening around her, to her family and friends and other people whose lives touched hers. She told him about her new relatives, life at Court, life in St Petersburg and Peterhof, the people she met, about the letters she had received from her husband and brother in Tibet, what they were doing, the people they had met on their travels, where they had stayed, and indeed, anything and everything she hoped might be amusing and stimulating to a man interested in geography, travel and human beings, yet never got the opportunity to indulge those interests except from behind an office desk, theodolite or draught-board.

'Why do you always write so much about everyone else and never of yourself?' he had once enquired.

'Because,' she replied, 'nothing ever happens to me and what I do in a whole week would furnish you with a letter of two sentences and would therefore be of no interest to you whatsoever!'

ii

The last two letters Sonya had received from her husband and brother had been sent from Gartok, a border town in Tibet. The date on both letters was 18 March 1899, eleven months ago. Absorbed in replying to their letters, Sonya was somewhat annoyed to be disturbed by a footman bearing a message on a silver salver. He had crept up behind her so stealthily, she had jumped in fright. Taking up the envelope, Sonya recognized her father's handwriting and seal; 'Please come at once, your mother is very ill and not expected to live.'

Sonya had not set foot in her father's house since her wedding day, estranged after the embarrassing scene he had engendered in her bedroom at Novgorod. While she dreaded seeing him again, she also knew she could not ignore such a plea where her mother was concerned.

Stepping from her carriage in Kirovsky Ploshad, she was caught in a sudden spring shower. Sonya glanced up at the sombre shuttered house, a cold fist clutching her heart. Her mother dying, could it be possible? Not an old woman by any stretch of the imagination, but a very unhappy one. Could a person die of a broken heart? Yes, Sonya believed one could.

Count Mikail was waiting for her in the salon, a despondent and equally unhappy figure who seemed to have diminished in grandeur and shrunk into the shell of an old man. His appearance was dishevelled, his high forehead shiny and pale. His hair, lank, greasy and plastered to his

100

scalp to disguise his increasing baldness, reminded her so much of Kolya and his decrepitude, that for an instant Sonya felt an overwhelming hatred against her father and not sympathy in this, his hour of need. After all, he was to blame considerably for her mother's misery. His transparent probing eyes beheld her for hardly a second – before he shifted his glance elsewhere, his hands clasped tightly behind his back and beneath his coat-tails so that their tremor might not be so noticeable. Sonya realized he had probably been over-working – and drinking. Nervous and embarrassed, uncertain how to address her, he began hesitantly, 'Thank you for coming so promptly, Princess.'

Sonya was relieved he did not come forward to kiss her and maintained her own distance. 'Father, what's wrong with mama?'

'I don't know exactly. A new doctor attends upon her since Pratikayit was dismissed. He's an Englishman and doesn't live in the house – and hardly bestirs himself when he's called.' Count Mikail turned and reached for his snuff box on the mantelpiece. When he had taken his snuff and replaced the box, he seemed a little more in command of himself. 'The doctor – don't ask me to pronounce his heathen name – seems to think your mother has suffered an effusion of blood into the brain – he called it a cerebral embolism.'

'Oh no! But how . . . why? I mean, that's a conditon of old people, surely?'

'As I said, I don't think the doctor himself knows. They're all the same, these medical quacks, pretending to a little knowledge while charging the highest in the land for their services. However, let me explain all that has happened from the very beginning. It only occurred after we received bad news concerning Kolya and Kirsten. Prepare yourself not only for your mother's condition, but also to the news that Kolya's surveying-party has met with disaster. Take off your wet cloak while you sit, otherwise you too will be ill.'

Sonya did so, obedience to her father's wishes a conditioned reflex in her and as automatic as his remark concerning her health – courtesies done from habit, nothing more. She did not interrupt him as he went on to explain;

101

'The Tsar sent for me to give me the facts. Barakov's Legation arrived in Lhasa without undue mishap – only the usual things besetting a lengthy journey; sickness, food shortages and the loss of some pack animals. In Lhasa itself the Legation met the Dalai Lama and a favourable treaty was implemented between our country and Tibet. Barakov's party thereafter returned to Russia via the route by which they had entered Tibet, while Kolya led a surveying-party across the Chang-Tang. Kolya's group was never seen or heard of again.'

After a protracted silence weighted with questions and conflicting emotions, Sonya said, 'Kirsten's dead . . . that's why mama has collapsed.'

Her father nodded.

'How do you know for certain Kirsten's dead?' Sonya asked.

'Barakov's scouts brought back news of the remains of a Russian camp and signs of funeral rights conducted in the primitive frozen conditions of the Chang Tang. The belief, generally, is that our men had been attacked by a Mongolian raiding party and the bodies of those killed were dismembered and left for wolves.'

'How could they be certain everyone was killed? Surely there could have been survivors, injured survivors?'

Count Mikail shrugged. 'There were no survivors, injured or otherwise. Any man left stranded in those frozen conditions, without food, medicines and protection, presumbly injured, would not survive even for a few hours.'

'But couldn't some of them have been taken prisoner by the Mongolians? Barakov's scouts need not necessarily have been accurate in what they believed had happened to Kolya's men.'

In a jerky, abstract movement of head and hands, Count Mikail reached again for his snuff box. 'There were Tibetans in the Thok Daurkopa area where Kolya made his last camp. They bore out the statements made by Barakov's scouts.'

Sonya's thoughts and feelings were confused – almost as if she were unaffected by the tragedy – or had she suddenly become like her mother, numb with shock and refuting all logical evidence to the contrary? That Kirsten's body had not been chopped into little pieces and left for wolves or vultures, Kirsten's young, handsome, athletic body so full of life and vigour. 'What does the Tsar intend to do now?' Sonya asked.

In a despairing gesture, her father sat down, clasped his hands between his knees and stared into space. 'Negotiations between the Tsar and the Dalai Lama are finely balanced at the moment. The Barakov-Dorjiev Mission was so successful in winning us Tibetan support and co-operation, the Tsar does not want to make hasty and unecessary accusations against the Tibetans by over-reacting to what befell Kolya's surveying-party, thus jeopardizing the treaty.'

'We are talking of men's lives, father, not precious treaties! Men who might be injured or unwilling prisoners of hostile tribesmen under the rule of Tibet and China. From the information of a few scouts who happened to stumble across some signs of a skirmish, who could so easily have formulated their own theories and hasty conclusions because they wished to put the Chang Tang behind them as quickly as possible, the Tsar is now turning his back on Kolya and his surveying-party when they might be in urgent need of his help!'

Her father glanced up at her after this heated rendering. 'Dear girl, I feel exactly as you do. I, too, would wish the Tsar to organize another delegation straightaway to find out the absolute truth of the matter, but he can't do it – not yet, anyway. He's meeting soon with Dorjiev and Barakov, when he intends to establish the full facts concerning the tragedy. Afterwards, I'm sure he'll decide one way or another.'

'On the assumptions of a few scouts who weren't even material witnesses to what really happened to Kolya and his men on the Chang Tang! Father, you and I both know ice has a habit of burying the truth!' Sonya added bitterly. 'The way I see it, the Tsar doesn't really want to be bothered because he doesn't care. He's more interested in pandering to the whims of a few Tibetans, their trading agreements and pushing out his frontiers as far as possible, than in establishing the absolute facts concerning his own Russian people – just little folk who don't seem to matter to him. I think Mr Lenin is right about our Emperor! Tsar Nicholas is only a weak man and like all weak men, perversely listens to one side of the argument only, his own.' Sonya got up and walked to the door. 'I'm going upstairs now to see mama. Is there anything else I should know?'

'No . . . I think that is all. The doctor will inform you about her exact condition – as near as can be ascertained in the circumstances. I asked him to wait here until you arrived. He called to see her about an hour ago and informed me there was no change in her condition.'

'How long has she been like this?' Sonya asked from the threshold.

He looked up, his expression vague. 'Oh, let me see, three days now . . . the day I saw the Tsar.'

'Why didn't you send for me sooner?'

'I did not think, Princess, you wished to be bothered by us anymore.'

Sonya, at a complete loss for a suitable answer, turned on her heel and went upstairs to her mother's bedroom. She stayed an hour. Torn between compassion, loyalty and her own inadequacy, Sonya was dismayed by the sight of her mother, once a very attractive woman, now just a tiny helpless victim of circumstance lying like a pale tortured fish in its vast ocean-bed. The doctor, not an Englishman as her father had mistakenly assumed, but a Scotsman with a brogue that could be cut, answered her questions with cautionary jargon; 'A've nae idea, Princess, whether she will or she won't get better. 'Tis in the lap o' the gods. If y'maether's tame is nigh, then she'll nae tarry fer lang, fer there's nae arguin' with th'Almighty. But raight noo, she's gude an' dead tae th'world . . . though tha's nae tae sae she kenna open her bonny blau eyes bae ta'necht an' gi' us all a wee thrill.'

'Thank you, Doctor MacDiarmid,' Sonya said, gazing with concern upon the slack pallid face of a woman prematurely aged, rosebud lips dribbling saliva into her pillow. No cousin Sasha now to admire the burnished hair, flushed cheeks, light in the eye and latest ballgown – for yes, her mother could be a pretty flirt with the right man. Sonya, utterly demoralized, had to leave sooner than later, Anna's accusing grunts and scowls indicative of what she thought of Sonya's lack of filial duty. 'I'll call again tomorrow morning,' Sonya told her father when, an hour after Doctor MacDiarmid's departure, she took her leave. From the back of the sofa where she'd thrown her cloak, Sonya retrieved it and put it around her shoulders. 'If there's any change at all in mama's condition, good or bad, please send word to me at once. I can get here in just over an hour.'

He nodded; Kolya's horses were indeed swift. His profile all she could see of her father standing before the long windows of the salon, Sonya knew his attention was beyond her, his unseeing eyes and thoughts only upon the tall golden spire of Peter-and-Paul Cathedral.

iii

Before she returned to Dubrovka-Dvaryets, Sonya had some chores to do. First, she went to the great library on Ostrovsky Square, off the Nevsky-Prospekt. A complete collection of books and manuscripts was to be found here, with translations in and from every language. Sonya asked the librarian to search out as many books as were available on the geography, history, culture and customs of Tibet. He was more than helpful, and when she was satisfied, he tied them together and promised delivery to Dubrovka-Dvaryets that same afternoon. Then she went along to the Institute of Linguistic Studies where she enrolled in classes teaching the Tibetan and Sanskrit languages. Afterwards, still in a mood of exploration as it gave her something to take her mind off the combined tragedy of mother, brother and husband, Sonya enrolled at the Institute of Botanical Studies. Then she went home.

Two weeks later Sonya found the man she had been looking for, Chao Sui Yuan, who had been an Amban at Lhasa. Without delving into his reasons for seeking political asylum in Russia, Sonya engaged him because his credentials were perfect. He offered to teach her, over and above the Institute of Linguistic Studies in St Petersburg, everything she required to know about Tibet and China.

Sonya could have stayed in her husband's private apartments opposite the Winter Palace in St Petersburg while she studied there, but she preferred to travel every day to her classes, despite the length of the journey. She was also able to visit her mother every week day. The weekends and evenings were hers alone, to study, revise and practise Tibetan and Chinese with Chao Sui Yuan.

Grandmother Lizaveta wrote, 'Your botanical studies sound admirable, petroushka.' (Sonya had made no mention either to her grandmother or Lewis Joyden about her interest in Tibet, only that she was studying Botany.) 'Reverend Joyden and I will know who to come to now when we require the professional name of a species of plant or flower, and what to do with it! I would have thought, however, music lessons would have been more advantageous to you, or are you bent upon finding another kind of rare blue poppy that grows somewhere in the Khang-Yul . . . aha, dear girl, I'm not as senile as I look and I can still put two and two together. Don't worry, I shan't say a word to your parents about there being an ulterior motive in all this diligent search of plants and things via the encyclopaedias, but don't do anything foolish, dear child. I'm glad your mother is slightly improved, and I pray for her constantly. Your visits every day, must have encouraged her no end and given her a purpose to live again. Do you know, petroushka, I have the same feeling as you describe to me of yours concerning Kirsten. Neither do I believe he's dead. When one is close to someone, one knows instinctively whether they're dead or not. I had that feeling about your grandfather. He was in East Africa when he died – and yet I, in England, knew exactly the hour of his death, miles away, and long before the telegram arrived.'

The letters continued between Abingdon, Peterhof and Dehra-Dun, letters that had become as much a part of Sonya's life as the Tibetan letters and numerals she was trying to master with the help of Chao Sui Yuan.

In two years, all but a month from the day of her collapse

106

over Kirsten's fate on the great frozen Chang Tang plateau of Tibet, the Countess Marya was well enough to raise a spoon to her mouth, and feed herself again. Only coherent speech was still denied her, reminding Sonya of Grechen, her maid and Lala's daughter, born with an ugly harelip and speech impediment that had made her a laughing stock and the butt of cruel people's jokes. Determined her mother would not be put into the same category as an imbecile, because she was unable to articulate coherently, Sonya sat with her every day and re-taught her basic sounds and sentences, all the time encouraging the Countess to respond once more as a normal human being.

After a morning's work at the Institute of Botanical Studies, an hour's break for her lunch, then an hour spent with her mother at Kirovsky Ploshad, Sonya had just enough time to spare one afternoon to visit her priest before her session commenced at the Language Institute. Inside Peter-and-Paul Cathedral, where she had been united with Prince Nikolay Dubrovka by this very same priest, she attempted to untie the knot in an intense discussion with him – intense from her point of view, less so from his. 'How long, Father, until it can be safely assumed I'm no longer married to my husband?'

'For life,' he murmured, not looking at her but at his feet peeping out from under his black cassock.

'But I last saw my husband three years ago!' Sonya protested.

'For life,' he murmured, reaching up to scratch his head under the rim of his black ecclesiastical hat of the Orthodox Church, his eyes fastened upon the huge gold cross shining brilliantly above the high altar.

'But supposing he really is dead?'

'For life. Unless his body can be recovered and it can be proved beyond doubt to be that of your missing husband.'

In desperation Sonya sought a more reasonable alternative. 'But supposing that's not possible? Supposing wolves or vultures in Tibet had devoured his body, how then could I possibly obtain that proof?'

The priest examined his spotless fingernails. 'For life, Princess Dubrovka.'

'But can't I obtain a dispensation of my marriage on the grounds of desertion?'

'Why desertion? Duty called him away, not desertion.'

'How long has duty to call a man away from his wife before his wife is free?'

'Life.'

'And desertion?'

'Never – in the eyes of Mother Church.'

'But even the Tsar assumes Prince Dubrovka is dead.'

'God assumes nothing, my child, neither does Mother Church. In the eyes of the Church marriage is for life, unless of course there is a dead body to prove beyond doubt that the couple have been parted by God's hand. Holy vows taken before the Altar of God, cannot be broken.'

'Then what about a divorce?' Sonya asked desperately.

'There is no such thing as divorce in the eyes of Mother Church.'

'But the marriage was never consummated.'

'Ah then!' said the priest, his eyes at last upon her, his index finger uplifted like a pointer to the Word of God. 'That is different. That is a matter on which to pause and reflect. A marriage without consummation is not a marriage at all in the eyes of Mother Church, for, without heirs, Mother Church herself will die. But the matter will have to be examined carefully and the circumstances of your case brought before the Holy Synod.'

'How long will it take?' Sonya scarcely dared hope.

'It will be protracted.' The priest re-examined his finger-nails. 'I know of a case where both parties concerned have died before their marriage could be annulled on the grounds of non-consummation.'

'Thank you, Father.' Sonya, with a sigh of exasperation got up to leave. 'I can't wait around a lifetime while the Church decides my future. I've things to do in the meantime.'

Chapter Seven

Chao Sui Yuan had become Sonya's confidante – up to a point. In his black satin robe embroidered with silver dragons, hands tucked into his wide sleeves, he stood respectfully in his black satin slippers, upswept at the toes, and gave his opinion in answer to her question, 'Well, what do you think, Chao?'

'In two years Princess, you mos' intense pupil Chao ever teach. Now you spea' li' one who live in Tibet many years.' He beamed and the twin points of his whispery grey beard leapt forward in agreement.

'Then you really think I'm proficient enough to hold a conversation with any Tibetan?' Sonya asked eagerly, wanting to be absolutely certain what he thought of her ability without flattery entering into it.

'Oh no! No' anybody in Tibet! Many ignoran' people live in Tibet,' said the Chinaman pedantically. 'Princess li' you, mus' spea' only with educated noblewomen li' yourself.'

Sonya judged the moment, and decided she would let him know her intentions. Without looking at him, but keeping her head bent to the exercise book in which she was translating a passage of Sanskrit, she said; 'I'm going away for a little holiday, Chao. I've decided to go to Central Russia to carry out some botanical field-work.'

'Princess li' you, it does no' seem correc' to dig in cotton-fields like peasan',' Chao replied seriously and Sonya laughed.

'No, no, no, Chao!' She put aside her pen and flexed her aching fingers. 'I'm not intending to work in the fields like a peasant . . . well, on reflection, perhaps it might come to that if I run short of money, but I hope not. I'm going to see how many new flowers and plants I can discover in the Zeravshan valley. Who knows, I might even discover a rare golden lily the Botanical Society will name after me. Think of that accolade!'

. 'I understan',' said Chao, regarding her unblinkingly. 'You, Princess, are mos' worthy and clever woman, mos' ambitious. Chao very impressed with pupil li' you.'

'Thank you Chao, that's kind of you.' She continued cautiously; 'I've no idea how long I shall be away, perhaps six months, a year, or even more, depending on circumstances. I'm telling you all this now, so that you can make other arrangements regarding your accommodation and employment. You will, of course, receive from me three months salary in lieu, since your contract with me is not fully expired.' She gave him a charming smile, a dimple in evidence at the corner of her mouth. 'You'll agree, I've made swift progress in my language studies, so now I must do some work for the Botanical Society as I wish to gain my doctorate in the subject.' She toyed with a ruler. 'I heard that the Institute of Asian Languages in St Petersburg has recently lost one of their Chinese tutors, so, if you wish, I'll put in a good word for you.'

'Thank you. Mos' kind of you, Princess.' Chao bowed stiffly from the waist. 'I will do my utmos' to be worthy of your recommenda'ions.'

ii

Sonya found herself short of ready cash. Kolya had been more than generous in the monthly allowance he had allotted her, but other than that financial arrangement, she had no other source of income. All the housekeeping bills for an establishment the size and prestige of Dubrovka-Dvaryets were taken care of by secretaries and the major-domo, Prince Nikolay's trusted servants for generations. Sonya had had no wish to upset the apple-cart when she had first arrived at Dubrovka-Dvaryets as Kolya's green and frightened child-bride, so she had left things as they were. Now she wondered where she could raise the necessary funds to finance her expedition through Russia, as her allowance was swallowed up by private tutors and tutorials.

In the end, she secretly managed to sell one masterpiece by Titian she discovered in store, three icons, a pair of Catherine the Great vases and the sable coat Kolya had given her as an engagement present. She added to her greatly improved funds by pawning a few pieces of not so valuable jewellery. The valuable family heirlooms handed down from generation to generation of prestigiously wealthy Dubrovkas, and poorer but ambitious Vremyas, were always kept in a safe, and accounted for to someone else every time the safe was opened, so she could not lay her hands on that source of revenue without raising suspicion. But, she told herself sensibly, beggars couldn't be choosers! Kolya had promised she would never have to go without, and since he had not provided her with sufficient funds, she was now taking matters into her own hands! With those sentiments in mind, she salvaged her conscience whilst preparing for her solitary journey across Russia.

In the spring of that year, 1902, Sonya received certificates of proficiency in Tibetan Studies, in the Tibetan and Chinese languages, and also in Botany, which allowed her, on passing that examination, to be able to sit for her doctorate in the subject. She informed the Institute of her intended field studies, with a promise to continue with her doctorate when she returned. To her surprise, Sonya received a hand-written letter from the Tsarina congratulating her on her achievements, and inviting her to address a group of Russian Society women on 'The Changing Role of Twentieth Century Womanhood.' The Tsarina hoped (duty permitting) she would be able to attend Sonya's talk with the Grand Duchesses in the Rastrelli Room at the Winter Palace.

In reply to such an honour Sonya stated that she would be delighted to oblige the Tsarina, but unfortunately she would be away on the date the Empress had decided upon, as she intended doing some research-work in the Zeravshan valley – her ambition being to find a rare blue poppy known to be growing somewhere in the remoter parts of Central Asia.

A few days later, Sonya received another letter from the Winter Palace, this time from the Tsar himself. Hearing from the Tsarina of Sonya's ambitious project, he wished not only to congratulate her on her recent achievements in Tibetan and Chinese studies, and also her Botanical work, but to offer his support and encouragement in all aspects of her research. If she required letters of introduction from him, he would be only too delighted to oblige. He expressed his disappointment that she would be unable to deliver her talk to 'women of a seeking mind', but hoped she would be able to do so on her return to St Petersburg. He added that he and the Tsarina found her 'courage and thirst for knowledge, very commendable'. Sonya chuckled and said smugly to Chao; 'How very useful the Tsar's letters of introduction will be.'

Chao smiled unblinkingly; 'Very commen'able, and mos' enligh'ening, Princess. Your search for many plan's and flowers will ma'e this world a sweeter smelling place, an' I wish you much success with your projec'.'

'I hope so, Chao, I hope so,' Sonya murmured, her thoughts racing ahead. She wished to set out on her journey not later than this present month of May. She had not breathed a word to anyone of the true nature of her journey through Russia, not even to grandmother Lizaveta or Lewis Joyden. Sonya felt afraid that, in knowing of her intention, someone, somehow, would prevent her from doing anything as foolhardy as setting off on a hazardous journey, all by herself, to regions where even angels feared to tread. Neither had she closed her mind to the dangers that sort of venture entailed, but had prepared herself to meet those dangers head on. What she was not prepared for was that others should spell out those dangers for her and put on the brakes. With the Tsar and Tsarina's blessings, and their letters of recommendation and introduction to 'people in high places' Sonya realized the time had come to tell her parents of her jaunt into the unknown. Since the

112

Royal family now knew of her intentions, news was bound to reach the ears of her father, himself a member of the inner court circle.

Much to her relief, her father was not at home the afternoon she called at Kirovsky Ploshad to inform her parents of her imminent departure from St Petersburg. Sonya felt it would be easier to put her mother in the picture first, and to leave a note for her father. She knew she was being a coward, but felt she could not cope with his temper, and would much rather be at Peterhof when he found out about her solitary pursuit of the rare blue poppy.

'Mother,' Sonya began, taking up the cold pale hand lying on the eiderdown while the pink gas lamps hissed noisily above their heads, 'I've something to tell you . . . something important to me.' Sonya realized this was going to be the hardest part, and searched for the right words of reassurance. 'Darling mama, more than anything in the world, you'd like to see Kirsten again, wouldn't you?'

The Countess Marya nodded, tears gathering in her faded blue eyes. Anna had braided the Countess's hair into two long plaits that hung down over the frail shoulders. She reminded Sonya of a pathetically aged child. Sonya tried once more; 'Mama, I want to find Kirsten and Kolya, and that's why I'm going away for a little while. I'm qualified to do botanical research work of my own, and I want to collect some rare specimens to bring back for the Botanical Society. I'm going to do my research work in Tibet.'

Sonya was aware that behind her, Anna had stopped sewing. In the full length swing mirror that had been pushed close to the Countess's bed while her hair was being dressed, Sonya could see the peasant woman's black eyes wide open in astonishment, her needle poised in mid-air as she sat cross-legged on her iron cot. Catching Anna's eye, Sonya said sweetly: 'And since mother can't say anything to father as her speech has not recovered to that extent, if Anna Andropova breathes one word to anyone – especially to Count Mikail – when I get back I shall have her tongue cut out . . . and you love your food, don't you Anna?'

Anna scowled viciously. Bending her head to her sewing, bulbous joints worked the needle furiously through the

113

material, headscarf slipping forever backwards from the brown egg-shell dome of her speckled forehead. 'Take care my tongue won't give you a poisonous bellyache when it's put in a sandwich for you to eat on your return, Princess!' Anna muttered.

Sonya chuckled to herself, and turned her attention to her mother – Anna, she knew, would be as silent as the grave. In the Countess's eyes, Sonya detected comprehension – even if the Countess could not formulate a coherent reply, she knew she had her mother's support. 'Mama, I need your blessing. It would be so much easier for me to know you will not be upset. Father will not support me in what I intend to do, so I don't want him to know anything until I've left Peterhof. I'll give Ropa a letter to hand to him once I'm safely aboard the train for Moscow. I'll find Kirsten, I promise. I don't believe he and Kolya are dead – neither does grandmother Lizaveta. I can't explain the feeling I've got, but I know they're alive somewhere in Tibet and I mean to find them. I want you to be very brave, and not miss me while I'm gone. Kirsten and I will be back sooner than you think, you wait and see. We both love you dearly.' She spoke to her mother as she would to a child.

Icy fingers squeezed hers for an instant, then tears splashed from the Countess Marya's tightly shut eyes.

'Don't cry, mama,' Sonya said gently as she wiped away her mother's tears, 'you'll only make me cry, too!'

After a while the Countess took a deep breath and, opening her eyes, gave Sonya a tremulous smile, her lips contorting with the effort. Sonya leaned forward and kissed her mother's forehead. 'Thank you, mama,' she whispered in relief, 'you don't know how much that means to me.'

The Countess Marya wanted more. With an effort of will the weak lips puckered again and Sonya realized her mother wanted to kiss her. Lowering her head, she felt the moist touch of her mother's lips on her forehead. Sonya stood up and still clasping her mother's hands said as cheerfully as she could; 'Next time I come to see you I'll have Kirsten with me. In the meantime you must do as Anna says. Eat up all your food, take your medicine, and exercise your limbs by walking as often as you can around the bed until

114

you're fit enough to play croquet with Kirsten and me, as we all did in Abingdon when Pratikayit wasn't looking, remember?'

Her mother nodded. Then, with a supreme effort the Countess drew Sonya's hands closer, so that when, for the second time she bent her head to her mother, she understood the gist of what the Countess was trying to say; 'You and Kirsten . . . my children . . . mean more to me than your father . . . take care, Sonya . . . '

'I will . . . now I must go.' Sonya, emotionally incapable of handling heart-rending scenes turned aside to Anna as the Countess, physically drained, sank back onto her pillows and closed her eyes. 'Look after her Anna,' Sonya said, hoping desperately she had not gone too far in making vain promises concerning Kirsten. But now, at least, the Countess had a hope to cling to, the hope that her beloved son might not be dead, that she might see him again before she herself should die. Sonya left her mother in Anna's good hands, thankful that moments of lucidness came to her mother's erstwhile befuddled brain more and more frequently now, which must mean she was well on the road to recovery.

Her private affairs settled – a letter given to Ropa to hand to Count Mikail the moment Ropa heard she was safely aboard the Moscow bound train – all that was left for her to do now was to get her faithful maid Grechen to post certain letters at regular intervals.

'Look here Grechen,' she told the ugly mute girl who was nevertheless a treasure Sonya was loathe to part with, 'in this compartment of my desk are twelve letters addressed to my grandmother in England, and in this next one, the same number addressed to a Mr Joyden in India. What I want you to do is post one to my grandmother and one to Mr Joyden on the twenty-fifth day of each month. In the corner of each envelope is a pencilled number, one, two, three and so on, so that the letters get posted in the correct sequence – the first two letters to be posted on the 25th of this month of May, the next two on the 25th of June and so forth, until both sets of twelve letters have been posted a year from now. Do you understand?'

Grechen nodded. Her intelligence unimpaired despite her disfigurement, Sonya trusted Grechen completely – she only wished her loyal little maid would dry her tears. 'Grechen, I need you here at Dubrovka-Dvaryets! Without you to do this thing for me my plans will fall apart. You'll make me very happy if you don't hinder me by crying like this, otherwise you'll set me off, too!' Grechen mopped her eyes and nodded her head.

An elaborate plot, perhaps, but Sonya knew her father would only view this venture as an extraordinarily foolish one, the kind that had got her talked about on the streets of St Petersburg. He would do his utmost to prevent her from reaching Moscow, let alone Lhasa. The Tsar, had he realized she was going beyond Samarkand and the Zeravshan river, would also have forbidden such a venture, despite his letters of introduction to 'people in high places' – namely the Governors of the various provinces she would be travelling through. Her first letter to grandmother Lizaveta informed her that she was about to embark on a field study of rare plants and flowers in the Zeravshan valley. 'I wish to gain a Professorship in the subject – that is, after gaining my Doctorship, which I will do if I show ability in my chosen field of study. However, each month I'll write to you from whatever place, town, district or mountain-top I happen to be stranded at the time. Your letters, of course, won't reach me as I shall be constantly on the move, so if you do still wish to write to me while I'm absent, then address your letters in the usual way to Peterhof. My letters to you will be sent first to Peterhof, and Grechen will re-address them – one can't expect a Turkman or Uzbek to be cognizant with the English language!'

Sonya wrote in similar vein to Lewis, but with more interesting highlights: 'Father thinks Kirsten and Kolya are certainly dead by now as we have had no news to the contrary for over three years. But I don't share his views – and neither does grandmother Lizaveta at Abingdon. Their bodies have never been identified, and loose bones can belong to anyone – including a yak! The Tsar himself vacillates as usual between one opinion and another without making up his mind on the best course of action to take.

Barakov and Dorjiev (that silly man who was once a Buddhist monk at the Drepung Lamasery) differ in their own versions of what befell my husband's surveying-party, and his Tibetan Holiness, the Dalai Lama, pleads total ignorance of the whole affair. Dorjiev – who travelled separately via India back to Russia – met secretly with the Tsar at a place called Yalta to tell him all about the Tibet Mission to the Dalai Lama, and what treaties they had managed to negotiate between Russia and Tibet. Isn't it exciting? I believe I wrote and told you about Dorjiev in one of my previous letters. He is, apparently, the power behind the throne (the Dalai Lama's throne) and is the one responsible for all this to-ing and fro-ing between St Petersburg and Lhasa. Rasputin and Dorjiev are as thick as thieves, both monks well versed in the black arts in my opinion. My father was present at the meeting between the returned Tibetan Legation and the Tsar, who wished to know every minute detail of the expedition which was so successful from his point of view – even to the Dalai Lama's reaction to the holy clerical garments embroidered by the Grand Duchesses! I can't help feeling the Tsar should get his priorities right, and instead of dressing up the Dalai Lama in the vestments of the Russian Orthodox Church, should look to the interests and safety of his own people. Not only are the workers and peasants (with Mr Lenin behind them) posing a threat to the Tsar here in St Petersburg, Mr Lenin has even set up his own Social-Revolutionary party . . . '

The letter to Lewis Joyden told nothing of her own actions, but, as usual, only those of others. Having put her house in order, Sonya, with butterflies in her stomach, woke early the following morning, before even sleepy-eyed Grechen crept in to wake her for the morning train to Moscow, the first stage of her journey into the unknown.

117

Chapter Eight

INDIA
August 1902

L ewis, beneath the deodar trees, hovered on the fringes
of Lady Curzon's summer ball. Dressed as Robin of
Sherwood in 'an under-ripe plaintain-green, not Lincoln-
green!' costume he had had words with his tailor about,
Lewis was wondering whether he could slip away without
being noticed, when Lady Curzon appeared beside him
dressed as Queen Elizabeth I. She whispered from behind
an ostrich feather fan; 'How George *hates* Simla! I've told
him to try looking out of the windows more often and take
solace in the view. The women and padres get his goat
oftener than anyone else. Do you find, Lewis, that the
Simla crowd resembles cold tapioca pudding?' Lady Curzon
gazed about her myopically and Lewis, running a finger
inside the collar of his plantain-green costume wondered
how best to answer such a question. While he was thinking
up a suitably diplomatic reply, Lady Curzon carried on
regardless; 'I do wish he'd stop scribbling in his office all
day and half the night! Sometimes he doesn't know I exist,
and all I have to talk to are the Lincrusta pineapples on the
walls of the Lodge. I've a good mind to get the place
redecorated.' She sighed in exasperation and changed the
subject. 'But since you already know what a workaholic my
husband is, let's talk about something else. How clever of

you and Miss Lucy Denton to win the pair of Waterford crystal goblets in yesterday's treasure-hunt! Are you going to split them apiece, or marry each other?' She gave him a sly dig with her elbow.

At that moment, a liveried bearer brought a message on a silver salver and Lewis was saved the embarrassment of answering her question. Lady Curzon gave the envelope a cursory glance before handing it to Lewis. 'It's for you, from George's office. What did I tell you? George, you see, is still hard at it, and now he wants to bore you by gubbing the night away on politics. You'd better go, but do change out of that costume first. I don't think George will appreciate such a bilious colour at this time of night.'

Lady Curzon drifted away in an aura of heaven-born scent and ostrich plumes while Lewis, smiling broadly to himself, dashed up to his suite to change. Lady Curzon was absolutely right, a bilious banana in danger of spearing itself with bow and arrow, was not the way to confront the great man in his office. Ten minutes later, dressed in the more sober elegance of an evening suit, the Viceroy's overworked Private Secretary ushered Lewis through double doors flanked by two impressive Indian Chaprassis standing to attention.

'Hope I haven't dragged you away from the evening's entertainment, Joyden?' Lord Curzon waved Lewis to a comfortable leather armchair.

'No, indeed. I was about to go to bed in any case,' Lewis sat down, carefully tweaking the knees of his new evening trousers to keep the creases.

'Good Lord, is that the time already?' murmured the Viceroy, looking at the clock, aware, for the first time, the lateness of the hour. His handsome full face below the high dome of a noble forehead was pale and moist. Slightly protuberant eyes, dark with fatigue, seemed to have absorbed the whole of India. The greatest power after the King of England, Lewis was aware that nothing ever escaped the attention of Lord George Curzon and automatically his left hand reached up to straighten his hastily tied bow-tie. But the Viceroy's attention was centred upon office work – one thin file open on his desk, another, bulging and heavy, supporting his elbow. The Viceroy pondered the thin file in silence for a moment then, looking up, cleared his throat and said, 'I didn't know you'd compiled a rather prestigious anthology of verse, plus having a volume of your own poems published.'

'Yes sir . . . er, sometime ago now, at Aedes Christi.'

'Hmmm, a man of many talents – poet, historian, geographer and an expert in Chinese and Asian studies – which is why I've asked you in here tonight.' He snapped shut the thin file on Lewis Haga Joyden and putting it aside, opened the thick one marked clearly and in large red capitals; TIBET. 'You'll be leaving Simla tomorrow morning, and I wish to pick your brains before you depart. There won't be time in the morning to talk to you privately as even whilst I'm on holiday a never-ending stream of plaintiffs and petitioners slog up the hill to seek me out.' He looked unsmilingly over the file at Lewis. 'Have you enjoyed your holiday, or has my wife exhausted you with her endless fancy dress parties?'

'As always, I've enjoyed my stay very much thank you, Sir . . . and of course, thanks, too, to Lady Curzon.'

A fleeting smile touched the bloodless lips. 'Harrovians always were better liars than Etonians . . . however, back to the subject in question. My predecessor was full of praise regarding the way you handled the '95 Manchu affair. The young Dalai Lama's life was saved in the nick of time, thanks to prompt action on the part of our chaps.'

'Yes, Sir.' Lewis examined the sole of his left shoe as he sat with one leg across the other. He realized he would soon have to buy a new pair of shoes, the leather on these was almost transparent. 'Lucky we managed to foil the plot to assassinate him during the Samye Ceremony. The scapegoat – a chap dressed up as the King of Impurity to take away the troubles of the city – was a Chinese political agent given the task of sticking a knife into Thupten Gyatso – which would not have been very amusing for Asia in general had he succeeded.'

'Indeed.' The Viceroy then proceeded to the real reason for having called Lewis away in the middle of a party. The subject of Thupten Gyatso's foiled assassination was in the past, and before his time. But the Tibetan question had again raised its ugly head, and this time it was his task to handle it in the most diplomatic way he could. 'Now then, Joyden, since you're an expert on Chinese and Tibetan matters, give me your opinion of this newspaper article.' He handed a cutting across the desk and whilst Lewis was scanning it the Viceroy said; 'When you were in Peking, I believe you met the Emperor Kyaung Hsu.'

'Yes Sir.'

'What did you think of him?'

'Kind, educated and most sympathetic towards our policies.'

'Can he be trusted?'

'No, Sir.'

'I didn't think so either. Today's gossip concerning that piece from a Chinese newspaper has been humming around my head all day. It was forwarded to me by Sir Ernest Satow, our Minister in Peking. I'm correlating all the information I can get concerning Russian interests in Tibet, and want your opinion on that article. How much do you think is the truth and how much Chinese propaganda?'

Lewis read the newspaper cutting, the only noise to disturb the oppressiveness of the room coming from the whirring black fans on the ceiling. He absorbed the twelve clauses of what was supposed to be a treaty between Russia and Tibet and finally handed the cutting back to the Viceroy who tucked it away in the copious Tibetan file.

'The most significant clause to my mind, Sir, is the one regarding China's role in all this. The fact that China, who, for hundreds of years has held suzerainty over Tibet, has suddenly undertaken to relinquish, quote, "her interest in Tibet to Russia in return for Russia's support in maintaining the integrity of the Chinese Imperial Empire" makes me suspicious. Whether it's a piece of propaganda, or the whole truth and nothing but the truth, some people on our northern border are going to become very restless when they realize how deeply Russia is involved in Tibet's affairs. If China does participate in Russian mining and railway enterprises, as well as having her goods only lightly taxed, or even exempt from taxation altogether, then I think we're going to let ourselves in for a whole lot of trouble. Non-intervention, because we choose to take the viewpoint that this treaty between Russia and Tibet is only Chinese spice and propaganda, will make us lose face.'

'My sentiments exactly,' said Lord Curzon. 'We can't afford to remain complacent with something like this going on on our back doorstep. While I've no immediate fears that Russia intends to invade India at this moment – St Petersburg being too far away in any case to make such a war feasible from the Russian viewpoint – nevertheless, hostilities on the Himalayan borders of this country cannot be tolerated. Another thing that perturbs me is Russia seeking to establish Government Officers in Tibet to control their affairs, while China has the right to station Consuls in the country. We cannot allow even fabricated rumours to cause feelings of unrest, thereby jeopardizing India's safety politically, geographically, morally, socially and economically – we've enough trouble with the Frontier and the Afghans at the moment!' Lord Curzon concluded; 'I want to know Joyden, if, in your opinion, this Princess Dubrovka's husband and brother have been stationed in Tibet as the Tsar's representatives. After all, you've had your eye on them for years now, and should know more about their affairs than the rest of us put together. What, too, of this Dorjiev fellow? And can Princess Dubrovka's information be relied upon?'

Lewis wondered which question he should tackle first. 'Sonya Dubrovka has had no reason to write untruths,' Lewis said stiffly. 'Her letters are written in the utmost innocence, with no knowledge that I er . . . pass on the information she gives me. Her grandmother's information is not so reliable – and one would not expect it to be as she's an old lady whose memory is failing. However, Sonya Dubrovka is right in the thick of things, moving as she does in Court Circles and St Petersburg Society – her father has a Ministerial post in the Department of Foreign Affairs. The Princess knows just about as much as anyone can know who is not in the Tsar's immediate confidence. But her snippets of gossip are usually related to the highest in office, and she would have no reason to embroider her facts. Her letters, as are her grandmother's, are based on friendship and trust.' Lewis did not feel any better for having betrayed Sonya Dubrovka and her grandmother Lizaveta's trust and friendship – but those thoughts he kept to himself. They were too personal to bear scrutiny, and anything of a personal nature he had long ago driven from his life. Besides, the Viceroy would be the first person to censure the slightest hint of familiarity where the Russians were concerned; Lewis knew full well how Lord George Curzon had an absolute phobia about anything Russian.

The Viceroy pretended to be hypnotized by the revolving fans which kept the temperature in the room as cold as an icebox, freezing the perspiration on one's body – hardly good for one when stepping straight outside into tropical heat – no wonder he always felt as if he had influenza. 'Forgive me for asking this question, Joyden, but it's necessary – this girl . . . woman, I should say, Princess Dubrovka, what is the exact nature of your relationship with her?'

'I'm not in love with her, if that's what you're implying, Sir.' The cool edge of Lewis's tongue and his chameleon stare would have daunted a lesser man than Lord George Curzon.

'I had no wish to be impertinent on the subject, but I have to be absolutely certain of my facts. I prefer, also, to seek them out for myself rather than have them spelled out to me from a file. You'll appreciate Joyden, this is the first time I've been able to judge for myself where you are concerned – and one can't let personal feelings cloud one's judgement, can one?' His marble eyes met Lewis's hazel ones. The two men regarded each other steadily and with cool detachment. 'And her feelings for you, can they in any way be interpreted as . . . er, romantic?'

'Good Lord, no!' Lewis declared vehemently. 'Sonya and I are merely good friends, that's all. Besides, she's someone I can only ever consider in the light of . . . of a child, a schoolgirl I once met in the line of duty.'

'She's twenty-one,' the Viceroy stated briskly, 'not a fourteen-year-old schoolgirl any more – and one, might I add, who almost succeeded in drowning one of our best

123

agents!' The Viceroy appeared to find the picture amusing. His bloodless lips twitched in a fleeting smile. 'What a loss it would have been to the Survey of India had one of their top topographers been drowned by the enemy's sister while trying to make contact!'

The Viceroy had a delicate sense of humour after all. Lewis, forcing a tepid smile, said; 'Can I just say this, Sir, regarding Princess Sonya Dubrovka – as far as she and her grandmother are concerned, every word written by them has been in the purity of friendship and with no ulterior motive. If, for one moment, I had suspected Princess Sonya of . . . er, any romantic illusions because of something I might have said or done, then I'd have been the first to terminate our correspondence. Besides, she's a married woman.'

Lord Curzon let that last naive remark pass. Married women, in his opinion, were far worse in their romantic aspirations than any single female – something Lewis Joyden, as a man of the world, seemed curiously obtuse about. The Viceroy changed the delicate subject. 'I want to know about this Russian fellow Dorjiev. Give me his general background and then tell me what you've managed to pick up regarding his recent activities.'

'He's a Buriat Mongol. Back in the '80s he went on a pilgrimage to Lhasa, eventually settling at the Drepung Monastery where he devoted himself to religion, philosophy and history. He qualified, brilliantly I believe, in metaphysics. Shortly afterwards, he became tutor to the adolescent Thupten Gyatso. Dorjiev seems to have made contact again with Russia sometime during that period because, in '98, he returned to Russia to gain financial and religious support for his monastery.' Lewis scratched his neck thoughtfully, as the Viceroy listened intently and without interruption. 'I believe,' Lewis continued, 'it was at this stage Thupten Gyatso also came into his own. Repeated attempts on his life left him with a firm resolve to exert his own authority and influence on his government, the Kashag made up of High Lamas wielding very great power through Tibet. The Dalai Lama sent Dorjiev back to Russia to win the support of the Tsar. My man, H20, was put on Dorjiev's tail around this time, because each time Dorjiev decided to cock a snook at us by travelling through India...'

'Good God!' The Viceroy looked suitably astonished, and annoyed. 'How did he manage that?'

Lewis shrugged: 'That Sir, is not my department.'

'Whoever was responsible for issuing Dorjiev with the appropriate papers allowing him to travel freely through India deserves imprisonment! God knows what spying that Russian did while in this country. All right, Joyden, get on with your story.' The Viceroy directed a tetchy finger at Lewis while making a mental note to jump on the Indian department issuing entry and exit permits within the next twenty-four hours.

'H20's information was that the Tsar was seemingly attracted to the Buddhist religion, and made promises that Russia would never seek to overthrow Buddhism in Tibet, nor desecrate holy places with their railway and mining undertakings. The Dalai Lama, in return, favoured the Tsar's idea of a Russian Imperial Prince as Russia's representative in Lhasa.'

'Prince Nikolay Dubrovka!' The Viceroy was quick to pounce, his tired eyes suddenly alive and gleaming because the jigsaw puzzle that had been bothering him was beginning to fall into place at last.

'I don't think so, Sir,' Lewis said. 'We have no proof that Prince Nikolay Dubrovka, or indeed Count Kirsten Vremya, are the representatives of the Tsar's Government in Lhasa. The last reports coming out of Tibet concerning those two were that they were missing, believed dead.'

'Then you, Joyden, as a political agent of some repute, find me conclusive proof of either their deaths, or their whereabouts!'

'Yes Sir.'

The whole of India might tremble at that tone of voice used by Lord George Curzon, but Lewis remained impassive. The Viceroy, no older than he, was an old man in a young man's body, and Lewis knew perfectly well how his high-handed ways had made him hated throughout India – why, even indomitable Simla Society stood in awe of him! Lewis also realized the lightness with which the top brass viewed pundits, men who risked their lives every day to

125

further the British cause but who gained precious little recognition for their efforts because their skin was brown and not white. No doubt, when his time came, he himself would also be considered 'expendable' by the likes of Lord George Curzon. So Lewis remained aloof from the Viceroy's demands, he would do things his way, and to hell with Curzon!

'How much of a hand has that monk, Rasputin, in all this?' the Viceroy asked.

'Undoubtedly he has a large part. The Tsar and Tsarina are greatly under his influence, while Dorjiev, as the Dalai Lama's former tutor, holds an equally favourable position inside the Potala. Between them, the two monks seem to be manoeuvring Russia and Tibet towards a mutual goal.'

'And I know what that goal is!' The Viceroy, in an angry gesture, swivelled his chair away from his desk and stood up. He went to the open windows, Simla's tropical night filled with stars and the scent of Himalayan cedar and pine, unmarked by him. Laughter and music, in muted strains, burst like annoying little bubbles across his thoughts. 'India . . . Russia wants India! Not through open warfare, but by a much more subtle route, infiltration; infiltration, Joyden, bit by bit. Afghanistan in the north-west, Tibet to the north-east, and then where will our hill states of Bhutan, Sikkim and Nepal be? Where will our Empire be? Do you know that Russia is extending her frontiers by over fifty miles a day? A day, Joyden! Think of it. It cannot be allowed. No longer can this threat to us be allowed to go on!' He slammed one fist into the palm of the other hand, his feelings so strong on the subject of Russian infiltration, Lewis, with a grim smile, could not help reflecting that the old boy was paranoid about Russia.

The Viceroy turned around and in a much calmer tone asked; 'What's your opinion of Younghusband, Joyden?'

Warning bells clanged in Lewis's head – diplomacy was required here. 'I think he's a . . . a nice enough chap, Sir. Though I don't know him well enough to pass judgement on him. I've only met him on one or two social occasions when we happened to be on leave together in England. I attended a lecture of his at the Royal Geographical Society

126

and it was delivered competently enough – though I couldn't help but feel Major Younghusband's facts were sometimes inaccurate . . . more coloured by personal feelings than by rational assessment.'

'Thank you, Joyden, your remarks are most enlightening. However . . . ' The Viceroy turned away again and delivered his verdict. 'I'm thinking of sending him to Tibet at the head of our own Diplomatic Mission to meet the Dalai Lama. If Tibet is going to side with one of the great powers, it might as well be us. I've already mentioned all this to Major Younghusband, and he has agreed to act as our Commissioner to Lhasa. What I want you to do, Joyden, is to keep up your good work from your listening-post at Dehra-Dun, and to supply Younghusband with as much support and back-up as possible through your pundits. If all goes well, by this time next year we ought to have a telegraph station inside Tibet itself.' He turned back to regard Lewis, his mood one of excitement and urgency now that he had established the facts of the Tibet file. 'Thank you for your co-operation and time, Joyden. No doubt you're dying to see your bed, so goodnight.'

Without apologizing for the lateness of the hour, the Viceroy shook hands and Lewis tried hard not to let his disappointment become obvious. Disappointment, deflation and frustration because he had honestly supposed the purpose of the Viceroy's invitation – in Simla jargon, 'to gub' – was the invitation to do something inside Tibet along the lines of the Manchu Assignment which he, Lewis, had handled years ago. Now Younghusband had pipped him to the post! What had been the dividing factor? The way Lewis saw it, obviously Clifton College and Sandhurst were the choices of the moment, Harrow and Oxford, nix. Admittedly Younghusband was a dashing enough figure – if a little under-sized – in the Dragoon Guards, but why, Lewis pondered, did a mission of this nature require a military leader? Surely Curzon was only stirring up trouble for himself by putting Major Younghusband at the head of a peace mission to Lhasa? Lewis glared at the Lincrusta pine-apples on the bedroom wall, his hands behind his head, the clock now showing three am.

127

Anyway, he told himself by way of consolation, the 'better man' had won so there was no need to get worked up about it. He ought to cheer for the 'other pawn' in this, 'The Great Game', swallow his pride and supply Younghusband with all the hard-gleaned intelligence he could lay his hands on, so that afterwards Younghusband could go home to England and rest on his laurels – won, in the end, no doubt, by Joyden's hard earned intelligence work! Lewis cursed his luck and his wagging tongue – and his pen-friendship with Sonya Dubrovka that had supplied him with valuable information while losing him an assignment in Tibet he'd have given his right arm for!

ii

Two months later, the middle of October, Lewis had settled back into his humdrum routine at the Survey of India, his two weeks annual holiday at the height of the Simla season among the deodars merely a pleasantly irritating memory, when a strange intelligence report came his way. Thoughts of glory and Lhasa tucked well out of his mind for the past two months, suddenly his heart leapt and the stagnant blood in his veins began to respond once more. One of his pundits on a 'surveying assignment' in a remote part of the Karakoram mountains had met a Burusho caravan that had arrived at the Hunza capital of Baltit to over-winter there after being away some months in the Hunger Steppe. A Russian woman (keeping company with a handless Hunza youth acting as her guide and escort) had joined that particular caravan of mountain people at Samarkand, and was now with them in Baltit. Subsequent investigation had led to the fact that the disguised Russian woman was Princess Nikolay Dubrovka from St Petersburg, identity papers issued under that name stamped at Samarkand prior to the continuation of her journey through the Karakorams to Ladakh.

Puzzled, Lewis searched out Sonya's last letter: It was dated, and posted, from Peterhof, 25th September, 1902. How on earth, Lewis wondered, had she managed to get from St Petersburg to Baltit in three weeks? Impossible, he thought. So, it could not be she – the pundit was mistaken. But was he? Lewis preferred to believe one of his professionals, every one as reliable as GMT. What if . . . ?

Lewis, his excitement mounting, looked at the map of Asia on his office wall and traced a route with his finger – St Petersburg, Moscow, Tashkent, Samarkand, the Karakorams . . . Ladakh, then on to Tibet? What if her next intended port of call happened to be the border town of Rudok in Tibet?

Lewis sent a ciphered message to the Viceroy's Office in Calcutta; 'Intelligence reports our Russian contact in disguise, heading for Tibet. If the Lord is my shepherd, we can't afford to lose this sheep now.'

A ciphered reply from Calcutta came almost immediately; 'Despite divine intervention, an Englishman must do his duty according to his God-given conscience. But, I deny your intelligence as many times as Peter denied his Lord – and Saviour. Good luck.'

Grinning at that piece of typical Curzon rhetoric, Lewis put a match to the cryptic telegraph message received from the Viceroy. The man was too clever by half in this, 'The Great Game', played on the desk tops of Russia and Great Britain – and as always, Lord George Curzon wanted, by proxy of course, to be the indisputable winner! Well, if that was the case, then to hell with Younghusband, Lewis reflected whilst clearing his own desk, the race for Lhasa had restarted, so it was now up to the best man to put his best foot forward!

PART TWO

The Tibetans

Chapter Nine

Suspended forty feet above a raging torrent, the rope bridge swayed and bucked in the icy wind whistling through the granite gorges of the Karakoram mountains. Narrow rounded logs, some rotten to the core, most green and slippery and permitting no firm foothold, presented the only solidity between life and certain death.

'Follow me, Princess, put your feet where I put mine,' Joonu, the guide, urged.

Fear of drowning in the turbulent river below too real to be easily ignored Sonya fought down her panic as she struggled to free herself from the string-bag holding her life to ransom. Terrified of putting her feet anywhere except on *terra firma*, Sonya could only stand sideways in a cataleptic trance, both hands clinging desperately to the ropes serving as handrails.

'I tell you,' said Joonu laughing at her, 'if you would wear pantaloons like we men instead of skirts like my great-grandmother in Baltit, you too, Princess, would be able to walk without fear like we men.'

His lordly air irritating at a crucial moment, Sonya shut her eyes tightly and tried to get a grip on herself. 'This is hardly the time to discuss my wardrobe, Joonu, so get along and leave me to make my own way across.'

Breathing through her teeth, she edged herself along sideways, inch by inch. A Burusho peasant with a struggling sheep in his arms dug her in the back and sent the rope bridge swinging even more erratically. 'Joonu . . . go . . . don't stand there blocking this man's path,' Sonya whispered, afraid even to raise her voice lest echoes reverberating off the mountains added to the danger. Standing perfectly still, she held her breath. The Burusho peasant placed one leg round her and then the other in a skilful manoeuvre to get past, the sheep in his arms bleating pathetically as it too sensed danger.

Sonya wished she had not been quite so cocksure of herself; she wished she had gone with the more sensible Hunzakuts who had taken the longer route through these mountains, and she wished she had not allowed herself to be sweet-talked into saving time and miles by Joonu the unreliable. She wished she were back in St Petersburg. Too late she realized those wishes were her own folly.

The Burusho peasant with his sheep, at last in front of her, skipped off across the wet logs behind Joonu, neither of them holding the hand-ropes. For a reckless moment Sonya was reminded of the fairytale of Big Billy Goat and Little Billy Goat Gruff she and Kirsten had read about in the nursery. One slip, one extra deep sway of the hammock-bridge and they would all go hurtling through the air to be dashed to pieces on boulders where white water crashed. Sheer madness to have attempted it . . .

Joonu desosited his back-pack on the narrow shelf of the mountain and came back for her, springing along dangerously like Little Billy Goat Gruff to set everything in motion again.

'Don't! Don't run Joonu . . . walk. Walk very slowly . . . please,' Sonya implored breathlessly.

'I will carry you like a sheep,' Joonu laughed, 'otherwise we shall be all night and I am not happy about sleeping on this bridge.'

'I can manage.' She gritted her teeth and took another shuffling sideways step.

'Then give me your hand.' Joonu put out the stump of his left arm, his right hand holding the rope. 'Go on Princess, take hold of it – it won't bite you,' he commanded as only Joonu could command while waving a stump arm.

134

Hysteria welled in her.

'Open your eyes, Princess, and look where you must put your feet. You will see how easy it can be with two eyes, two hands and two feet . . . after all, you are whole while I am but half a man,' Joonu said laughing.

Another peasant came along, but this time without a sheep in his arms. 'Go!' He shouted, cheerfully nudging Sonya towards Joonu.

'Do as he wishes and give him your hand. I will take hold of your belt and together we'll go as mountaineers,' said Joonu.

'What's he saying, Joonu?' Sonya asked desperately.

'He says a great-grandmother with bandy legs could make a better job of crossing this bridge than you who are my mother,' Joonu translated.

Sonya, determined to put an end to the ordeal, sought the only solution. She went forward. Somehow the three of them managed to reach the rock ledge, the Burusho peasant pushing her along from behind and Joonu dragging her forward by the hand.

Her breath ragged, perspiration cold on her, by the time they reached the other side of the steep gorge, she never in her life wanted to see another suspension bridge between mountains and raging rivers. Sonya sank to her haunches, thankful to be on firm ground once more. With a sigh of relief she removed her pack, the straps of which had cut into her shoulders for the past four hours.

Mountain people shuffled past on the narrow shelf of rock to gain the steep path to the bottom of the gorge, and from there to ascend once more on the face of another mountain. She and Joonu remained where they were and made camp. Joonu lit a small fire and brewed tea for them. Presently he handed her buttered tea in a wooden bowl. 'Drink it, Princess,' he said anxiously, 'it will help to calm your bad nerves.'

'There's nothing wrong with my nerves.' Hot tea slopped over the sides of the wooden bowl and into her lap.

'You are my mother, who am I to argue with my mother?' White even teeth in a bronzed smile of disbelief, teased her.

135

'Then kindly start treating me with a little more respect.'
She glared at him. 'My hands are cold, that's all.'

'Take off your wet gloves and put them over the fire,'
Joonu said sensibly. Her fingers frozen, Joonu assisted by
easing off her gloves, finger by finger, using his one good
hand he could perform miracles with. Sonya blew on the
steam wafting up from the bowl of tea. Her face was sore
and chapped from icy winds and the hot steam only made
her cheeks sting more. But Joonu's buttered tea always
tasted so good, so refreshing, after long hours of trekking.
Sonya did not know what she would have done without her
Hunza guide these past few months; Joonu meaning Best
Beloved, the name suited him. Sonya thought back to that
first day they had met.

From Moscow she had travelled on the single track Great
Siberian Railway as far as Orenburg, and from there had
transferred to the Trans-Caspian that would take her as far
as Tashkent. The journey had been long and tedious, nine
days altogether, with frequent stops and breakdowns. But
her first-class accommodation had been clean and comfortable enough, even if the tepid food in the dining-car had
left much to be desired. The boredom of the journey had
been relieved by reading, eating, sleeping or desultory
conversations with other passengers, so that she was
infinitely glad to reach her destination. Sonya had found
Tashkent to be a miserable town, recently rebuilt after an
earthquake had all but destroyed it. She had no enthusiasm
for the ugly squat mud-dwellings thrown up haphazardly by
a populace with no heart for rebuilding a town in constant
danger of earthquake destruction. But Sonya had enjoyed
the colourful endless stream of camels and caravans
traversing the crossroads between Asia and the Orient. She
found transport in one of the camel-trains heading for
Samarakand, and thereafter, Tashkent had faded into insig-
nificance.

On her third day in Tamerlane's wonderful city of
Samarakand, she had spent the morning delving into the
treasures of Islamic culture. Returning to her hotel via the
Turkish bazaar, Sonya had stopped at one of the fruit stalls
to buy some oranges. Searching in her copious shopping

bag for her purse containing not only money but personal papers, Sonya, with mounting horror, realized it was missing. She gazed about in distraction, hoping to find a policeman who could help. In the circumstances she did not know how he could help since she had no idea how or when her purse had been stolen – and that surely, was what must have happened!

'I'm sorry,' she said in English to the Turkman holding out the oranges, 'I haven't any money to pay for them . . . I think my purse has been stolen.' She felt foolish.

The stallholder had eyed her up and down boldly, and replied in English, that universal language, of which even he had a smattering; 'Instead of money, I will take the ring you are wearing.'

Sonya had made haste to depart with her diamond and sapphire engagement ring. 'Keep your oranges.' In the circumstances, she felt the best thing to do would be to go to the Russian Consul to sort out her problem. Sonya turned away from the stall. Opening her parasol, she felt her elbow pinched from behind. 'Please don't do that!' Indignantly she whirled round to confront her molester.

'Preety English lady wish for guided tour of city?' the youth asked, wide black eyes and a marble-white smile beguiling her.

'No thank you. I've seen enough of this city for the time being.'

'Preety English lady wish to buy cheap pomegranates in other better market than this one?'

'No, thank you.' She eyed the youth up and down, noting the traditional *shalwar khameez* costume; ragged red pantaloons, shabby woollen kaftan with its colourful but frayed embroidery, and the small red toque perched on his long black hair. Sonya wondered where he had learned to speak such good English.

'You are not Engleesh, but you answer me in Engleesh.' The youth shrugged, his grin enchanting – at least, he tried hard to enchant her, but she was in no mood for his chatter. 'I catch you out,' he said, gleefully wagging a finger at her, 'you are Russian, I theenk, but pretend otherwise. You are here incognito?'

137

'I am nothing of the sort,' Sonya suddenly wished she hadn't been quite so forthcoming.

Provided with a new opening, the youth did not disappoint her. 'Ah, then I am right!' Black eyes fished and danced. 'Your anger makes me believe you do not tell the truth. See, you are Russian like I said. I theenk you are a Russian Princess who can speak good Engleesh like me. From now on then, we will speak both languages.'

'We will do nothing of the sort.' Sonya turned her back on him. 'I've no wish to talk to you in any language, so please go away.'

'I speak every language of worthiness,' he said loftily, skipping along behind her.

Sonya stopped twirling her parasol over her shoulder and turned again to the undesirable, buzzing around her like a bluebottle. 'Will you please leave me alone, otherwise I shall call a policeman.' She caught sight of an ugly stump in the boy's left sleeve. 'What happened to your hand?' she asked despite herself.

'I did not drop it in the market place like your purse, Princess,' he said cheerfully, and from under his capacious kaftan withdrew her purse.

Sonya snatched it from him. 'So, you're the thief! How dare you . . . I shall call a policeman immediately.'

'But you dropped it. I picked it up for you, and now I give it back. That does not make me a thief, Princess Dubrovka!' He evinced injury.

Outraged, she turned on him. 'How do you know who I am?'

He shrugged. 'I can read.' He wagged his right forefinger at the purse she clutched tightly. 'I wished only to see the person's name to whom so much money belonged, so that I might return it all to them. I could not help finding many important letters telling me who you are and from where you come. It is not difficult to be a detective. You cannot be angry with me for being an honest man, Princess. If you will now give me a rouble, I will buy you the oranges.'

At a complete loss, she could only view the culprit with a mixture of anger, frustration and helplessness. 'I asked you

138

what happened to your hand,' she said once more in utter defeat.

'The Turks, they chop it off – chunk!' He demonstrated the ferocity of the chop by bringing his right hand hard down on his left arm. 'They do it with a blunt meat-cleaver and it hurt very much for many days. Then they seal it with hot tar and . . .'

Before he could go on further with such gruesome relish, she said, 'Thank you, I've no wish to know any more.' But drawn to him despite all her good intentions, she asked; 'Why did they chop it off?'

'Because I borrow the wallet of a rich man to give back to him at a later date – how am I to know he is the Grand Vizier?'

Sonya had the distinct feeling he was laughing at her. 'So, they cut off your hand for stealing, how thoughtless of them!' She turned away, but the youth persisted.

'Better that than slowly rotting in one of their prisons,' he declared, skipping in front of her and pulling a face. 'But now, Princess, check your purse. See for yourself that I am no thief, for not so much as a kopeck have I taken.'

Sonya took stock of the contents of her purse. All seemed to be in order and she breathed a sigh of relief. 'Very well, I'll give you the benefit of the doubt. I won't call a policeman – yet! What is your name?'

'Joonu, it means Best Beloved.'

'Well then, Best Beloved, if you don't want to lose your other hand, just behave yourself from now on and stop following me around.'

'But that is my job,' Joonu protested. 'I like to follow rich ladies . . . and princesses are even better. Princesses are usually well-bred and so have better manners. They do not hit me on my head with their parasols. I *hate* peasants, pah!' He spat his contempt on the paving stones.

Sonya walked on, hoping she had seen the last of Joonu the Best Beloved, but still he insisted in dogging her footsteps. 'Joonu,' Sonya said in exasperation after having endured his stealthy bare feet behind her for ten minutes, 'please stop following me and go home. What do you want from me? Food, money, pomegranates?'

139

'I do not want your money or your food,' Joonu answered in an aggrieved tone. 'I only want your friendship, Princess.'

'Why?' She turned around to look at him.

'Because you are very beautiful and I would like an opportunity to fall in love with you. I think you also need a guide to show you around Samarakand. Very good guide I am, and very cheap. I will show you many tombs of Tamerlane the lame warrior. I am like him in many ways, for I, too, have a disability that will not get the better of me.'

'How many tombs does one man have – or did he have a separate one for his disability?' Sonya tried hard to keep a straight face. 'And don't change the subject Joonu! I want to know why you follow rich ladies and princesses. I want to know why you were able, so conveniently, to pick up my purse when I know for certain I didn't drop it anywhere but inside my shopping bag, which was on my arm at all times. I would have thought that you had learned your lesson already by having one hand chopped off for stealing – or are you such a glutton for punishment you don't mind losing the other one as well?'

'I am not a thief Princess, I swear it. I am an honest man.'

'How old are you?'

'Twenty-one.'

'Twelve, I think.'

'Never. I am a man of age.'

'Come, Joonu, speak the truth for a change.'

'Then I am nineteen.'

Narrowly, Sonya assessed him. Joonu backed down. 'Well then, if you must know, I am eighteen.'

'Whatever your age, Joonu, you're still a silly boy, so we won't make an issue of it. How old were you when they cut off your hand?'

'Six.'

'I see, a ruffian all your life.'

'I am a man from the Hunza!' he declared hotly, squaring his undernourished shoulders to look her straight in the eye. 'My people are the Burushos from the central part of the Hunza, a very well-respected people, Princess, who are able to look sixty when they are a hundred-and-sixty!'

'What a pity they didn't respect you enough to teach you better ways and so prevent your hand from being chopped off by the Turks.' Sonya, her purse and bag held tightly under her arm, continued on her way. She made a mental note to buy a money-belt she could wear underneath her petticoat, where the Joonus of the world could not reach! She made haste to get away from this squalid part of town, thankful that Joonu had at last seemed to have taken the hint and disappeared.

But a few minutes later, the now familiar voice came after her again; 'Wait, wait, Princess . . . you forget your oranges and I have them for you.' He came panting behind her.

Sonya sighed deeply. 'Keep them. They haven't been paid for and I don't wish to lose *my* left hand.'

'They are paid for now,' Joonu insisted. He skipped in front of her, dodging his way round other pedestrians thronging the narrow alleys. Joonu held out the bag. 'Here, take them, I am no thief but an honest man of the Hunza. These oranges are paid for with honest Hunza money; a woollen scarf my great-grandmother in Baltit wove for me.'

Sonya, a lump in her throat, endeavoured to ignore him. 'Then they're your oranges, Joonu, not mine. Please go away.'

'A princess on her own, it is a bad thing. Many men will become suspicious and wish to ingratiate themselves with you. They will try and fleece you of many things, including your virtue. Look . . . see . . . there is an evil man ogling you right now as we walk this street. And there are many more who peer at you from under their fezes and from behind their carpets.'

'They're watching you, not me. Wondering to themselves why you're stealing oranges and my money,' said Sonya, increasing her pace. She began to wonder if, after all, it wouldn't be more prudent of her to call a policeman rather than engage in conversation with a criminal. But the sight of Joonu's mutilated stump set her against any such brutal

141

action – if his story of the hand-chopping could be believed. He was certainly not above putting about such a wretched lie in order to gain sympathy from all sorts of stupid and soft-hearted females such as herself. 'Joonu,' she said frostily, 'where are your parents?'

'Dead. I have no family. I have no brothers, sisters, aunts, uncles or cousins. I am alone in the world.'

'You told me just now you had a great-grandmother in Baltit, wherever that is.'

'Baltit is in the Hunza, it is the capital of the Burushos.'

'If you're from the Hunza, what are you doing in Samarakand?'

'We take our animals to the grazing land of the Steppe in the summer months and return home in the winter. We take back salt, butter, tea and flour in exchange for our woollen shawls, blankets and fine oil made in the mountains from our Hunza apricots. It is a clever arrangement.'

'Very clever,' Sonya murmured from beneath her parasol. She brushed the back of her cotton glove across her face to wipe away the perspiration from the striking heat. 'Tell me about your great-grandmother.'

'She is one hundred and twenty years old, the oldest person in my city, which is a little town really. But my people are the wonders of the world, for they live to be great ages in the mountains. My great-grandmother – who might even be my great-great-grandmother for all I know, since we are not closely related, she is hard-working and thrifty like myself. I will be sorry when it is time to return to her in Baltit, because she is very ancient and angry all the time with Allah who has forgotten her and keeps her living on the mountain. All her family are dead except me, so I have to work for her, too. She expects me to mash her noodles which makes me very sick because it is like killing white bowel-worms. You wish to see the tomb of Bibi Khanym?'

'I have seen it, thank you.'

'Then you know why it is necessary for a preety woman like you to wear the veil, huh?' He whispered close to her ear; 'Men are staring at you. Bibi Khanym was Tamerlane's Best Beloved. He was lame and she was his Chinese

142

mistress who made him a monument of love when he was away fighting the wars.'

'I know the story, Joonu, so save your breath.' Sonya, almost running, still could not shake off the persistent Hunza youth.

'Then I am like Bibi Khanym's builder,' he said coming close beside her to take her arm under the parasol. 'I have fallen in love with your beautiful eyes and would wish to kiss them, but I am afraid to leave the mark of ardour on your face. That is why Tamerlane makes all his women wear the veil, so that the mark of Bibi Khanym does not show from the builder's hungry kisses on her pure white cheeks and red lips. So now I am so much in love with you, let me show you the tomb of Ulug-Bek. The Englishman you write to in India, is he your lover?'

'Joonu!' This was the last straw. Disentangling her arm from his, Sonya could only stop and glower in dismay. Her attitude was unrelenting and brittle as she confronted him. 'How dare you!' Joonu fell back several paces, the point of Sonya's parasol dangerous as she directed it at his belly. 'No, he is *not* my lover, and I'll thank you to mind your own business. If you don't go away and leave me alone, I'll call a policeman to lock you up!'

Sonya folded the parasol, turned on her heel and having reached the Registan, ran the rest of the way to her hotel. Joonu had taken the wind out of her sails. She was discomfited that through his pilfering ways he had come to learn more about her than was good for either of them.

The following morning Joonu was back again, sitting cross-legged outside the door of her suite. 'No! Oh no!' She put her hand to her head in disbelief. 'I thought I told you to leave me alone.' In desperation she looked around for one of the hotel staff to rescue her, but the corridor was deserted. 'Joonu, how did you get in here?'

'I walked, Princess, how else? The Hotel Proprietor is a very good friend of mine. When I am not with my people and our grazing flocks, I am painting his wrought-iron balconies and watering his window-boxes of dried-up flowers.'

Sonya stepped over the lanky and, despite everything,

143

likeable youth, determined that the Manager should toss Joonu into the street. She had had enough of him.

'I bring you your oranges,' Joonu said, juggling three of them remarkably well with only one hand and stump. 'I have not eaten a single one even though I am very hungry, but I bring them to you because they are my gift to you.'

Unable to cope with such a waif, Sonya paused at the head of the staircase. Over her shoulder she said: 'If you were *that* hungry, you'd have eaten the oranges, gift or no gift.'

He stopped juggling to look at her with a forlorn expression, very subdued for a change. 'I do not like oranges, Princess.'

'Then what do you like?'

'Pomegranates.'

'Very well, here's a rouble, go and buy some pomegranates.'

She tossed him the coin and with a bright smile Joonu leapt to his feet. Treading on the over-ripe oranges rolling in the corridor, he said gleefully, 'I knew you were a real princess the moment I saw you. For this,' he kissed the rouble, 'I will be your guide throughout the whole wide world.'

'That won't be necessary. Now will you please go somewhere else for the day, I've business to attend to.'

'I will get you the necessary papers to enter Tibet so you do not have to approach stupid officials who only argue with you,' Joonu said swiftly and again Sonya had cause to view him in alarm.

'Joonu, your snooping ways offend me. I don't need forged papers thank you.'

'Do not be upset, Princess, I am a good fellow really. I will be your guide because I know you will remunerate me well.'

'How do you know I wish to enter Tibet? For all you know, I might be on my way to India to . . . to see the gentleman who writes to me.'

Joonu grinned wickedly, 'I think not. I observe you now for three days, Princess, and watch what kind of things you buy in the market-places. By now I think you have the complete disguise of a Ladakh widow-woman.'

Sonya did something she had never done in her life, she stamped her foot. 'Joonu, you are incorrigible! I promise you, I'll see you behind bars before this day is through.'

'Do not be angry with me, Princess. I am here only to help you. To be a Ladakhi widow-woman is a good disguise – as far as Ladakh. To travel in Tibet, you will need to be a Tibetan noblewoman on pilgrimage, and here I can be of great assistance to you. I have travelled in Tibet many times and know the customs.'

'I don't believe one word.'

Joonu shrugged indifferently. 'Whether you believe me or not makes little difference to me, Princess, but it will make a great difference to you. I have learned a lot about you – your purse reveals many secrets.' He grinned broadly. 'I read letters in Russian and English. From them, I know your husband and brother travelled this way four years ago. They were on their way to the Forbidden City. They were never heard of again. But now you go to look for them because you do not believe they are dead. Am I not right?'

What could she say? 'Joonu,' she said at last, 'I do not know who or what you are, but only that you're a spy and a monster!'

'I am also in love with you, O Bibi Khanym. Yes, it is true, I am a spy. I spy everywhere I am required to earn my bread and butter. It is a good living being a spy because it is an exciting life. But it pays me nothing.'

Sonya closed her eyes in despair. 'I thought you were a shepherd-boy from the Hunza.' She opened them again to glare balefully at him.

'I am that, too.'

'If you're a spy, who pays you? Who has asked you to spy on me?'

'Nobody. I am my own master. I only supply His Worship, the Mir of Baltit, with my information since he is a good friend of my great-grandmother's. But he is a poor man and cannot influence my career greatly. I would one day like to be employed by the British or Russians, but they won't have me because I have a disability. In Samarkand there are many foreign spies – the British and Russians call it "The Great Game", but it is more like "The Great Hoax". The British are here as they do not wish the Russians to get any closer because it makes them nervous on the other side of the Himalayas, and the Russians do not take any notice of the British because they are only nervous of the Great White Khan who desires to rule the whole world, including the British.' Joonu, a smile splitting his roguish face, rubbed his right foot against the back of his left leg. Over-long sleeves hanging below his wrists, one of them pathetically handless, presented such a ludicrous picture of grand espionage, Sonya burst out laughing.

'Bravo Joonu! I had a brother like you. He got himself into trouble one day, and was never heard of again.' She changed the subject abruptly. Her anger dissipated in the light of innocence, reminiscent of the purest choir boy on earth, she finally succumbed to the winning ways of the Hunza youth beneath his coat of dirt. 'Very well Joonu, I'll hire you as my guide – but you'll only get paid when we arrive in Lhasa.' Sonya turned and began to descend the stairs.

'That will suit me, Princess.' In delight he followed her into the narrow dark street outside the hotel. 'But I do not think the disguise of a Ladakhi widow-woman is a good one for you.'

'Oh, why not?' She put up her parasol and, dodging a donkey-cart, proceeded towards the Registan.

'You must be a Hunzakut noblewoman – I will teach you how. And you must be called Shaim Khanym, the beautiful sister of the wonderful Bibi who never knew she had a sister – neither did Tamerlane, but wished she had, then he could have had her, too.' He grinned. 'It is a good name for you and one most suitable for a noblewoman from the Hunza as we are of the Mohammadan race. In that way no one will suspect you are a Russian spy.'

'I am *not* a Russian spy!' She glared at him from under her parasol. 'I think you're getting a little carried away on all this nonsense, Joonu, so kindly stick to the specific.'

'Yes, Princess, I will be very specific. I will be your son. In that way we can both travel through Tibet without raising British suspicion.'

'British?'

'They are everywhere in their border-posts listening and spying and stopping everyone about their legitimate business. I do not like the British very much, they are so superior – or like to think they are. I prefer the Russians because if they wish to kick a dog they kick him in broad daylight. The British do it at night so nobody sees.'

Sonya said; 'I don't think the British in their border-posts will believe you're my son – a noble Hunza boy who tends sheep, eh Joonu?'

'It is true, the British are far from stupid. They are always sending their spies to Baltit to watch what my great-grandmother and the Mir are doing. We are sometimes afraid to blow our noses with them watching. The British are frightened that we in the mountains might go to the side of the Great White Khan, or the Afghans, or the Turks, or the Tibetans or the Chinese. So we shall both be humble pilgrims on a journey to Lhasa, to pray at the tomb of my noble father.'

'I doubt we'll find it, the Tibetans don't have tombs, which makes me suspect your story about being in Tibet many times is only another lie.'

'I wish you would trust me, Princess!' He sighed melo-dramatically. 'I have been in Tibet many times on pilgrimage and seen the bellies of foreign-devils ripped wide open and stones shoved inside them by High Lamas who do not like foreign-devils.'

'Suspicious, no doubt of Mohammadans embracing Buddhism!' she retorted.

'Trust me, Princess,' he nevertheless insisted. 'The Hunzakuts are on their way back to the mountains – that is why you find us in Samarakand after spending the summer in the Steppe. We are taking our animals home for the winter, so you are very lucky to find me to be your guide. Another week and I would not have been here, but much further along the caravan route. Before the heavy snows arrive to cut off all the passes, we will be in Baltit. There we will stay with my great-grandmother, and you can mash her noodles and be sick instead of me as she splatters her food up the walls just like a baby. Afterwards, when the snows

147

begin to melt, some Hunzakuts will come again this way, others will go to the rich pasturelands of Ladakh and Tibet. We will go with those.'

He seemed to have worked everything out perfectly. 'And how much do you yourself intend to make from me?' Sonya asked. 'I'm certain you're not rearranging my life out of love and charity, since we hardly know each other.'

'Princess,' he announced with a touch of honesty at last, 'I would wish to be a rich man one day and marry a noble-woman richer than myself, one like you. I am what is called an opportunist, and that is why I like you. You will give me the opportunity to go far. I do not wish to stay a humble shepherd all my life.'

'You won't Joonu, I'm certain of that! It will definitely be either a palace or a prison for you, depending on how many purses you can get away with.'

'I like you very much, Princess, that is why I am prepared to risk my life for you,' he informed her with a certain amount of redeeming grace in his impish grin.

ii

'Come,' said Joonu, expertly repacking everything with one hand, assisted by the blind end of his stump. 'If you are sufficiently rested, let us go. We do not want to be left behind. It is still a long way through the Indus valley to Leh.'

Agreeing wholeheartedly, Sonya adjusted her disguise. 'Joonu, is my headdress straight. Do I look all right?'

'Your face is smudged a little. Wait a minute . . . ' Joonu rubbed the palm of his hand against a rock and transferred the dirt to her face to give her the bluish tinge of a true Tibetan. 'It will do for the moment. When we stop again, I will make some more dye for your complexion because we do not want you looking like a snow-leopard to give us away to the British. Sometimes their political officers come into these passes to spy on us and to see we do not contra-vene any trading laws.'

Adorned with cheap jewellery purchased in Baltit, Sonya did not feel the least like a Hunza noblewoman in her heavy

148

woven skirts and loose coat, an embroidered and quilted toque on her braided hair over which a veil of heavy muslin was draped. She asked Joonu anxiously, 'talking of political officers, what are we going to say to the officials at the border-posts? We're not pilgrims, traders or even proper Hunza shepherds, so the excuse of looking for fresh grazing ground cannot be ours.'

'You worry needlessly,' Joonu replied. 'Leave the worrying to me, Princess, we are not at the Chinese border-post yet.'

Sonya reserved judgement as they rejoined the rest of Joonu's people seeking springtime pasture for their winter-starved animals. If Lhasa was to be her goal, then, she told herself, she ought to start trusting her guide.

Chapter Ten

D espite dazzling glaciers, snowy mountains, waterfalls
cascading between granite rocks, edelweiss and
gentians carpeting the lower slopes of the green valley,
despite the sun shining upon the Burusho peasants cheerfully cooking breakfast in the open air, Sonya remained in a
state of disquietude. With troubled eyes she watched their
yaks and goats wandering contentedly in the meadow
through which a stream ran, devouring everything in their
path – including tents – her thoughts far away upon a
distant goal.

'I always know when you are angry,' Joonu said, lolling
unconcerned on one elbow in the lush damp grass, a sprig
of thyme between his strong white teeth, 'you become like
an ice-maiden, your grey eyes silently condemning, face red
as an alpine-rose, and then I am very afraid.'

'Your people are going no further than this valley. I'm
not stupid, Joonu, I know they're going nowhere near
Lhasa.'

'I never said anything about my people going near
Lhasa!'

Sonya put down her bowl of tea before she threw it at
him, and walked swiftly away across the springy turf. Joonu
caught up with her. 'Go away, Joonu,' Sonya said,
disgusted and disappointed with him. 'I ought to have
realized the Tibetans, unlike the Ladakhis, would not allow
foreign devils – which is what your people are despite all

your grandiose claims to the contrary– to graze on their pastures, however near the border!'

'What is wrong with you this morning, Princess?' Joonu said in exasperation. 'Have I not devoted my whole life to you these past few months? Have I not risked heart and limb to bring you this far?'

'This far is not far enough, Joonu, can't you understand? I must get to Lhasa – soon! I don't want to have to spend another winter mashing noodles for your great-grandmother in Baltit, I want to find my brother and my husband!'

'Follow me please, Princess.' Joonu ran ahead of her, up the steep valley slope, shouting back; 'Come, I want to show you something. We will take this path . . . I want to show you how close we are to the Tibetan border. I never told you before, because I wanted you to rest before pushing yourself further.'

They panted heavily as they ascended the steep path. Sonya, her ears ringing in the rarefied atmosphere, only hoped he was not imagining things again, and that the Ladakh-Tibet border was indeed in sight.

Presently, a bend in the mountain-path brought them to a spectacular vantage-point from where they were able to look down into the valley. 'There!' said Joonu triumphantly, as he pointed to the near blue distance. 'There is the Ladakh-Tibet border, and the pack road which is the main Silk Road of Tibet from Khotan in the north, to Demchok and Gartok in the south. You can see the Dogra Raja of Jammoo's flag flying at the Ladakh outpost, and there you will also find the Kashmiris. A little distance beyond, lies the Rudok border-post where the Chinese or Tibetans will interrogate us – High Lamas make sure you are well and truly inside their country before torturing you.' And on that disconcerting note, Joonu began to descend the mountain, loosening more stones that scattered in front of him in gravel showers.

'I'm sorry. Perhaps I was a little hasty in my accusations, forgive me, Joonu.' Always unsure of Joonu, truth and lies merging in the sunniness of his disposition, she forgave him as swiftly as he forgot to bear grudges. 'Joonu, what *am* I to do with you . . . and without you!'

He turned and grinned, and it was like seeing the sun after a thunderstorm. 'You may kiss me mother, and leave upon me the mark of Shaim Khanym.'

'I'll do nothing of the sort,' Sonya said more cheerfully. 'But as soon as we get back to camp, you can beg, borrow or steal – I don't mind which method you choose – as much food as you can cram into our packs. I've a nasty suspicion we're going to be very lonely, cold and hungry while we're losing our way to Lhasa.' She still did not trust him!

ii

Three days later a Kashmiri custom officer, with barely a glance at them, stamped their papers issued in Samarkand, and they walked through the border-post unscathed.

Afraid of being turned into a pillar of salt if she dared look behind her, Sonya, at almost running pace, kept her attention pinned upon the busy Silk Road ahead, and only when the Kashmiri post was a hundred yards behind, did she crow; 'Joonu, it was so easy!'

'Yes, it was easy,' Joonu said, catching up with her, 'but we have not reached the Tibetan post yet. It is there, about fifty paces in front of us. Wait until we are over the actual Tibetan border, Princess, and then you can sack me if you wish.'

More soberly, Sonya approached the Tibetan customs shed, her heart beating so fast and loud she thought everyone would hear it. Far busier here, and more daunting than on the Ladakh side of the border, traders, pilgrims, businessmen, soldiers, peasants and animals were tripping over each other, Sonya and Joonu stumbling amongst the Tibetans.

'You are from the Hunza?' asked the Chinese officer with lazy slant eyes staring hard at Sonya. He spoke Tibetan and Sonya, forgetting every word she had learned with Chao in St Petersburg, waited for Joonu to do the answering. He seemed to have lost his tongue too, and the Chinese officer impatiently repeated the question.

'Yes,' Sonya answered in more of a monosyllabic grunt than a real yes.

152

'You speak Tibetan in the Hunza?' asked the Chinese officer pedantically, his black slit eyes probing.

'Yes.'

'No!' Joonu in Burushaski whispered urgently behind Sonya. He dug her in the back and when she turned to look enquiringly at him he made urgent signals with his eyes and silent mouth.

Sonya turned back to the Chinaman and smiled an apology. 'My son is not in possession of all his wits . . . no, we do not speak Tibetan in the Hunza,' she replied in Tibetan.

'Then what language do you speak in the Hunza?'

'Many . . . er, Burushaski . . . Shina . . . '

'Of what religion are you?'

'Ortho . . . Moslem . . . ' She swallowed and pulled her confused thoughts together. 'Bud . . . Buddhist.'

'If you do not speak Tibetan in the Hunza, how is it you can speak it now?'

'I . . . I speak Tibetan . . . my husband, he was a Tibetan nobleman.' Her head reeling, Sonya wished Joonu would say something to rescue her from this Chinaman's awkward questioning.

'From which Province?' he asked next, his eyes like granite blades slicing her nerve.

'From . . . from Po Yul . . . '

'Tsang!' Joonu hissed behind her.

'Tsang!' Sonya bending forward with the weight of her pack looked straight in the Chinaman's face, her honesty and innocence manifest.

'Make up your mind,' he said tersely. 'Why do you wish to go to Lhasa?'

'To pay homage to his Holiness, the God-King,' said Sonya, finding her tongue at last. 'And to make a pilgrimage to my husband's chorten. He died in Lhasa in service to the Kashag. He was a well-respected nobleman. After his death I returned to my homeland in the Hunza, the capital, Baltit. Now my son and I return to Tibet to pay our humble respects on this pilgrimage.' She smiled again, her grey eyes soft and beguiling.

'Have you anything to declare?' asked the Chinese officer

153

growing tired of them. The rubber stamp hovered over their papers and Sonya, shaking her head, held her breath as the officer's eyes strayed to a sudden commotion in a corner of the customs shed. A group of High Lamas of the Yellow Hat sect had entered the premises. They began to rip open sacks and prise the lids from wooden crates.

'They are the very worst,' Joonu declared hotly in a whispered aside while everyone's attention was centred upon the rumpus. 'I hope they will not come over to ask us our business. Now what are they doing with that poor old man?' They watched anxiously while an aged crippled peasant-farmer with bowed back, sores and rags, was taken by the scruff of the neck. Led to a corner, he was forced to kneel with his hands on his head before being searched. But his person revealed nothing except lice and more sores, so his sack of turnips instead was ripped open against his feeble protests.

The rubber stamp in the Chinese officer's hand banged down, approving their papers to allow entry into Tibet. Sonya and Joonu were jostled by the next group waiting impatiently. Eager to get away from officials and Yellow Hats, they never did find out what became of the unfortunate peasant-farmer.

In Tibet at long last, Sonya, in a superstitious little gesture, took up a handful of soil and trickled it into her pocket for luck. Then she and Joonu took the Silk Road, heading for Demchok, a hundred miles away.

'Joonu,' Sonya said angrily once they had resumed anonymity among the traders, pilgrims, pack-animals and other motley characters on the road, 'why on earth didn't you open your mouth and say something to help me in front of that Chinese customs man?' But before he could answer, Joonu suddenly grabbed her arm and drew her urgently off the road. 'Quick, we must hide!'

He dived into some bushes growing below the level of the dusty road. 'Come quickly, Princess, do not stand there with your mouth open. Soldiers, Tibetans this time, not Chinese as in the customs shed. Many of them are coming along this road riding horses with bells – that is how I know them to be Tibetan. I hear them before we see them which

154

is just as well, Princess; they are the worst – after the High Lamas. Soldiers travel the country and know everyone's business. They can sniff out a foreign devil from miles away, and I have no wish for my belly to be filled with stones if they should take us before the Ponpo.'

'Ponpo? What's a Ponpo?' Sonya asked, keeping her head well down beside Joonu in the bushes.

'A district Governor or Magistrate. A Ponpo has very great powers, and could torture us if he wished to exercise his sadistic will . . . shh! They come abreast of us now, so be silent until they pass.'

Crouching with bated breath among the prickly thorn bushes, Sonya had a chance to take stock of the situation and marvelled she had come so far in the circumstances. Perhaps it had been her very naivety, combined with a determination not to look beyond the immediate moment, that had brought her at last to this pass in the Tibetan mountains, a wondering victim of Joonu's capriciousness. 'Joonu,' she said when the soldiers had passed along the road to the north and they had scrambled back up the slope to the elevated roadway, 'sometimes I have this strange feeling that I was meant to meet you in Samarakand.'

He grinned. 'Princess, you should have been a Mohammadan.'

iii

That night, not wishing to camp beside their fellow travellers for fear of too many awkward questions being asked, they separated from the crowd with the excuse that they wished to cover as much mileage as possible through the bright moonlit night. The bond between fellow pilgrims being what it was, the excuse had to be provided to avoid suspicion, a certain camaraderie existing on the Silk Road. It reminded Sonya of a story by an Englishman named Chaucer she had read on holiday at Fairmaster Manor entitled, *The Canterbury Tales.*

Camp sites were plentiful along the road, blackened stones and rubbish, landmarks of previous travellers.

'We will go to that mound of stones on top of the hill

155

over there,' said Joonu, indicating a vague black hump on the horizon. 'I'm tired and wish to rest. That place is too far and too steep for most people to want to climb to, when there are plenty more convenient resting places along the route.' He seemed perfectly sure of what he was doing. Also very tired and footsore, Sonya allowed herself to be guided by Joonu, the perfect night lit by a myriad of stars begging them to call a halt to the day's travels. Their water-bottles filled from a mountain spring an hour before, Sonya did not worry about camping close to a stream as they usually did. Once they had climbed to their rocky eyrie, she realized Joonu had been right about its solitude: It was too inconvenient a resting-place when one was tired and hungry.

Joonu lit a campfire within the circle of white walls reflecting the moonlight, and soon they fell upon their bowls of buttered tea flavoured with salt and thickened with tsampa. Afterwards they settled down in the lee of protective walls and slept. It was one of the most peaceful and restful nights Sonya had spent for many weeks.

In the dawn light she awoke refreshed. Joonu was already awake, the campfire relit and tea brewing. He crouched on his haunches, looking very much like an Arab stall-holder in a bazaar, amid an assortment of clothes laid out neatly on the grass.

'What on earth are you doing?' Sonya asked, struggling to sit up on her bedroll.

'Making breakfast,' he replied laconically.

'What are all those old clothes?'

'Old clothes.'

'Come on Joonu, you're up to something. Where did you find those garments?'

'Along the way.'

'They're filthy, so you can dispose of them along the way.' She began to roll up her bed. 'Really, Joonu, I wonder about you sometimes.'

'You do not smell the clothes, Princess,' he said, rolling his eyes and grinning widely so that she knew he was up to mischief. 'What you smell are the odours of the departed.'

'I don't know what you're talking about!'

'Drink your tea, Princess, before it gets cold.'

156

Sonya looked around her, not liking Joonu's secretive manner one bit. 'What is this place?' she asked, all at once noticing the paper prayer flags fluttering on top of the walls. She went closer to examine their surroundings. In horror Sonya saw tiny clay images with paper faces stuck haphazardly in niches – these were not stone walls, they were walls of human bones! 'Joonu, we've been sleeping in a crematorium,' Sonya said angrily.

'Do not worry, Princess,' he answered cheerfully, 'the spirits were at peace last night.'

'Did you know this was holy ground?' she asked, accusingly.

'Oh yes. There are many such cremation places in the mountains – I've seen the monks gather the bones of the dead after they've been cut from the flesh and picked clean by vultures. Then they grind them with the ashes and mix it all together with holy spit to form the replica of the departed. But do not worry, they will not harm us. Now eat up and let us move on. But please change your clothes first for these I have procured for us.'

'They are disgusting and I've no intention of donning garments you picked out of the gutter.'

'They are clothes I managed to borrow from those who argue about the taxes on salt and tea in the Customs post at Rudok,' Joonu said with a world-weary sigh. 'From now on we must be real Tibetans from Tsang Province, so put on these clogs and this headdress, please Princess.'

'Why Tsang?'

'All the best Tibetans come from Tsang Province – and it is near enough to Lhasa for us to be heading there.'

'Joonu, please tell me what's wrong with this Hunza costume you insisted I should wear? It has been acceptable until now.'

'Acceptable yes, safe no. It is much like the dress of Tibetan women and that is why no-one asks too many questions – so far! So far, most people have been ignorant peasants.' He spat contemptuously for effect. 'When we meet with the real quality who are less ignorant, they will become suspicious and start asking all kinds of rude questions. For that, we want to be prepared, as I do not

157

wish to eat stones. It will be much simpler and swifter to travel as Arjopas who are Tibetan pilgrims.' All the time he had been patiently explaining, Joonu had been dressing himself in a long, dirty-brown toga-like robe. Made of sacking-cloth, it was put over a loose sleeved blouse of hideous yellow. Joonu had removed his Hunza toque, stuffed it into his pack, and then, with his penknife, began chopping his hair off into ragged stooks. Afterwards, he smeared the exposed areas of his body with the last of their yak-butter. Gone was the shepherd of the Hunza and in his stead was a blackfaced grease-smeared Tibetan youth – only that Joonu was going to attempt to get away with murder by declaring himself a novice from a Monastic Order collecting alms for his Lamasery!

Reluctantly Sonya donned the smelly costume Joonu had 'managed' to obtain for her from the customs post at Rudok. An enormous front pocket acted as a most useful pouch on the front of the Tibetan dress. She put on the heavy headdress of bamboo and beads Joonu had also managed to pick up so conveniently, and finally squeezed her swollen feet into wooden clogs. By the time they reached the main road again she had hung the clogs on the side of her pack and regained the comfort of her soft sheepskin boots purchased in Baltit during the winter.

'Your costume suits you,' Joonu nodded in approval. 'You are now a lady-sorcerer from Kham Province.'

'Just now you said we came from Tsang!' Sonya argued in some confusion.

'We do. But we must always say we come from somewhere remote – as far away as possible from where we are at a particular time. When we reach the Province of Tsang, we will say we come from Amdo, or if we reach Po Yul, then we must come from Tsang, do you understand?'

'No.'

'Then you must try. We have to be what we are not. We must also confuse our fellow travellers by coming from a region they themselves have no knowledge of. In that way, total ignorance can protect us.'

Sonya sighed in exasperation. Truth and lies, it was all the same to Joonu. She gave up trying to understand him, but accepted him for the companion she needed on this long hazardous trek to Lhasa. 'Joonu,' she warned, 'don't ever make me sleep in a chorten again, otherwise I myself will haunt you.'

Joonu grinned. 'There is a proverb in my country – offend not nobility or yak, otherwise they will attack! As I have no wish for my tail to be pulled, I will try not to offend the Princess any more.'

Chapter Eleven

Chapter Eleven

It took Sonya and Joonu ten days to reach Demchok, and a further three weeks to the outskirts of Gartok, a border-trading post and major milestone on their route to Lhasa. By mutual consent they did not linger in Gartok where they were likely to meet officialdom in all its various forms, something Sonya wished to avoid at all costs. They decided to replenish their dwindling stocks of essential food-stuffs once Gartok was behind them.

The Silk Road stretched before them like a ribbon lacing the mountains. They did not pass anyone willing to barter tsampa and butter for a handful of walnuts and a wooden spoon, so they decided, as the day progressed, to come off the main Silk Road and take a lesser track in the hopes of finding a farmhouse where they could obtain food. Sonya even contemplated parting with a whole silver tranka for the vital ingredients of flour, butter and tea, but in the end, was dissuaded by Joonu from doing anything so rash. 'If you wish to throw away your money, then do it in my direction, Princess, since I have received no remuneration from you for nearly a year.'

Suddenly, with a jerky cry, Joonu dived off the narrow path they had been pursuing and scampered into the shelter of an ash grove, crying urgently over his shoulder; 'Quickly Princess, we must hide.' He disappeared into the protection of the trees.

'Really, Joonu . . . '

'Shhh!' He put a warning finger to his lips. 'The Red Caps . . . they are sharing this track with us. Wait here, I will see what they are up to.' Joonu shrugged off his pack and shinned up the mountain ash under which they stood. A few minutes later he slid down with urgency. 'There is a chorten half way down the slope, I think they are going there as it is a funeral procession. There are hundreds of them spread out all along this path and halfway down the valley. Some of them might even come into this glade and see us. They will capture us if they think fit.'

'Is there no other way back to the main road?' Sonya said anxiously.

'Not one I could see, but then I did not stay long enough to examine our surroundings in detail . . . hsht! I hear twigs crackling underfoot, more monks come this way. Can you climb trees, Princess, because that is our only hope?' Joonu tossed his pack into the protection of the lush undergrowth. Sonya did the same with hers, answering Joonu with a grim determination, 'If you can climb trees with one hand, I'm sure I can manage with two. You go first.'

'Put your feet where I put mine, there are plenty of stalwart branches for you to cling to.'

Sonya followed him closely, and, out of breath, perched beside Joonu. They had a good view of the valley and surrounding countryside. 'I am sure the monks have come from that lamasery up there on the opposite side of the valley.' Joonu squinted to the distant mountain, the sun so blinding that he had to shield his eyes with his hand. He pointed out the squat square buildings in orderly rows terracing the mountain on the other side of the valley. 'I think they do not wish for their own mountain to be haunted by the spirits of the dead and would rather take pains to convey the body to this side where only the villagers in the valley will be tormented.'

Sonya smiled. 'I'm sure you must be right, Joonu. I hope we're not going to be stuck up here for long, it's very uncomfortable . . . and dangerous . . . owee!' She almost lost her balance on the branch they shared, and hung on for dear life as, with great interest, she and Joonu observed the antics of the Red Caps.

'The village and its people must be owned by the lamasery,' Joonu said thoughtfully, 'so we will have to be extra careful when we pass through it. We do not want the monks knowing our business. It is a pity we cannot stop there for our food, because it looks a prosperous place. Now what are they doing?' Joonu almost fell out of the tree as he craned his neck too far forward to get a better view of the chorten.

The funeral procession had come to a halt on the tableland immediately below the ash grove. A doleful chant of monks reciting the Mantra drifted up to Sonya and Joonu in their leafy hideout. Suddenly, *en masse,* the lamas and lesser monks prostrated themselves on the stony ground of the chorten. To her horror Sonya could now clearly see in their midst a massive cauldron perched on top of logs and brushwood into which a yellow liquid was being poured by monastery servants. But the real horror of it all came from the realization that into the cauldron had been placed a human body.

Sonya clung dizzily to the branch on which she precariously perched, a sense of mounting horror destroying rationality. Beside her Joonu stifled his snorts. 'Do not worry, Princess, I think he is already dead.'

The lama in the cooking-pot looked too alert to be dead and Sonya flinched, goosepimples breaking out all over her as she witnessed such a bizarre rite, all her finer instincts telling her this was just not happening! But she did watch, despite herself, incredulity getting the better of squeamishness.

In his monastic robes and the distinctive red winged-cap by which the sect was known, the lama sat bolt upright with arms dangling nonchalantly over the sides of the cauldron. A brown-robed servant carrying a lighted torch approached the cauldron and touched the flame to the brushwood. Fire leapt into the air as the bone-dry fuel assumed a life of its own, hungrily to devour holy flesh.

The hot bright noon became black with acrid smoke drifting up to the ash grove. Sonya and Joonu coughed and spluttered as the pungent fumes seared their lungs and gathered chokingly in their throats. The laden air filled with

162

the hypnotic chant of the Mantra, the snapping crackle of dead wood and dancing flames fuelled by oil bubbling over the funeral urn in which human flesh was being melted became all too much for Joonu. He began to giggle hysterically.

'Stop it, Joonu!' Sonya said as the sublime turned to the ridiculous. Smoky tears streamed down her face. 'You'll give us away with that silly noise. Let's get out of here . . . come on . . . ' She made a move on the branch and Joonu, unbalanced in more ways than one, crashed through the mountain ash into the undergrowth twenty feet below.

'Oh my goodness! Joonu, are you hurt?' Sonya scrambled down the torn trunk of the ash, almost falling on top of Joonu who was laughing his head off in the tangle of foliage that had broken his fall.

'I am unharmed,' Joonu reassured her, a nasty graze on his forehead. He rubbed his hand across it carelessly. 'It is nothing, only blood. Let us rest here awhile since we cannot go anywhere while the monks are boiling their comrade in yak-butter. Later, when they disperse, we can make a move to the village, for now I am very hungry.' He opened his pack and took out a handful of walnuts, all they had left to stay the pangs of hunger.

Relieved that Joonu was unhurt, Sonya settled herself beside him in the green glade, but declined the walnuts. She was not hungry – not after what she had seen in the chorten below.

Sonya rummaged through her medical-pack for cotton wool and iodine. 'Now hold still while I attend to your damaged head,' she told Joonu.

Several hours later, just as the cooler air of evening started to spring up in the mountains, Sonya and Joonu descended from the ash grove to the deserted path, the Red Caps having returned to their lamasery. All that was left of the lama in the cauldron were his bare bones left to dry on the mountainside. In the village, Sonya and Joonu encountered several brown-robed monks of a lesser order than the Red Caps, together with the servants from the lamasery loading heavy sacks on a procession of mules and donkeys.

'Either it is taxation day, or the lama boiled in oil was a great man who is deserved of a grand feast tonight,' Joonu commented wryly. 'Now there will be no barley-flour or butter for us.'

'Just as well. We are not buying butter here!' Sonya insisted. 'Heaven knows what they do with the melted butter left over from their cremation pots. Oh goodness! I thought the last of the Red Caps had reached the monastery by now, but that one there is going to take all night!' she wailed in horror.

They drew back cautiously beneath the tattered awning of a shop while the devout Red Cap left behind all the others, prostrated himself in the dusty street. Sonya realized he was practising Kayapdo, a ritual Chao had described to her. '*Om mani padme hum! Om mani padme hum!*' The Red Cap stood, then prostrated himself once more on the filthy refuse-laden ground, over and over, one laborious prostration followed by the next. A servant walked solemnly behind carrying his master's prayer-wheel, trident and rosary.

'The one whose bones will be gathered as holy relics for his lamasery, must surely have been a great reincarnation for all the devotion he is receiving,' Joonu whispered as the Red Cap came not ten paces from where they crouched in purple shadows stretching across the narrow street.

Sweat, dirt, tattered locks and shabby clothing joined Joonu to the brotherhood of Arjopas, and Sonya, stealing a sidelong glance at him, hoped she did not look as repulsive as he, while realizing that their very repulsiveness might be their only salvation. They had both come to resemble the parts they were playing – and not in a trifling way, but in deadly earnest. She hoped now, they would be able to pass through the village unnoticed, she and Joonu just tired pilgrims who deserved alms and shelter in return for an Arjopa's blessing. Sonya waited impatiently for the Red Cap to get a move on so that she and Joonu could proceed on their way, but they were out of luck.

'*Ohgai, Oghai!*' said a deep voice startling them from behind. A handsome grinning Tibetan with brawny arms and smooth muscled chest stuck his tongue out in greeting.

'You have undergone much hardship,' he declared in the usual friendly acknowledgement of strangers.

They too stuck out their tongues, Joonu cracking a low remark beside Sonya who replied according to custom, 'We have suffered no hardship like you.'

The day had been hot. The man wore only an unfastened sleeveless yak-skin waistcoat that revealed his bronzed torso, a stiff skirt to his knees and soft yak-skin laced boots. He was bare-headed and his thick black hair hung in greasy plaited ropes to his shoulders. 'You are Arjopas?' the shopkeeper asked.

Sonya and Joonu nodded dumbly.

'You have come from far away?' He eyed Sonya's bamboo headdress furtively, as though he were half afraid of it.

Again they nodded in unison, dark eyes and light ones wide and fearful upon the handsome shopkeeper. But he was kind and hospitable. 'Come then,' he said, drawing aside the sacking curtain across the entrance to his premises, 'it is getting late for you to travel, so you must rest here. Tonight is the marriage-feast of my daughter and you are welcome to share in our joyous celebrations. It is an auspicious day all round,' he added jovially, 'for a High Lama has also been reincarnated, so we must give thanks to the good spirits who protect our village. Come, follow me, Holy Mother,' he bowed respectfully before Sonya.

The Tibetan shopkeeper led them through the dark interior of his ground floor, on one side of a narrow corridor the shop that sold everything from food to fuel, and on the opposite, a storeroom for his grain and an animal pen, the stench of which hit them in passing. At the back of the squat clay and stone house was a small back yard. He stood aside to let Sonya pass first up a narrow outside stairway to the flat roof where a party was in progress. Prayer-flags and flowered wreaths gave the place a festive air. They were offered a flagon of barley-spirits which Sonya tactfully removed from Joonu's hand. She set down the earthenware flagon out of his reach.

'You are truly a spoilsport, mother!' Joonu protested.

'Maybe. But I don't want to carry you along the road tomorrow morning.'

The bride's mother offered them turnip soup, filling their wooden bowls to capacity – again and again and again.

'I am sick of turnip soup, Princess,' Joonu whispered in disgust through the unmusical noise made by a primitive band in the corner. The wailing oboes and lamentable singing not to their taste at all. 'I would have thought that on this occasion they could have given us something more befitting!'

'Hush Joonu! Be thankful for small mercies.'

'I am thankful, and sick to my stomach of turnip soup.' He reached across her for the more desirable flagon of pure alcohol. 'And don't look at me like that, Princess . . . you know by now I am not a good Mohammedan.' He grinned back at her cheekily.

After the turnip soup they were offered tiny honey-cakes fried in yak-butter and Sonya tried hard not to think of the cremated lama on the hillside. The bride, flanked by the groom and those whom Sonya took to be the bride's brothers, was seated crosslegged on a cushion placed in the centre of the unswept floor. She smiled shyly at Sonya and offered her another honey-cake. Then the inevitable questions started. 'You come from which Province, Holy Mother? On what kind of pilgrimage are you engaged? Is your companion your son, your brother or your husband? From where did you get such handsome jewellery for we have never seen such a necklace, earrings or bracelet? Why can't your son speak properly, has he a speech impediment? What has happened to his hand? Do you like my daughter's wedding dress? Is she not remarkably beautiful? Do you not think her husbands fine men?'

'Husbands?' Startled, Sonya looked at the bride's entourage more closely. 'How many husbands does she have, Joonu?' Then, before he could answer, the unbelievable occurred. The shopkeeper, grinning widely and displaying a mouthful of cracked black teeth, ushered in the Red Cap who had been saying his prayers in the street outside. The Red Cap's servant hovered at the top of the staircase, thus cutting off their mode of retreat.

'I have brought the Holy Father to bless the bride in our midst,' the shopkeeper beamed. 'Cast away any evil spirits that linger here, Holy Father, so that tonight my daughter might not be infertile for her husbands.'

Joonu put his head in his hand. 'Life is a continuous wonder to me, Princess,' he moaned to the soles of his feet.

'Oho! A woman-sorceress of some spirit, I see!' said the lama, his straggly white eyebrows arching into his red winged cap. 'Only ignorance or supreme faith would allow a headress like that.' The lama coughed delicately behind his hand as he eyed Sonya's headdress, much as the shopkeeper and wedding-party had done. All at once his mood and tone changed alarmingly, 'I have observed you and this fellow,' he kicked Joonu with his sandalled foot, 'Skulking in the shadows. Now tell me, what is your motive for this sham-pilgrimage, as I know you to be *philangs* by the mode of your dress, and not true Arjopas.'

'I'm on pilgrimage to my husband's cremation-ground, and afterwards to gain the blessing of His Holiness, the God-King.' Really frightened by the vindictive old man, Sonya realized Joonu had spoken the truth regarding holy men being the most suspicious of the lot. She turned to Joonu, but he only drooled and whimpered at the lama's feet, playing the idiot right to the end.

'What is this fool to you?' asked the Red Cap as he seated himself on a cushion behind them.

'He is my son.' Sonya was greatly troubled by the suspicious monk, although she had no idea how or when Joonu and she could have given themselves away. It was as though the wrinkled hunchbacked old man had been lying in wait for them – and yet that seemed ludicrous, for their disguises had so far carried them through remarkably well. But the Red Cap was being a thorough nuisance. 'Then I take pity on you,' he mumbled as he took the flagon of home-brewed *chang* the shopkeeper hospitably offered. 'But he is too big to be your son, and you are far too young to be his mother, unless of course the girl-children in your unknown province give birth when they are themselves in the cradle.' A straggly white brow quirked in her direction. Sonya was too perturbed to answer, afraid she might further give herself away in the eyes of this inquisitive lama who bothered her in more ways than one. She could not explain the feeling he engendered in her, even to herself, but it was as though he were deliberately provoking her in order to judge her reaction to him as well as to her surroundings. And, having latched on to her, he now seemed unwilling to relinquish her company. Sonya avoided the penetrating look he gave her, and he, chuckling to himself, turned his attention back to the flagon of potent spirits, after which he performed an elaborate 'blessing of the bride' ceremony.

'Ahh!' said the Red Cap, runnels of silvery liquid slipping down his unshaven chin, and gathering at the corner of his mouth. He hoicked in his throat and spat. 'The shopkeeper brews strong stuff. His little daughter will be happy tonight with her four husbands, eh, Sister-Sorceress? All for one and one for all!' In a lewd gesture he dug Sonya in the ribs.

Sonya smiled tautly and kept her own counsel.

'Master, I think it is time we were returning to the lamasery,' said the mendicant monk, attendant in the shadows.

'Think what you like Geyog, but it is I who give the orders around here,' growled the Red Cap. 'Go back to sleep, fellow, and let me get to the root of these *philangs* – as they undoubtedly are. Geyog will be the death of me,' muttered the Red Cap as he thrust his wart-encrusted whiskery face close to Sonya who recoiled at the musty stale odour emanating from his clothes. His face, hands and feet slimy with rancid yak-butter, he was a totally unprepossessing character. 'Adelphic polandry – you have this thing in your unknown province?' he asked Sonya as he peered into the bottom of the empty flagon. 'Hoi there, shopkeeper, fetch another.' He glared at Sonya over the rim.

'I . . . I . . . ' she stammered foolishly.

'Speak woman! Adelphic polandry,' he grunted impatiently. 'How many husbands is it permissible for a woman of the north to possess?'

'One.'

'Only one?' The Red Cap guffawed, slapping his thigh boisterously. 'No wonder you go on pilgrimage to your husband's chorten! Overworked in all probability, the poor man. But with four husbands, like our blushing bride over there who has to take all four brothers in the family, the

168

work-load is shared – especially the night shift, eh, Sister-Sorceress.' His throat working convulsively, he drew gustily from the replenished flagon of *chang*.

'Princess,' Joonu hissed in her ear while the Red Cap was preoccupied, 'do not look with such a face which gives you away. It is acceptable for a man of the cloth to drink so in Tibet – as it is for Tibetan women to take many husbands.'

Sonya stood up abruptly.

'Where are you going?' the old monk asked as he wiped the back of his hand across his mouth and glowered up at her.

For a moment, suspended in time, Sonya imagined the old man's face had slipped a little.

'Downstairs . . . to the yard,' Sonya said breathlessly.

'Sit down!' He dragged at the hem of her skirt. 'Do they not teach you manners in your country? Stay and listen to me and you might learn a thing or two. For instance, what becomes of those who disobey the laws of my country. Where do you make your pilgrimage?'

'To Lhasa.'

'Why Lhasa?'

'To pay my respects at my dead husband's chorten, and to his Holiness, the God-King.'

'And for what other reason?'

'Those are my only reasons.'

'It is also the reason for our decline . . . ' the lama mumbled drowsily and Sonya held her breath. With luck, Sonya hoped the second flagon of barley-spirits would do its work and send the old man into a stupor from which he would be unlikely to awake until morning – by which time she hoped she and Joonu would be well away from here. Joonu snored gently beside the mendicant monk and carefully Sonya edged her way towards him. Her finger prodding Joonu awake, he turned onto his back with a groan, crossed both arms on his chest and promptly fell asleep again.

'Joonu, wake up!' Sonya murmured in his ear, one eye still intent upon the sleepy lama. 'Joonu, for heaven's sake wake up!'

'I have made a study of it,' the Red Cap jerked bolt

upright and peered shortsightedly at her, everyone except the lama in that careless drowsy aftermath which follows an over-indulgence in food, alcohol and pleasure. 'Come here woman . . . ' Again the Red Cap forcibly drew her to him by tugging her skirts. 'Listen to what I have to say. I am one of the chosen few – one of the educated. The High Lama of my monastery requested a study of adelphic polandry to go into the annals of our country. I was the educated one chosen to make a study of it!' He tittered noisily. 'There are too many . . . too many men given to too few women. There are also too many men who have taken the vows of celibacy, you understand? The new-born children, I have discovered, are few and far between in these last two . . . few decades. It is a foolish custom, this poly . . . poly . . . I myself . . . I am not celibate . . . it is a waste of a man's . . . ' Slowly, like a myriapod, the strange lama curled up on his knees, dead to the world.

'Quickly Joonu!' Sonya forced Joonu's sleepy body to the top of the stairs, dragging their packs with her. 'Now, Joonu, now! Otherwise I swear I will leave you behind.'

The threat worked. Joonu reluctantly gathered his wits together and with a supreme effort got himself and his pack after her down the stairs.

At the bottom they were greeted by the smiling shop-keeper. Unlike the others on the rooftop, he was wide awake. He held a yak-butter lamp in his hand and said cheerfully, 'Come Holy Mother. I have made preparation for you and your son to be accommodated more comfort-ably this night. This way, please.' He ushered them into his indoor animal pen, holding the light high to illuminate the thick darkness. He bowed, placed the butter-lamp on the floor and shut the door on them.

Resigning herself to the strange customs of this strange land, Sonya said to Joonu; 'As soon as it's quiet outside, we'll creep away. Sooner or later our friendly shopkeeper is bound to need some sleep himself.'

'Why did you not tell him we did not want to sleep with his pigs and goats?' Joonu grumbled. 'I cannot even put my pack on the floor because it runs with urine and other unmentionables. The smell is truly horrible!' He wrinkled his nose in disgust. Arms folded, sulkily Joonu stood with his packsack hanging heavily off his shoulder.

'It won't be for long, Joonu. We must accept what we're given. You know pilgrims are considered bodily unclean. He will not allow us to sleep in his grain-store as that is considered holy ground – I expect the lama and his servant will occupy those premises. If we start being fussy, they're all going to become suspicious of us – not just the Red Cap – so please try and be humble like the Arjopas we're supposed to be.'

'Humble yes, insulted no. I am insulted by being shoved in here to look at the back end of pigs which are unclean animals and contrary to my religion. I am going, Princess, whether you wish to stay or not, otherwise I shall be very ill with the smell.' Joonu turned to the door, lifted the latch, jerked it, rattled it and finally kicked it. 'There! Now you see how much I am insulted – he has locked us in.'

'Don't be ridiculous!' Sonya herself rattled the latch. 'Maybe it's stiff.'

Joyful inebriation having given way to bad temper Joonu said angrily; 'Maybe it requires cremating in yak-butter to oil its rustiness. It is locked I tell you, so believe me. *Allah Akbar*, Princess!' He slumped down on the oozing mud floor with his pack.

ii

Four hours later the barn door opened. On the threshold stood the Red Cap, his servant, and the shopkeeper, still smiling. 'Come,' said the Red Cap, 'it is time for us to go.'

'Go where?' Sonya asked in some trepidation.

'To the Ponpo of the District, where else, *philang*,' said the Red Cap. 'Put out your hands so that they can be tied together . . . no, on second thoughts, the dumb one lacks not only his wits, his tongue, but also a hand, so fasten the rope around their waists, Geyog.'

In the street, the lama climbed upon the shopkeeper's mule. 'You are a worthy and obedient servant, fellow, unlike Geyog. Ho there, Geyog, give the shopman a silver

171

piece for his cooperation in helping us to apprehend these *philangs*.'

The shopkeeper bowed low from the waist. 'I have only done my duty, master. It was fortuitous the *philangs* called at my house at the exact moment you were at Kayapdo, otherwise they might never have been apprehended. I had a bad feeling the *Mig Kar* of the white eyes was not a professional holy woman, and you confirmed my suspicions, Holy Father.'

Joonu snorted in disgust. The vow of silence too much for him, he threw caution to the winds; 'Sons of leperous offal, may you fall off your donkeys and break your necks!'

'Ha!' said the Red Cap raising a finger in delight. 'It is as I thought. They are truly foreigners in our country, shopman. Anyone foolish enough to sleep on his back, catching flies with his mouth open, cannot be anything else. Come, we've wasted enough time, let us go.' He urged the shopkeeper's mule forward, the rope tying Sonya and Joonu together, jerking them painfully forward behind the Red Cap who retained the end of the rope in his leathery brown hands.

Arms tucked into her capacious *amphag*, her pack heavy on her back, Sonya was pulled relentlessly towards a distant mountain, her sense of direction lost in the numbness which overtook her halfway up the steeply tortuous path. Her legs wanted to let her down, her rationality sailed away in confusion. Fatigue and hunger dominated her whole being while her breath came gratingly in the rarefied atmosphere and her ears hurt. With each jerking step, Joonu stumbling along behind her and the mendicant servant-monk behind him, Sonya willed herself to go forward without giving the Red Cap the satisfaction of knowing she was only, after all, a weak woman.

Her arms inside her *amphag* grew heavy as she worked the blunt blade of her eating-knife against the coir-rope binding her to the lama. Halfway up the mountain, the frayed rope finally broke. 'Run, Joonu, run!' Sonya slapped the Red Cap's mount on the rump before lashing out with the knife as the mendicant monk darted forward to

172

stop their flight down the mountainside. She gashed him across the back of his left hand while Joonu, stupidly, did nothing. Sonya did not dare look behind her as the Red Cap slid sideways off his mule to land with a thud on the scree slope while the mendicant monk lunged at Joonu to prevent him from escaping too. Sonya just kept on blindly running.

173

Chapter Twelve

Sonya reached a fork in the tortuous path. Many paths
scored the face of this mountainous ridge, some wide
and well used, others only narrow goat-tracks. Her greatest
desire being to put as much distance between herself and the
Red Cap, Sonya did not pause to reflect upon anything,
least of all Joonu's fate. She had given him the opportunity
to flee, and yet he had hesitated. In that moment of
hesitation beside the Red Cap, Joonu had forfeited freedom
– something Sonya puzzled about all the way down the
mountain when she soon discovered herself to be irretriev-
ably lost.

From her packsack she withdrew map and compass and
retraced the Silk Road with her finger, committing key-
towns and distance to memory. It was noon by the location
of the sun in the sky. According to the compass, she was
facing due south instead of east, heading deeper into the
mountains. Range after range spread before her like the
blankly identical convolutions of a spreading fan.

Sonya set off again. She also puzzled to herself why the
Red Cap had been leading Joonu and she away from the
lamasery on the mountain-top instead of towards it. If it had
been his intention to take them before the High Abbot of
his lamasery and thereafter the Ponpo of the District – as
he had intimated along the way – then he had got his
bearings all wrong. Whether by design or accident was
another matter that confused her. A great many things did
not fall into place concerning the two holy men she and

Joonu had unwittingly encountered outside the shop-keeper's premises. For the moment, however, she realized that if she were to catch up with Joonu again, she would either have to give herself up to the Red Cap, or hope that Joonu had gathered his wits together, escaped from the clutches of the two monks, and that he would meet up with her again somewhere along the Silk Road.

On her left the mountain terraced gently away into lower green valleys. To her right a solid wall of rock kept her hedged on the narrow track she was following. Presently, as she turned another bend in the path, far below she could see animals grazing. Her heart leapt. Where there were yaks and goats, there she was bound to find a herdsman of the mountains. The *dopka* would be able to give her directions so that she could get her bearings and could head back towards the Silk Road.

Keeping the mountain wall now to her left, she followed the pathway which soon turned back on itself so that the valley below her was once more on her left. Descending lower and lower to that elusive valley, now to the right of her, now to the left, her pack-straps began to cut deeply into her sore shoulders. She also felt a sharp stone digging into her right instep. The path was hardly two feet wide, just a dangerous rocky ledge. But she had to stop and take off her boot to remove the stone. Sonya unlaced her soft sheepskin boot. The shifting scree slid from under her as she balanced on one foot. The weight of her pack further unbalanced her and both feet shot from under her, precipitating her over the edge of the precipice.

Gorse and thorn ripped past her. Her pack-straps broke and her pack fell free. Sonya and her belongings tumbled downwards. Stretched out on her stomach, Sonya scrabbled wildly for a grip on something to break her fall. Then her right foot crashed against a boulder and the breath was knocked out of her.

ii

Sonya lay unconscious for two hours.

When she eventually came round, the sun was going

down behind the mountain. Someone was washing her face – no, not someone, something . . .

She opened her eyes and turned her head cautiously, wincing with every movement. Her whole body was encompassed in a red mist of pain.

The black-faced goats thrust their soft moist noses at her, and again started to dribble over her as they explored her face, tickling her with tongues and tufted beards. Sonya struggled to sit up, pushing away the curious animals. Her right boot had gone missing and her foot was three times its usual size. The pain of movement as she flexed her toes made her dizzy and cold perspiration bathed her when she realized she had perhaps broken her ankle. Oh no, she moaned to herself, the awful realization that she might not be able to walk for months ending all her hopes of ever gaining The Forbidden City of Lhasa.

'Oghai, Oghai!' A man came up behind her, gathering his animals together for the night. He stood towering over her and for a moment she was unnerved by his hostile appearance. Then his mouth opened in a black-toothed smile of sympathy as his dark eyes reflected his concern for her. 'You have suffered much hardship.' He stuck out his tongue in friendly greeting.

'Yes, very great hardship.' Sonya did not have the strength nor inclination to disagree. She pushed away the nuzzling goats and attempted to regain her feet. It was hopeless, red-hot pokers seemed to be thrusting their way through the bone and flesh of her injured foot. She peered helplessly into the gathering dust to see if her pack was somewhere nearby. She might just be able to find something in her medical pack to ease the swelling and pain.

'You are an Arjopa?' enquired the herdsman.

'Yes . . . and an initiated sorceress.' She thought it best to perpetuate that formidable image even though her headdress had come off and was lost in the grass.

The *dokpa*, reading her woebegone expression, came to her rescue. 'Do not worry, Holy Mother, I came across your broken pack and headdress and many other items of yours scattered in the meadow. They are put safely with my

176

yak. I knew then I would come across their owner before long. You are badly hurt?' He glanced dubiously from her scratched face and torn clothing to her bleeding swollen foot.

'I don't know . . . I don't think I can walk.' She began to pick out the gorse needles stuck into the palms of her hands before using those hands to lever herself off the ground. Again she fell back weakly.

'From which Province do you come?' asked the *dokpa*.

'Tsang,' she replied, not caring one way or another. Tsang, Amdo, Po Yul, it was all the same now that she could not go anywhere on her two feet.

'A noble province . . . but you are badly hurt and shaken, Holy Mother, and for now you must rest before proceeding on your way to Tsang. My mountain home is humble, but you are welcome to share what my wife, children and I possess. Wait here, and I will fetch my yak for you to ride.'

He ran off barefoot through the lush grass while Sonya held a fleeting uncharitable thought; had the impoverished *dokpa* been about to make off with her possessions as she lay concussed at the foot of his mountain? Glancing at that mountain now, it did not seem nearly as steep looking up as looking down into the valley from the narrow path she had been following. The talus of the mountain was grassy and covered with alpine flowers as well as the gorse and acacia that had caused her so much damage. Unfortunately too, the slope had been strewn with boulders, loose rock falls from a previous avalanche. All that, and not the actual height of her descent had done the damage.

Sonya looked with distaste at the fearsome long-haired, long-horned beast she was supposed to ride. Recalling Joonu's words about never offending a yak, she allowed the *dokpa* to assist her onto its back. With a very undignified shove, he thrust her bottom up and sideways onto the yak over which lice heaved and flies settled. Sonya, with bloodied sore hands, clung desperately to the yak's shaggy coat and disregarded the wildlife inhabiting it. She only wanted to lie down somewhere and sleep off the pain.

177

The *dokpas*' accommodation consisted of four crudely built stone walls over which a suspended yak-skin provided a roof of sorts. Daylight filtered in between walls and roof and Sonya wondered how on earth these mountain people managed to survive the harsh ice-bound winters. She was relieved, however, to discover the herdsman had a gentle wife and six rowdy children as he had boasted, and if their home was primitive, their hospitality was at least civilized. Sonya, overwhelmed by all that had happened to her since meeting the Red Cap, gave herself up now to the kindly *dokpas*; Phagpa and his wife Sera, who made her comfortable, warm and welcome.

Sera put some smelly brown linament on Sonya's injured foot and bound it tight with strips of yak-skin and the heartfelt assertion that all would now be well with the Holy Mother! In the absence of real medical attention, Sonya still did not know if her foot was broken or not, only that it felt broken. Sera gave her a leaf to suck, 'to take away the pain', she informed Sonya. Sceptical of any leaf being able to take away the kind of pain she had, Sonya took the leaf and sucked it since she had no wish to offend the kindly mountain woman's feelings. In a little while she slept peaceably and, remarkably, when she awoke the pain was indeed far less. She asked Sera for the name of the plant with such analgesic properties, but Sera did not know it, only where it could be found.

As the days passed, her cuts and bruises slowly healed and with the healing process she began to fret about Joonu, wondering what had become of him. Autumn would be upon them soon, with all hopes of reaching Lhasa before the winter set in with a vengeance diminishing day by day.

One evening Phagpa returned to find Sonya kneeling beside the outside fire, stirring the soup. Her right foot very much better, she could at least limp around on it now with the aid of a stick. 'Where is my wife?' Phagpa asked, settling himself beside Sonya on the grass.

'She's tending a sick goat in the fields,' Sonya tasted the

watery soup before adding more salt to the turnips. 'Are you hungry, Phagpa?' she asked with a smile.

He returned the smile, his black pointed teeth horrible in his mouth. 'A poor man of the mountains is always hungry, Holy Mother.'

'Supper won't be long,' Sonya reassured him, adding, 'Thank you for mending my headdress, Phagpa.'

'I gain blessings for assisting a holy woman, Mother.'

Sonya had heard similar words before. She also remembered how swiftly Tibetan hospitality could turn to hostility where *philangs* were concerned.

'The taxes are high for us at present,' Phagpa said conversationally. He took his wooden bowl from the *amphag* of his short yak-skin tunic tied tightly around his waist with string, and handed it to her to be filled. 'Yesterday the Ponpo of the District came to my village and demanded another burdensome levy to help furnish an army that is being raised against the nation who dwell on our Himalayan borders.'

Sonya's ears pricked up. 'The British you mean?'

'Aye.' Phagpa slurped his soup noisily.

Sonya had discovered that Phagpa and his family did not lead nearly the isolated existence she had at first imagined. The man of solitude knew far more about current events than most pilgrims on the road, his information gleaned from goodness only knew where!

'How is it you know so much about everything Phagpa, you who lead such a lonely existence in the mountains? You have no newspapers or books, no neighbours during the summer months, and yet you hear things even I as a pilgrim on the road do not hear.'

Phagpa shrugged, and put out his bowl for more of the thin vegetable soup. 'We have a precious gift, Naljorma, and that is the ears and confidence of people everywhere. I am part of a communication system that is better than any modern one of wires the Urusso are seeking to decorate my country with. You think I am lonely, I am not. Every day someone crosses my path in the mountains – you are one such person only. I have many pilgrim-friends who tread the same path year after year. I have friends from my village

179

who climb up here when there is something of importance to tell me – as yesterday when I was brought news of the extra taxes and the war that is presently to start between my country and another.' He picked his teeth contemplatively. 'We must fight evil spirits with force. The holy men will see to it that we are not overrun by heathen invaders.' He cleared his throat elaborately before spitting on the grass.

Sonya took a deep breath. While Phagpa was in such a talkative mood, she decided to probe him further. 'During my pilgrimage, I've heard many strange rumours about the Urusso seeking guidance from his Holiness, the God-King. They not only wish to bring with them their strange wires of communication, but also the iron-railway, carriages with wheels, and many other such things. Four years ago, the white Urusso sent a mighty delegation to meet with the God-King and his Kashag so that all these things might be discussed and implemented. I heard that many of the white Urusso were killed on the great Chang-Tang as they were returning to their own country.'

Phagpa nodded. 'I too heard such rumours.' He tossed more dried yak-dung nuggets onto the fire and brought it to life.

Sonya was irritated by five of the children returning with grubby fingers and faces, screeching for soup while chasing each other round the cooking-fire. Hoping Phagpa would not be put off from further conversation by his noisy brood, she quickly dished out their supper, each child handing over their own wooden bowl licked clean according to Tibetan custom from the previous meal. 'Phagpa,' her head was beginning to throb with excitement, 'could there have been any survivors?'

Phagpa wiped out his bowl with bread before reattaching the bowl to his person. Then he relaxed, chewing upon a tobacco-leaf while resignedly awaiting his wife's return. 'Survivors?' He brooded on Sonya's question. 'Aye, there were survivors. A legend has grown up since from the rumours that we all heard four years ago. It concerns the noble lord, Kuma Sidheong, who took as his serf one of the white Urusso survivors.'

Sonya felt the blood rush to her head. 'Kuma Sidheong?'

The children started screaming and misbehaving again. Now that she at last had a name to go on, Sonya did not want Phagpa to stamp away in temper because she could not control the children in Sera's absence. In desperation Sonya gave them her watch to play with – an article that had aroused much interest and curiosity when she had first brought it out. She had told the unsophisticated yet intelligent Phagpa – so as not to arouse his suspicion – that it had been given to her by a wealthy trader in exchange for magical rites to save his sick daughter's life. He had believed her, while she prayed forgiveness for the lies she had to tell in order she herself might survive!

'Kuma Sidheong is a great Lamaist Commander in the service of the Dalai Lama,' Phagpa said when the children were silently engrossed in listening to the ticking watch and observing the movement of its hands.

'Does he live near here, Phagpa??'

'He lives in Tsang, the noble Province.'

'This serf . . . of . . . Kuma Sidheong's, is he part of the legend?'

'It is he who created the legend whilst in Kuma's employ.'

'Then . . . then they did not get set upon by Mongol hordes? That was the rumour I had heard.'

'I do not know what kind of rumour you heard, Holy Mother, I am only telling you what I heard. The Lamaist Commander, returning from manoeuvres in the north of the Khang-Yul, came across the white Khan's people struggling across the frozen plateau. In seeking to lend them his support and assistance during part of their journey together – they were in a bad way, I believe – they turned upon him with their firearms. Kuma Sidheong lost men in the fight, but finally his superior force vanquished the hostile Urusso, the survivors of a larger party returning to their homeland on the same Silk Road you were taking to Lhasa before you lost yourself in my mountains,' Phagpa jabbed a twig into the soft earth as though it were a dagger.

'And the legend, Phagpa?' Despite Phagpa's tired irritability, Sonya just had to keep him alert so as not to lose the story of Kuma Sidheong.

He jerked wearily, and fumbling in his *amphag* for more

tobacco said; 'It is getting dark. Sera and the eldest boy should be home soon . . . put on more soup, Holy Mother.'

'Phagpa, tell me about the legend first.' She risked arousing his suspicions by such fervent interest in his story, but did not care.

'I can tell you no more,' he grunted sleepily, and then realizing she was a holy woman and what was more, a holy sorceress capable of casting spells and calling up devil demons, said begrudgingly; 'The white Urusso, the leader, was taken prisoner and hostage by Kuma Sidheong, and for a little while was a serf in his household in Tsang. But the serf showed remarkable powers so that the holy men soon came to acknowledge him as the reincarnation of a greater being than mere man. Today he is a respected Tulku, and the legends surrounding him are legion.'

'Do . . . do you know the name of this man, Phagpa?'

'Tulku . . . I have just told you Holy Mother.'

'Does he also live in Tsang Province?'

'Yes.'

'What is the name of the town, Phagpa? I only ask because I would wish to make the acquaintance of such a great Tulku who has earned the respect of holy men. In meditation with him, I, too, will be able to improve my art for the sake of other holy women sharing the lives of their holy men.'

'Thug-Phul. It is near Gyantse. I am surprised you have not heard the name before, Holy Mother, as it is in your noble Province too, and was once on everyone's lips. Made famous, of course, by the Urusso of supernatural powers, so that it has now become a place of pilgrimage.'

'Yes, of course, how silly of me not to remember the name, my memory is bad,' said Sonya quickly. She gave Phagpa a charming smile, her dimples deep. 'Thank you for talking to me for so long, Phagpa. I fear I've tired you with my questions, so now I'll go and make some more soup for everyone.' She took her watch firmly from the children before they broke it, and turning on her knees to Phagpa as she could not bear weight on her injured foot as yet, added, tonight I will write out many prayer-flags for you to put around the walls of your house. They will be powerful prayers to ward off any evil spirits.'

'Thank you, Holy Mother, you too are an education and blessing to me in my humble abode.' Phagpa went inside his primitive hut, curled over on his knees, pulled a blanket over his head, and settled to sleep.

Not ten minutes later, the bright sun going behind the mountain in rugged shadows of purple and grey which cast the green valley into the damp fist of night, Sera came panting up the path. 'Nepo, Nepo,' she cried out to her husband, 'we have more guests . . . three *trapas* coming up the mountain . . . a *gelong* and his two servants . . . one without a hand. Hurry please and provide them with hospitality lest we offend the spirits.'

iv

Sonya was paralyzed with fear as she watched Sera and her eldest son approaching the *dokpa* hut. Then, jerking to her feet, she quenched her cry of pain as she stood on her injured foot and hobbled inside the hut. Phagpa was still curled up with the blanket over his head, snoring loudly in deep rhythmic grunts. Without a moment's loss, Sonya heaved her packsack through the gap between the sagging roof and the back wall of the hut. Then she wriggled out after it, up and over the wall, her injured foot forgotten.

Attached to an iron ring embedded in the stone wall of the hut was Phagpa's lame mule. Sonya unfastened the mule, transferred the rope around its neck to use as a set of reins, then heaved her pack on her back. Perspiration broke out on her forehead, tears of pain and effort starting in her eyes as she clambered onto the animal. Clicking her teeth and jabbing the mule hard with her left foot while her right hung useless, she urged it to get going in the opposite direction to Sera's visitors. The children, too, were all gathered at the front of the hut in curious anticipation, so Sonya was able to ride away across the back meadow without being noticed.

As daylight merged with darkness, protected by sinister

183

shadows cast by the mountain, Sonya took an ascending path away from the *dokpa* hut. It would be cold on the mountain tonight, she knew that much, and only hoped she would find a cave or some such shelter until she had worked out what to do next.

Chapter Thirteen

Joonu saw Sonya leave the *dokpa* hut, and had no doubt at all the Red Cap and his servant had also witnessed her hasty departure.

'We will catch her now!' said the Red Cap triumphantly as he paused to survey the mountain and the slight figure on the mule merging with the twilit shadows. She will go up, and what goes up must come down, since I know full well there is only one escape route on this mountain, the *dokpa* path! So, we will catch her. Come, let us settle here for the night as I'm fed up with chasing her for the past four.' He made Sera fetch them soup, bread and tea and afterwards show them to their sleeping places.

Joonu was secured to the Red Cap, as he had been every night since his recapture. Having fought tooth and nail with the mendicant as they slithered together down the mountain path, in the end, he had been overpowered by the wiry and athletic Geyog. The Red Cap now took his red sash, customarily worn across the breast of his ochre *shamtag*, and over one shoulder. He looped it around Joonu's neck, the other end in his hand. The art of Gomthag had proved a powerful deterrent to Joonu following in Sonya's footsteps and many an hour had passed for Joonu in meditation with the Red Cap while the servant slept. Geyog, the mendicant monk, was the only one who appeared able to sleep anywhere and at anytime. Even through the terrible storm that night, he slept like a baby. While Phagpa, Sera and their children were kept awake by the lightning flashes and thunder crashes, both holy men were dead to the world, one in meditation and the other in dreams. 'It is the change of seasons,' Phagpa muttered to Sera while wearily struggling to keep the holy men dry under the sagging yak-skin roof, they and their children pushing off the water by vigorous up-thrusts with fists and poles as the fast and furious rain-water collected. 'Winter will be early in the mountains this year . . . the Holy Sorceress, she will have to make powerful prayers for herself, this night.'

'Shhh, Nepo,' Sera warned with anxious and meaningful glances toward her visitors, especially wide-awake Joonu, 'Do not speak of such things, the Sorceress has brought us bad luck. Let us hope the roof holds, for we do not want to further incur the lama's displeasure.'

In the dawn light, as the last of the thunder rolled away beyond the mountains, the mendicant stirred. He sat up, yawned, stretched, and said to Phagpa and Sera; 'Last night I had a dream. I dreamt the Sorceress was inside the belly of a whale. Today we will find her because she is sick. She is swallowed into the mouth of a dark cave where she is burning with a great fever brought about by the lashing wind and rain.' He smiled benignly at his host and hostess. 'You have not slept all night,' he observed, 'but do not be perturbed, your animals are safe, your home is safe and the evil spirits depart. You and your family will be safe if you listen to me and my master. Do not aid the *philangs* in our custody. Give me your mule, the one in the Sorceress's possession at this moment, and I will say prayers for you to vanquish the evil that has come into your lives since taking in the *Mig Kar*, the woman of the white eyes.'

Phagpa and Sera humbled themselves on the ground before the mendicant, and Phagpa said; 'There is indeed a great cave halfway up the mountain – the *Mig Kar* would be bound to find it if she searched for shelter last night. Keep the mule, holy monk, for your need is greater than ours.'

ii

'Will she die?' asked Joonu, peering over the mendicant's shoulder while he attended to Sonya's infected foot.

'No, she sleeps the sleep of the weary. But I've put upon her the flavours of the blue poppy-flower found in this valley. It has a healing and soothing property. In a few days she will be as good as new.' Geyog and Joonu wrinkled their noses in disgust as the monk unwrapped the yak-skin bandages Sera had put on Sonya's foot. 'What a pity,' murmured the mendicant, 'that the ignorant peasant-woman used a yak-dung pack to fuel the fires of infection.'

'Is that bad?' asked Joonu anxiously.

'Only when there are cuts and grazes, as there were in this case. Otherwise the pack would have reduced the inflammation. Now it is infected and that is what has given her a fever, combined with the chilling she received in last night's thunderstorm. But the fever will burn itself out.'

'How do you know?'

'I studied medicine in my monastery.'

'Then why are you the Red Cap's servant if you are so much better educated than he?'

'He is my master. I cannot argue the fact, for he is richer than I. His parents were from a more illustrious background than mine. I studied to get where I am, but my master inherited his credibility.'

'But he is foul-mouthed and flea-ridden, whereas you seem to be more cultured than he.'

'That is how life goes, young man. But he is still my master, for his station in life is greater than mine.'

'Then you should push him down the mountainside and be rid of him,' said Joonu with feeling, and made the mendicant smile.

'You are only a youth,' he said gravely, 'and one who must learn many things before he can be a man to air a suitable opinion.'

'My opinion, youth or man, is that the Red Cap should be pushed over the mountain so that the world be well rid of him. Why does he wish so desperately to take us before the Ponpo?'

'Because you are foreign devils, and, as such, are not allowed to enter my country to make a pilgrimage to Lhasa.'

'Why are we not allowed?'

'It is forbidden,' answered the mendicant patiently.

187

'Why?'

'Because our boundaries are closed to outsiders.'

'Why?' Joonu insisted perversely.

The mild and cultured Tibetan smiled his gentle smile:
'You are only a young man as yet. And, in the way of all
young men, curious about life itself. So, I will endeavour to
answer your questions honestly. As a small Buddhist nation,
we of Tibet have a genuine fear that our religion and culture
might become diluted by foreigners of other religions and
customs.'

'Then you cannot have much faith in your religion or
culture,' Joonu retorted.

The mendicant bowed his shaven head: 'Maybe. But it is
the law of my country. Decreed by their Holiness the Dalai
Lama and his shadow, the Panchen Lama. Tibet must
preserve its identity in order to survive . . . the woman, she
is stirring. Pass me the drinking-water so that she can be
sustained.'

iii

Sonya opened her eyes. It was very dark all around her,
only a pinpoint of light far away, as though she were staring
down a long tunnel. Someone offered her a sip of water.
Desperately thirsty, she struggled to sit up so as not to
spill any. It was only as her eyes accustomed themselves to
the gloom, the meagre light from a butter-lamp on the floor
beside her falling upon the thin black scar on the back of
the man's left hand, did Sonya become aware of the Red
Cap's servant holding the water-pouch to her lips, and her
heart sank.

'Where am I?' Without any more pretence, she spoke in
Russian.

'In a mountain cave, Princess.' Joonu's shadow loomed
large over her.

Infinitely glad that Joonu was back beside her despite the
ignominy of falling once more into the Red Cap's clutches,
Sonya closed her eyes and fell into a deep, restful sleep.
When she awoke again it was morning and her fever had
subsided.

'She will be all right now,' the mendicant declared, and thereafter had left Joonu and Sonya alone in the cave.

Four hours later they were still alone and Sonya, very much recovered and drinking the buttered tea only Joonu could make so well, asked; 'Where are they, Joonu, the Red Cap and the mendicant?'

'Oh, don't sound so strong and cheerful, Princess,' Joonu said gloomily, 'we are still their prisoners. They are not far away at all. The mendicant sits outside the cave, while his master climbed to the top of the mountain this morning in order to find a patch of snow to practise the art of *Thumo Reskiang* – at least, that's what Geyog told me.'

'What's *Thumo . . . Reskiang*?'

'Our mendicant friend tells me it is the art of generating internal heat so that one does not feel the cold. The old one practises it regularly, having learned the mystic performance from a reincarnated Guru in the Himalayas. He climbs a high mountain, finds a place of snow and ice, takes off all his clothes and meditates for long hours . . . sometimes days, Geyog says.'

'Without his clothes on . . . the Red Cap?' Sonya marvelled at the old man's fortitude.

'Yes. It is the habit of the mystics.'

'In all the snow and ice?'

'So Geyog tells me.'

'It sounds incredible. I must see for myself how it's done.'

'I would not, Princess. The Red Cap without his clothes on must be an even more repulsive sight than with them.'

After a little pause she asked; 'How can you and the mendicant speak together in such depth when neither of you understands the other's language?'

'We converse in the universal language, Princess, English.'

'Geyog speaks English?' Sonya asked in amazement as she put her bowl down on the floor.

'Yes. He learned it at the Drepung Monastery from where he comes. He is returning there now after being on pilgrimage through Tibet collecting alms and favours for his monastery. It is near Lhasa.'

189

'What about the Red Cap? We know his abode is at the lamasery overlooking the village of Tsu where we attended that unfortunate wedding.'

'And that is where the Red Cap intends to take us, first to see the High Lama of His lamasery and afterwards the Ponpo of Gartok. Geyog will escort us to the Red Cap's lamasery in fulfilment of his duty as he offered to be of service to him when they crossed each other's path at Demchok. After which, Geyog will continue on his way to Lhasa. He told me to tell you we would be better off seeking the protection of the Chinese Mandarin at Gartok, for he is the Tibetan Ponpo's overlord. The Mandarin, who is sympathetic to any country not Tibet since the Tibetans gave him much trouble, would treat us with more respect than the High Abbot or the Ponpo who would sooner fill our bellies with stones than send us back to the border with an expensive escort.'

'Geyog told you all this?' asked Sonya in astonishment; she still only half-believed anything Joonu said.

'Every word, Princess. I swear it on my noble mother's grave in Baltit.'

'Joonu,' she said thoughtfully, 'I . . . I've a funny feeling concerning the Red Cap. I don't think he is all he makes out to be.'

Joonu scoffed. 'Princess, he's worse than he makes out to be, believe me. He would as soon fill our bellies with stones himself than leave it to the Ponpo.'

She changed the subject. 'Joonu, who removed my clothes?' She was beginning to feel very exposed beneath the mendicant monk's blanket.

'Geyog and I. But do not worry, Princess. We are both men of the world and did not see anything we have not already seen before. I think your clothes will be dry now, we put them in front of the fire. You must have been out in the storm a long time before you found this cave.'

'The mule found it, so they're not such stupid animals. I don't remember much about anything.'

'*Allah Akbar*, Princess,' Joonu replied. 'It is just as well, otherwise you would have died of an even worse headache.'

190

At noon the Red Cap reappeared, eager for his midday meal.

'Aha!' he greeted them boisterously, 'a silent trio, I smell corruptness in the air! White-eyes is awake, good. Now we can retrace our steps to Gartok. You have led me a merry dance for a week, *Mig Kar*, and I am impatient to regain my lamasery. So, let us all eat up quickly and be gone from this place of solitude. You have done a good job on the *philang*'s foot, Geyog, so tonight I wish to celebrate her recovery by sleeping one step nearer the Ponpo!'

Joonu scowled as he dished out the thin soup made from only a wadge of tea with the addition of salt and yak-butter. Sonya had a momentary vision of her father's dining table groaning with the weight of food at Kirovsky Ploshad and at his hunting-lodge at Novgorod. It was no good, she told herself sternly, to let her mouth water for real food. If her recovery had given her the appetite of a horse, then she had to curb that appetite like a good Arjopa and use her new-found strength to get her to Lhasa. With a welcoming smile, just like a true Arjopa, she asked Joonu to refill the Red Cap's bowl.

They started down the mountain half-an-hour later. The Red Cap rode one mule and refused his servant the other. 'The *Mig Kar* is to have the *dokpa*'s mule,' the Red Cap instructed, brandishing his mule-stick at Geyog. 'Tie her on so that she does not escape again. She will ride behind me and you and the idiot-youth can walk behind her, only this time, Geyog, have your wits about you and don't dream. Just keep your eyes on the two of them, and not your holy texts!'

Joonu trudged along behind Sonya. Several lengths of flax rope joined together, bound him, arms behind his back, before passing twice round Sonya's waist and then twice round her hands held in front of her, so that the Red Cap could be aware of what they were doing. The rope was finally looped twice round the neck of the Red Cap's mule.

'Son of scrofulous pig-offal,' Joonu had declared hotly at

the time of departure, 'I wish the rope were around *your* neck!' But then, receiving a warning frown from Sonya, Joonu had fallen silent.

They reached the *dokpa* hut that evening. To Sonya's relief, the Red Cap decided not to stay there for the night, but to pass on to the village in the valley since the *dokpa* hut offered no security for his prisoners. Sonya was unable to look at Phagpa or Sera as she passed them, both of them observing her with sad eyes and strained expressions as they saw their wealth, in the shape of their mule, confiscated from under their noses. That she had been the cause of their misfortune was very hard to bear in the face of their hospitality and goodness. She hung her head, and only lifted it again when they dismounted at a resting place for the night. The Red Cap had decided, after all, not to risk village curiosity regarding his prisoners, and dispensed with indoor accommodation. They camped at a convenient spot by a waterfall drumming into a narrow gorge. The bright moon rose above the margin of the mountains and threw the late-summer landscape into breathtaking relief.

'It will rain by morning,' the mendicant observed, 'the moon has a halo.'

Which is more than can be said of your master! thought Sonya.

It did rain that night. The deluge all but washed her out from under her tiny yak-skin tent. The Red Cap and his servant, seemingly impervious to the weather, crouched in the entrance like dark eagles while they took turns in keeping guard. But, as no-one was able to sleep that night, the Red Cap decided to press on as soon as the gloomy grey morning presented itself in mountain mists and steaming alpine meadows. The torrent of water in the gully had risen several inches overnight.

Joonu, soaked to the skin, his black hair plastered to his scalp like a ragged thatched roof, grinned as they set off in the half-light. 'With luck, Princess, tonight we will be sleeping beside a warm kitchen fire. I do not think the Red Cap cares much for real hardship!'

192

Chapter Fourteen

They came into another valley. The damp mists of the day had vanished, bringing the evening clear, warm and heartening. Tree rhododendrons, thirty feet high grew in the lush valley through which a broad river flowed in silvery rose-tinged evening light. Pear trees, climbing yellow roses entangling the branches, camellias and peonies the size of dinner plates, ferns and evergreens; it was a place of unreal quality, a secret garden at the foot of snowy mountains. A song-bird trilled lustily overhead in the branches of a maple under which they paused to get their bearings.

'It is the voice of the *djolmo*, the Tibetan songbird,' Geyog whispered confidentially to Sonya.

'Have you travelled this way before, Geyog?' Sonya whispered back, an intimacy in their conversation instigated by Geyog himself.

'Only once before. The mountain pass was cut off one winter as I was returning to my monastery. I remember this pretty village from before . . . '

They were interrupted at once by the uncouth Red Cap. 'Come,' he ordered, pointing with his mule-stick, 'we'll try that house over there!'

The four of them descended the steep path, and came to a squat clay-bricked house at the head of the valley. It stood alone, the rest of the dozen or so houses comprising the village, too far away and crowded for the Red Cap's liking.

Down the long valley through which the river carved its tumultuous passage Sonya could see another lone house set amongst fields and orchards, a much larger, prosperous dwelling which the Red Cap chose to disregard because it meant crossing the dangerous river.

The home of the local muleteer consisted of one room and a thatched shed in a tiny back yard. He came to his door and greeted them by placing both hands palms up to show he carried no weapons before holy men. Wearing his long Tibetan robe drawn up to the knees, from his belt hung his eating bowl, his mule-whip, tobacco and skin-bag of tsampa. The top half of his robe had been unfastened and hung down over his back to leave his torso exposed, the long sleeves tied around his waist. He was dirty, smelly and covered with sores. After greeting them, he showed them to their sleeping quarters, all the while energetically scratching his grimy chest. The room was divided in half by a sacking curtain, and Sonya flinched when a rat ambled through the filth, plump and practically tame.

'I would not sleep here if they paid me,' Joonu said in English, adding in Russian, 'neither would I let him touch my donkeys with a barge pole.'

'Mules, Joonu, not donkeys. Mules and donkeys are different breeds.' Sonya, for want of a better remark in the light of their horrible accommodation, took comfort in a forced flippancy.

'Muleteer and Red Cap, they are of the same breed if the reverent fellow chooses to sleep here tonight!' Joonu spat in disgust while observing the muleteer scratching his armpits.

The Red Cap changed his mind when he, too, saw the fat rat, 'tell me if there is an inn here, man,' he growled at the muleteer.

'There is no inn, master. I can vouchsafe that,' Geyog interrupted. 'I stayed here many years ago, and I doubt they have built an inn since then.'

'In this same flea-pit?' The Red Cap glowered at his servant.

'No master. I stayed in the farmhouse across the river. It means getting across it, I know, but there is a ferry. The farmer has four daughters . . . all were unmarried when I

194

was last in this village. The farmer, however, looks after his daughters well in the absence of a mother – she left Rika, the farmer, to live with another man when I was last here as she found Rika's farm too much work for her liking. But the daughters are comely maidens and the eldest one is a good cook. The farmhouse is very clean, master . . . and much larger than these premises.' Geyog gazed about him with harmless myopic eyes.

'Come then,' said the Red Cap, 'let's leave this pig to his pigsty and go to Rika's farmhouse. You will receive no blessings from me, man, for you are nothing but an insult to humanity!' The Red Cap scowled at the muleteer before stamping out of his squalid house.

'You will have to wait a very long time for the ferryman to see you and take you across the river,' the muleteer said from his doorway.

'Then we will wait,' said the Red Cap mounting his mule. 'Geyog, what a pity we untied these two thinking we'd be staying. Tie them up again, we don't want them getting any ideas about escaping before we reach the ferry.'

'The slings are not safe . . . the ferryman does not grease them well enough, for he is a mean man with his yak-butter,' the muleteer shouted, following them down the cliff path, put out because he had been deprived of an opportunity to earn himself prayers and blessings while giving hospitality to holy men.

'Geyog is not as daft as he makes out,' Joonu whispered to Sonya as they came to the ferry. 'That bit about the farmer's daughters . . . did you see the way the lustful old goat's eyes lit up? I refer to the Red Cap of course, Princess.'

'Shhh, Joonu! Don't give us away again. The Red Cap will start wondering what's going on between we three, and we mustn't arouse his suspicions. I'm sure Geyog has a plan in mind once we're across the river and in the farmer's house – why else was he so persuasive? A chance to escape might present itself, and that is perhaps what Geyog is hoping for where we are concerned.'

'Perhaps, Princess. Like the moon rising to take us across her ungreased shoulders to paradise,' said Joonu dashingly.

The river was not wide, no more than twenty feet across, but it was of such ferocity and between such high cliffs, Sonya soon realized that in a small craft it would be like trying to defy rapids. Even so, she was totally unprepared for the kind of crossing she was to endure. Not a conventional wooden raft in sight nor even a yak-skin coracle, but only ropes loosely strung from landing stage to landing stage. Two ferrymen had to operate the apparatus, one at each crossing. A half-cylinder of wood, a foot in length, was notched on its upper surface to accommodate leather thongs threaded through to act as handles. The concave edge of the cylinder was greased to pass easily along the rope loosely suspended across the river. Observing the mules kicking in mid-air as they were ignominiously suspended aloft on the sagging rope, Sonya decided she would not follow.

'Very well,' said the Red Cap, 'then we shall go together. Geyog can bring the idiot-youth with him. Ferryman, tie us together. Give me the pair of thongs that pass under the thighs. I shall sit and swing while the woman can be suspended by the arms so that she does not cut the rope to pieces with her nifty fingers.'

Realizing it would be grossly undignified to kick and scream against her captor, Sonya outwardly maintained her composure, while inwardly her dislike of the Red Cap increased a thousandfold. Suspended in mid-air, leather thongs passed cuttingly under her armpits and her hands frantically sought the slider above her head.

'Do not touch the rope!' the ferryman warned, 'otherwise you will have no flesh left on your hands by the time you arrive on the other side.'

At once she removed her hands from the rope, keeping them only on the handles attached to the greased slider above her head. The Red Cap was made secure, his pale hairless calves exposed and curiously ageless compared to his hands when he hoisted his *shamtab* skirts. A set of thongs was passed under his thighs to support his weight. The ferryman shouted, '*Go!*'

Sonya's scream was involuntary, the air rushing out of her lungs with the impetus of their flight across the river.

Only as the rope sagged at the other end, lowering them to the landing-stage, did she let out a vast sigh of relief.

ii

The farmhouse looked warm and inviting. Brass butter-lamps placed at the open squares of ground floor windows lit up the yard. Like the Tsu shopkeeper, the farmer appeared to be a little more prosperous than the average Tibetan. Visions of the muleteer's fly-blown premises and lice-ridden person made Sonya infinitely thankful she had braved the river crossing despite the Red Cap's silent heavy breathing in her face while he held her much too tightly for comfort. She still could not explain to herself the odd feelings he stirred in her, vibrations designed to confuse her utterly in their familiarity. Somehow she sensed he was not the genuine article, yet knew it was absurd to assume other-wise. It was as though he were watching and waiting for a false move on someone's part, and she also sensed it was not entirely due to she and Joonu being foreign devils his vigilance, and vindictiveness, verged on the manic. Absurd, yes, but there was no getting away from the fact the wrinkled Red Cap in his shabby padded robe had displayed moments of weakness – his sweating mobile face, his unusually leathery hands, his pale athletic legs, and above all, mannerisms that brought back memories of a forgotten time. Sonya shook herself clear of such agitated thoughts. First gentle Geyog with his mild brown eyes, who used his left hand to remind her of someone else, and now the Red Cap, absurd! She was becoming unhinged on the fresh Tibetan air! Sonya pulled herself together and concentrated on events of the moment.

Joonu and the mendicant arrived with the four packs. Awakened from his sleep, Rika the farmer, once the customary courtesies of receiving his guests were out of the way, left his daughters to feed and settle them all for the night with the apology, 'excuse me, holy people, but I sleep as soon as it gets dark and rise as soon as it gets light. My eldest daughter who has taken the place of my wife will give you supper.'

197

'And this one will take the place of my wife, so put us a bed together on the other side of the fire so that she cannot escape from me again,' the Red Cap instructed with grim determination.

'What does he mean, Princess?' Joonu asked with sixth sense, looking hard at Sonya.

'I think he wants me to sleep beside him tonight in return for our freedom . . . at least, that is what he intimated on the way here.'

Joonu's eyes widened in astonishment, 'Princess, you are willing to sell yourself to that lustful old goat?'

'Trust me, Joonu?'

'Trust you, Princess! What about him!' Joonu spluttered. 'I saw the way he was clutching you on the rope-ferry and it wasn't only due to his fear of falling off it. I swear I will kill him if . . . '

'Joonu, please!' Sonya said in exasperation. 'Don't be such a goose. Of course I haven't promised myself to him, but he thinks I have. He wanted to talk with me, or rather, make a private bargain with me, but don't worry . . . I have a plan, so trust me.'

After supper the girls started undressing for bed, observed unwaveringly by Joonu and the Red Cap. Without the least embarrassment they took off their loose blouses worn over hessian skirts and, with no undergarments whatsoever, the fourteen and fifteen year old exposed pubescent pink breasts.

'Joonu, you're dribbling your soup – and I thought you were a gentleman,' Sonya accused. 'Why don't you turn around and go to sleep . . . where's Geyog?' She was aware suddenly that he was missing from the party gathered around the smokey fire and wondered when he had slipped away.

'No doubt he is saying his prayers . . . ' Joonu, in openmouthed asbtraction watching Rika's daughters, scarcely spared her an answer, and, because the Red Cap, too, was noisily slurping his soup with one eye on the impromptu floor show, Sonya got up and went into the next room used as a grain store. It led out onto the front yard. In the open doorway Geyog sat with his prayerbook on his knees.

198

'Geyog, it's too dark to be able to read without straining your eyes. Why don't you come for your supper?' Sonya said from behind him.

'I am not hungry, lady. And I do not have to see to read. I know it all off by heart. This is the age of oddities let loose, where different talents find their different marts; You'd best begin with truth, and when you've lost your labour, there's a sure market for imposture.'

Sonya froze. 'What did you say? What . . . what . . . did you mean about imposture? I know those words – what you just quoted is from *Don Juan* by an English lord.'

'Yes lady, I know,' he murmured softly.

'Who and what are you, Geyog,' she whispered, a sudden dread upon her.

'I am a monk. Servant to the Red Cap, and I come from the Drepung Monastery.'

'I don't believe you. I'm . . . I'm certain . . . ' Fearfully, her voice trailed away.

'Of what are you certain, gentle lady?' He kept his shaven head bowed so that all she could see of him was the paleness of his neck as moonlight held him in the doorway and the white blossoms of the syringa growing around the farmhouse door dispelled a breathtaking perfume.

Sonya took a deep breath; if he wished to play games, then so could she. 'I am certain you are not who you say you are. I know, that you know of my real identity. Yes, I am a Russian princess searching for her husband and brother lost somewhere in Tibet. I am here for no other purpose bar that – I need your help, Geyog . . . Geyog!' She smiled. 'And since we are alone we ought to resolve this thing right now. You speak perfect English . . . despite the accent you put on. So I'm curious, what nationality are you Geyog?'

'Tibetan, as I told you.'

'I don't think so. I think you're English.'

'It is half true,' Geyog admitted almost shamefacedly. 'My mother was an English missionary in China when my Tibetan father met and married her. He was a nobleman from Kham province. I am thus a Tibetan, since I, too, was born in my father's province.'

'Don't do this to me please, I beg of you!' she pleaded in an urgent whisper over his shoulder. 'I know who you are. I am certain, and yet I cannot be certain! I want to believe it, but I can't believe it. I don't know how, what, when, or why you are here, only that I have this extraordinary feeling about you . . . you, and your companion, the Red Cap. Who and what are you both? What sinister purpose makes you follow me? Yes, I am Sonya Dubrovka, despite my grotesque costume and appearance . . . the girl you saved from old Father Thames . . . it is Lewis, isn't it? You are so much like him, your height, your build, your eyes, your hands, you are Lewis Joyden in disguise, aren't you?'

'Lady, lady!' said the monk, turning to her with a kindly smile, 'you talk to me in riddles.'

'Oh, don't deny it!' she said wringing her hands in frustration. 'Despite your wonderful disguise and all your Tibetan mannerisms, I know you and the Red Cap are concealing something. He, too, is disguised to resemble what he is not. I know, I saw his limbs on the rope-ferry and they were not the infirm limbs of a raddled old man. I sense what lies beneath the surface of you two monks. Look at your left hand, scarred by me : . . . all clever men are left-handed, I remember saying to you once at my grand-mother's house in Abingdon. You quote *Don Juan* to me. I had never heard of *Don Juan* until you introduced me to the *Canto*. How did you guess I was coming to Tibet, Lewis? Did you not receive any of my letters from Peterhof? Did my grandmother tumble to it, and write and tell you accordingly? How, Lewis, why Lewis? Are you and the Red Cap British spies operating secretly in Tibet?'

He grabbed her hands to quieten her. 'Keep your voice down . . . listen to me . . . whatever you do, the Red Cap must not be aware of . . . '

'By the light of all that's holy! What are you two doing holding hands in this fashion?'

She and Geyog had been so engrossed with each other they had not heard the stealthy approach of the lama. The Red Cap wrenched his servant's hands from Sonya's. 'Have you taken leave of your senses, Geyog? What is this woman to you, that you should forget your vows? Make no

200

mistake, the High Lama of the Drepung will get to hear of this, and you will be publicly disgraced. As for you, *philang*,' he almost snarled, 'you want my servant as your lover, too, eh *Mig Kar*? Isn't one man a night enough for you, you must make promises to two? Come! I will show you who is more of a man than my poor celibate Geyog!'

'Lewis . . . don't let him . . . !' Sonya cried as the Red Cap dragged her forcefully into the yard.

Then, as if she were viewing the whole scene from across a deep dark treacherous cavern, Sonya saw the mendicant rise off the doorstep, lift his right arm, and slice downward to the back of the Red Cap's neck. The lama dropped like a stone into the mud.

Sonya felt no elation, only that, somehow, she had betrayed Lewis Joyden.

She ran back into the dark smelly kitchen. The farmer was still fast asleep, his three younger daughters, their smooth creamy-bare arms around each other, also slept peacefully with dreamy smiles on their bland faces. What Joonu and the eldest girl, Dorjee, were doing together made Sonya rush out of the kitchen in confusion, back to the storeroom and the open yard.

There was no sign of the Red Cap or his servant. One of the mules was also missing. Sonya hovered on the doorstep, peering into the darkness while a cold clammy hand seemed to gather her up bodily, squeezing the air out of her, the life out of her . . .

Murder or the murdered, whichever way Sonya looked at it, the man she now believed to be Lewis Joyden had lost out because of her. If the Red Cap recovered from the blow to his neck and remembered who had struck him, the consequences all round would be too dreadful to contemplate. If the Red Cap died at his servant's hands, Geyog, alias Lewis Joyden, would be a hunted man, the killer of a holy lama – and his punishment would be grotesque if he were caught. If he himself were to die at the Red Cap's hands, Sonya did not know how she would be able to live with herself for having been the cause of the quarrel between master and servant.

It was almost morning when Sonya finally lifted her head off her knees. Her body locked in icy numbness, she had difficulty in raising herself from the step to go inside. The strange drama of the night rushed in upon her senses, and she asked herself for the umpteenth time, what on earth was Lewis Joyden doing in Tibet when he was supposed to be in Dehra-Dun? That question, as well as many more, burned her consciousness when she crept back into the warm kitchen. She had hoped to return unnoticed, but the farmer was already awake, prodding the fire to life while his eldest daughter, having disentangled herself from Joonu's arms, sleepily prepared the breakfast. 'Oghai!' said Rika yawning, 'you are up early Holy Mother.'

'Yes – but I've slept well,' Sonya reassured him, on tenterhooks for him to depart with his daughters so that she could speak to Joonu alone.

'Come then and join me in taking tea and prayers. Wake the others, Dorjee, and let the Holy Mother bring us blessings.'

While Joonu slept on in a deep slumber from which nothing could disturb him, Sonya, as she had observed others like her do in fulfilment of holy duties, put on her headdress, tossed maize grain into the fire, and placed cake and milk in the four corners of the room to propitiate any evil spirits that dwelt in the house. Then she scribbled out a few prayer-flags which she handed to each member of the family. Rika seemed satisfied. Beaming at her with the black hole of his smile, he slurped the last of his tea, tied his bowl to his belt and stamped off to his field with his three younger daughters. Sonya ignored the presence of Dorjee stooping over the cooking-pot on the fire and roughly shook Joonu's shoulder. 'What is the matter, Princess?' He sat up anxiously.

'Joonu, there was a fight last night between the Red Cap and his servant. Geyog struck the lama who collapsed unconscious in the yard. I haven't seen either of the monks since.'

Joonu had paled dramatically. 'Where was I when all this

was going on?' he asked stupidly as he tumbled out of his bedroll and hurriedly gathered together his things.

'Showing a side of you I had never seen before.'

He glanced over his shoulder at her, 'You are not angry with me because of Dorjee, are you, Princess?'

'Yes, I'm angry. You were not there when I needed you, Joonu. And now poor gentle Geyog will be hunted down as a criminal, all because he wished to protect me from the Red Cap.'

Joonu looked at her sympathetically and was about to say something when he seemed to change his mind. Silently he fastened the straps of his packsack and heaved it onto his back, the Red Cap's pack as well as Geyog's still in the corner of the kitchen where they had been left.

Dorjee thrust a handful of apricots and walnuts at them. '*Kale pheb*,' she said sadly in Joonu's wake. He didn't seem to hear her as he marched off in the direction of the ferry with Sonya almost running to keep pace with him.

The sun was just beginning to creep over the rim of the eastern mountains, bathing the misty valley in mellow golden light. The white syringa tumbling over the doorway had lost its perfume of the night before and now appeared crystallized in a cocoon of spiders' webs that had been woven in the dawn.

'Joonu,' said Sonya anxiously, 'where do you think the Red Cap and Geyog might have got to?'

Still he said nothing, his normally cheerful expression set into an implacable pale mask that unnerved her, for here again was another side of Joonu she had never seen before.

'Joonu, where are we going?' She caught his sleeve.

'To the ferry, Princess, where else? We must escape from here while we can.'

'We cannot leave yet, Geyog might need us.'

Again Joonu seemed about to say something, again he changed his mind. He forged ahead to the river, engrossed in thoughts he seemed not to want to share with her. A crowd of people had already gathered on the wooden landing stage, and more people hugged the shore to obscure the river view.

'They are busy this morning,' Joonu commented wryly.

'Stay here, and I will see how long we will have to wait.' He ran off down the path. Suddenly he stopped, turned around and made signs to Sonya to get out of sight before plunging off into the undergrowth. Sonya fled into the shelter of some alders growing along the river bank and waited impatiently for Joonu to rejoin her. Ten minutes later he came panting back. 'Prin . . . Prin . . . ' Unable to get the words out, he doubled up as if in pain.

'What's the matter?' Sonya asked in alarm.

'One of them has drowned with a knife in his back . . . the ferryman and Rika are fishing him out of the river now . . . I do not know which one . . . '

'Geyog, it's Geyog, isn't it? The Red Cap must have recovered from the blow, and paid Geyog back.' Her mind riveted to a man and a girl drowning together, that same man who had twice risked his life for her succumbing in the end to an element all her life she herself had dreaded, raging water, Sonya did not hear or heed Joonu, her heart had frozen into a solid block of ice.

204

Chapter Fifteen

All the water in the world could not wash away the red stain of murder. Geyog floated face down in the river, his robe slashed, revealing the knife still in his back. That the knife with its glass-jewelled hilt, was purchased in Samarkand by Joonu, who thought he had lost it when he had fought Geyog on the mountain path at Tsu, further added to the tragedy. Geyog's body was dragged ashore by the muleteer and the farmer, demonstrative villagers weeping and wailing for fear of evil curses on their village because a holy man had been murdered in the water they drank, washed in and lived by. Geyog's body was left uncovered for all to peer at, his opaque eyes staring up at the clear blue sky, his mouth a grimace of pain frozen at the time of his death.

Only Joonu's steadying hand on her shoulder brought Sonya to her senses. He said something strange; 'Princess, whatever transpires now, it will be better to place our faith in the Red Cap, who is after all, an honest rascal. I never trusted Geyog.'

'What do you mean?' Sonya stared at Joonu in amazement.

'Geyog was far too smooth to be genuine. Always slyly pumping you for information which you were willing to give him because he ingratitated himself into your feelings.'

She dashed his hand aside furiously. 'How dare you, Joonu! How would you know what is genuine or not? You have no concept of anyone's finer feelings, have you? Geyog happened to be a friend of mine.' And without saying another word she turned on her heel and ran from Joonu – straight into the arms of the Red Cap.

He rode the shopkeeper's mule in company with the Ponpo of the District seated on a fat sleek pony with jingling silver harness and bells,and a contingent of foot soldiers bearing firearms. Sonya had no doubt in her mind that the lama himself had gone in search of the Ponpo.

At once she and Joonu were detained by the District Official on suspicion of being foreign devils. The Ponpo harried the soldiers and villagers to tie them up in Rika's yard.

Dorjee wailed non-stop on the doorstep.

Joonu, pale and too frightened to say anything, looked at Sonya with pleading dark eyes and she misinterpreted the look.

'Joonu . . . it's going to be all right, please don't look like that,' Sonya implored as they were jostled by the Ponpo's soldiers. 'They can't pin Geyog's murder on you, no matter how hard they might try. You were with Dorjee last night, and never left the kitchen once. The farmer and his daughters will bear out the truth.'

'They were all asleep, Princess, as you well know.'

Well then, Dorjee was not.'

'The knife, Princess . . . '

'Joonu, don't you see! The Red Cap stole your knife and stabbed Geyog with it to make it look as if you killed Lew . . . the monk. He wants to get rid of us from Tibet, and is trying everything in his power. But he won't get away with it – not murder.'

'Try convincing the Ponpo, Princess. I am already convinced I am a dead man.' Joonu fell silent.

Dazed by all that had happened so swiftly, Sonya was hardly aware of what was taking place around them. The Red Cap seated himself next to the Ponpo on mats and cushions the farmer's daughters brought into the yard. From then on, she and Joonu were precipitated into a nightmare trial based on false accusations and betrayal. Rika, his daughters, the muleteer and ferrymen, all swore they had seen Joonu fighting the mendicant in the river for possession of the jewelled knife that Joonu had stolen from a rich man, and the mendicant had wished only to restore to that man! Everyone admitted to having seen the two strangers – whom they had always suspected to be foreign devils and not true Arjopas – enter the village to steal, cheat and abuse, the Sorceress herself having performed grave magical rites to call up demons.

Tibetan justice was swift and to the point, the Ponpo and the Red Cap acting as judge, jury and executioners. The punishment for stealing, stabbing and drowning a holy man was death by scourging and mutilation.

'No!' Sonya, in shock and disbelief, cried out as Joonu crumpled to his knees with a moan and placed his forehead on the ground in front of the Ponpo and Red Cap. 'How dare you all!' She set her shoulders and faced the hostile crowd. 'How dare you judge and sentence us in such a barbaric fashion! If we are to die, then we are entitled to a fair trial in Lhasa, not here in this yard! I am a Russian princess. If news of this kind of atrocity comes to the knowledge of the Dalai Lama who is a friend of the White Khan, my ruler, all of you will be condemned by the Kashag and your land and property confiscated. If you kill my servant and me in this place, then the White Khan will join forces with the British who already gather on the borders of your country to wage war. Against superior forces, Tibet will not win and you will all become the prisoners of white men, and those of you taking part in this sham trial today will be imprisoned or sentenced to death. So think very carefully about what you intend to do with us, because I have the power to bring more curses on all of you.'

In silence they had listened to her, a Russian princess who did not tremble before the High Magistrate or the Red Cap lama. One or two people in the crowd fidgeted uneasily and glances were thrown upon Sonya's elaborate headdress, the headdress of a Sorceress with great powers. The Ponpo too, seemed to hesitate. He demanded aggressively; 'What powers have you got, you who claim to be a princess from the White Khan's country, but are only a *philang* in this country?'

'I have a letter of authority from the White Khan to his Holiness the Dalai Lama. If the God-King does not receive it within a specified time, he will wonder what has happened to me, and will send his soldiers to find out. The God-King is the only one in this country who has the power to question and punish me and my servant – no one else. He has given his word to the White Khan in a treaty made between the Urusso and the Tibetans several years ago. The Dalai Lama will not be at all pleased to know his people have taken power into their own hands to make him appear inferior to the White Khan.'

'Where is this letter purporting you are a Russian princess and an emissary of the White Khan?' asked the Red Cap stroking his stubbly dirty chin. But he eyed her with less hostility than before, almost a kind of sympathy in his pouched bloodshot eyes now that sentence had been pronounced.

'In my *amphag*.'

The Red Cap asked Dorjee to fetch it, but the Ponpo snatched at the Tsar's letter first. He examined it without being able to understand anything except the impressive Romonov crest of black eagles. The Ponpo handed the letter to the Red Cap who said: 'I believe the *philang* has more letters in her *amphag*, fetch those too.'

Dorjee dutifully obeyed.

'They are written in English,' Sonya enlightened the Ponpo and the Red Cap, 'and like the Russian one, you will not understand those either.'

'What kind of letters are they?' asked the Ponpo peering over the lama's shoulder.

'Love letters I believe,' said the Red Cap with a smirk in Sonya's direction, adding, 'You have brought these all the way from Russia with you?'

'That is none of your business.'

'Everything is our business where it concerns a *philang*. You must be very much in love with this man to harbour his letters in English, eh *Mig Kar*?'

'They are the letters of a dead man,' Sonya stared the Red Cap in the eye, unafraid of anything he could do to her now. He averted his gaze, and she knew then, as she had known all along, it was he who had committed murder, no-one else.

The Red Cap muttered something in the Ponpo's ear, and presently the Ponpo looked across at them. 'The holy man pleads for clemency in this instance so I will allow it where the woman is concerned. Two lashes for her, then deportment with an armed escort to the border. The death sentence for the youth stands, by scourging and mutilation.'

'You will not touch a hair of his head!' Sonya raised her own voice in shrill admonition. 'I will not allow it!'

'The youth will die,' cried the over-fed and richly clad Ponpo. 'If only to teach other *philangs* a lesson. The laws of my country are to be obeyed and I, as Officer of this District, must uphold the law. Come, help me up.' He raised fat dirty hands to the two soldiers flanking him. They helped the overweight Ponpo in his fur robes to his feet. The Red Cap was also given assistance from his lotus-position on the ground and together they went into Rika's kitchen for refreshment.

Sonya had no conception of how long she and Joonu sat in the muddy farmyard while everyone around them treated the day as a holiday and a festival. A small fire was lit in the yard, pouches of tsampa and tobacco opened. Tea was made, tobacco was smoked or chewed as everyone patiently waited for the Ponpo and the Red Cap to come out of the farmhouse. Two hours later they emerged, flushed, jocular and with glazed eyes.

'The floggings will take place at once,' announced the Ponpo. 'Make it swift, muleteer, for I am a busy man and have no time to waste. If the youth does not die today, then it shall be tomorrow. The woman will be flogged first. Tie her to that tree.' He brandished his crop at the silver birch growing close by, which, in that moment, reminded Sonya painfully of Novgorod.

Only when her arms were tied around the argent markings on the slender birch trunk, and the back of her thick dress ripped wide open by the muleteer's filthy hands, did extreme reality present itself. She closed her eyes fearfully. She would not cry out, she told herself. She would not beg for mercy, and least of all would she tremble before such brutal peasants. If Joonu died at their hands, then she would somehow survive to vindicate him and extract punishment from everyone, but most especially the Red Cap! She braced herself for the first stroke of the muleteer's yak-hide whip, an instrument whose scars his animals bore in brutal reminder of the cruelty of their master. The whistle of leather thongs through air left her unprepared for Joonu's shriek as he, in a frenzy, struggled against restraining arms to fling himself on her, thus taking the full force of the lash that had been intended for her. Sobbing like a baby, he spread his body against hers, and would not be dragged away by soldiers' kicks, shouts or rifle-butts.

The muleteer lifted his arm once more and asked if he should strike again, despite the youth who had got in his way. 'Do not hurt her, I will take her sentence upon myself,' Joonu sobbed.

'No, Joonu, No!' Sonya cried, pain and rage engulfing her. 'Please don't be a fool, Joonu, please don't, they will beat you to death . . . ' By now, she too was sobbing, her face pressed against the rough hard bark of the birch tree, and she heard only the soothing velvet rush of warm breezes in the trees at Novgorod, the pleasant deep brown reassurances of a man's voice through rushing water . . .

Joonu's tears against her bare back and the Red Cap's intervention jolted her back to the present with all its sinister and tragic implications. 'Enough,' he said, sensing the watching crowd was growing restless. He had dealt with crowds more times than he cared to remember, and they were always the same. He had seen how soon a crowd could turn like an animal of many heads and limbs, transforming a trial of justice into a lynching mob, and he did not want that to happen here. 'Cut the Urusso woman down since it would be a crime to scar such an appealing back which could be put to better use. The youth takes her sentence upon himself, so be it. I myself will escort the *Mig Kar* back to Rudok with an escort of soldiers.

The crowd groaned, whether in sympathy or disappointment Sonya did not know nor care as she was cut loose from the tree. She only saw Joonu tied up in her place.

210

Sonya would never forget the slicing sound of the muleteer's whip on Joonu's back. Food and drink nauseated her, sleep eluded her and, sitting in front of Rika's fire, she could only think of how she and Joonu had been betrayed by all of them, including Dorjee. Joonu's beating had been severe. On the seventh stroke, the thin flesh on his back had opened to reveal torn muscle and he had fainted. Then the Red Cap and Ponpo had conferred together for several minutes. Another heated discussion seemed to be going on between them until the Ponpo, shrugging his shoulders in resignation at the forceful Red Cap, announced; 'The holy man again sees it his way, enough for today. There is no purpose in flogging a dead horse, he is unable to feel anything. Tomorrow, when this murdering youth is once more conscious of his evil-doing and feels pain again, then we will carry out the rest of the sentence. So, muleteer, put away your whip for today, and go home to sharpen your axe. The *philang*'s one hand will be removed first, then his two feet, so that he might never again trespass on our soil and kill holy men. The Urusso *Mig Kar* herself will again observe the kind of punishment her servant receives so that she can return to her own lands without wishing to return to Tibet ever again. That is the kind of punishment we must mete out to foreign devils, murderers and thieves who seek to corrupt our holy country. The *gelong* will be avenged!'

The Ponpo turned his pony's head and rode away. Joonu had been cut down from the birch tree, taken into the farmer's house and placed face down on a sleeping mat in front of the kitchen fire where, only the night before, he had spent such a happy time in Dorjee's arms. Now she did not go near him but like Rika and the other girls, kept herself distant and cold while Sonya bathed Joonu's wounds. How swiftly, Sonya thought, did the world and its people change, blown by fickle winds, shallow as puddles, and dangerous as a typhoon at sea. Lewis Joyden was dead, why? Joonu was about to die, why? What had suddenly happened to change her quiet, harmless journey through Tibet into a nightmare of cross purposes? 'I want some of that blue-poppy ointment Geyog carried in his pack to put on Joonu's back,' Sonya said to the Red Cap dozing in front of Rika's fire.

Absorbed in his own meditations the lama shrugged indifferently. 'It is poor reward to my servant murdered at the hand of your servant,' he mumbled stupidly, 'but do as you wish.' He flicked a derisive hand towards Geyog's belongings still in the corner of the room.

Sonya's indignation got the better of her. 'How can a holy man like you possibly be so cruel? How can you lie and cheat, murder and delight in acts of barbarism as you did today? You know who the real murderer of Geyog is, as I do, yet why you've let Joonu suffer like this for your sins, I don't understand.'

'There are many things you don't understand, *Mig Kar*. It is not for me to explain the principles of Bon-culture to you who are only a foreign devil and of little consequence in my country. There is a greater understanding of life in my country than ever there is in yours. What is a little pain in this life when there is eternal glory and painlessness after death? So do not worry about your little friend and servant should he die of his injuries. Tomorrow he will be born again, reincarnated to a greater glory and standing than he enjoys today . . . maybe he will be the master and you his slave in the next life, eh, *Mig Kar*? As for me, I serve my conscience, my country and my Gompsa on the mountain. That is enough for you to know and understand, for you are only a woman, ungrateful to the last for having had her own hide saved by me!' He went off into a trance then, taking neither food nor drink for the rest of the day, but sleeping upright in the lotus-position in the corner of the room while the Ponpo's soldiers guarded the farmhouse and Joonu slept off the worst of his thrashing.

Sonya rifled through Geyog's packsack and found the blue-poppy ointment with such amazing properties which she smoothed over Joonu's raw back lacerated with crusty black streaks where the blood had dried. He flinched, consciousness and pain returning slowly, but did not wake fully. Sonya allowed him to sleep on for as long as possible while she mended her torn robe. In the early dawn the Red

212

Cap stirred, spat and with as much noise as possible so that he might wake everyone, demanded bread and tea from Dorjee. The girl, too frightened to disobey, was also too frightened to do things silently in her nervousness and soon the kitchen was filled with awakened Rika, his other daughters and the soldiers.

'Time for us to go,' said the Red Cap, glaring piercingly at Sonya from beneath his straggly white eyebrows as he gustily sipped his tea. 'Hurry and eat up, *Mig Kar*, it's a long way back to the border.'

'I'm not going anywhere with you,' she replied, softly determined as she smoothed more ointment onto Joonu's back. 'Is this the way a holy man who sees visions lives his life? Only to take pleasure in the sufferings of others? Go yourself back to your monastery, I will stay here with my servant, and so be it, we shall die together.'

'Courageous words, O noblewoman, but they will serve you nothing. The law must be obeyed. Punishment only comes when one breaks the law.'

'I hope you will remember that in your Gompsa on the mountain-top,' Sonya said bitterly. 'You murdered Geyog, no one else.'

'Indiscretion like that will get you nowhere except into trouble, *Mig Kar*,' said the Red Cap, adjusting his monk's cap with its distinctive flaps either side, reminding Sonya of devil's horns.

'I'm not coming . . . '

'*Bring her!*' commanded the lama, brooking no more nonsense from her. Two soldiers immediately sprang on her and gathered her up bodily while Rika and his daughters moved to a far corner of the room where they could watch without becoming involved. 'You two men will accompany me back to Rudok to guard this Urusso *philang*,' said the Red Cap jabbing a finger at two of the soldiers, and without sparing poor suffering Joonu a backward glance, stepped over him and through the doorway.

Joonu, one tear-stained cheek pressed to his sleeping mat, his stump protective of his face as he lay on his stomach, raised his head a fraction and opened his swollen sticky eyes before dropping his head down again with a heartfelt sigh.

213

Sonya knelt beside him, disregarding the hostile Tibetan soldiers in pursuit of their duty with outmoded matchlocks. Joonu's lips quivered. Sonya bent her ear closer to him. 'Princess,' he whispered in Russian, his eyes screwed tight with the effort of talking, 'do not be angry with the Red Cap who, as you rightly guessed, is not all he appears to be. But he only does his duty. Trust him, and obey him, all will be well, he knows best. I can say no more, it is not my place. But I do not intend to die, I promise . . . so go with him now before it is too late.'

iii

For three days Sonya travelled beside the Red Cap like a woman in a trance. The only facts to penetrate her consciousness were that they were progressing higher and higher into the mountains and on the third day the weather changed. Flurries of snow began to hamper their progress, giving way to a full snowstorm before the day was through. But the Red Cap urged them forward remorselessly, beating the Tsu shopkeeper's mule and striking the soldiers on foot with his mule-stick when they could not keep up. 'We must make haste before the mountain passes are blocked by the snows.' The lama, blowing hard, his red wrinkled face turning purple with effort, forged ahead while Sonya, flanked by the short-limbed Tibetan soldiers, struggled after him on Phagpa's increasingly lame mule. Dimly Sonya registered the fact that they must be lost since they ought, by now, to have retraced their steps to Gartok and the lama's Gompsa on its great pinnacle of rock. Then her mount, completely lame, collapsed and had to be abandoned. 'Someone will find him and gobble him up,' declared the disgruntled Red Cap poking the fallen animal with his toe. 'I'd skin him myself only we haven't time.'

The poor *dokpa* would never get his humble possessions back now, Sonya reflected, keeping her head bent against the icy gusts blowing in her face. Neither were Phagpa and Sera likely to be recompensed by the odious creature who had disrupted her life. Why, she wondered, did the good die young, while the wicked went on through life perpetrating their acts of evil? And what on earth had Joonu meant about trusting the Red Cap who was not all he was supposed to be? Obviously Joonu had been hallucinating, after-effects, no doubt, of his beating and the drugging properties of the blue poppy. Still, there was something very odd and erratic about the Red Cap's behaviour! Sonya tried hard to put Lewis Joyden out of her mind but failed. She promised herself that when she got back to Russia her first visit would be to the British Ambassador in St Petersburg to tell him exactly the fate of a British subject in Tibet. Lewis and Joonu would be avenged even if she had to start the war against the Tibetans herself!

By late afternoon visibility was nil, darkness was approaching and six inches of snow lay on the mountain path.

'There is a *mi-deussa* further along . . . I know this route well,' announced the Red Cap. 'I have travelled it many times to and from my Gompsa. We will shelter in the *mi-deussa* until the snowstorm abates. Tonight there will be a moon, and with the snow to light our way as well, we can continue our journey through the night.'

But the wayfarers' shelter was already occupied. Within its roofless stone walls not an inch of space was to be had as pilgrims clustered together round the central cooking fire someone was feeding with nuggets of yak-dung, the fire having been lit under an awning of yak-hide to prevent it from going out while the snow fell.

'Oi, make way there!' The Red Cap dismounted and elbowed the Arjopas aside. He took the prime position next to the glowing fire, dragging Sonya along to sit beside him. The soldiers were given the task of attending to the Red Cap's mule and pitching Sonya's yak-tent so that she might be contained and guarded for the night.

Oblivious to her surroundings, she sat numbly by the fire thinking about Joonu and Geyog, the strange mendicant monk who had left the burning question in her mind, had he *truly* been Lewis Joyden? Was she not getting carried away by a vague image of a man she had built up in her own mind over years of corresponding with him, imbuing that man with characteristics she herself had wished to find in him? If so, then why was Lewis here in Tibet in disguise?

Why? What had he been doing in Tibet? Why had he been so brutally disposed of by the Red Cap – if indeed it had been the Red Cap who had been his murderer? It might not have been of course, for it could easily have been the muleteer, Rika, or the ferrymen . . . any number of people with a grudge against Geyog, for hadn't he said he had visited that village before? The whole situation was too perplexing for her to fathom, all she wanted to do was sleep without thinking about Lewis Joyden or Joonu, who, in all probability had died of his injuries by now.

'Come, eat up!' the Red Cap said heartily when he saw her staring into space. 'You haven't eaten for three days and I don't want you dying of hunger and being more of a nuisance to me than you already are.'

'I'm not hungry.' The smell from the cooking-pot slung on a metal tripod over the fire was enough to destroy anyone's appetite. Sonya moved away from the lama and the fire and went to crouch in the lee of one of the stone walls. An old harridan, muttering incessantly to herself, a tattered shawl covering her head, scratched at the frozen ground beside Sonya. For a little while Sonya did not take any notice of her, but her actions were so futile yet so determined, Sonya could not help observing her in fascination as, with long curved talons the old woman systematically dug into the snow. After a while she uttered a triumphant grunt and withdrew from the shallow hole she had made with her bare fingers a bundle of frozen entrails, pulling and parting the shiny red viscera, heart, lungs, liver, intestines and stomach. Sonya would probably have thought no more about it except that the old crone gathered up the revolting bundle, wandered over to the camp fire and flung the mess into the cooking pot. Five minutes later one of the soldiers carried a bowl of steaming broth over to where Sonya huuddled in misery. He thrust the bowl under Sonya's nose. 'The Tsawai Lama gives you the honour of his bowl and begs you to eat lest you die,' the soldier said.

Not only the smell, but also the bowl's contents made Sonya retch. She dashed the bowl from the astonished soldier's hands, 'Damn the Spiritual Father and the old hag's soup! Damn all of you . . . ' She scrambled to her feet, tears streaming down her face. The Red Cap was beside her in a trice.

'Sit down! Go soldier, fill the bowl again and bring it back.' Keeping a firm grip on Sonya's arm, the Red Cap hissed in her face. 'You will eat what is given to us by the graciousness of these poor people even if I have to force it down your throat!'

'I can't . . . I'll be ill . . . '

'Then be ill, but eat it first . . . here . . . ' The soldier brought back the replenished bowl, and the Red Cap took it from him, forcing Sonya to sit down and eat. 'In this cold weather you will die if you go another day without food.'

'Then let me die, but I can't touch that stuff . . . My God, I can't!' Her last reserves of strength snapped, she put her head in her hands and began to sob hysterically. 'I can't eat what they're eating . . . I'm not a cannibal. Human entrails, that's what that old woman dug out of the ground, human entrails! I watched her. Then she put it all in the cooking-pot, and you expect me to eat human entrails . . . I'd rather die.'

'You will not die. You will eat first, *philang*, and die on the way to the border, not in this *mi-duessa* to harbour your evil spirit. Take the *philang*'s arms, soldier, and I will pour the soup down her ungrateful throat . . . '

With a cry of outrage Sonya flung herself from the soldier and the lama before they had a chance to grab her and taking up one of the matchlocks lying on the ground used it to dash the cooking pot from its tripod, knocking everything into the fire and extinguishing it with a steaming hiss of spilled soup. Wielding the matchlock she defied the Red Cap and the soldiers to come any nearer while the frightened Arjopas stared at her as though she were raving mad. 'The gods ride her!' they whispered fearfully among themselves.

'Joonu was innocent and you know it!' Sonya cried out in ringing tones as she turned on the Red Cap. 'You know it because you are a white man's murderer! Geyog was no Tibetan monk but an English explorer in disguise . . . the man whose letters you have kept along with Tsar Nicholas's. Why did you murder him, why? It surely cannot

217

be because he struck you in order to protect me from your vileness? You're wicked and unscrupulous and I will make sure the Dalai Lama as well as all these humble pilgrims, knows what kind of monk is being harboured in one of their monasteries. I will return to Russia to convey to the whole world how Tibetan monks murder innocent people in order that they themselves can grow fat on the land as well as off the backs of these poor ignorant pilgrims . . . '

'The gods do indeed ride her!' roared the Red Cap above Sonya's pitiful cries. 'Observe her behaviour, she has become a *Pamo*! Take hold of her everyone, force her to the ground so that the evil spirits possessing her might be cast out, and I will explain the reasons for her behaviour.'

Obedient despite their fear of a woman possessed by demons, many willing hands soon forced Sonya to her knees while the Red Cap told the Arjopas, 'The demon who speaks through this woman's mouth is the evil spirit of her departed servant. He died three days ago for having committed a terrible crime, that of murdering my servant, a humble mendicant who caused no harm in this world, only good – and all for the sake of a glass-handled *phurba* he was brutally killed! Now the spirit of the idiot-youth, who was this *philang's* servant, wishes to avenge itself on me and on all of us gathered here. But I will not let the demons have their way. Bring me holy water from my pack, bring me my rosary, trident and prayerwheel. With prayers and alms, together we will exorcize this poor woman's devils.' Then the Red Cap began an elaborate ritual to cast out Sonya's demons, using his money-fed prayerwheel and selling his paper prayer-flags to the Arjopas who were all too willing to avail themselves of a holy man's blessings and to be rid of the demons haunting their resting place. 'Yaks' milk will protect us within these walls,' the Red Cap grunted as he paraded around the *mi-deussa* sprinkling milk and touching the prongs of his silver trident to the four corners of the shelter. 'The odours of the demon-spirits will not trouble us again tonight . . . look, see the mad woman is already calm and foams no more at the mouth. Put her in her tent and my soldiers will guard her. Pick up your cooking-pot, put snow in it to melt and retrieve your meat off the ground which has been blest and is therefore clean again. Relight the fire and eat. I am going to the mountain to converse with the gods who will watch over all of you this night despite the *philang*'s presence.'

The Red Cap picked up his wooden bowl, put it in his *amphag* and poking his head into the tiny yak-skin tent under which Sonya sat shivering, thrust his whiskery red face close to hers. In a mellifluous voice she could not fail to remember from her days at Abingdon so that she wondered how on earth she could ever have mistaken Geyog for Lewis Joyden, he said in English; 'In saying the very least, the yak's a remarkable beast. From fly-whisks to butter, you won't hear him utter – so neither will you at this feast! And when the next batch of yak-soup is ready, you'll eat it, my girl, or by God, I'll skin you alive for almost having given the whole damn show away!' He stamped off into the white night, leaving her utterly dumbfounded.

Chapter Sixteen

Sonya sat in the entrance to her tent. She stared out at the frosty stars perched on the rim of the mountains. It had stopped snowing and the night was clear and bright. The old crescent moon on the wane was rising in front of her and Sonya wondered why. It should be coming up in the east, just before the sun, not the west where Gartok lay along the Silk Road. Yesterday, she had thought they might be lost, although the Red Cap was obviously not going to admit to any failure on his part. Well, let him get thoroughly lost in these mountains! Sonya registered the fact, too, that all the Arjopas were asleep as well as the soldiers supposedly guarding her. Around her tent, bodies were humped on the ground, heavy Tibetan skirts and woollen blankets drawn over heads making her feel like the shepherdess to a flock of black sheep. Her hands and feet were still tied. Beside her a tiny yak-butter lamp flickered dimly, casting none of its own light since the moon far surpassed anything the lamp could do. But it did have a flame, and Sonya, in grim determination, held her hands over it, hoping it would not go out before it had a chance to burn through the cord around her wrists.

Half an hour later her hands were free, smarting badly where she had burned herself. She untied her ankles, and still not a soul stirred in the sleeping camp. She was not afraid any more of Tibetan soldiers, she had seen what kind of rusty weapons they possessed. By the time they could ignite the powder and aim, she would be out of range.

It was a simple matter to follow the Red Cap's footsteps. It had not snowed to any great degree since he had announced his intention to converse with the gods and only a light powdering covered his tracks. Half-way up the mountain moonlight silhouetted him on a glacis not far from the path. He stood defiantly tall with arms outstretched to the stars, his body dark against the brilliant snows. In that rarefied atmosphere Sonya's breathing was harsh. When the sound of her laboured gasps disturbed his lonely meditation, he turned to look down on her. He was stark naked, his pleated *shamtab*, sandals and cap lying on the path at her feet, his body hardy and athletic. '*Mig Kar*!' he said, as astonished as she. 'You look surprised. Don't tell me you haven't seen it all before – you who are a married woman!'

She turned away, ready to leave such a man without sense nor feeling, but he called out sharply, 'Wait! Don't go!'

She hesitated, then her voice rang out clear and frosty as the night air; 'What are you, Lewis Joyden, other than a butcher of lives and feelings?'

He slithered down the glacis and came beside her, unabashed by his nakedness and shaven head. He stooped to retrieve his sodden robe from the snow. 'Yes, *I* am Lewis Joyden, Sonya, not Geyog – I'm sorry. But I've had to maintain this grotesque charade for reasons I know you will not believe at this stage. Let me explain . . . '

Sonya turned away despairingly, her breath catching in her throat, hurting her chest. In that moment she could have struck the Red Cap for everything he had put her through.

In confusion Sonya turned to him again when he had donned his robe, padded to give him a bulky shape, and the red wrinkled face of the round-shouldered Red Cap stared back at her grotesquely. 'I think I am going mad,' she said.

'No, no you're not . . . ' He put out his hand to her but she dashed it aside and said fiercely; 'I can't believe you are who you say you are . . . ' Her voice faded, she remembered she had said exactly the same thing to Geyog and in remembering Geyog and Joonu, everything she had built in

221

her memory of a handsome young man performing heroic deeds burst like a poisonous bubble, shattering once and for all any illusions she had ever had of Lewis Joyden. 'I can't believe it . . . I don't want to . . . ' She shook her head, tears dangerously close. 'Geyog . . . murdered, and Joonu . . . '

'Trust me, Sonya.'

'*Trust you*! Oh . . . after . . . after what you have done? After . . . after allowing Joonu to be whipped so brutally . . . oh no, I cannot believe Lewis Joyden would do any such thing, he was a man of honour . . . wasn't he?' Her voice broke pitifully, her mind split between the Tibetan lama and the Englishman.

The man standing before her straightened his back, lifted his hands and began peeling away the edges of his face, stripping the rubbery substance that disguised him so completely from neck to forehead.

'It takes me two hours to put on another real Tibetan *phisog* like this . . . for that reason I hardly ever remove it.' He gave an amused little grunt.

The face underneath began to appear faintly familiar and Sonya wondered then how she had ever imagined Geyog to be Lewis Joyden when this was the face she had held dear in the tunnel of time, the picture of him at her grandmother's house, looking up at her through rhododendrons with a certain smile on his face as he teased her. And ever after she had held that picture of him close to her heart, no-one else; like an Icon seen through the perfumed haze of an incense candle, sometimes near, sometimes far, but always held in reverent devotion. She could only stand and stare at the transformation, the face and the man suddenly very dear to her in that alien place, and with the cry of a lost child centering on the immense conflict within herself, she flung herself at him in utter hopelessness. 'Why Lewis . . . why?' she wept against his shoulder.

'No questions, Sonya, not yet.'

After a moment or two she composed herself, and stepping away from him tearfully shook her head and said, 'I'm not going to be sidetracked by you after the outrageous way you've behaved.' She scrutinized the face of shaven-headed Lewis Joyden, the man who treated human beings with impunity. 'You've put me through purgatory, and that I shall never forgive.'

'What do you think you've put me through?' he said, looking at her sadly. 'I never wanted it to happen this way . . . and it would not have, had you not opened your mouth to Geyog.'

'I . . . when did I open my mouth to Geyog?' she asked in bewilderment.

'The night you and he sat in the moonlight beneath orangeblossom and you got carried away by his sweet double-talk. Geyog was dangerous. He was pumping you for information. But it's a very long story and this is neither the time nor place to relate it as I'm frozen.' He grinned sheepishly, his lop-sided smile reminding her of a time gone by in England. 'The art of Thumo Reskiang only works when one's concentration isn't shattered by a woman. I'm sorry, Sonya, about Joonu; I know how much he meant to you. I will explain everything later. For now, you really must try and trust me. I have to be the despicable Red Cap in order that people I meet along the way dislike and fear me, and therefore prefer to shun my company. Only in that way can I do what I'm here to do. I want you now to go back to the *mi-deussa* and fetch both our packs, as well as my trident and prayer-wheel . . . the prayer-wheel is most important. Then return here as fast as you can. I'd go rather than you, but I daren't show my English face and it will take too long to put on my Tibetan one.'

'Supposing someone wakes and sees me walking away with your things?'

'Then think up some excuse, I'm sure a potent sorceress like you can come up with something. If you really can't get away, I'll wait a couple of hours and then return to the camp with a new face – I always carry a spare box of tricks in my *amphag* just in case my pack should go astray.' He patted his breast pocket. 'Anyway, enough explanations for now, just do as I say, there's a good girl.'

'I'm not a child Lewis, nor a girl, so please don't talk to me as though I were. Whatever you do or say now won't compensate for what happened to Joonu . . . '

223

'Sonya, I swear, I'll kill you too if you give the game away now!' Strong fingers bit into her arm.

'Oh, don't worry, Lewis Joyden, that won't be necessary.' She cast him a scathing look. 'I'm still your prisoner, remember? Now please take your hand off me and I'll do my best to obey your instructions. I will return, so don't worry about my giving the 'game' away because I want to make absolutely certain of your part in Geyog's death. And I, too, swear, that if you're responsible for what happened to Joonu, I'll denounce you to the nearest Ponpo and watch you being flogged as he was.'

ii

Arjopas and soldiers were still dead to the world in their curious sleeping positions, the freezing night keeping everyone under cover. Sonya took the packs, prayer-wheel and trident but had to leave her invaluable yak-tent behind. Unmolested, she left the *mi-deussa*. Lewis was waiting for her in the same place, his shaven head covered by his distinctive red cap so that when he came down the path to meet her with his English face and English smiles, she could hardly believe he was the same man she had been travelling with for more days than she cared to remember.

'Good! Now let's put as much distance as we can between the Ponpo's soldiers and us. Thank God it's stopped snowing.' He shrugged his pack on his back and went in front of her. 'Follow me, keep up and don't ask me a single question until we stop to rest. You'll need every ounce of breath for these mountains.'

The Red Cap's authority was all there in his relentless attitude, and Sonya, still perplexed and sore about many things, bit on her tongue. Time would tell, but right now she knew she had to concentrate all her energy on keeping up with this man who appeared to know the mountains like the back of his hand.

'You weren't taking me back to Gartok, were you, Lewis, so what were you intending to do with me?' Sonya asked in a moment when they were able to walk side by side through a narrow but sheltered pass overhung by towering cliffs.

'Hoping to string you along for as long as possible, *Mig Kar*.'

'In which direction?'

'Towards Lhasa.'

'In your odious capacity as the Red Cap, I don't think I would have survived the journey.'

'And now?' Looking down at her, he raised a quizzical dark brow.

'I still don't think I'll survive.'

'You'll have to . . . but make no mistake, Sonya, the Red Cap will come into his own again once we leave these uninhabited mountains.'

'These mountains aren't so very uninhabited, we've just left a *mi-deussa* full of people.'

'All wayfarers' shelters are bound to be occupied, that's what they're there for. And we're still not that high up in the Himalayas – these are really only foothills. But we'll be taking a route not many people know about . . . I discovered it on one of my previous sorties into this country. Following this pass, we'll come out the other side of the Manasarowa Lake between Nepal and Tibet where we'll once more pick up the Silk Road to Lhatse and thence Gyantse.'

'You're very sure of yourself, aren't you, Lewis?'

'I have to be, otherwise I'm a dead man.'

They said nothing more until Lewis announced that there was a deserted *jong* further down the pass where they could rest for a while.

'What's a *jong*?' Sonya asked.

'A fort. It's built at the convergence of two passes into India, only it's in ruins since the Chinese abandoned it some years ago.'

'How do you know so much?'

'I had to redraw the boundary, my dear girl.'

'Oh, I see. Is it coincidence we both met here in Tibet, or is there something going on I don't know about?'

'No coincidence – I've been on your tail ever since Rudok.'

'Rudok?' she asked in amazement.

'Yes, Rudok. You and Joonu would never have got past

those interfering Yellow Caps had I not caused a diversion.'

'You? How?' She stared up at him disbelievingly.

He chuckled. 'I was the messy old peasant whose sack of mouldy turnips was hacked to pieces by Customs Officials searching for opium.'

'The one full of sores?'

'The very same.'

'My goodness, you are a master of disguise! And that realistic mask of yours, if it takes you two hours to put on, what on earth is it made of?'

'A new kind of resinous amalgam derived from Malasian rubber. It sets like wrinkled skin when it's mixed with other properties . . . secrets I'm not divulging to you which would risk the life of other pundits!'

'I never meant to risk anyone's life – Geyog's or Joonu's.'

'Geyog was not a pundit.'

'I'm not sure I know what a pundit is, but what are you doing in Tibet, Lewis, because I know now it's nothing to do with geography.'

'I'm a spy, Sonya, a British Agent, and it's everything to do with geography.'

'Espionage! So that's the mystery surrounding Lewis Joyden!'

'No mystery, only danger . . . to you as well as to me.'

'Why me?'

'Because you are who you are, and because your husband and brother are engaged in activities the British Government don't like one bit.'

'What on earth are you talking about?' She stopped and stared at him in dismay. 'What have my husband and brother to do with all this?'

'Everything. But let's not stand here freezing to death, we'll talk when we get to the *jong*.'

'I want to talk now, Lewis!'

'Very well, but you'll have to talk to yourself.' He strode ahead purposefully, leaving her at a loss for a suitable answer.

Once inside the deserted fort that reeked of urine and yak-dung, Lewis lit a fire on the hard damp stone floor of

226

the principal room. 'One thing I'll say about the Tibetans,' he grinned above the flickering match, 'they're always considerate of other travellers. The old woman in the *mi-deussa* was only digging up fresh yak-meat preserved in ice by a previous band of wayfarers for those who followed them, so that they might not starve. There's more yak-dung fuel over there in the corner, so could you kindly fetch a little over here? Thanks.'

'Lewis, I want to know what you meant about my husband and brother,' Sonya said, realizing now how greatly she had gone to pieces inside the *mi-duessa* by imagining Tibetans were cannibals! She seated herself before the feeble fire.

'All in good time, Sonya. Can you make Tibetan tea?'

'No.'

'Then I suppose I'll have to do it.' From his pack he took out a wad of tea and sliced it with a knife before tossing the piece into a small brass cooking bowl that had belonged to Geyog. 'Now we'll have to wait until it reaches eighty-five degrees centigrade before it boils since we are approximately fourteen thousand feet high.'

'Is there anything you don't know?' Sonya asked, but her sarcasm was lost on him.

He raised his hazel eyes to her and said cheerfully, 'I am an ignorant fellow in many ways, *Mig Kar.* For instance, I want to know what your purpose is in Tibet.'

'That, Lewis, is my business.'

'And mine, *Mig Kar.*'

'Please don't call me *Mig Kar.* My name is Sonya.'

'Not in Tibet it isn't. When I call you Sonya, it's a slip of the tongue, and slips of the tongue have come to me more readily since I fell into your company. After all, we're all human and partial to a pretty face – God knows they're rare enough in this place! However, carelessness is not a good habit to fall into in my profession.'

'The profession of a killer?'

'A government agent, *Mig Kar.* What do you know about Dorjiev?'

'Lewis, is this another one of your bizarre jokes?' she asked, getting angry.

227

'I assure you, *Mig Kar*, joking is the farthest thing from my mind right now . . . ahh! The water bubbles . . . hand me over that bamboo funnel. Thanks. Now then, where was I?' He vigorously stirred the tea. 'Dorjiev, right. So tell me all about Dorjiev. Where, when and how you two met in St Petersburg. Tell me what your brother and husband are doing gun-running and tell me where you stand in all this.'

Sonya watched him pour the tea through the latticed bamboo funnel in which he had placed a lump of yak-butter. The hot tea melted the butter, after which Lewis removed the inner basket of strained tea-leaves, added a pinch of salt to the brew in the outer funnel, which he then whisked long and hard with a wooden disc on a long handle until the buttered and salted tea frothed and bubbled like champagne. 'I met Dorjiev only once,' she said, keeping her eyes fixed upon his dexterous hands. 'Not in St Petersburg, but secretly . . . at my husband's country estate at Tula. We were on our honeymoon at the time. I don't know what transpired between Dorjiev and my husband, only that they both left shortly afterwards for St Petersburg. A few weeks later Kolya left for Lhasa.'

'With Dorjiev?'

'No, with Barakov.'

'Do you know what was discussed?'

'I've no idea.'

'When did this secret meeting take place?'

'In the summer of my seventeenth birthday,' she said with a distant look in her grey eyes. 'Five years ago, if you must know.'

'Yes, I must know, Sonya, it's important.' He handed across her bowl of buttered tea. 'Tea like Joonu never made,' he said softly and realized at once he had said the wrong thing when she bowed her head over the bowl and sat as stiff as a wooden doll. 'I'm sorry . . . '

Presently she raised her head to look at him. 'Why Joonu?' she asked in a muffled voice. 'Couldn't you spare Joonu in your grand game of espionage?'

'Sometimes, Sonya, in my line of work, one person's life is deemed expendable in order to save many more lives.'

She gazed at him in horror. 'No. I don't believe you can

228

say such a thing! Is that why you killed Geyog?'

'Geyog was dangerous. He was a counter-spy. While pretending to work for the British, he was actually working for your lot – like Dorjiev.'

'My lot! Is that what you classify me as, Lewis – your lot?'

'Sonya . . . !'

She got up and left his presence.

Finding a crumbling stone staircase, she ascended it to a narrow parapet overlooking the moonlit snow-filled valley overshadowed by the mountains. Mountains, mountains everywhere, tangible and intangible and all insurmountable! Lewis came behind her.

'Sonya,' he said, his voice hard. 'One day I'll be able to explain the real reasons for my presence in Tibet, but not now because too much is at stake. Try to understand.'

'Oh, I understand all right. I understand that two good men were considered expendable by you, in fulfilment of your *duty*!'

'Sonya, believe me when I tell you I killed Geyog in self-defence. He tagged on to me soon after Rudok. He had a shrewd idea of who I was but couldn't prove it. We led each other along in a game of now you see me, now you don't. Please try to understand. The night you and he talked so freely, you let slip many things. Geyog was no fool but the best in the business – the business of espionage. Yes, he was educated at the Drepung like Dorjiev. His father was a Chukpo-Kudak, a rich nobleman who married an English missionary. Geyog was trained in turn by the British, then the Tibetans and lastly the Russians whom he chose to serve like his counterpart, Dorjiev. Geyog was put on my tail to find out what I was doing in Tibet and when the time was right, to get rid of me before I reached Lhasa. He could speak English, and he knew all about my habits because he had been tutored accordingly – even to using his left hand! That's why he could spout to you bits of Byron and I dare say other literary greats given the chance. At the farmhouse you were swayed by his charm and kindness after what I'd put you through . . . and that was my folly, because I'm not used to handling women in the midst of business. You virtually told him who I was and after that, it was him or me. We fought each other in the river . . . and he lost. There it is, Sonya, believe or disbelieve as you wish.'

'And what about Joonu? Why did poor innocent Joonu have to be your scapegoat?'

'That was never my intention . . . '

She rounded on him. 'Never your intention? Tell me, Lewis Joyden, what then was your intention? It was you, wasn't it, who went to fetch the Ponpo to try Joonu and me for a murder you committed?'

'You think I went for the Ponpo?' he asked in amazement.

'Didn't you, Lewis, didn't you?'

'No, Sonya, I did not! The muleteer fetched the Ponpo. He had witnessed Geyog and me fighting down by the riverside and, wanting to get even with me because I shunned his rat-ridden house and withheld blessings from him, he took full advantage of the situation by bringing the Ponpo on the scene. I was returning for you and Joonu to put you both in the picture when things were taken right out of my hands by the appearance of the Ponpo.'

'I can't believe such a story. Why would you choose to fight where the muleteer could so conveniently see you both?'

He sighed in exasperation. 'I never chose to fight anywhere. After Geyog hit me on the back of the neck he carted me down to the river on the back of one of the mules. By then I began to wake up a little. Geyog had Joonu's knife which he decided to use on me. The Survey of India taught me many things, and along with my geography lessons I learned the art of self-defence.'

'In other words, you murdered Geyog in the line of duty?'

'Yes, Sonya, if that's the way you want to look at it.'

'I don't want to, Lewis; you leave me no choice. You keep evading the issue of Joonu. Is it a guilty conscience? Was Joonu your expendable person? I want some answers, Lewis, before I can conceivably believe anything you say.'

'Yes, Sonya! Joonu was my expendable person.'

It was a long time before she felt like speaking to him or

looking at him again. In the white night she gazed upon the dead valley from the parapet of the ruined *jong*. 'We are enemies you and I, Lewis Joyden,' she murmured.

'No Sonya. I don't believe that. Our countries might be at variance, but you and I understand each other.'

'Do we, Lewis? I don't think so.' She climbed down from the parapet, and descended the staircase back to the room with the fire. Reseating herself before it, she extended her hands to its welcome warmth. She was cold, her fingers and feet frozen, her heart as solid as a lump of ice that refused to be taken in by any sugary words. Sonya stretched out her bedroll and crept into it.

Lewis settled himself in a far corner of the room and pretended to meditate. 'Do you love your husband?' he suddenly asked from his shadowy corner.

'No, Lewis, I do not.' Sonya pulled her sleeping bag up to her chin.

'He's alive, here in Tibet, don't you want to know where he and your brother are hiding out . . . or do you already know?'

'No, I don't know. I came to Tibet to find out.'

'Kirsten is living on the outskirts of Gyantse, at a place called Thug-Phul. Your husband is in Lhasa, inside the Potala to be exact.'

'I won't ask you from where you glean your information. You are engaged in espionage, and beyond that I don't want to know anything more about you, Mr Joyden.'

'Fair enough. I know I haven't treated you well, but believe me when I say there was nothing I could do about the stripes you were to receive at the muleteer's hands. If it's any consolation to you, it hurt me terribly to see you ill-treated, but I could do nothing about it without giving myself away. While the Ponpo and I were in Rika's farmhouse I got him drunk, and in doing so managed to persuade him to reduce your sentence, otherwise the muleteer would have drawn blood on the first stripe you were to receive. Joonu was another matter altogether . . . but I was grateful to him when he rescued you from those two lashes just in the nick of time . . . '

'*In the nick of time*?' Sonya raised her head to stare at

231

him. 'Is that all you can say? My God, Lewis Joyden, what code of ethics do you go by? I was about to be severely beaten, maybe scarred and injured for the rest of my life, Joonu was brutally flogged, the sentence of mutilation hanging over his innocent head for a crime you committed, and all you can say is, *in the nick of time*!'

'Look here, Sonya, if I hadn't bribed the Ponpo and muleteer and got them convivially stupid in the two hours we sat in Rika's farmhouse before the sentence was carried out, your fate would have been far worse. The Ponpo would have made sure you received more than just two lashes of the muleteer's whip had I not put in a good word on your behalf. Joonu's loyalty and regard for you saved you from even that much. Had I interfered any more regarding you and Joonu, the Ponpo and the rest of the villagers would really have become suspicious of me and would have uncovered me for what I am, a British spy. I couldn't risk that.'

'How convenient for you a raw uncultured youth turned out to be the gentleman I had always imagined you were! How much did you part with in bribes for our sakes, thirty pieces of silver?'

'Sonya, I . . .'

'Please don't call me Sonya any more. I'm Princess Dubrovka to you, Mr Joyden.'

'So you would rather have had Geyog the cunning monk here in my place, is that it? You would rather have been his prisoner than mine?'

'Why would Geyog have kept me a prisoner? You told me he was working for the Russians, so surely he would have aided my cause, that of finding my husband and brother?'

'Perhaps, though I doubt it. Geyog would not have wished to have his style cramped by a woman tagging along with him. He would have got rid of you as positively as he wanted to get rid of me – eliminate is the word. Men like Dorjiev and Geyog, in the end, are only their own masters despite the fact they are trained in monasteries all over Tibet to help take this country out of its material backwardness while still maintaining its ancient religion and culture.

232

Russian innovation rather than Chinese suppression is the Dalai Lala's policy, and with the blessings of the High Lamas, educated Tibetan men are brainwashed to see things Russia's way. Geyog studied mysticism as well as the humanities at the Drepung, the very dichotomy of his education made him a radical and dangerous thinker.'

'So men like Dorjiev and Geyog, who are doing for Tibet what Vladimir Lenin is doing for Russia, must be "eliminated" by Englishmen like yourself because they are radical and dangerous thinkers. Is that what you're saying?'

'All I'm saying, *Mig Kar,* is that it works both ways in this "great game" of nations. Tibetan policies lean towards Russia rather than Britain, but Geyog had a very personal reason for hating the British. His mother was an English-woman, and when Geyog was about four years of age his noble Tibetan father died. Geyog's mother couldn't be bothered with a small child and put him into a monastery to be brought up by monks while she carried on with her missionary work of converting the heathen Chinese. Geyog never saw his mother again. He was a hard and dangerous man who would as soon have stabbed you in the back when he could get no more information from you – about me, yourself, about your brother and husband or anyone else in whom he was interested.'

'I only have your word for it as Geyog's dead . . . stabbed in the back by you . . . '

'In self defence, *Mig Kar.* Would you begrudge me my life?'

'Did you do anything to save my poor servant Joonu, Mr Joyden? So what do you intend to do with me, assassinate me, too, since I am classified as the enemy?'

'Don't be harsh and shrewish, *Mig Kar,* it doesn't become you. I know you are not that kind of woman.'

'How do you know what kind of woman I am?'

'You'd be surprised. Your letters over the years told me what kind of lady you are, and I have a deep respect for you. You are intelligent and brave, loyal and compassionate, warm-hearted and caring; why else would you have risked your life to come to Tibet to find a good-for-nothing brother and a dolt of a husband unless you were all those things? Why else, *Mig Kar*, tell me, please. Is it that you do love your husband, after all, and cannot live without him?'

'Yes, Mr Joyden.'

'I don't believe you, Princess, Sonya Dubrovka. Sonya, Joonu won't die – I hope. I also bribed Rika and his girls to get Joonu away as soon as my back was turned.'

An icy blast from the open door cut short any further conversation between them. Two figures muffled up in ragged fur-skins entered the *jong*.

'Oghai, oghai!' said a young man pulling aside his wrappings to reveal a glowing red face and wide friendly smile, 'you have undergone much hardship!'

'Not as much as you,' growled Lewis, shrinking into the shadows and becoming the Red Cap once more as he loudly recited the Mantra over his rosary beads.

The Tibetan put out his tongue in greeting, joined Sonya beside the fire and only then noticed his companion still standing by the door letting in the icy draught. 'Come inside, wife,' he scolded. 'The Holy Mother and Tsawai Lama are not going to eat the baby!' He turned to Sonya as his wife shut the door. 'My wife is a nervous creature and did not want to come on this journey. You see, Holy Mother, my wife was delivered of our son eight days ago. But my sick mother who lives in the next valley sent word that she is dying and wishes to see her new grandson. As I am her only child, this is my mother's first grandchild and so my wife and I had no choice but to obey. Now I hope we will reach my mother before she dies or before the weather gets much worse.'

Sonya regarded the young husband in horror. 'You have a newborn baby with you and a wife much too soon out of her lying-in bed! In these mountains with the bad weather upon us, what are you, mad? Surely the sensible thing would have been to visit your sick mother alone?'

'I told him that,' said the young wife falling on her knees beside Sonya, 'but he wouldn't listen . . his mother is the all important one to him. Now the baby cannot feed from me as my milk has dried up and he is angry with both of us because I'm tired and make slow progress while the baby does nothing but scream for milk.' The girl unwrapped the squalling bundle next to her breast and thrust the infant at Sonya. 'What am I to do, Holy Mother, I am empty and exhausted?'

'Give it yak's milk,' said the Red Cap from the shadows.

'But where will I get yak's milk, Holy Father?' asked the distraught girl.

'From the yak . . . give her some of our supply, Holy Mother,' he said to Sonya.

'We have no more yak's milk, Tsawai Lama,' Sonya reminded him as she rocked the crying baby in her arms. 'You gave the last of our yak's milk to placate the demons from that mad *Pamo* in the *mi-deussa*.'

'So we did, Holy Mother! Then give the infant buttered tea which is very good for the digestion, we have plenty of that, haven't we? The child obviously has the wind.'

The young parents smiled gratefully at the lama in the shadows, touched their foreheads to the ground and while the husband made preparations to sleep, pulling his long hessian skirt over his head together with his reindeer skins and wool blanket, the wife implored Sonya, 'Please nurse the baby for a little while, Holy Mother. Already it is daybreak and I am so tired and wish only to sleep before resuming my journey to visit my mother-in-law who will get angry with me if the baby is hungry.'

Sonya, utterly exhausted herself, nodded helplessly. She could do little else but oblige the weak and frightened girl who would never make it to the next valley unless she rested. The wife settled down beside her husband and Sonya angrily said to Lewis; 'How am I expected to feed a new born baby who hasn't learned how to drink from a bowl?'

'Dip your little finger in the brew, then stick your finger in the infant's mouth. Only make sure the tea isn't boiling otherwise you'll burn the child's tongue.'

Sonya bit back her retort and instead tried to soothe the hungry baby who pathetically and greedily sucked her finger. Every time Sonya removed her finger from the child's mouth to dip, the baby began its feeble wailing cry that, after an hour, began to get on her nerves. 'What now, Tsawai Lama?' she demanded. 'It's not hungry any more as it has finished off half a bowl of tea and its stomach is now quite distended.'

'Put it across your shoulder and bang its back.'

'Are you sure?' Sonya asked dubiously as she lifted the baby over her shoulder.

'Quite sure. It has wind, so rub its back. It'll be all right and will go to sleep once it's comfortable.'

Amazingly the baby did nod off and Sonya, nursing the child in her lap found her head dropping over it as she, too, was unable to keep her eyes open. She jerked herself upright. 'Shall I put the baby back with its mother?'

'Not yet. Give it a little while longer in case it wakes up again and starts yelling. By that time I'll have finished putting on my lama's face, and won't feel so nervous when those two start looking at me by daylight.'

Two hours later Sonya woke from her intermittent dozing. Gone was Lewis Joyden the Englishman, to be replaced once more by the Red Cap lama with his red wrinkles, slant eyes and scowling mouth, although it was impossible for the new mask to imitate exactly the features of the last one. But it was enough to give Sonya a nasty jolt seeing the Red Cap peering over her shoulder.

'Put the baby back with its mother, *Mig Kar*, and get some sleep yourself,' he hissed. 'All three are out for the count and look as if they're going to be snoring their heads off for the rest of the day, so you try and get some rest, too. You'll be needing it if we're to get to Thug-Phul.'

She looked at him in amazement. 'You're taking me to Thug-Phul?'

'Why not? It's on the way to Lhasa. You did come to Tibet to find your beloved brother, didn't you?'

She didn't know what to say. Sonya picked up the sleeping baby to put it with its mother but something made her look at the infant more closely. A purplish-white ring was very noticeable around its mouth and the infant was so still Sonya gave it a little shake. Then she touched its cheek, both cheeks, then its forehead, lips, and feverishly she loosened its tight swaddling clothes. 'Lewis!' she said sharply, her eyes round and wide upon him. 'It's not moving!'

'What do you mean it's not moving?'

236

'I don't know what's wrong with it, but it won't respond.'

'Shake it.'

'I've done that . . . it's not even breathing.'

'Then shake it again . . . no don't, let me see . . . ' He came beside her and felt the baby. 'Lord, Sonya, it's dead! Quick, put it back with its mother . . . no, not under her, beside her. She'll wake up and think it has died from the cold . . . but we've got to get out of here, fast.' He began stamping out the fire, scooping up brass bowl, tea utensils and everything else belonging to them. 'Quick, the packs, let's get out of here before they wake up.' With one hasty glance around to make sure they had not left anything of theirs behind, he slipped open the door and ushered her out into icy bright daylight.

Sonya, shattered by what had happened so swiftly, dragged along by the hand to keep her from falling behind or ending up in a snowdrift, her heart pumping in her ears, felt herself becoming lightheaded. 'Lewis,' she gasped, a terrible stitch in her side, 'Please slow down, I can't go any further.' They had been stumbling through the snow for two hours and she felt they had put enough distance between themselves and the young Tibetan couple with their dead baby.

But Lewis was remorseless. 'We'll stop long enough for you to regain your breath, but then we must press on. We must find some shelter before tonight otherwise you'll freeze to death out in the open.'

'What about you?'

'I'm all right, I'm used to the snowy mountains.'

It was then that Sonya realized he had been walking through the snow in only his open rope-sandals. She gazed up at him in astonishment, only the tip of her pink nose and her large luminous eyes showing above her scarves and shawls. 'Aren't your feet frozen?'

'Watch!' And he placed one foot deliberately in front of the other. When he lifted it, the imprint of his foot on the crystallized snow steamed as if boiling water had been poured on the frozen ground.

Disbelieving her eyes, Sonya said; 'It's a trick!'

He laughed. 'Yes, it's a trick all right, *Mig Kar*. One

taught me by an ancient and experienced Guru of the Himalayas, a mystic who could dwell among the high mountains clad only in a thin cotton shift and sometimes nothing at all. And when I talk about high mountains, I mean high mountains! Those like Everest and Kangchenjunga that are so high men cannot climb them because they are unable to breathe properly in the rarefied atmosphere of those summits. Like the baby who died back there in the *jong*,' he concluded on a sobering thought.

'Is that what you think happened to it, Lewis, lack of oxygen?'

'I'm not God, Sonya, so I don't know for certain. But yes, I dare say it was something to do with the altitude which its tiny newborn lungs couldn't cope with. But that young couple aren't going to know that, all they'll think of is that we had something to do with it and word will spread to all and sundry about a Nagspa wearing a male Sorcerer's headdress of human bones, and then we'll both be brought to trial.'

'What on earth are you talking about?'

'You, *Mig Kar*. A real Nagspa, a most feared kind of sorcerer who has magic at his command and who is able to call up demons and wears the kind of headdress you're sporting.'

'Bones . . . you said human bones.'

'That's right.'

'But the one I'm wearing is made of bamboo . . . Joonu told me.'

'Then Joonu told you wrong. What you're wearing on your head is made from one-hundred-and-eight tiny human bones. Some of them I dare say come from dead babies . . .'

With a cry of disgust Sonya swept off her headdress and tossed it away with all her strength so that it flew like an ugly bird into the far distance.

'Now your head will get cold,' Lewis laughed.

Sonya pulled her shawl round her head and glared at him. 'Could that baby possibly have died of your buttered tea and not altitude sickness?'

'Not unless your finger was poisonous. I shouldn't worry about it any more, *Mig Kar*. What's happened has happened and we've just got to be doubly cautious until we're out of the area.'

'But how could it possibly have died so suddenly and so quickly? It was hungry, but that was about all; it appeared perfectly healthy otherwise.'

'I've no idea, *Mig Kar*. I don't know why some babies die at high altitudes and others don't; I don't know why some babies starve to death in desert regions and others don't. But it must be something to do with the evolutionary process of natural selection, the strong surviving while the weak go to the wall – you know, all that controversial stuff Darwin stirred up years ago. Oh, before your time, was it? Well then, let's change the subject and put our best foot forward towards Gyantse.'

'When will we get there?'

'Next year – I hope.'

Sonya gave him a dour look from above her frosty scarf. 'If you're being facetious, Mr Joyden, it's not appreciated. I'm in no mood for your Red Cap humour – now or next year.'

He came to stand in front of her, where she had found a boulder on which to rest. Placing his hands firmly on her shoulders he peered into her face. If she did not know the face which lay behind the mask was a more human one, she would have flinched. But now she stared the Red Cap coolly in the eye when he said; 'Let's get one thing straight shall we? If we're to travel together for the next few months, this Red Cap's spouse has got to be above reproach. From now on, you're not a sorceress, a *philang*, a *Mig Kar* of the white foreign eyes or any other such rubbish, but my Jetsunma, my Reverend Lady. And no more of this Mr Joyden business, understood? I am to be called Tsawai Lama at all times by you, Jetsunma, got that?'

'I understand perfectly, Tsawai Lama. But it's a great pity this Jetsunma must travel to Lhasa with a spouse who *isn't* above reproach!' She got up from the rock, picked up her pack and put it over her shoulders before walking off ahead of him, a small stalwart figure who defied the might of the snowy Tibetan landscape while, behind her back, the Tsawai Lama smiled applaudingly.

PART THREE

The British

Chapter Seventeen

'How swiftly the days pass when one's vision embraces only happy things,' Sonya reflected aloud one morning as she plucked wild red berries from a bush before tossing them into the stewpot.

'Who wrote that?' asked Lewis.

'What do you mean who wrote it? I just said it.' Sonya sighed in exasperation. She took up the wooden spoon to stir their evening meal, and tasted the soup tentatively. 'It needs more salt . . . we haven't any more salt, Tsawai Lama. Never mind, it's now the middle of October, we've travelled together since the summer months, and I'm no nearer my goal. Why won't the water boil, Lewis?'

'Tsawai Lama to you, Reverend Lady.' He chewed the end of his pencil, his brows drawn together in deep concentration as, lying inside his warm bedroll, he settled his head more comfortably against the weight of his pack and continued scribbling in a notebook.

'We're not fifteen thousand feet any more, Tsawai Lama, or even twelve. We are now in the lush valley of the Manasarowar where autumn still reigns supreme and the treacherous mountain snows have not yet reached, so why won't the water boil?'

'Try lighting a fire under the cooking-pot, *Mig Kar.*'

She struck him on his red cap with her wooden spoon. 'You promised not to call me *Mig Kar* any more. Anyway I'm sick and tired of the eternal snows and cooking outdoors where the water takes so long to boil. I want to get to Thug-Phul and see my brother again. I want to sleep in a proper bed and eat a proper meal at a proper table. We've passed plenty of wayside inns, why can't we lodge overnight in one of them?'

'Too dangerous. Be patient, Reverend Lady, and you'll be able to spend Christmas at your noble brother's table.'

'Christmas! Why, that's another two months away! I'll never survive until then . . . not with my clothes in rags, my hands and feet raw with chilblains and blisters, my tongue swollen from poisonous berries and iced-tea, and . . . and nowhere to take a decent bath . . . ' Sonya's voice petered away on an unusual plaintive bleat which made Lewis look up and pay closer attention.

'What's wrong, Sonya?'

'Nothing is wrong, Lewis!'

'I can tell by your tone of voice something is upsetting you; I want to know what.'

'Why can't you ever be more specific about anything? Why can't you tell me exactly where we're going, when we'll arrive, the reasons for your being here; just the truth Lewis! Instead, you palm me off with half-truths the whole time – next year, Christmas, sometime, never! Why can't you ever be honest with me?'

'I don't like giving away classified information to the Russians – especially attractive aristocratic Russian women with chilblains. In my line of work it's called pillow-talk . . . ' Laughing at her, he ducked, his hands shielding his head as she threw the spoon at him. 'All right, don't hit me again, I'll talk. Would you like to hear what I've written just for you?'

'No.'

'Very well then, come over here and sit beside me. I'll forget my poem if you'll forget the dashed soup . . . I've got something far better for an emergency like this.' From his *amphag* he withdrew a spirit flask. 'As one gazes upon the luscious peach, hanging from the top of the peach-tree, out of reach, so I gazed upon the maiden of noble birth charming and full of youthful vigour . . . Maiden towards

244

whom my heart leaps, could'st thou but be mine – Tsang Yang Gyatso was a romantic old Dalai Lama after all was said and done. Here you are, brandy to warm the cockles of your heart, so come sit beside me and tell me what's troubling you apart from altitude sickness.'

'I hate your face, Tsawai Lama,' Sonya said, smiling despite herself.

'Then why didn't you say so!' Without further ado he began peeling off his false face. 'Only for you would I do this, Princess Dubrovka,' he said as the real Lewis Joyden began to reveal himself once more. 'As we're still so far from civilization and I, too, am growing bristly and sweaty beneath the mask, I'll come clean. There! Satisfied?' He grinned disarmingly. 'On this benign autumn evening, ensconced as we are in our secret valley away from the world, let's sit together and enjoy the song of the *djolmo*.' He patted his bedroll invitingly. 'Could'st thou but be mine!' He sighed.

'Lewis, have you already been drinking that stuff?' Sonya asked suspiciously.

'Me? Goodness, no! I never drink on duty – not unless I have reason to. You are sad this evening and I wish to know the reason. I know I'm not much of a travelling companion, ugly to boot and without the drawing-room conversation a lady of rank would require, but I do my best.' He reached across for her hand and laced his fingers in hers. 'We've been together night and day for a very long time. We've talked long hours, all day and all night sometimes, and never have we grown tired of one another. Not only is that a revelation in itself – which must mean something – but you and I have also been pen-friends for a good number of years now, and in all that time we've never had reason to fall out . . . '

'You've forgotten Joonu.'

'Were you in love with him?' He leaned closer, his dark eyes searching, and the way he was looking at her Sonya found most disturbing. Her heart began to beat a little faster, her breath caught in her throat, and she could not bring herself to meet his eyes.

'Don't be absurd,' she said angrily.

'He was in love with you then?'

'Joonu was my faithful servant.'

'It has been known for a faithful servant to fall head over heels in love with his mistress.'

'Whatever you're implying, I don't like it!' She withdrew her hand from his.

'Why else would a faithful servant lay down his life for his mistress unless he loved her to distraction?' Lewis insisted, half teasingly, half serious and altogether in a mood Sonya could not pinpoint. He seemed almost reckless, and she would have believed it had she not known Lewis Joyden better. He drew her firmly to him, his hands reaching around her waist to pull her down beside him. 'You're frozen,' he said, opening his bedroll wider and moving aside to allow her room to lie beside him. 'It's cold out there in the big wide world, so let's get to know each other even better while keeping the world at bay.'

Against her feelings of propriety and the right and wrong thing to do, she was drawn to him and his strange mood that highlighted their mystic world of mountains, magic and danger. Lying beside him with the blanket drawn up to their chins, her hand in his, he said; 'Listen to the *djolmo*, Sonya. The *djolmo* is a Tibetan songbird. In your grand-mother's house at Abingdon did you ever lie in your bed at night and listen to the nightingale in her garden? Well then, listen now to an English nightingale in the throat of a Tibetan *djolmo*. The music of Chopin, Liszt, Wagner all rolled into the one song of the earth.'

She turned her face into his shoulder, her voice and tears muffled; 'Lewis, oh Lewis, I think I love you . . . I think I've always loved you . . . '

'Sonya, hush.'

'No, I can't . . . I must say what I feel. I'm not an Englishwoman brought up to hide her feelings. I'm Russian, born and bred, despite the fact of having an English grand-father. I have to be honest with myself . . . and with you, Lewis. Ever since you dragged me out of the River Thames and became angry with me afterwards for pretending to die on you, I've loved you. I loved the look on your face then, and I love it now . . . even while I ask you not to look at me

246

with that pained expression in your eyes. I never asked for this to happen, and even now I can't believe it, that we are both here in Tibet together, drawn together by fate . . . '

'Drawn together by my government and yours, Sonya.'

'But still the instruments of fate, kismet, destiny, whatever!' She flung up her hand dramatically.

He smiled above her head. 'Nothing so fanciful. I don't believe in such things, Sonya, only in the practicality of our lives. You came to Tibet in search of Kirsten and Kolya because you love one and want to be free of the other. I came to Tibet because I was detailed to find out what you, your husband and brother were up to – as I was detailed all those years ago to find out what they were doing in England. Fate, kismet and destiny didn't land me in the River Thames, but Her Britannic Majesty's Foreign Office in Whitehall. One way or another I had to establish contact with your father or your brother. I did so one midsummer afternoon in England with the aid of a frayed mooring rope. I knew you and your family came along there at weekends, out for a Sunday afternoon's jaunt on the river in *The Belle Dame Sans Merci*, so I manoeuvred our meeting – or rather, the meeting with your father and brother. My encounter with you was incidental to the plot and, incidentally, almost wrecked it.'

'Am I still incidental to your plot?' she asked, gazing up at him with expectation and a quizzical smile. 'Or have I ruined everything with my protracted schoolgirl crush?'

'You're not supposed to ask me such things,' he said, returning her smile ruefully.

'I know, Lewis, I know.' She patted his shoulder reassuringly before pushing aside the blanket to climb out of his sleeping-bag. 'I'm being very unfair to you. You're here on a political assignment – that of eliminating my brother and husband to stop the flow of Russian arms to the Tibetans so that Great Britain can walk in unimpeded via the Chumbi Valley to take Lhasa for the British. I'm sorry I'm in the way. I'm sorry I've ruined things for you by emotionally attaching myself to you and I'm sorry I've ruined our supper because all the water has boiled away in the stewpot, and the juniper berries and the duck you shot all those days

247

ago on the shore of the Manasarowar have left only the high smell of charred bones – which somehow represents to me the smell of Tibet!'

'Sonya . . . come here, please don't go.' He drew her back. 'Don't be angry with me. I know I'm a clumsy oaf at times, but you mean more to me than I can say. I want you to know that you're like no other woman I've ever met, and that I admire and respect you deeply; you must know that. But this is neither the time nor place for us to throw caution to the winds by becoming emotionally dependent on one another. We're in great danger, both of us. I don't want anything to happen to you before you return to Russia . . . or before we can again pick up the threads of our lives in England where we can make rational plans and know they will continue to fruition.'

'Plans, Lewis? What plans?'

'Just trust me, Sonya, that's all I'm asking.'

'I trust no one. All the trust I ever had has been betrayed time after time. The only one I trust is myself.' She turned her head away, but not before he had seen her grey eyes moist, accusing him of further betrayal. His forefinger turned her chin again to face him. She met his eyes, and Lewis read there what he hoped to see, yet, at the same time, was perturbed at the depth of her feelings. 'Lewis, Kolya and I are not really husband and wife. Our marriage was never consummated. I don't know what physical love is, only what I feel inside which has nothing to do with admiration or respect – but an intangible wanting that always ends up with my seeing you in Kolya's place.'

'God, Sonya!' he said, falling back and clasping his forehead as he looked up into the fading branches of the peach tree under which they lay, 'What am I supposed to say to that!'

'You don't have to say anything. I don't love Kolya. I couldn't care less whether or not I ever see him again. I came to Tibet to find Kirsten for my mother's sake, and to find out if Kolya was dead – for my sake. My marriage exists in name only, but because Kolya and I are still tied by the Church, I'm not free of him until his death can be proven. I know I will never be happy with him. If he is still alive and wants to remain here in Tibet, then I have every right to ask him to divorce me so that I can start my life anew.'

'Supposing he won't agree to such a thing?'

'Then I have tried, and what transpires afterwards will not be entirely my fault.'

'Why did you agree to marry him in the first place?'

'Oh, Lewis . . . there were reasons, so many reasons which I don't want to talk about now. All I know is, there has only ever been one man for me – and that's why destiny mocks me by throwing you in my path again after all these years. If happiness is to be found for only a very short while here in Tibet of all places, then I accept that scanty measure because it's you I love and always have done – since I was a girl who knew nothing about love.'

After a while he drew her head against his shoulder while he gazed up into the fretwork of branches above them. 'Are you really that skinny precocious little girl I salvaged from the Thames all those years ago?' he asked, marvelling.

'The very same one.'

He looked down at her and traced her lips with a wondering forefinger: 'Isn't nature astonishing! I wonder what you really look like under all that Tibetan clutter and with your hair loose.'

'Why don't you find out?'

'Samsâra,' he murmured on the flirtatious quirk of a dark eyebrow before he began to unpin her long thick braids.

'Lewis,' Sonya said laughing as she stayed his hands for a moment while her eyes gave her away. 'It'll take me all evening to redress my hair.'

'That's all right, I'm not going anywhere this evening.' With the gentle hands of a lover he untied the waist-cord of her *amphag*. 'Destiny does indeed mock us so that even the lotus trembles.' His lips were close to hers. 'What a fool your husband must be.'

ii

In December they came to Gyantse. Lhasa was now only one hundred and twenty miles away. It had taken Sonya nineteen months since leaving St Petersburg to arrive on the outskirts of the fortified town of Gyantse that, together with Shigatse a short distance away, comprised the only other two places of any note in Tibet apart from Lhasa. Thug-Phul, where her brother was supposed to be living, lay on the outskirts of Gyantse, a hamlet according to Lewis, ruled over by the Lamaist nobleman and soldier, Kuma Sidheong. Sonya's impatience to reach Thug-Phul could scarcely be contained and so she chafed at the delay Lewis imposed on them by insisting on dallying in the town of Gyantse itself.

'Jetsunma,' he said, standing with her on the iron bridge going into the town, which was adorned with prayer-flags that fluttered in the stiff wind blowing across the plain, 'I'm sorry, but we must part company for a few days. It won't seem right for us to be seen in each other's company so much, not with so many people about.'

'But am I not supposed to be your wife?' she argued fiercely, terrified of suddenly being left alone in such a big town. 'Husband and wives are supposed to live together.'

'On the road itself it was probably safer to be together, but here in town we must separate. You and I have grown too close these past few months, and two *philangs* in town are bound to give themselves away sooner or later. Please don't make it harder on me, Jetsunma, you know how much you mean to me. And we both know that a Red Cap's spouse does not stay with him overnight in his monastery, so we must abide by Tibetan rules.'

'Then why can't we both lodge at the local inn?'

'Because we can't – and there's an end to it!' His voice was coldly resolute in his role as the Red Cap, whose wrinkled face drove her to despair. 'Come on, Reverend Lady, don't sulk. I'm only leaving you for a little while.'

'Why must we remain in Gyantse at all? Why can't we go straight to Thug-Phul?'

'I have . . . things to do in town. No more arguments please, so let's go. I'll deposit you with the nuns and come for you when it's time for us to set off again for Thug-Phul.'

'Supposing the nuns discover I'm not really a Reverend

250

Lady at all? Supposing I can't maintain my disguise while I'm shut up in some grotesque Tibetan convent? Be honest, are you tired of me now you've got what you want from me?'

'You're behaving stupidly, Sonya . . . Jetsunma, and you know it!' he said angrily. 'And I doubt you'd have got this far on that kind of stupidity. If you are discovered to be a *philang* by some shortsighted and ignorant Tibetan nun, then that's your fault, not mine.'

'Do you love me, Lewis?'

'You know I do.'

'No, I don't! You've never actually told me you love me . . . '

He shook her fiercely by the shoulders. 'Don't be absurd – you're beginning to make me very annoyed! What have I been doing all these weeks if not proving to you in so many different ways how much I love you?'

'Inside your bedroll, yes . . . oh, I'm sorry! I shouldn't have said that.' Angry and confused, too, she viewed his hurt expression and cursed herself for humiliating him as well as lowering herself in his esteem. 'Forgive me, I'm just tired and strung up, that's all. Very well, show me to my convent and I'll try to put on a brave face as your absent spouse.'

'That's my girl.' He turned and shuffled off along the bridge, acting the part of the decrepit old monk he had not been for many weeks in the solitude and intimate privacy of their travels together. Behind him she asked meekly; 'Tsawai Lama, aren't you going to kiss me before we part?'

'Yes. If you catch me up and stop behaving as though I were divorcing you.' He stopped and waited for her.

More cheerfully then, and determined to hide her fears, Sonya fell into step beside him. 'I'm sorry, forgive me, Tsawai Lama. I am once again your obedient spouse who will wait for you forever if need be at the gates of her convent.'

'Glad to hear it,' he growled, taking her elbow firmly to lead her along, but with a softer expression in his hazel eyes as he glanced sideways at her.

For three days Sonya endured the overtures of the Mother-Nun in the hot smelly kitchen where she assisted with the convent meals, and then she rebelled. Not one single word had she received from Lewis, and she began to grow anxious.

'I wish to leave the convent, Reverend Mother,' she said to the sturdy and smelly Mother one morning. The Mother shoved briskly into a primitive charcoal oven the bread she had been kneading and then without wiping her sticky black fingers, used them to caress Sonya's brightly woven shawl, making no pretence that she envied Joonu's great-grand-mother's gift to the Jetsunma.

'Why, Jetsunma, are you not happy with us?' asked the Tibetan woman blowing her nose on the hem of her skirt and eyeing Sonya warily.

'Yes, very happy. But I need to go outside for a breath of fresh air. I think I'll take a walk in the town. Is there anything you want me to buy for the convent larder?'

'Jetsunma, the only thing I want is your shawl . . . it is so pretty.'

'That is not possible. It was a present from a very dear friend of mine. His grandmother made it especially for me,' Sonya said emphatically.

The Mother began to sulk as she always did when unable to get her own way. 'I will inform the Tsawai Lama you leave our protection. He gave me plenty of alms to make sure you would be well looked after until his return and so I cannot give you permission to leave these walls until he comes for you himself.'

Sonya took off the shawl. 'Here, have it with my blessing. Now I am going. If the Tsawai Lama comes for me in the meantime you can tell him I've gone to do some shopping for you in the town.'

With a triumphant smile the Mother took the bright heavy shawl and tossed it around her humpback shoulders. 'We have run out of milk to keep away the evil odours. Perhaps you can fetch me some from the town, Jetsunma, since our yaks have not enough milk for our needs.'

Keeping her thoughts and temper to herself, Sonya let herself out of the small convent, which was also a temporary refuge for pilgrims, and took the road into town half a mile away. She avoided the narrow smelly alleys, but kept to the broad main street, walking up and down for fully an hour before she recognized a figure shuffling into the inn. She knew Lewis's gait and mannerisms well enough by now. Certain the Red Cap entering the inn was none other than he, she followed.

Inside, the stench overpowered her. Filled with traders, soldiers and pilgrims, the gloomy place was rife with spitting, laughing and drinking Tibetans who mercifully took no notice of her. In a corner of the room a cockfight was in progress, feathers flying everywhere. Sonya could not see Lewis in amongst the raucous Tibetans, yet she could have sworn the old Red Cap monk who had entered was he. She marched up to the overworked innkeeper behind his bar and before her courage deserted her asked; 'Where is the Holy Father who came in here a moment ago?'

The innkeeper scratched his thick rope locks and looking her up and down said; 'Jetsunma, there are many holy men here, which one do you seek?'

'The old one, the Red Cap. He is my neglectful spouse and I wish to ask him for more money to keep me in my convent in a manner to which I'm accustomed.'

'In that case, Jetsunma, he is in there.' The innkeeper jerked his head in the direction of a tattered sacking curtain behind the counter. 'But he must not be disturbed, those are my instructions. He is in consultation with other holy men who make plans to save our town from the British. The High Lamas congregate on the orders of Kuma Sidheong himself who will defend Gyantse with his soldiers, so Jetsunma, we must leave important men alone to settle their important business as they know best.' The innkeeper sighed heavily, rubbed a grubby cloth over his wooden counter and shaking his locks continued to bemoan the fate of Gyantse. 'The *trapas*, the soldiers, the holy ones themselves, they all come to my humble house because the valleys are filling with warring nations and nowhere do the townsfolk feel safe but here. Gyantse will not fall to the *philangs*, of that I am sure. And if Gyantse does not fall, nor will Lhasa since they must march through this valley to reach the God-King's holy citadel. Now Jetsunma, what more can I do for you? A bowl of milk perhaps while you wait for your holy spouse to finish his secret meeting with those who will save our town from the enemy?'

'No . . . no thank you.' Sonya, in a dilemma, turned aside. Lewis was engaged in something that augmented no good for the Gyantse innkeeper and the rest of the Tibetans innocently gathered here, of that she was sure. But what could she say or do when, in her heart, she was in love with the enemy? To give him away was to give herself away, for, without him, her life would be empty. She hesitated before turning back to the garrulous innkeeper. 'When the Tsawai Lama who uses his left hand to drink his buttered tea re-appears, please tell him I have gone to Thug-Phul to the home of my relative.'

'Of course, Holy Mother, that is a simple matter,' said the innkeeper, reverently bowing his head before more customers claimed his attention. 'And many blessings upon your holy family, Jetsunma.'

'And yours,' she murmured before leaving his inn.

Sonya, unwilling to return to the convent to collect her packsack, decided to press on to Thug-Phul without it. Later on, she would get one of Kirsten's servants to collect it – provided of course Lewis had not been lying to her and Kirsten was indeed to be found at Thug-Phul. She asked directions to Thug-Phul and crossed a narrow wooden bridge out of town, the prayer-flags on the bridge fluttering with the inscription, *Sarva Mangalam* – Joy To All Who Are Soulless. With that thought in mind, Sonya wondered what lay in store for her at Thug-Phul.

Chapter Eighteen

Kuma Sidheong pushed back his gilded chair, wiped his mouth on his brocade sleeve and belched. Rubbing his distended belly, he beamed benevolently at his famous son-in-law, the *Tulku* once christened Kirsten Mikail Andre Vremya, and happily declared to his host; 'That was a fine meal, Kudak, thanks be to the women of your household. Now I must be away to my own house as I have important military matters to attend to. You are sure the armaments will reach us soon?'

'I am sure,' Kirsten replied laconically, refilling his silver goblet with wine, then clicking his fingers at a servant standing in the doorway to see that Kuma's pony was resaddled for the half-mile journey home.

On the threshold Kuma turned back and with a hesitant approach to another subject close to his heart asked; 'How is my dear daughter keeping? Is she with child as yet? I only ask because I am a father soon to be embroiled in war and like any father approaching the imminence of death, require to know that someone of his own blood will follow after him.'

'Have no fear on that score, father, you will not die since you are too savage a soldier.' Kirsten tossed back the wine. 'As for Dolma,' he added after his thirst-quenching draught which he repeated by again filling the goblet, 'you know very well she's barren and cannot conceive children. Why else would she have been discarded by her former noble

255

husbands?' A sardonic eyebrow raised, he quizzed his father-in-law.

Kuma, in embarrassment, smoothed down his tunic over his stomach. 'Well, I must be off . . . '

'But don't worry, father, I am still working on her,' Kirsten laughingly quaffed his wine and eyed his father-in-law over the elaborately chased goblet. 'Don't forget, I am a *Tulku* whose magical powers can defy even the gods themselves. Who knows but one of these days I might sire a little Kuma who will save the Khang-Yul from the *philang* invader, eh?'

'You make fun of me, Kudak,' Kuma growled disgruntled, 'and I don't like you when you are in this mood. You have drunk too much wine – an increasing habit of yours I am beginning to find disconcerting since it leads to impotence in a man. Just make sure your Russian people deliver my guns on time, otherwise you might find yourself once more a serf.' Kuma turned on his heel and curtly left his son-in-law's presence.

As soon as her father had gone, Dolma appeared on the threshold. 'What have you been telling him? You have made him angry again. I know, I heard him stamping and swearing from the house. You are always making fun of him and you know how upset that makes him. My father has no sense of humour, yet you insist on riling him. Have you two been making another deal between yourselves – another one that involves me?'

'Shut up, Dolma darling, and go to bed. What your father and I say between us is no business of yours. Your business is only to lay your pretty little backside on my bed and leave the rest to me . . . now what does that old crow want?' Dolma's nurse poked her head around the door and whispered something in her mistress's ear.

'She says there is a Jetsunma at the door who wishes to interview the Rishi possessed of supernatural powers who is my husband.'

'What I love about you Dolma, is your ability to communicate the simple in the most elaboratel terms possible,' Kirsten told her, adding carelessly; 'Tell the Reverend Lady to go away. I'm conducting no more magical interviews tonight. Tell her I am in session with my *Yidam.*'

'She has come a long way, my lord and master. She has been going round and round in circles for the past few hours trying to find your whereabouts.'

'Then that's her bad luck.'

'We cannot send her away without food and rest.'

'We cannot, but I can. I'm going to bed.' Kirsten, yawning, removed himself from his dining table and staggered into the entrance hall of his large house where a ragged pilgrim-woman, dead on her feet, had been kept waiting.

'Kirsten, is it really you?' she asked, incredulity in her voice. 'Is it really you behind all that paint, costume and nonsense?'

'Sonya . . . *Mon Dieu*! It cannot be . . . yet only my sister can speak with a voice like that . . . ' He came before her and placing his hands on her shoulders stared disbelievingly into her grimy pinched face . . . Jetsunma . . . Reverend Lady, what in God's name are you doing here, Sonya?'

'I might well ask the same of you, Kirsten Vremya,' she said stiffly. 'I've been standing here for the past hour while they only wished to send me away again since you were dining with gluttony. Who was that man who pushed past me so rudely? I must say, Kirsten, in our father's house, the servants always knew their place.'

He groaned while ushering her away from Dolma and the nurse staring ogle-eyed at them. 'It is you . . . My God! Do you know we'll both be hung drawn and quartered if Kuma discovers you are here . . . come in here. Go to bed!' he hissed at his wife and her nurse. 'Go to bed otherwise I'll perform *dragpoi-dubthab* on both of you.' They scuttled away at once.

'What did you threaten them with that they should both disappear so promptly?' Sonya asked with a little smile as she sunk into his chair and eyed the remnants of his meal while Kirsten, suddenly sober, shut the door on his household and poured himself more wine.

'A magic rite to bring about injury and death . . . now, do you want some wine before you tell me what you're doing here of all places?'

'Yes please.' She took the silver goblet eagerly. 'I got lost. No one told me it would be so difficult to locate your house. It really is in the back of beyond, so why are you in hiding, Kirsten?'

'Sonya, for God's sake, what are you doing in Tibet?' he asked, cutting her short in utter exasperation.

'I came to look for you. I always knew you weren't dead. It was a feeling I had about you. When we were children we always said we would stay close to each other even unto death in view of father's aggression and mother's incompetence to cope with her life and ours. She's sick, perhaps even dying, Kirsten, and she wants you to come home.'

He clapped a hand to his white-painted brow. 'I'm sick! I'm imagining all this. My sister comes two thousand miles to tell me this . . . Sonya, I'm my own person, you have no right to hound me so far on a whim of yours . . . '

'Oh, it was no whim, Kirsten, I assure you. I spent two years studying the Tibetan and Chinese languages as well as the culture and customs of this country. I've spent almost another two years integrating myself into the ways of Tibetan life while travelling. You are in trouble, I sense it. I want to help you, that's why I'm here.'

'The only way you can help me is by getting out of here again, fast!'

'Are the Tibetans keeping you a prisoner, Kirsten? Are they blackmailing you? Tell me what really happened after Barakov sent you and Kolya on that foolhardy journey across the Chang-Tang. Were you made a prisoner? Did they force you to acquiesce to their demands on fear of punishment and death? Why are you doing this to mama and me?'

'No, no, no!' he moaned, closing his eyes and sinking dramatically into the gilded chair Kuma Sidheong had previously occupied. 'Oh, oh, oh, I don't believe this to be true! I have become a victim of my own magical powers! Often I have dreamed of you and mama buried away in Kirovsky Ploshad, weaving away at the mouldy tapestry of your lives, and now I'm being confronted with the rein-

258

carnation of my own shortcomings. I want to be free, Sonya . . . do you understand that?' He rounded on her fiercely, his grey eyes so much like hers narrowed and filled with conflict and aggression. 'I want to be free of the trappings of our kind of civilization, I want to be my own man!'

'By being a prisoner of another man? A tribal soldier who holds you to ransom?'

'You don't understand. I'm nobody's prisoner. For once I am my own person. Not mama's, not yours, not papa's, not Kolya's or even the Tsar's. I am me, Kirsten Vremya, and I'm very happy in my role as *Tulku*-supreme in a primitive land that nevertheless has great potential.'

'You always were a very good actor, Kirsten,' Sonya said in disgust as she put down the goblet on the table. 'However, I don't believe a word you say. I want to know the real reason for this grotesque charade of yours, the reason why you turned your back on Russia and the people you love. You cannot be what you are not! You are not a Tibetan, a *Tulku*, or even a man to be respected because you are nothing but a sham who has caused great heartache to the people who love you the most. We all thought you were dead – even Princess Irene, your erstwhile mistress in St Petersburg – you remember her?'

'There you go again, lowering me closer to the floor than a cockroach. You did it once before, Sonya, in the matter of Ivan Ivansky for which I never forgave you. Don't do it again. Leave me alone, Sonya, and go back to St Petersburg.'

'No, Kirsten. Not until I'm satisfied that you're truly happy in what you are doing. I know you're engaged in a dangerous pursuit – gun-running, as it appears to be called. You're supplying Russian artillery to the Tibetans in order to prevent the British from occupying Lhasa . . . '

'Who told you that?'

'Never mind. I found it out on my travels through the country.'

'Is such a thing so very bad? For God's sake, Sonya, whose side are you on?'

'I can see this is getting neither of us very far,' Sonya

259

said, tired beyond belief. 'I suggest we resume this discussion – rapidly becoming a confrontation – in the morning.'

'What a good idea,' he said with irony. 'Meanwhile, how am I to explain you away to my wife and her father?'

Sonya smiled. 'I am a holy woman, a Jetsunma whom your noble wife must automatically respect. I will ask her for a bed for the night.'

'Do that. But if you breathe one word about our true relationship, I'll see you back on the road to Rudok faster than you can say Sonya Vremya!'

'Sonya, Princess Dubrovka,' she reminded him.

'And that's another thing, all the time you've been here enquiring into my business, you've never once asked about your husband, Prince Nikolay Dubrovka! Sometimes I just don't understand you, Sonya.'

'You can tell me about Kolya in the morning. Just now I'm so tired I could drop. Please ask Dolma where I can sleep – and Kirsten, don't think I've come here to interfere in your life. I'm only happy you're alive, well and happy. I just had to make sure, that's all, my dearest brother.' Rising from her chair, she went to him and kissed him on the forehead. 'Kirsten, I know you have never forgiven me for what happened over Ivan, that's why I've travelled two thousand miles, to beg your forgiveness.'

'I don't believe you; you're a little liar and blackmailer,' he said gruffly, nevertheless clasping her hand tightly. 'You've always been your own person, Sonya, and that's what I envy most about you, your ability to pick yourself up and start all over again without bearing a grudge. That's what I'm trying to do, trying to start again in a new land. Yes, we will talk again in the morning as I, too, am tired and confused. And Sonya . . . ' He drew her back for an instant. 'I'm glad you're here, dear sister of mine.' He kissed the back of her hand in a gently chivalrous gesture before dismissing her into Dolma's keeping.

ii

The voice of the white-faced *Tulku* from his gilded chair was strange and guttural, speaking in a trancelike fashion, terrifying to Dolma's ears. He had made objects fly around the room and had put a curse on a servant who had offended so that the man had suddenly appeared with bulging eyes, swollen throat and terrifying pains in the groin. Dolma had already, very early, placed bowls of milk throughout the house to placate the evil spirits, and now, walking inadvertently into the main room of the house, she saw her husband, the *Tulku*, rise up out of his chair like a great gold and scarlet bird with wings outstretched, ready to fly across the ceiling, able to devour her with scarlet mouth, tear her limb from limb with scarlet talons painted with the blood of the dead. With a screech of fear, Dolma dropped to her knees, her forehead pressed to the floor so that she might not look upon the *Tulku*'s magical rite and be blinded for her boldness – as he had once promised.

'I am the great Rishi-Kudak, noble sage of Ozymandious, possessed of supernatural powers, so look on my mighty works, O ye of little faith, and tremble . . . by tonight, Dolma darling, I will have beside me, sitting right here at my right hand, my little sister reincarnated from the *Bardo* of emptiness. I will do this thing, for I am what I am, the great Rishi-Kudak whom people seek from far and wide so that I might teach them my magic. But no one is like me. Only I am able to bring back the dead to become again the living, because I am who I am, half-man, half-god. You will welcome her, won't you dear wife? You will see to all her material comforts, won't you, my treasure? You won't believe one single word she says about me, will you Dolma, my pretty one? And above all, you'll never breathe a word to your father about her, will you, darling?'

Dolma, still with her arms wrapped around her head protectively as she knelt at her husband's feet, alternatively nodded and shook her ornate silver and jewelled headdress in accordance with Kirsten's demands. His arms folded beneath his elaborate cloak, he stood over her, looking down on her cowering mound with amusement. Three times he walked round and round her and then commented, 'You're in a very interesting position, my love. I think I'll take you right now on the floor. But first let me hang up my boots outside the door to let the rest of your Tibetan

261

peasants know who's in possession of their noble mistress.'

Later in the day, Sonya was surprised and touched by the friendliness and consideration Dolma showed her. She was given a small bedroom to herself rather than the straw pallet she had occupied the previous night on the floor of the nurse's room, and a bunch of dried thyme appeared some time during the day, placed on her pillow, a perfumed reminder of Dolma's change of heart towards humble pilgrims. At the evening meal, she, Kirsten and Dolma sat companionably round the table laid with silver bowls and goblets and clean white linen. Kirsten said with seeming indifference; 'Dolma darling, you see what I can do with my magical powers? You see how potent a person I can be? I told you, didn't I, my pretty, that tonight the Jetsunma would become my noble sister, called up from the *Bardo* of emptiness where the dead go? Go on Sonya, say something to my wife. Tell her who you really are and where you've come from. Oh, don't look so astonished, my dear, Dolma won't breathe a word to anyone, will you, my precious?' He squeezed his wife's plump cheek affectionately and made her blush.

Sonya, suddenly uncomfortable and deeply embarrassed in the presence of her amorous brother and his docile wife, looked from one to the other in some confusion. Kirsten, with an exaggerated air of insouciance, and grinning broadly, continued in lordly fashion; 'You see, Sonya, you are now a reincarnated being in Dolma's eyes. You have become my beloved sister with one fell stroke of my magic wand. Dolma believes everything I say and do – which is as it should be where a dutiful wife is concerned. The only problem is she's barren and hardly in the first flush of youth any more. Before me, she had three other noble husbands who all abandoned her to the wolves because she was so useless in bed. When Kuma got his hands on me and found out from what kind of noble house I came, his attitude towards me changed remarkably. Overnight I was taken from his pig-pen into his daughter's bedroom where he begged me to sire a little version of himself so that he

262

could go away to fight the British with peace of mind, knowing that if he died in battle, his noble house would have an heir. The trouble is, air is all we've managed to produce so far since nothing else appears to be going on in Dolma's womb.'

'Kirsten, I don't think I ought to remain here listening to all this,' Sonya interrupted unhappily. 'It's embarrassing for me and for Dolma.'

'I thought you wanted to hear about what befell me on Barakov's Mission?' Kirsten replied peevishly as he poured red wine into his goblet.

'I do. But I'd rather you kept your marital problems to yourself.'

'I have no marital problems, darling girl, so don't be such a prude. Dolma certainly isn't. She'd go with anyone who'd make her father happy. And he admires me so much, he even gave me this ugly stone box in which to sire a noble grandson. All right then, we won't talk about my wife, we'll talk about me instead, since I'm the great *Rishi-Kudak* to all these ignorant Tibetan peasants.'

Kirsten, Sonya noticed, drank and talked with a kind of desperation, and so she stayed with him rather than abandon him there and then to his self-pity and the morbid release he found in insulting his wife while drinking far too much.

'If I'm to explain what is going on here, we'll speak Russian – I've almost forgotten how after all these years of grunting primitive sounds, so it'll give me great pleasure to talk to you in our native tongue – oh, don't worry about Dolma, she'll ogle at us doltishly while admiring our magical powers in being able to converse in a language known only in the *Bardo* of emptiness,' Kirsten scoffed before embarking on his story. 'All went well until the return journey to Russia. Your husband and Barakov fell out over a difference of opinion. Kolya thought the whole Legation ought to stick together as there was safety in numbers. Things weren't going too well for us, what with sickness, death and shortages of food and pack-animals. You've probably gathered by now that hell isn't hot or centered in the bowels of the earth but is right here in this frozen ice-cube they call Tibet. However, I digress. Kolya was ordered to take a surveying-party in one direct line from Lhasa to Khotan across the Chang-Tang, a journey of some eight hundred miles, in order to chart the area for the Russian Geographical Society of which father is President, as you well know. However, Barakov was uncooperative and showed his mealyness by giving us the minimum of supplies and men. Our party consisted of some twenty men with thirty pack-animals and three quarters of those numbers were lost before we reached Thok Daurakpa. While we were licking our wounds, Kuma's men found us. They did not believe we were a legitimate enterprise sent from the Tsar to the Dalai Lama's Court and shot us up with their rusty rifles. No one was seriously hurt, but five men against sixty was suicide. We surrendered – thereby boosting Kuma's ego. He took us to Lhasa as his prisoners. By then the Tibetans had done a volte-face as is their custom when the Chinese and British tread on them. They ignored the treaty we had made only a few months previously and we were treated as spies and worse. To show us they meant business, two of our party were treated to a stay in the scorpion's den below the Potala, the third died of a fever while Kolya himself remained in the hands of the High Lamas who brainwashed him into believing he was a reincarnation of Chenrezig. Kolya always was a bit unbalanced.' Kirsten took a deep breath, replenished his goblet and sighed. 'And I was brought here as Kuma's vassal – it's a Tibetan habit called the spoils of war.' He smiled benignly at Dolma. 'Lucky girl, eh, sweetheart?' He squeezed her hand – too tightly Sonya feared by the expression on Dolma's face.

Sonya cleared her throat. 'It's an extraordinary story, Kirsten.'

'Dear girl, it gets even more bizarre. Do you want to hear the rest?'

'Of course.'

'Well then, after being beaten to death every day, in between scraping out the pig and yak muck on Kuma's farm, working a thirteen hour day and falling asleep beside more rats and lice than I care to mention, he decided to put me to stud with Dolma here . . . not that I minded in the least, *Mon Dieu*, no! But it was rather a shock to the system to be taken one day from the underside of a yak to the topside of a voluptuous woman even if she did smell like a Parisienne tart in high summer. So, at the time, I wondered what his little game was. I now know. While I behave myself with Dolma in the bedroom, I'm treated with respect. Kuma, you see, still lives in hope.'

'Forgive me, Kirsten, but you've lost me. How did you get involved with all this magical rubbish, earn yourself a reputation far and wide for being the greatest *Tulku* for miles, as well as getting caught up in supplying arms to the Tibetans?'

He shrugged. 'Simple really, it was a matter of survival. After one year in Dolma's bed with no son and heir produced, I had to think of something very quickly lest I was relegated back to the pig-pen. This is a country of mysticism and magic and I studied, observed and practised the art of deception to such a degree, I can even fool myself at times. It's all a hoax really. I know it, but they fortunately do not. The fellow you saw this morning with his neck swollen and his unmentionables seized up, has epidemic parotitis which has developed into orchitis – if that sounds too clinical for you, dear sister, at the Kutuzov Barracks we called it mumps and inflammation of the testes. No curse from me, only an act of God, but I play on these people's ignorance and superstition, and for the past few years I've got by splendidly.

Kuma Sidheong shows me respect and, I think – at least I hope – a certain amount of fear. I play on that, too. The costume and make-up help, it impresses people. They come from far and wide to ask for my assistance if they want a neighbour to drop dead or a sick yak cured of milk-curdling disease. It's all in the mind, Sonya.'

'Yes,' she murmured remembering Lewis Joyden's bare feet melting the snow and his naked body shining on a glacis at midnight, 'someone I know does a similar thing. Tibet is indeed a strange land. How did you get caught up in supplying Russian arms to Tibet?'

'Ah! That was my most strategic and brilliant move in

265

this whole game. Dorjiev set up the deal for me. Russian arms get here via Afghanistan, Dorjiev and I get our cut and Kuma Sidheong gets his obsolete weapons. Gunrunning is a very lucrative business all round, believe me. The most wonderful part of it all for me is to do it under the noses of the British while Kuma thinks he's getting good up-to-date weapons from Russia to stop any aggressive advance the British might make. Many noses will be put out of joint when the time comes and everyone finds out what's been happening – and I can sit on the sidelines laughing my sides out because I've earned myself respect and a veritable fortune in the meanwhile.'

Sonya kept her opinions and fears to herself. 'Is Kolya still alive, Kirsten?'

He shrugged. 'Yes, I think so. Last time I heard anything about him from Kuma, he had apparently walled himself up like an ascetic with only a tiny opening allowing for food and water to be passed through to him. It was of his own volition, Kuma assured me. It's what very devout lamas do here in order to gain their special heaven – some of them living in such holes for forty years or more without seeing the light of day. If Kolya's gone off his head, then mercifully he won't have to do his penance for forty years since he's already a-hundred-and-ten.'

Sonya shuddered while Kirsten drank. Dolma looked at them with kohl black eyes and smiled every time she caught either her husband's or Sonya's eye. 'If you'll excuse me, I'll go to bed now,' Sonya said, leaving the table. 'Kirsten, could you send a servant to the convent at Gyantse where I've left my belongings. If I'm to stay here with you and Dolma, I shall need a change of clothing – although I've very little clothing left to change into.'

'Dolma will lend you something now she knows who you are. After all, she has a rich husband now who can buy her all her heart desires. I'm far richer than I ever was in Russia. Not only do the Tibetans, Chinese and Russians pay me, but also humble peasants and *trapas* when I cure a constipated yak or hand out magical incense sticks. And all through my own initiative and astuteness! What a clever *Rishi* I am to gather such a stockpile of gold, silver and jewels to get me out of this hole one day. I ought to have been a doctor like Pratikayit; I'd be even richer in this god-forsaken place where nobody can tell a sick bat from a sheepskin.'

Sonya left her brother to his moroseness and went to bed. She did not know what time it was when Dolma awakened her, only that it was very dark outside and the rest of the occupants of the house were still asleep. 'Madam-sister, madam-sister, a holy man is asking for you. He says you were his devout companion along the journey and now he only wishes to make sure you are safe and well. What shall I do?'

Sonya was wide awake instantly. 'Dolma show him in here. Don't let my brother know this man comes, promise me?'

Dolma nodded vigorously, her two heavy braids jerking like belt-ropes.

'Don't tell anyone else either!' Sonya hissed in her wake.

Presently Dolma ushered in the shuffling stooping Red Cap and the moment she had closed the door behind him, he pounced. 'What the devil are you playing at, Sonya?'

Sonya, clad only in a thin sleeveless shift, her knees as well as the bed covers drawn up to her chin, could only welcome with happy relief the man who had seated himself on the end of her bed. His face was in darkness and she was relieved that she could not see his Tibetan profile, but only the Englishman in shadow.

'I thought you'd never come,' she whispered.

'You were supposed to wait for me at the convent! I told you not to move from there until I came for you. How on earth did you find your way here alone?'

'With great difficulty.'

'Why did you leave, Sonya?'

'You never came to the convent and I thought you'd abandoned me, so I made my own way here.'

'You little fool.' His voice was hollow as he reached for her hand in the darkness. 'I was out of my mind wondering what had become of you. The innkeeper told me you'd been enquiring after me otherwise I wouldn't have known for several more days that you'd left the convent. You haven't told your brother about me, have you?'

'What kind of woman do you think I am, Lewis?' she asked coldly, but just then the bedroom door opened and Kirsten, a brass butter-lamp in his hand, stood on the threshold.

'I heard noises,' he said in that electrifying moment when Lewis, his head low and in shadow seemed to shrink into himself while Sonya, aghast, could only stare speechless at her smiling brother.

'What's going on here, Sonya? Who is this man?'

'I . . . I . . . some . . . someone I met on the journey. We . . . we were very close. He protected me along the way, Kirsten . . . ' Wildly she searched for words and excuses.

'My name is Geyog. I am from the Drepung where I am returning after collecting alms to support my monastery,' Lewis said with great presence of mind in a strong clear Tibetan voice Sonya did not recognize, all the time keeping his head averted and giving the impression he had eyes only for the woman in the bed. 'I called at the convent in Gyantse where the Jetsunma was staying and they told me she had forgotten her packsack. I have brought it to her as I know she will have need of it. Forgive me, *Rishi-Kudak*, but I know who you are, for your fame has spread far. Don't be angry with us, this woman and I are merely friends. I had no wish to disturb your household at this time of night hence my stealthy approach. But I am no thief in the night, only a holy man with high intentions whose heart has been affected by the things the gods send to try us all. I will go now.' He made to move from the bed but Kirsten said with amusement and, Sonya sensed, a great deal of enjoyment;

'Don't get in a coil about it, *Rimpoche*. I have the feeling my sister and you have an understanding which is no business of mine. It's about time someone taught her a few things about life . . . she always did have a preference for older professional men. Let him stay if you both wish it, Jetsunma; Dolma will be glad of his blessings. However, I won't be here after daybreak. I've got to meet a yak-train of hardware ten miles on the other side of Gyantse so I'll say *adieu* now.' He went out and shut the door, chuckling to himself.

They waited five minutes and then Lewis got up and put a chair under the door handle. 'He's gone, thank goodness.'

'He called you *Rimpoche*, Lewis? Why would he address you as Precious One? Do you think he suspects something?'

Lewis shrugged. 'It's only a polite form of address when speaking to an unknown lama.'

'But he was making fun of us – laughing at us. I've never known Kirsten to be sarcastic before . . . what are you doing?' He stood by the open window, watching the approach to the house, his left hand suspiciously concealed inside his *amphag*. With a muffled cry of fright she flung herself on him. Taken by surprise, Lewis stumbled in the darkness and banged his head on the window-frame.

'Sonya . . . what's the matter with you?' Breathing deeply, his hand over her mouth and his lips close to her ear he said huskily; 'For God's sake, what's got into you?'

She mumbled something behind his palm and he eased the pressure of his fingers. 'I . . . I thought you were going to shoot him as he left the house . . . that's what you're here for isn't it? "Elimination" is the word you used!' she hissed back in his face.

'Don't be ludicrous! Come on, you're distraught, get back into bed, you're trembling.'

She took hold of his wrists fiercely. 'If you kill my brother, I swear I'll denounce you for the British spy you are!'

He picked her up and flung her back onto the bed. 'I came here for one reason and one reason only. You! You little Russian idiot. Do you think I'm mad enough to jeopardize everything by shooting your brother in the back, in his own house, with Tibetans around every corner? Please give me credit for more sense, Sonya. When and if I want to "eliminate" your precious brother, rest assured I won't do it under your nose. I don't think I'll even bother with him since he's only a self-opinionated stupid little pawn in a greater man's game, and it would only be a waste of my time.'

She had turned her face into the pillow, sobbing quietly, while he, on his knees beside the bed, whispered furiously into the same pillow. 'I know darn well what kind of hard-

269

ware he's meeting on the other side of Gyantse but that yak-train of Russian guns is, as of this moment, lying at the bottom of a deep snowy gorge smashed to smithereens. Now, do you want to go and tell him all that before he leaves the house? You have a choice, Sonya, Kirsten or me?'

For fully an hour she did not move or speak to him again while he sat on the floor beside her. When she was certain Kirsten had left the house with some of his servants, she sniffed into her handkerchief. 'I hate you!'

'No you don't.' He got up from the floor, went to the window and closed it. Then he peeled off his Tibetan mask and robe and came beside her. 'You love me, Sonya, and I want you. Why else did you think I risked my neck tonight? Move over, we've got all the time in the world. He won't be back for three days and by that time we'll both be on our way to Lhasa.'

His body hard and cold against hers, she tried to quell the rashness of her turbulent feelings for him. 'I've no intention of going to Lhasa with you.' She turned her tear-stained face away as he tried to kiss her.

'Oh yes you have. You and I are committed in far too many ways now to give each other up. Kiss me, damn you, otherwise I'll leave you here and now.'

Obediently she did so and knew the reason why. 'Lewis . . . I . . .'

He silenced her with hard-mouthed obstinacy. She could only salvage the brief moment life had lent them by joining him in the kind of lovemaking that had stormed and illuminated their relationship for the past two months. He had opened to her vistas she hadn't imagined, while every step of the way had been agonizingly foreshortened. She had no wish to reach anywhere anymore; she only wanted to remain cherished and encapsulated in this fragile bubble of harmonious time with him alone. His body finally replete against hers, he fell asleep, his head cradled against the hollow of her throat while she held him possessively, lives entwined as daylight patterned the ceiling and time ran out.

Dolma called softly through the closed door; 'Madam-sister, are you awake? There are two more holy men here from the same lamasery as the one who came in the night. They want to talk to him most urgently. They know he is still with you, for they have been watching the house.'

In a little while Sonya had the courage to say, 'Let them wait, Dolma, he is still sleeping. When he wakes of his own accord, he'll come out to them.' She closed her eyes and slept with him.

Chapter Nineteen

Chapter Nineteen

In the ground floor main room of Kirsten's house, two men with shaven heads, humble monks from a lowly Tibetan Order, waited impatiently for the Tsawai Lama to appear. They were offered buttered tea, goat's cheese and honey cakes, and, from time to time in the heavy silence exchanged embarrassed and impatient glances.

Upstairs, Sonya was perturbed by Lewis's casual reception to the fact that two strange men awaited him. 'But they might be here to kill you, Lewis!'

'They might be – on the other hand, they've had three hours to shoot me or stab me in the back while I lay here in bed with you.' Washed, dressed and with a new face, he came beside Sonya sitting up in the bed with a blanket around her shoulders and, smiling down at her, kissed her briefly on the cheek.

'I'd better not keep them waiting any longer, you ought to have woken me when Dolma first told you they were here – on the other hand, I'm glad you didn't:'

'Lewis . . . ' Sonya held up her arms to him as he turned away. 'Don't go downstairs, it might be a trap. It's not such a great drop into the yard. You could easily make your escape from the window without them knowing . . . '

'Dearest Sonya, why would I want to do that and risk breaking a leg?'

'Then these men are known to you, aren't they, Lewis?' she accused angrily. 'And you have the nerve to invite them here to the house while my brother is away, you really are the limit!'

He chuckled as he sat down again beside her. 'Sonya, Sonya . . . if you had my welfare so much at heart, why then didn't you wake me and tell me about them in the first place? By now I could have put nearly four hours distance between us.'

She bit her lip. 'I . . . was afraid. I thought they might go away and leave you alone rather than try anything here in a magic house owned by a powerful *Tulku*. You, as well as I, know how much Tibetans dread stirring up "evil odours" as they call them, and so I knew they wouldn't harm you as long as you remained here inside this room. I just hoped they would go away when they got tired of waiting. Neither did I wish to . . . to . . . ' Her voice faded away, the look in his eye burning her as their bodies, together, had done just a short while ago.

'To what, Sonya?'

'Never mind.'

He tilted her chin and made her look at him. 'You're blushing. To what?'

'Do you know what day it is, Lewis?' she asked almost tearfully.

'Yes. Christmas Day. That's why I came here on Christmas Eve like Good King Wenceslas to bring you your Christmas present. Didn't you like it?'

Her blushes deepening, she pushed him away angrily. 'Go then!'

Grinning broadly through his mask he slid a hand over her unclad breasts, and kissed her. 'I enjoyed mine. Stay here, I'll be back later for more.' He got up, and left the room.

Sonya scrambled out of bed, quickly dressed and hurried downstairs on bare feet. Dolma, behind her, caught Sonya's arm. 'No, no . . . it is no good to listen at the door, the *Tulku*, my husband, has made sure no one can hear anything through it. Come with me.'

Hating herself for wishing to eavesdrop on Lewis, Sonya realized that for Kirsten's sake, she just had to find out what Lewis was doing. Dolma led her upstairs again and into a little cupboard where she pointed out a hole close to the floor. 'This place looks over the room where the holy men are talking. It has a strange echo and every word can be heard. You can also see what is happening if you put your eye against the crack. I come here when I wish to know what my husband is keeping from me – it is the right of every wife, madam-sister.' Her heavy silver earrings sweetly musical, Dolma closed the door with a knowing smile and left Sonya in total darkness. Below her she could see two shaven heads and Lewis's red winged cap gathered around the table. Their voices carried to her as clearly as though she were in the same room with them, and then, in total frustration, she realized they were speaking a language she did not understand. Sonya, biting her thumb, sat on the floor and cursed Lewis Joyden a thousand times.

ii

Lewis, his voice tautly controlled yet conveying all the fury he felt, spoke in Hindi to the two pundits disguised as Nepalese monks. '*Who* sent you here, who dammit? You were supposed to contact me at the Gyantse inn!'

'Forgive us, sir, but we waited there. Then we found out you had come here . . . '

'How did you find that out?' Lewis snapped. 'Have I become so very careless?'

The two stocky Nepalese monks looked uncomfortable and exchanged glances. Lewis's hand banged down on the table, startling them.

'We followed you, sir. We recognized you from the photographs the Colonel-Sahib showed us.'

'Do you know how long it's taken me to perfect this disguise, do you?' Lewis ground his teeth in anguish. 'And you two have now destroyed my cover!'

'Forgive us, sir, but it was imperative we contacted you without further delay. We have come all the way from Tuna on the Colonel-Sahib's orders. He wishes to know "what you are playing at" – those are his words, not mine, forgive me, sir.'

'Then you can go right back to Tuna and tell Younghusband I'm not one of his little soldiers, and he knows damn well what I'm playing at. Tell him also, my authority comes from one far higher than he and my instructions were to chart the area from Gyantse to Lhasa in the van of his so-called peaceable expedition. So what has happened to change those plans?'

'It is feared that the British expedition cannot proceed in a peaceable capacity any longer in view of Tibetan aggression along the way. The Escort-Commander has now crossed the Tang La with the Sikhs because news has reached winter headquarters that the Tibetans are massing a great army in the Chumbi Valley to prevent Colonel Younghusband from reaching Gyantse . . . '

'I know all that,' said Lewis irritably. 'It was I who sent him the information in the first place via my man, H20, so tell me something new. Why have my orders been countermanded by Younghusband?'

'He was not specific, sir. All he said was, "make contact, and bring him back to Tuna with his damn prayer-wheel before he loses Lhasa for us".' The Nepalese monk reddened with mortification for having been ordered to repeat the words of his superior officer.

'He said that?' Lewis asked in amazement.

'Yes sir.'

'And what if I refuse to return to Tula with you?'

The two monks again exchanged awkward glances. 'Then, sir,' the braver man said, 'we have orders to arrest you, and if you resist arrest, to shoot you on the spot.'

'I see. How very commendable of the Colonel. You then, presumably, are to return to Tuna with my compass, sextant, prayer-wheel, rosary and trident whilst leaving my dead body behind as proof of Tibetan aggression?'

The monks shifted uncomfortably and said nothing.

Lewis removed himself from the table. The monks jumped up in alarm and indecisiveness. 'Oh, don't worry, I've no intention of bowing disgracefully out of the Colonel-Sahib's life by getting you two to shoot me for disobeying orders. I know he wants me out of the way for reasons all of his own. I shall return to Tuna with

275

you, knock his teeth out, and then continue my journey to Lhasa uninterrupted. Now I'm going upstairs to fetch my things – including my prayer-wheel which nobody lays their hands on. Excuse me, gentlemen – and what a good job the master of the house is taking the country air on the other side of Gyantse.'

Lewis returned to the bedroom where Sonya was waiting for him. By his face she saw all was not well, but braced herself without displaying her worst fears.

'Sonya, something unforeseen has cropped up. I've got to leave immediately. But don't worry, I'll be back shortly, a couple of weeks at the most. Stay here so I know where to find you.' He began to gather his things together.

'Can't you tell me about it, Lewis?' she asked softly.

'No, I cannot. The less you know about me, the better. If someone then wants to question you about me, you can truthfully say you know nothing. Now kiss me and let me go before I change my mind about knocking someone's teeth out.'

Putting a brave face on their parting, she watched from the upstairs window as he left the house with the two strange monks whom she had known, from the start, had meant nothing but bad news for them.

iii

On a glacial plain 15,000 feet above sea-level, four companies of pioneers, Gurkhas, Mounted Infantry and Madras Sappers froze to death. The cold was so intense oil set solid into rifle-bolts which jammed in the breeches. Locks from the Maxim guns had to be removed at night and so, too, the leather bucket-sheaths attached to saddles in which the cavalry carried their carbines. The men slept with their weapons under them in order to be able to use them on the morrow. Poshteens, Gilgit boots and thick underwear was not sufficient to keep out the intense icy temperatures and men died at an alarming rate, frost-bitten, pneumonic, dispirited. Less than ten miles away across the plain, and clearly visible, the Tibetan army, several thousand strong, opposed the British expeditionary force.

On the day Lewis was shown into Colonel Young-husband's quarters at Tuna, eighty miles from Gyantse, a violent storm was raging across the plain. 'You are mad!' were the Colonel's first words to Lewis, looking him up and down in amazement. He saw him without his Tibetan mask, white with frost, yet wearing only a ragged Tibetan *shamtab*, a red cap and sandals on his feet while he himself was muffled to the ears in his thick winter garments. Then with a grim smile he reinforced his general idea of the man he had sent for. 'There must be truth in that adage after all, that where there's no sense there's no feeling and that's precisely why I've recalled you, Joyden.'

'Nobody recalls me except the Viceroy,' Lewis retorted equally tersely. 'I'm not in your army, Colonel.' As far as Lewis was concerned, this man's temporary promotion from the rank of Major to Colonel, did not give him the authority to pull rank on him!

'You're part of this Mission whether you think so or not, and since I've been put in command of it, you're in the army for the duration!' Colonel Younghusband snapped. Only a small man, five feet six, he looked up into the face of Lewis Joyden and realized why he disliked him so much. He was only ever his own man. 'An expedition as important as this one, only has one commander, *me*! So I'll thank you not to take matters into your own hands and ruin every chance we've got of successfully reaching Lhasa.'

'What do you mean?' Lewis, baffled, stared at Young-husband. 'Haven't I been doing my bit by supplying you with every scrap of intelligence that comes my way.'

'No, you have not! You have not relayed me one single account of what I'm supposed to find at Gyantse. And that, I suppose, is because you're too busy fraternizing with the enemy.'

Lewis took a deep breath and calmed himself. 'May I sit down, please? I think I'm thawing out rather fast, so I'd prefer to sit and talk this out in a more dignified fashion.' He placed himself in a canvas chair and looked Colonel Younghusband perilously in the eye. 'What precisely do you mean, Colonel?'

'Precisely this, Joyden. The Tibet Frontier Commission

might regard you as a two-footed wonder but I do not! What, I wonder, would His Majesty's Foreign Office make of an official Blue Book report concerning your disloyal behaviour with a certain Russian woman whose husband happens to be a spy working for the Russians right inside Lhasa itself? I could get you court-martialled, by God!' For some reason, Lewis Joyden always managed to ruffle him, and so Colonel Younghusband, conscious always of his small stature when up against men of greater height and talent, maintained his superiority in the only way he knew how, by utter dedication to the military code of conduct and recourse to 'The Blue Book' procedure.

Lewis remembered that this man always did have a penchant for opening his big mouth first and then thinking about it afterwards. 'Are you calling me a traitor?'

'I'm calling you a fool, Joyden, and I don't tolerate fools gladly.'

'Then let me remind you, sir, I am a civilian attached to the Survey of India and all knowledge of my activities with the Tibet Frontier Commission, the Foreign Office or any other official department concerned in the affairs of Tibet will hotly be denied, right up to the King himself, so anything you may report about me in your Blue Book will be ripped out according to official policy. Therefore, a court-martial, in my case, will not be applicable. And, as far as fraternizing goes, how the devil else do I screw information from the enemy?'

Taken aback, Colonel Younghusband said; 'Then Princess Sonya Dubrovka means nothing at all to you except that?'

'Exactly that.'

'You would make that official?'

'Certainly – and I dare say you already have as I can smell your stenographer busily writing everything down in his Blue Book behind that half-open flap. Lord Curzon already has on record my feelings upon the subject and if he wasn't happy with the situation, I doubt he would have given me his assignment. I have been acting on orders from the Viceroy himself, Colonel – though he left the actual methods of gaining intelligence up to me entirely.' Lewis grinned without humour, more a tightening of the nerves and muscles of his face as he surveyed Younghusband. 'Now, if that's your only reason for bringing me all this way, to find out exactly who I've been keeping warm with, I'll be on my way back to Lhasa to do what else I can to smooth your passage.' He got up.

Colonel Younghusband cleared his throat. 'I admit I was greatly put out when pundit-reports reached me about your affair with the Princess, since I felt it would jeopardize our own position. If the woman really does mean nothing at all to you except a means of gaining vital information concerning her brother's and husband's activities, then I'm prepared to accept your word and the matter is closed. However, now you're here, you can make yourself useful. There are several things I want you to do for me, including handing over your intelligence regarding Gyantse, which we'll start with.'

Lewis took up his prayer-wheel, released the outer silver casing and from the inner revolving drum withdrew a roll of paper containing, not prayer-inscriptions, but a graph. 'This gives the altitudes of your route. From Kala Tso you will descend from this fifteen thousand feet plateau of Tuna and Guru, down towards fourteen thousand at Kangma and into the Gyantse Valley at thirteen thousand feet. There, the maximum range and velocity of your bullets will be slightly less than at this level, but the trajectory of them more accurate.'

'That's some consolation,' Younghusband agreed. 'At the moment our riflemen are only obtaining high-flying results. What's the land like beyond Gyantse?'

'It rises again very sharply to sixteen thousand feet at Ralung and seventeen at Karo La where your marksmen will have to readjust their sights yet again if they want to hit the enemy. Gyantse itself is like the rock of Gibraltar, on top of the rock the fort and monastery. It does not appear to be too much of a climb from the south, the direction you'll be approaching, but it will be difficult to assault since the fort itself is built into solid rock at a steeper ascent to the north. On the plain below lies the town, a veritable labyrinth of alleys and lanes, all filthy, so warn your men. The Nyang

Chu river flows through the plain which is remarkably green and pleasant.'

When they had finished discussing the maps, drawings and distances Lewis had calculated and managed to keep hidden whilst travelling in Sonya's company through Tibet, Colonel Younghusband remarked, 'I appreciate all this stuff, Joyden, you've done well.'

'I'm only doing my job, Colonel, but thanks anyway. Appreciation does help a little when one remembers the things the Tibetans would have done to me had they found this kind of information in my possession. By the way, while I wandered around Gyantse doing my bit for my country . . . ' he noticed Colonel Younghusband's flush, 'I was allowed to look around the fort. Inside, there's a room full of skulls – men, women and children's – the victims of Tibetan tortures. I thought you might like to know in case any of you fall into Tibetan hands. They have no mercy, believe me. Now, after I've written my official report which you can despatch for me via your couriers to the Viceroy, I think I'll get going, if you don't mind.'

'Yes, I do mind,' Younghusband said intransigently. 'It's not convenient for you to leave at the moment. Tomorrow morning I want you to get out of that garb you're wearing and to put on some sort of uniform in order to accompany me to Tibetan headquarters at Guru where you will act as interpreter for me.'

'Good God, sir, you're not thinking of walking straight into the lion's den, surely?'

'Why not? They send their delegations here every other day,' Younghusband retorted smugly, his clipped moustache twitching impatiently, 'so I'm only returning the compliment. I want to talk peaceably with the Tibetan General, come to terms with the fellow, ask him to hand over Guru without making a song and dance about it. So don't leave the camp tonight, will you, Joyden? Otherwise my sentries will shoot you on the spot.'

Lewis believed it.

Chapter Twenty

Designated the rank of temporary Staff Officer, Pioneers, and supplied with army issue winter clothing plus snow boots, Lewis very reluctantly accompanied Colonel Younghusband and two other officers to the Tibetan camp less than ten miles away at Guru. In his mind the enterprise was foolhardy and lacking in proper judgement, but he kept his opinions to himself since Younghusband was in charge and did not take kindly to advice once his mind had been made up.

The village of Guru lay at the foot of a hill, a shabby little place where, in the main house, they were ushered into a smoky room warmed by a yak-dung fire, around which sat several High Lamas from Lhasa, the Tibetan Commander and some of his senior officers, as well as a representative of the Chinese Amban. Buttered tea was offered, and while Younghusband and his men thawed out after their breathless trek on stalwart ponies across the icy plain, the atmosphere surrounding the Tibetans became more and more chilly.

Colonel Younghusband opened the proceedings by explaining to the Tibetans that he had come without an escort, on a friendly basis, in order to resolve difficult matters so that he could proceed to Gyantse with peaceable intent.

Lewis, translating, gave Younghusband the Lhasa General's reply: 'He says that if you want an amicable settlement, you must go back to Yatung and renegotiate.'

The Colonel chose to ignore the General's reply. 'Ask him why Tibet is so hostile to Great Britain while indulging in close relations with Russia.'

'They say they have no truck with Russia.'

'Then why does the Dalai Lama send letters to the Tsar via Dorjiev and other Russians, while refusing to receive letters from the Viceroy of India?'

'They dislike the Russians as much as they dislike the British. They have nothing to do with the Russians. There are no Russians anywhere near Lhasa and Dorjiev is a Buriat Mongol, not a Russian.'

'Tell them, Joyden, that I believe differently. Tell them that our intent is to send a peaceful mission to Gyantse for the purpose of settling our commercial treaties once and for all. The Tibetans have ignored our goodwill, our trading agreements and have violated our frontiers.'

'The British have no good will towards the Tibetans. They seek only to change the religious laws of Tibet.'

'Then tell that officious lama, if that were the case, why haven't the British interfered in the numerous religious structures of India?'

'I think, sir, we ought to watch our step. They're becoming rather aggressive and we're greatly outnumbered here.'

'You're here in the capacity of interpreter, Joyden, not advisor.'

'Very well – they say we have broken the rule of the road. We ought not to have entered Tibet in the first place. They say we ought to get out before it's too late.'

Suddenly one of the Gyantse officers, Kuma Sidheong, stood up and abruptly left the room.

'I think we ought to keep smiling, sir.'

'Then tell them I'm only following the orders of my government and we're not here to make trouble.' Smiling with frozen politeness, Colonel Younghusband picked up his bowl of tea and sipped from it with amazing nonchalance and his men followed his example. Lewis could feel the hairs on his forearms prickling coldly in the ominous atmosphere and had the fleeting thought that none

282

of them would get back to Tuna at this rate. To be taken hostage now would be the end of everything.

'Joyden, I want them to know that I respect their wishes and just as they have to follow the advice of their government I have to do the same. Tell them I have a wife and child in Darjeeling and my greatest wish is to be with them, not here. But I will relay their directives to the Viceroy, and if he orders me back to India, I will willingly go.'

'The General says he will send a messenger back with us to Tuna who will wait there for the Viceroy's answer. The lamas wish to know the date of our withdrawal from Tuna.'

'At the moment, I cannot answer that.'

Feeling the time had come to beat a hasty but dignified retreat while the going was good, Colonel Younghusband stood up to shake hands with the Lhasa General, who ignored Younghusband's outstretched hand, and instead stuck out his tongue according to Tibetan custom. High Lamas continued to scowl and would not even rise from their cushions but continued to treat the British officers as beneath their dignity. Escorted to the door, and with fresh air blasting the icy grit of the plains once more in his face, Colonel Younghusband looked pale but elated. 'Whew! That was a close shave. Come on, mount your ponies carefully, and keep smiling. I don't like the look in the eyes of that grinning General, Kuma Sidheong, and his warriors.'

With smiling composure the Englishmen mounted, rode at a dignified pace out of the Guru camp where Tibetan soldiers were busy gathering yak-dung for their fires, and then galloped as hard as they could back to Tuna.

ii

Colonel Younghusband was in a morose frame of mind. Pacing up and down, he did not take kindly to Lewis's untimely intrusion on his thoughts.

'Sir, if you have no further use of my services, I wish to resume my journey to Lhasa . . . '

'Who said I have no further use of your services? May I

283

remind you, Joyden, you are now seconded to the Pioneer Corps and I have very great use for your services. For a start, I am not happy about cooling my heels here at Tuna in the face of Tibetan recalcitrance at Guru. Unless we can get past the bottleneck of the Guru garrison, we have no hope of proceeding towards Gyantse. That's why I need you here. Scouts like you are invaluable.'

'But Colonel, the main body of the army cannot advance towards Gyantse until the spring, it would be suicidal to do so. If I can get going now, I'll be back with all the information you require long before you set off for Gyantse.'

'What's your hurry, Joyden?' Younghusband glared up at him. 'Do I take it you're eager to fall back into the arms of Princess Sonya Dubrovka in order to . . . screw, I think was the word you used, more information from her?'

'The road to Lhasa is practically uncharted,' Lewis replied coldly, his chameleon eyes not masking a mutual dislike. 'Besides, I have an assignment inside Lhasa, with a deadline to meet. Those were my instructions from the highest authority. My contacts are not going to hang about unnecessarily, and if I can't get my intelligence reports through, you might find yourself in the unenviable position of facing hordes of savage Tibetans armed with sophisticated Russian artillery on a hostile and totally unchartered plateau.'

'You've made your point, Joyden. What sophisticated Russian artillery did you notice at Guru, eh? Matchlocks, broadswords, bamboo clubs. Not a sophisticated breech-loader or ten-pounder in sight, eh?'

'Thanks to the erstwhile efforts of my unrecognized native team, Colonel! That does not mean none will get through before the spring. Every week, yak and camel trains are bringing armaments via Afghanistan which we've a devil of a job to sabotage. I have my own kind of work to do, ensuring your march to Lhasa is as safe as it can be where an invading army is concerned.'

'Ours is not an invading army, Joyden. It is a peaceable mission on its way only as far as Gyantse for the time being, for the purpose of diplomatic negotiations over commercial agreements between Great Britain and Tibet.'

'With all due respect, sir, the Tibetans do not see it that way,' Lewis, trying hard to keep his temper, added, 'Do I take it, I'm under some kind of house arrest for a sinister reason I know nothing about?'

Colonel Younghusband seemed momentarily disconcerted. 'Of course not! But my better judgement tells me you are of more value here than elsewhere. At the moment I don't envisage advancing on Gyantse before the spring. As you so rightly said, it would be suicidal. I'm sure you're well aware that my Escort Commander and I do not see eye to eye and the atmosphere is er . . . rather cool between us, and so he is thinking of abandoning the project altogether. I've a real crisis on my hands – and this is for your ears only. I cannot turn back since we'd lose face, and I cannot go forward without risking war with the Tibetans. We're also encamping on Bhutan's borders, and you know how tetchy and pro-Tibetan the Bhutanese are. I don't want them joining forces with the Tibetans, so I'm only biding my time here for political reasons. Somehow, we've got to neutralize Bhutan's position in all this, and that's where you can assist me. I want you to be my interpreter and liaison officer with the Tongsa Penlop of Bhutan as well as Captain Jit Bahadar who is Nepal's representative in these negotiations.'

'Colonel, I only take my orders from the Viceroy. My role is to function in Tibet, not Bhutan.'

It was as if Younghusband had not heard him. 'Until I get a response one way or another from His Majesty's Government, my way is blocked. If you are caught in Lhasa spying for us, this whole Mission will fall apart before I get my reply from London. A great amount of public funds will be lost, as well as prestige – not to mention my men who have already suffered enough hardship in getting this far. The Tibetans will never trust us again.'

'I see,' said Lewis, controlling his feelings by breathing softly and rhythmically through his nose. 'So I'm made redundant because my superiors fear I might blab if the Tibetans found out what I was about?'

'Well, wouldn't you blab?' Colonel Younghusband turned to regard Lewis, his expressive eyes dark and faintly scornful, brows interrogative for the crucial answer. 'No one would blame you.'

'And what about other pundits who might "blab" under torture. What directives have they received?'

'You and I both know,' Colonel Younghusband snapped as he pointed a finger at Lewis, 'that you were sent into Tibet under extraneous circumstances. It is not normally British policy to involve an Englishman in pundit activities in this country, the political implication being that if you were caught, the consequences would be far more dire all round.'

'I see. Brown men are expendable, white men have to preserve face. The same kind of political reasoning that issues Gilgit boots to British officers while the lower ranks can get frostbite because they're not allowed them! Thanks very much, Colonel,' said Lewis, leaving the Colonel's bivouac in disgust.

iii

Kirsten, acting as if all the demons in hell were after him, ran into the house one morning shouting, 'Sonya, Sonya! Where are you? Come down . . . oh, there you are. I've got news for you.' Flushed and excited he grabbed her arm, pushed her inside the main room and slammed the door. 'Sit down . . . here, have a drink, I'm going to.'

'Kirsten, what on earth's the matter?' Alarmed by his manner, Sonya could only think it was something to do with the Red Cap she had had no news of since Christmas Day, eight weeks ago. Her thoughts always centering around Lewis, she knew she ought not to have expected him to contact her since that would only endanger his life, yet, in a tiny corner of her heart, she still expected it . . . and a tiny corner of her heart still denied the fact the man she loved was a paid assassin with no real feelings about love, commitment or any other refinement.

'Russia has declared war on Japan,' Kirsten enthused.

'Oh, is that all,' disappointed she clasped her hands in her lap.

'Don't you see! I must return to Russia, rejoin my Regiment, blast the Japanese out of Vladivostok . . .'

'Calm down, Kirsten, and think rationally. You can't return to Russia at the moment. Dolma needs your protection while her father is away fighting the British. I also need you here.'

'But you'll be returning to Russia with me, silly girl! There's nothing stopping us now. Kuma's away somewhere in the Chumbi Valley and I have enough money to buy our way back to Russia. Dolma can come with us if she wants, although I'd rather she didn't.'

'No, it's not practical, Kirsten. Not just now. Things are so unsettled here. At any moment the British might march into Gyantse . . .'

'That's the very reason why we ought to get out of here, Sonya! The British won't take kindly to us. They might lock me up, or shoot me as a Russian spy. You wouldn't want that to happen, would you?'

Sonya bit her lip. 'No, I should hate that to happen to you. But I can't leave Tibet yet, Kirsten. I must go on to Lhasa and see if I can contact Kolya. I must ask him to divorce me.'

'He won't even know what a divorce is. I told you, he's supposed to have gone off his head.'

'Then I must be certain.'

'Divorce is dirty, Sonya. You'd be better off to wait till Kolya's dead – he might be by now for all I know. But if you're a divorced woman, no one will want to associate with you when you get back to Russia and no decent man will marry you again.'

'Then I'll just have to take my chances with the indecent, won't I, brother dear?' she said with forced cheer, adding briskly; 'Kirsten, if you desire to return to Russia and Kuma Sidheong does not prevent it, then you go alone, I won't stand in your way.'

Over her small pale hand resting on the tablecloth, Kirsten placed his stronger one. 'Sonya, I couldn't go and leave you here alone.'

'I got here by myself, did I not? And I shan't stay here once you go? I shall head for Lhasa.'

'Without your *Rimpoche*?' he teased. 'I suspect he is your reason to visit Lhasa, not Kolya. What have you two

287

arranged between you? That you should call upon him at the Drepung, uh, you naughty girl? You've not seemed the same since he departed. Is the Rimpoche your heart's desire, Sonya? Tell me.' He winked above the silver goblet. 'I didn't get a chance to look at him properly in the moonlight, but is he handsome and wealthy and faithful?'

'Isn't it rather early in the morning to drink wine, Kirsten?'

'No, darling girl, it isn't! I bathe in it since the water is one step away from typhoid . . . ah, here's my dutiful wife with the cream cheese and honey cakes she brings every time someone sits down at this table. No wonder my reincarnated sister is putting on weight, Dolma. What are you trying to do, fatten her up like you, who has nothing else to do except eat and make love all day?' He pinched her as she set the tray down on the table. 'Dolma, tell Sonya what kind of lecherous men wear holy cloth. I do believe my reincarnated sister has fallen in love with a *Rimpoche* and he with her, and now she's trying to divorce her husband because of it. Dolma darling, what if I divorced you so that I might return to my native land in order to fight Japanese soldiers invading my country?'

With a screech she turned to him, anguish in her dark eyes.

'On the other hand, I don't really have to go to all that bother do I, since you're only what is commonly known as my common-law wife, eh, Dolma, my beauty?' He pinched her cheek and with tears in her eyes, Dolma fled the room.

'I wish you wouldn't treat her so badly, Kirsten. It's not your way at all. In St Petersburg you were always known for your gentlmanly ways and careful regard where women were concerned,' Sonya admonished.

'In St Petersburg I wasn't beaten like a dog, treated like a dog and made to bed like a dog,' he flung at her before leaving the table. 'And that's why I'm returning to St Petersburg with you the moment the opportunity arises and I can make adequate plans for our journey. Neither of us is staying a moment longer in this god-forsaken hole surrounded by primitive enemies!'

Chapter Twenty-One

Over-wintering on the Tuna plain had resulted in the total denuding of trees, every remaining scrap used as firewood. The independent state of Bhutan had been neutralized, with promises from its ruler that no interference would come from the Bhutanese as far as a peaceable British advance to Gyantse was concerned. When orders to advance were received in the spring, Lewis, sidetracked by Younghusband in the affairs of Bhutan, could only breathe a sigh of relief that he himself could now press forward to Lhasa even if Younghusband and his men wheeled right around at Gyantse and headed back to India.

Filling his lungs with the sweet sharp air of the early spring morning, he was reminded of acid drops on the tongue when, as a schoolboy, he had leant over the sweet-shop counter back home at St Anne's and wondered on what he should spend the penny the Rector had given him. Aniseed balls, humbugs, jelly mints; he had always opted for the pungent, pear-scented acid drops. Looking to the eastern mountains bathed in pale primrose light, their summits emerging through misty haloes like white-pated monks, the sky above as wonderfully blue as summer cornflowers in the Rectory garden, the sweet – and bitter – tastes of England returned. He saw a carriage plummeting down a steep hill, himself, the seventeen year old youth on the box, Beddoes the groom wrenching the reins away from his untried hands, the horses careering out of control, and his mother and twin sister lying dead in the ditch, carriage wheels spinning. His father's voice down the years, 'I told you, I warned you to leave the driving to Beddoes. But no, you had to disobey me, you had to prove you were the man you are not. What a price, Lewis, what a price you and I now have to pay . . . ' Lewis shook his head to clear it of those haunting dreams that hounded him, closed his senses to the scent and taste of acid drops . . .

Never really comfortable with horses any more, the jingle of harness, the creak of leather, the soft whinnying noises of ponies against the muted urgency of an army on the move again, he was only thankful, like the soldiers, that a long period of inactivity was over. The main body of the army having arrived across the Tang La with more yaks, donkeys, mules and sheep, the baggage and armaments train, medical, clerical and other ancillary units stretching for a mile back, the British Mission looked to be anything but peaceable.

Three miles south of Guru lay an outcrop of little rocky hills, at the foot of them a marshy lake, still frozen solid. From a ruined house that stood some way back from the lake the Tibetans had built a wall and several sangars, stony emplacements, to stop the advance of Younghusband along the old caravan route to Gyantse. It was no stronghold, merely a gesture. The Lhasa General had sent his messengers out several times to ask Younghusband to turn back and renegotiate terms at Yatung. The Tibetans did not wish to fight: Neither did the British, Younghusband had sent his own emissaries back to reassure the General.

It all started quite amicably. The Tibetan officers from Lhasa, Gyantse and Shigatse, dotting the hillsides in their yellow and green coats to match the gentle colours of spring, their mounts, gaily bedecked in vividly patterned saddlecloths, chased-silver harnesses, jewel encrusted sword hilts and guns, flamboyant headdresses set against purple and blue silken robes, banners and prayer-ribbons fluttering in the five sacred colours, red, blue, green, yellow and white, the Lamaist army, like some medieval pageant, was a sight to behold. It was like seeing the hills blossoming with the bright flowers of summer, eclipsing the heady splendour of springtime, until a reckless wintry wind swept across the snowy plain in khaki dust to leave the flowers mown down, crushed, dead.

'Clear the road! We give you quarter-of-an-hour!'

Nothing happened on the Tibetan side of the wall and the weather slowly changed, the sky turning from blue to grey. 'All right, men, march forward, hold your fire, don't shoot unless they shoot first.'

'This is madness!' Lewis turned to Younghusband riding beside him, the chill wind blowing ice-darts in their faces. 'You don't seriously expect them to walk through those barricades as though they were on a Sunday afternoon picnic?'

The Colonel smiled grimly. 'Bluff, Joyden, bluff! Nothing will happen. The Tibetans know when they're beaten.'

'Sir, they're outnumbering us by seven to one!'

'They haven't got Maxim machine-guns or Lee Metfords, Joyden. If you haven't the stomach for this, then get out of here.'

'I might do just that! I might even fill out a Blue Book report on the events in the Guru camp back in January when you decided to play God!' Turning his pony's head, Lewis wheeled to the rear of the infantry and artillery and from a small promontory observed the rest of the action as an outsider.

The rifles of the Pioneers covering the wall at point-blank range, Lewis was presently amazed, and relieved, to see the Tibetan soldiers jump over the wall to meet the British force with shy friendly smiles. Great comradeship of spirit was evident from both sides, British soldiers and Tibetans slapping each other on backs and shoulders, shaking hands, a great many Tibetan tongues displayed in their curious form of greeting, while the English officers ambled around the *sangars* taking photographs. Again, Younghusband's gamble had paid off, and Lewis had to acknowledge a certain amount of grudging admiration where the man was concerned. He saw Younghusband's orderly gallop off with a despatch, heading obviously for the end of the telegraph-line and presumably claiming a bloodless victory over the

Tibetans, since the Lhasa General sat on the ground in front of his wall with a very melancholy expression.

British machine guns still trained on the friendly Tibetans, hordes of them took a curious interest in weapons they had never seen before by climbing all over them, peering down the barrels, examining every piece of equipment the British had brought with them. And then, bored and tired of the whole affair, the Lhasa General sprang upon his pony as some of the sepoys were ordered to disarm the Tibetan soldiers in front of the wall. It led to total confusion, and Lewis guessed why. Each Tibetan soldier regarded his matchlock or sword as his own property, depending upon his weapon for hunting or shooting for his food and for his own protection. Told to put down their arms, the Tibetans rebelled, their weapons were personal property, not government. Blows were exchanged.

The Lhasa General spurred his horse into the middle of the fracas. His bridle was seized by a Sikh soldier and the General shot him in the face. Instantly, firing broke out. A British officer was hacked by a broadsword against the wall. Caught between the wall and the stone-throwing relentless Tibetans everything appeared grim for the British. Then, volley after volley, Sikh rifles peppered the wall, Maxim machine-guns like nervous teeth chattered revenge, Lee Metfords smashed directly into Tibetan lines, firing almost at point-blank range, shrapnel burst into the air like exotic firestars. The Tibetans broke loose. Backs to their own wall, they walked away through the hail of bullets as though they still believed their gods would save them.

'*Om mani padme hum!*' Lewis said, unaware that he had spoken aloud, shocked and revolted as he watched Tibetans walk away from the battle area, a confined space of less than an acre. He shuddered, it was horrible, just horrible – and he thought he had become immune to horror. It was all over in ninety seconds. On the marshy slopes of Guru, seven hundred Tibetans lay dead including the Lhasa General, one-hundred and sixty-eight wounded. British casualties in those few seconds, six wounded. Reviewing the scene afterwards, officer Hadow of the Norfolk Regiment murmured beside Lewis, 'I hope I never have to shoot men *walking away*, again.'

'Amen!' said Lewis, sickened. He went in search of the Colonel and threw down three Tibetan rifles at his feet. '*Here* is the Viceroy's spectre of Russian influence in Tibet! Three rifles with the imprint of the Imperial Arms Factory at Tula, the honeymoon home of Princess Sonya Dubrovka! I hope he, and you, are satisfied. I'm leaving. Just try and stop me and I'll tell the *Dail Mail* the truth. No official Blue Books this time, Colonel.'

High on a hill, a handful of Tibetan officers and High Lamas who had escaped the massacre, watched a lone figure in a thick *poshteen* hunched over his pony taking the Gyantse road, riding like the wind.

'I want that man,' Kuma Sidheong said without a muscle moving in his strong implacable face, 'I want him so that every Britisher here today can see what we, too, can do. *Give him to me*!'

ii

The frozen earth was thawing at last. In the fields around Thug-Phul serfs and peasants belonging to Kuma Sidheong, the great warlord and nobleman of Gyantse, tilled the fields by hand, pushing ancient wooden ploughs up and down in endless furrows for barley and bean planting. In the valley, half a mile away, Sonya could see Kuma's house, a large white flat-roofed building looking like a sketch from the paint-brush of a young child – more impressive and grand, however, than the dingy grey box Kuma had given to Dolma and Kirsten, shut away as it was in a dark poplar grove. Sonya liked to walk each morning in the fields, following a soft grassy path all round the edge of Kuma's estate, observing the Tibetans at work, thinking about Lewis, wondering what had become of him, since it was now three months since she had last seen him. Why did her head always tell her heart he was only true to his duty? She was dressed as a Tibetan noblewoman, sharing Dolma's clothes and jewellery, and in her heavy tapestry skirts and loose over-blouse with long sleeves, her elaborate lofty headdress and heavy silver earrings and bracelets, she elicited awe and respect but very little curiosity as the companion of the overlord's daughter. Sonya, pulling the thick cloak more closely around her to keep out the fresh wind, lifted her head to feel the warmth of the sun on her face. She passed a row of decrepit outhouses where winter fodder and grain was stored. The pathway, overhung by poplar trees and silver birch, reminding her so much of her father's hunting estate at Novgorod, she imagined the light was playing tricks on her when she saw a shadow jerk back suddenly from the threshold of an open barn door – or Kirsten. With a little laugh she quickened her step and called out gaily, 'Kirsten! Are you still playing your silly *Tulku* games? Come out of there and tell me what you've been doing in Gyantse for three days.'

Eager to catch him out before he pounced and scared the wits out of her as she passed the door, she ran into the barn. He grabbed her from behind and kicked the rickety door with his heel. His hand across her mouth, the urgent whisper was not Kirsten's. 'Don't make a sound, Sonya, it's me, Lewis.' He took his hand away.

'Lewis! Oh Lewis . . . ' He had drawn back into the shadows and she could barely see him. With all her senses honed to the realization of the moment she had been waiting for, she could only look at him in tongue-tied joy.

'Sonya, I need your help. I can't use the Red Cap disguise any longer. I want you to try and find me some old clothes, pots and pans, needles and threads, so that I can continue to Lhasa. I want you to come with me, a tinker's spouse.' He smiled wanly in the darkness.

She stared at him, joy turning to dismay, noticing that under his thick *poshteen* he wore a military uniform. 'I didn't know you were a soldier.'

'I'm not . . . I'll explain some other time. Will you do this thing for me?'

'Of course. But I can't come to Lhasa with you.'

'For heaven's sake, why not?' His whisper evinced exasperation.

'Kirsten . . . '

'Kirsten, Kirsten, all I ever get from you is Kirsten. I've risked everything by coming here to warn your precious brother to leave Thug-Phul before the British arrive – otherwise he might find himself in an Indian gaol!'

'Please tell me what's going on, Lewis.'

'Sonya, I've just ridden all the way from Guru. It's taken me three nights – it was too dangerous for me to travel in daylight. A battle took place at Guru which I'd rather not talk about. The British are supposed to negotiate peace and trading agreements at Gyantse, then turn round and go home. After what took place at Guru, it's not very likely this will happen now, since the Tibetans are up in arms over the losses they suffered there. Neither are the British very happy about finding Russian guns on the battlefield. Now I know your husband has an interest in the Imperial Armaments Factory at Tula and, while you might be totally innocent of what has been going on, your brother isn't! The British will interrogate you and Kirsten if they find you here, because, whether you like it or not, you are part of this set-up, married as you are to Prince Nikolay Dubrovka, a Russian agent working from inside the Potala itself! I don't want you imprisoned with your brother, that's why I'm asking you to come to Lhasa with me.'

'Lewis, Kirsten is already making arrangements to return to Russia. It's taking him longer than expected because he is still virtually Kuma Sidheong's prisoner. The Gyantse watchmen know all his movements so he has to bribe his way out of Gyantse very carefully in case Kuma realizes his intentions. He wants me to accompany him but I've refused. I still intend to go to Lhasa to find my husband, but I'm leaving it until the summer months when it's easier to travel.'

'That will be too late. The British are expected to arrive in Gyantse next month.'

She turned away. 'Let me go and find you a new disguise . . .'

'In a moment.' He caught her hand and drew her with him into the shadows. 'You don't know how much I've missed you.' He bent towards her but she held back rigidly.

'Lewis, I know it's dangerous for you to linger here, and

295

you mustn't. I'll be back shortly with the things you require . . . '

'Does my three days' stubble offend you? Or have you fallen out of love with me, is that why you won't kiss me?' His teeth shone whitely in the semi-darkness as he smiled down at her.

'No . . . none of those reasons . . . Lewis, please don't!'

His arms around her, he trapped her to him, her protestations lost. Then, all of a sudden, he released her and fell back a pace. With one swift-fire movement of his hand, he threw off her cloak to capture her in a coldly assessing scrutiny. 'So that's it! Your reason for not wanting to come to Lhasa with me. Why weren't you going to tell me, Sonya?'

She bit her lip, unable to meet his accusing eye. 'It would have been unfair on you . . . '

'When?' he asked curtly, his expression suddenly haggard in the meagre light filtering through wooden cracks.

'When did it happen, or when is the child due? The first time we ever made love, Lewis, in the mountains . . . our honeymoon baby, while the *djolmo* sang.'

'Oh Sonya,' he said after a while, 'I'm sorry.'

'Why? I'm very happy and so should you be.'

'Come here, come to me, let's talk . . . ' He drew her to the heaped luxury of the straw mountain in the corner where he had spent the night, and together they sank into its rustic privacy while he held her and let his hand settle on the soft mound of her gently enlarging abdomen. 'Why didn't you tell me at Christmas, Sonya?'

'I couldn't be sure, and I didn't want to give you an additional worry. So, as you can see, Lewis, I can hardly go to Lhasa in my condition to demand a divorce from my husband on the grounds of non-consummation of marriage – the only grounds I had.'

'And I've gone and messed things up for you, forgive me.' He sounded lost.

'No. I'm part of it, too, you know.' She smiled, and smoothed back his dark hair, grown again in the three months he had been away, and now boyishly untidy over his forehead. 'You look tired,' she said. 'Why don't you sleep for a little while? When the serfs go for their midday meal, I'll sneak out and bring you back some Tibetan clothing.'

'What a good idea,' he murmured, before settling himself more comfortably against her and closing his eyes.

When Sonya was certain everyone in the fields would be at Kuma's house for their midday meal, she eased herself away from Lewis, peacefully asleep with his head on her breast. He murmured something dreamily, turned over and resettled himself, curled like an overgrown foetus in a warm womb of straw. She re-covered him with his fur-lined *poshteen*.

Sonya opened the barn door gently and it creaked a little but did not disturb him. Pulling it gently shut again she turned, and in that instant shadows from the poplar trees took substance. Before she could make a sound, her arms were wrenched up behind her back, a broadsword pressed against her mouth . . . Instinct woke Lewis, the tiny muffled mew like a kitten in pain, he leapt to the door. '*Sonya*!'

Sound of the air rushing away, rented in two by the whiplash, searing fire as a snake-like thong curled around his neck chokingly. Tibetans grabbed him. The voice of the Yellow Hat lama seated on his pony under the trees was like a death-knell. 'Good morning Britisher, we trust you slept well. Our noble lord, Kuma Sidheong, regrets he cannot be here in person to greet you – as you and Younghusband so kindly did at the camp at Guru. He has, however, requested the pleasure of your company at the Jong in Gyantse so that all *philangs* daring to cross the iron bridge at Red Idol Gorge will be welcomed by your smiling face.'

Blood rushed from Sonya's head. The unborn child turned a somersault, pushing its head down, forcing her to her knees, to the pawing hooves of the lama's pony, sparing her, mercifully, in a numbing blackness, the sight of Lewis finally betrayed by his love for her.

iii

Dolma bathed Sonya's face with ice-cold water. When Sonya opened her eyes, it was growing dark outside. At first, full memory eluded her, and she wondered what was happening to her – Dolma washing her face, damping everything, her clothes clinging to her in hot stickiness while her hands and feet remained frozen. Then the terrible realization of Lewis's capture threatened to overwhelm her – floggings, mutilations, terrible tortures before death came as a merciful release. Memory of what Joonu had suffered on her behalf shocked her out of her apathy. Sonya flung back the covers; 'Lewis . . . my Lewis . . . don't hold me, Dolma . . . I must go to him, I must . . . '

Dolma did not fully understand but tried to restrain her. 'I think it is better you stay in your bed, madam-sister. This afternoon I sent for the Holy Mother from the convent. She is wise in the art of midwifery and often I have gone to her for words of advice. She told me you are known to her, for you once gave her a good warm shawl. Now she wishes to repay your kind deed. Her words of advice were, you should remain in your bed for a few days otherwise you may lose the Tsawai Lama's holy child. For the moment nothing is wrong except that the child turns his head down low, so that when the summer flowers bloom he will be ready to be born. If you get up now, you will kill him.'

'Oh no . . . ' Sonya sank back upon the pillows, unable to prevent the tremble in her hands as she held them over her face. Unwilling to relinquish her only link with Lewis, she could not face losing them both. Mastering herself at last, knowing full well that to go to pieces now would do neither herself nor Lewis any good, she began to think the matter through and finally asked Dolma; 'Where's Kirsten?'

Dolma looked blank.

'No . . . of course you don't know who I mean. Your husband, the *Rishi-Kudak*, Dolma, where is he?'

'Still in Gyantse,' said Dolma sulkily. 'He never comes home these days but prefers to spend his time in gambling-dens and whore-houses . . . '

'Fetch him, Dolma . . . please.' Sonya grasped Dolma's delicate wrists feverishly. 'Please Dolma, help me!'

Dolma looked perturbed. 'Madam-sister, I will not go into the places he does, it is unseemly. I am a noblewoman from the house of Kuma Sidheong . . . '

'Your father is about to destroy the man I love! Go to him for me and beg mercy, for my sake. Otherwise fetch my brother to do this thing. Both of you together might be able to save Lew . . . the Englishman I love.'

'Nothing can save an Englishman, madam-sister. He is doomed for what happened to my people at Guru.'

'Oh God . . . Dolma, listen to me, do you love my brother, do you?'

'Of course, madam-sister. If I did not, then my father would have had him put to death when he first came to us. It is only I who stand between him and what your lover will suffer.'

'You're cruel, Dolma, cruel like the rest of your tribe. I'll go to Gyantse Fort myself! Each moment I spend arguing with you is a moment lost in the Englishman's life.' Determined, she got out of bed again, scrabbling for her boots under the bed. 'But listen to this, if he dies, then I'll get my brother, the *Rishi-Tulku*, to bring curses on you and your family. Don't forget, I, too, am a reincarnated being with very great powers! Tomorrow morning, every yak, every mule, every animal on your father's farm will be dead. Whatever is planted in his fields will wither and die. He will lose all his wealth and prestige. Next month, he will be beheaded by the Dalai Lama when he loses the Battle for Gyantse and you will be afflicted with great sores to make you so ugly no man will look at you again after you lose my brother's love . . . because he will not love you any more if anything happens to the one I love. We are very close, the great *Rishi-Tulku* and me.'

It did the trick. Dolma pouted, fidgeted, looked uncomfortable and finally agreed. 'Very well, madam-sister, I will do as you ask. But I cannot go myself, so I will send a servant to bring him back.'

'Tell the servant to tell my brother I'm dying because my child comes too soon. Oh, and Dolma, the moment my brother is here beside my bed, I'll take back all the curses I've just made, so you needn't be afraid when tomorrow morning comes.'

Dolma smiled meekly and left the room. The moment the door closed behind her Sonya, feeling very much like a

299

Biblical phophetess, fell back once more on the pillows. She closed her eyes and breathed in relief, thank you, God! Thank you for creating some people simple-minded heathens . . .

Two hours later Kirsten stood beside her.

He bent down and peered at her. 'Sonya, are you truly dying?'

'Kirsten, oh, Kirsten!' She sobbed, springing awake though she had not been sleeping, only lying with her eyes shut against the harsh brutality of life.

She clasped his hands. 'Kirsten, you've got to help me.'

'Any thing, darling girl, but are you really dying, Sonya?'

'Yes, yes, inch by inch, every minute . . . Listen to me, Kirsten. This afternoon an Englishman was taken to Gyantse Fort. He is to be beheaded in order to teach the British a lesson . . . '

'Serves him right. Gyantse's buzzing with the news. But it's a relatively painless ordeal I'm given to understand.'

'Damn you, Kirsten!' She struck her brother on the shoulder with a fervent fist. Already half out of her mind agonizing over Lewis's fate, she could not bear Kirsten's drunken flippancy.

'I'm sorry . . . I oughtn't to have riled you at a time like this. But why take it so much to heart, dear girl? What's this Englishman to you, Sonya?'

'He's the father of my child.'

'*Mon Dieu*!' After a heavy silence, Kirsten, marshalling his confused thoughts said; 'I thought you were in love with a Tibetan monk?'

'They are one and the same, the Red Cap and the Englishman.'

Again the tangible silence as he tried to extricate truth from fiction. 'You'd better tell me everything,' he presently muttered, sitting himself on the edge of the bed.

'Kirsten, the man the Tibetans have taken to Gyantse Fort is an Englishman not unknown to us. His name is Lewis Joyden . . . '

'Sonya! Now I know you are out of your mind!'

'No, no! Listen to me, please listen to me, Kirsten! He's a British agent, a spy. He knows all about your armaments

300

deal with Dorjiev, everything. You remember I wrote and told you about Kolya's secret visitor to Tula when Kolya and I were on our honeymoon? Lewis even found that out. I had no idea at the time what Dorjiev and Kolya were up to, only that Dorjiev was polite enough to pay his respects to us since he was in Tula. Lewis Joyden knows all about Kolya's interests in the Tula Armaments Factory, and he came here to warn you to get away from Thug-Phul before the British arrive, otherwise you'll find yourself in an Indian prison. So you must help him, for my sake, Kirsten.' Sonya, clasping his arm in two hands, laid her head beseechingly against his shoulder.

After a while, Kirsten asked; 'Why did you allow yourself to be seduced by a British spy, Sonya, the enemy?'

'Because I love him.'

'You don't know him.'

'*Yes, I do, yes I do*! I've loved him since the first day I met him. I've loved him in all the years we've been writing and never saw each other, and I love him enough to beg you now to help us.'

Kirsten took a deep breath. One arm across his chest supporting the other, his hand fingering his mouth in perplexed contemplation, he asked; 'How? How am I supposed to help him?'

'You can, you can! If anyone can, you can, Kirsten! In your capacity as the *Rishi-Kudak*, the all-powerful *Tulku*. Kuma Sidheong will listen to you. You know how superstitious the Tibetans are. You can threaten them with all kinds of curses if they harm Lewis . . . '

He laughed scornfully. 'Sonya, grow up, dear girl! I'm an ordinary mortal when we boil it down to the common denominator – common sense. If Lewis Joyden is about to die because he was unlucky enough to put a foot wrong, then there's nothing I can do to save him. The Gyantse Fort is a rabbit warren of iniquity and I'd never find him, let alone whisk him out under the noses of the *Jongpen* and his guards.'

'Then go to Kuma. You and Dolma go to Kuma Sidheong and ask him to spare Lewis's life, please!'

'Kuma would give us short shrift for interfering in

301

military matters. What happened at Guru has incensed the Tibetans to such a degree that they are more determined than ever to teach the British a lesson. I'm sorry it has to be your lover.'

Lying back against her pillows, her eyes tightly closed, two wayward tears escaped and made their way down her cheeks. Sniffing loudly, she brushed her hand over her nose, and, scrubbing her face, determination braved defeat despite the fact her voice betrayed her in broken spasms. 'I loved you enough to risk my life to find out what had become of you. I thought you'd do the same for me, not turn your back when I have most need of you.'

'Sonya,' he took her hand, 'I am your brother, not Jesus Christ.'

'Then be Jesus Christ for me just this once, Kirsten. Do something, anything to help Lewis.'

Kirsten looked at her lying small, defeated and forlorn in the narrow bed, the empty room with its lime-washed walls, its stark pieces of furniture, a bed, a chair, a worm-eaten clothes chest and a lamp, and seeing in his mind's eye, Dubrovka-Dvaryets and the opulent splendour of her marital home, wondered what on earth had possessed her to turn her back on it all: surely it could not be solely on his account, or Kolya's? How much had it to do with Lewis Joyden? She was, after all, carrying his child, the little fool. Squeezing her hand tightly, Kirsten said at last; 'All right. I'll see what I can do. But no promises, mind. Kuma's a prickly character where justice is concerned.'

'Thank you, Kirsten,' she whispered before he took the butter-lamp, leaving her in total darkness.

302

Chapter Twenty-Two

To go to Kuma Sidheong to beg clemency for a British spy and no doubt Tibetan assassinator as well, would only result in his own beheadment. Kirsten was in a dilemma. He wanted to help his sister, but how?

In a small, totally private cellar where he could get away from Dolma and the rest of his household, he soused his head in a bowl of cold water and vigorously towelled his face dry, trying to rid his head of the muzziness resulting from drinking too much wine and brandy in Gyantse.

His jaded eye took in his *Tulku*'s cape, hanging on a nail struck at random in the stone wall, leaving an ugly scar of displaced masonry. Its scarlet and gold opalescence, so rich, so strikingly extravagant with thousands of tiny scintillating gemstones, hurt his eyes by its flamboyant brilliance. It would fetch a good price from another aspiring *Tulku*. The money would add to the wealth he had already accumulated, hidden away in a chiselled niche he had made in the stone floor of this very room, wealth that would soon buy him out of his misery.

Kirsten sat down in an old chair, its rattan seat in wispy tatters so that his bottom stuck through it uncomfortably. He took up a hand-mirror, the edges of which had lost the silvering, and shuddered at his reflection. Bloodshot eyes, purple thread veins resembling the contours of a map, crags and bags, wrinkles and lines that had not been there a year ago. Irene would never recognize him without his handsome luxurious moustache. Slowly his hand reached for a jar of cosmetic cream on the table in front of him. He smeared his face with the white paste. He drew round his eyes with kohl. The eyes that stared back at him were even more blood red – *Tulku*'s eyes. He painted his lips scarlet, sucked cochineal to redden his tongue, painted his nails crimson. He looked frightful, and he felt frightful.

He changed from his Tibetan nobleman's clothes into the garments of the *Tulku*, draping the heavy richness of the cape around his shoulders with loving attention to detail. He put on his headdress of a hundred and eight human bones, and finally took up his *Tulku* staff topped by a grinning monkey-skull. Kirsten stealthily left the house and took the swiftest pony he possessed.

Half-an-hour later Gyantse Fort rose in front of him, moonlight silvering it, a Knights Templars bastion perched on the last mountain in the world. He looked up at the great *Jong*, impressive and magnificent, and was filled with a sense of star-studded drama. Yes, of course! He was a crusader riding into battle to meet a great warlord, exert his influence, make history! He was Charlemagne, Roland of Roncesvalles, Peter the Great, Richard the Lion Heart, Hamlet, Prince of Denmark, all rolled into one wonderful Tibetan *Tulku*, half-god, half-man! In his capacity, he could even be the saviour of men, of spies, of nations . . . and Kirsten's response to the dramatic being that he could never resist playing the leading role, he suddenly had a very clear idea of what he was going to do.

He kicked his pony hard with his heels and urged it up the hill.

At the gates to the *Jong* he was challenged by the guards. 'Do you know who I am?' he roared, getting off the pony and thrusting the reins into the hands of a bemused watchman.

'Yes, O master,' muttered the Tibetans shamefacedly.

'Who am I then?'

'The great *Rishi-Kudak*, *Tulku* son-in-law of the great warlord, Kuma Sidheong.'

'Then open the gates! I come with a message from the great Kuma himself to the *Jongpen*. Where is he?'

304

'Asleep, *Jowo*.'

'Take me to him and wake him.'

Obediently they ushered him into the presence of the Fort Commander. Sleepily the old man sat up in his bed, wanting to know the reasons for being disturbed at such an hour. When he saw the *Tulku*, he was less querulous. 'Why do you come to me at this hour, *Rishi-Kudak*? Is there more trouble brewing?' he asked humbly.

'I have visions of trouble, *Jongpen*. How long have you known me?'

'Many years. Since you were first brought to this very fort as a Urusso prisoner, before they took you to Thug-Phul as a noble warrior-serf in the house of Kuma Sidheong.'

'Exactly. And I come now from the house of Kuma himself. He is afraid for his life. Soon there is to be a great battle for Gyantse. You have heard of what happened at Guru, haven't you?'

The harmless old man nodded anxiously. 'I am too old to fight anymore. I command only the keys to the citadel.'

'That's why I disturb you at this ungodly hour, *Jongpen*. Kuma has asked me to work my magic on the Englishman you keep here. You know I practise the art of *dragpoi-dubthab*, don't you?'

The white-whiskered Commander nodded fearfully as he regarded the *Tulku*'s garish face and devilish eyes. 'Do not harm me, *Rishi-Kudak*, I have done my duty faithfully. The Englishman was buried according to Kuma's instructions.'

'I am not here to harm you, *Jongpen*, but to elicit the truth from the Englishman. Truth that will save Kuma's life at the coming battle. Is the Englishman dead?'

'Oh no! That was not Kuma's intention in the first hours of the Englishman's capture. He is to suffer first before being put to death,' the *Jongpen* seemed unhappy about it.

'That is why I have been sent by Kuma, to hear and to bear witness to the things he says.' Kirsten hoped he would not be caught out in the lie. 'Before the Englishman dies, Kuma wishes to know more things from his wayward mouth, for the very thought of torture will loosen any man's tongue even before the pain afflicts him.'

305

'He will not talk. Even after many hours buried in the ice so that his skin peels from him, he will tell us nothing.'

'He will speak to me, *Jongpen*. That is why I am here now. Do you wish Kuma Sidheong to survive the battle for Gyantse – for the British are terrible in battle?'

'Yes, I wish it. Without Kuma, we have no leader, and without a leader we are lost.'

'That is why we must save Kuma's life. I must speak with the Englishman before he dies. No . . . you need not come yourself. You are an old man and the guardian of the citadel. You require as much rest as possible before the *Jong* fills with more British prisoners – for we will win the battle, *Jongpen*. We will win the battle if you assist me now. Your presence beside the Englishman will only confuse the vibrations of my magical rites. If you do not trust me, you may allow your guards to sit outside the cell door while I perform my magic art on the Englishman so that he will open his mouth and give away the secrets of his country.'

'I trust you, *Rishi-Kudak*. As you say, you have been with us many years. You have supplied us with guns so that we can fight the *philang*-invader. You have cured our sick animals and our children. You have kept Kuma's noble daughter happy . . . '

'And soon a noble child will be born in Kuma's household. I have done what other men have failed to do, reincarnate a child of Chenrezig himself! He will be born in the summer.' Kirsten raised a finger in the air impressively.

'Then you are truly the great *Tulku*, and my trust is in you.' The old man bowed his head in respect to one far greater than he. 'Take the keys, *Rishi-Kudak*,' he said, fumbling under his bedroll. 'Take them and make the *philang* tremble.'

After instructing the guards in what they should do, the *Jongpen* lay down again and went back to sleep.

Kirsten was taken to Lewis's cell through a maze of dark stinking passages beneath the stone fort. He would never have found it of his own accord. The guards squatted outside the heavy iron-studded door which Kirsten slammed in their faces. Once inside, he took a deep breath. Trained as a Hussar, he still had a streak of squeamishness in him and hoped Lewis Joyden was not too badly carved up by the Tibetans.

An iron brazier recently replenished with charcoals made the heat and stench in the tiny cell unbearable. No other light or air penetrated. Hanging by his thumbs, his toes hardly able to touch the floor, Lewis's head had dropped between his shoulder blades, his naked body pinkly glistening while he slowly roasted before the charcoal fire after being buried up to his neck in ice for several hours. He looked like a skinned rabbit, Kirsten thought. He cut him down and Lewis crumpled in a heap on the filthy earthen floor. Lifting Lewis's head, his complexion that of bad cheese, Kirsten knew he could not rub the man's tortured limbs to revive the circulation, and instead, placed a flask of brandy to his lips.

Lewis spluttered and choked, dribbling the amber liquid over his chin and chest. He screwed up his eyes against the stinging burns from the abrasive spirit on his raw flesh.

'Sorry, old chap, I sympathize utterly,' said Kirsten in a voice and language he had not used since Radley days as he carefully dabbed at the spillage with his handkerchief. 'When all the sensations start coming back you really have something to worry about. Brandy does help, y'know.' Because he could do little else just then except sustain the prisoner drop by drop, he talked to him in a way he knew Lewis Joyden would understand. 'Back at the Kutuzov barracks it was rather pleasant to roll in the snow after a hot bath, especially with a glass of vodka and a pretty girl in one's hands. I'm sorry I can only offer you cognac and the pretty girl is at Thug-Phul. Tomorrow it would have been the balancing act on a slippery log over a scorpion pit while they cut you to ribbons with red-hot swords. The day after you would have had to ride two ponies at the same time, both of them pulling in opposite directions while you only wished you'd stayed at home. Tibetan culture is infinitely imaginative I think you've gathered, so, by the end of the week, you'd probably have been glad to see your head at the entrance to Red Idol Gorge.'

Ten minutes later Kirsten saw Lewis's lips twitch. He was relieved to know the brain was slowly restoring its functions enough to establish a sense of the ludicrous. 'What . . . the hell are you doing here?' Lewis murmured with eyes tightly screwed up, tears escaping from the corners of them as he fought against the terrible pains of returning feeling racking him.

'It's called pulling together, dry-bob, blood being thicker than water. The Dalai Lama might have issued a decree abolishing all forms of scourging, mutilation and other nice things the Tibetans have done to their enemies down the centuries, but most of it doesn't seem to have got through to some under-privileged bastards living in the heart of the country. Now then, can you feel anything yet?'

'What am I supposed to feel, *Tulku*? except damn glad you're here.' He began to raise himself slowly off the ground but dropped back again with a groan when the fire in his joints became far worse than being humanly refrigerated. Kirsten covered Lewis with his *Tulku* cape as a rigor gripped the tortured man, his limbs and head jerking in involuntary spasms while his teeth rattled so that he bit his tongue.

'It'll pass in a minute. It's the blood returning,' Kirsten said, sweating before the charcoal brazier.

'D-damn . . . kn-know . . . all . . . '

After a while, Kirsten said, 'I don't want to rush you, old man, but we *Tulkus* have to creep back into our coffins at daybreak. If you want to beat Kuma to Lhasa, you'll have to pull yourself together a bit quicker.' Kirsten thrust a bundle of clothes at Lewis. 'Sonya said you wanted to be a Tibetan tinker so here's your costume. Sorry I couldn't include the pots and pans.'

'Sonya . . . ' Lewis set his teeth resolutely and with a grimace of pain forced himself to sit up. Slowly he reached for the clothes. 'How . . . is she?'

'In better shape than you. My sister is as strong as a horse, fed as she was for years on raw liver sandwiches and port-wine. She'll probably have a ten-pounder – your ten-pounder. I don't know what mama would say to all these goings-on; Kirovsky Ploshad was never like this.'

'Where have all the guards suddenly got to?' Lewis asked as he stiffly and tentatively dressed himself, the material of the rough garments chafing his raw and bleeding skin. He remembered the intense training he had received from the yogi of the mountains – mind over matter – an art that had miraculously saved his life during his hours of a living burial in the ice.

'I threatened them with *dragpoi-dubthab* if they pestered us,' Kirsten explained. 'Can you stand?'

'I hope so . . .'

'Well, take it easy. No point in rushing things so that you fall in a heap on the doorstep. Then we'll both be for the chop. Have some more cognac . . . take it with you, your need, Mr Joyden, being greater than mine right now.'

'Kirsten . . . have you thought about how we're both going to get out of here?' Lewis asked as, with Kirsten's help, he got to his feet. He stood swaying before the coals that tomorrow they would probably have done him further damage with, and moving away to the door, leaned against it, panting hard.

'You're going first, Englishman. I'll follow later,' Kirsten said. 'Here . . . smear this white stuff over your face, I brought it especially. It smells foul but is well worth it. Now, put on my cape and headdress and act like a proper *Tulku* without letting the side down! I've already paved the way for you. Nobody should ask you any questions since you're supposed to be me, but in case they do, glower, shout and keep your eyes on your chest while you recite any mumbo-jumbo that comes into your head. They love it. Just follow your nose, and you should find the way out.'

'I reconnoitred the place on a previous occasion,' Lewis said, 'so I think I've got a fairly accurate picture of its layout. I just hope I can make it. Right now my legs feel like overgrown rice-plants in a hurricane.'

'What damn bad luck, British spy,' Kirsten murmured. 'Things haven't been going too well for you lately, eh what? But you've only got to walk as far as the gates. Outside, there's a pony waiting for you, so you can ride all the way to Lhasa as a prosperous pedlar.' Kirsten, with an air of braggadocio, was bent it seemed, on treating the whole situation lightly, obviously viewing it as a means of enhancing his *Tulku* prestige and image in Tibetan eyes. In a way Lewis was glad, it eased the tension of being in the embarrassing position of owing one's life to the enemy, both of them very awkward in each other's company and pretending not to be.

Levering himself off the door with a great effort to stand straight, Lewis put out his hand, 'I'll let you know some other time how grateful I am . . .'

Ignoring Lewis's hand, Kirsten placed his own right hand on Lewis's shoulder. 'Every hero becomes a bore at last – as Emerson discovered about the British.' Kirsten grinned, his face taut and humourless. 'You see Mr Joyden, Radley did teach me something after all. Just tell Sonya not to forget to invite me to the christening. Now go on, get out of here before you undo all my good work and Kuma arrives with his broadsword.' He began to strip off his clothes before winding his thumbs in the frayed ropes. Winking at the departing prisoner, Kirsten dropped his head realistically, and Lewis slipped away disguised as the *Tulku*.

ii

Kuma Sidheong had slept well at his house. At midday he rode into Gyantse with his retainers, a good feeling in his breast. He smelled victory in the air, Tibetan victory. Outside the fort, a night watchman handed him the *Tulku*'s cloak. 'It was put on the back of a blind beggar, *Jowa*. He felt the *Tulku* place it round his shoulders in the early hours of the morning to keep out the cold. The beggarman knew it was the *Rishi-Kudak*'s garment because he had fingered and smelled it before. He thanked the *Rishi-Kudak*, the son-in-law of the great Kuma Sidheong, but because he was a little afraid of the cloak's magic properties, wished to return it . . .'

'All right, all right, get on with it,' said Kuma impatiently, his thoughts not on the generosity of his son-in-law, but how the Britisher had stood up to his treatment. 'Give it to me, I will return it to the *Tulku*.' Not trusting a servant with the priceless garment, Kuma threw it over his shoulder. He spurred his pony inside the gates and barked

310

at the guards. 'Tell the *Jongpen* I have arrived. I am going straight to the Englishman's cell, for I wish to see my orders have been carried out implicitly.' Kuma knew what a soft-hearted old fool the *Jongpen* could be, and hoped, this time, he would not catch him out by being lenient with the prisoner. Never had Kuma held such a prestigious hostage, his bargaining power with the British immeasurable! A real British spy caught in uniform, the secrets inside the Britisher's head would be invaluable when his tongue had been sufficiently loosened! After such a coup, the Dalai Lama would deify him, he, Kuma Sidheong, reincarnation of a greater god!

Kuma Sidheong discovered his son-in-law in the Englishman's cell. Seated on the floor beside the brazier Kirsten coolly consulted a pack of tarot-cards laid out in front of him along with the cell keys. Kuma turned purple with rage, the veins in his neck standing out like thick ropes. His eyes bulged when he tried to speak. 'What . . . ' he croaked, 'what have you done with him? Where is he?'

'Good morning, father. I trust you slept well. I did, although it's very warm and smelly in here. You look angry, what's the matter?' Kirsten's painted face innocently looked up at Kuma. 'Oh, I see you've found my cloak. Good show – as the British say. I lost it last night in a Gyantse whore-house.' He turned his attention back to the cards.

Kuma could not strike a *Tulku*, but he felt like it. Kuma, strangled by magic himself, afraid to offend the gods, demons and spirits dwelling in the *Bardo* of emptiness where the dead go, controlled his wrath. 'Where is the Britisher?'

'Dead,' said Kirsten.

'Dead?' Kuma's sense of loss was devastating. He felt a sharp pain stab through his heart as though he had been struck by a *phurba*, a magic dagger. He took care, and eyed his son-in-law warily. 'What have you done to him, Urusso?'

'I am the great *Rishi-Kudak*, a mighty *Tulku*, not a Urusso any more, father, for I am a reincarnated being,' Kirsten said, equally on his guard as he played out his hand, knowing full well he must not push Kuma too far. 'The

311

fortune-telling cards tell me there is soon to be a great battle. Red Idol Gorge will overflow with blood . . . it might be the River Nyang Chu . . . I can't see too clearly this morning.' He peered more closely at his cards.

At that moment the *Jongpen* appeared at the cell door nervously accompanied by more Tibetan guards alerted by Kuma's shouting. Kuma whirled on the Fort Commander. 'Who let him in?' he demanded, pointing an accusative finger before sweeping up the ring of heavy iron keys and flinging them disparagingly at the *Jongpen*.

'No one let me in, father,' Kirsten said calmly before the bumbling *Jongpen* could make a hash of everything. 'I let myself in. Am I not the great *Rishi-Kudak, Tulku* reincarnation of a great and mysterious power who can even spirit away human flesh?'

The *Jongpen* and the guards nodded vigorous assent. They looked at the empty ropes in which the Britisher had been hanging like a *rolang*, a corpse that stands up, and now he was gone. They flinched, and breathed deeply with fear in their eyes, wondering what the great Kuma would do now.

'Did you perform *dragpoi-dubthab* on the Britisher, did you, Urusso?' Kuma demanded, determined to get to the bottom of this and to catch out his son-in-law once and for all. Dolma would not save him now, he wished only to tear this impertinent Russian upstart limb from limb, *Tulku* or no *Tulku*. 'Did you perform a magic rite to bring about injury and death to such an important prisoner before I had a chance to interrogate him properly, did you?'

'Yes, father, I did.'

Kuma flung Kirsten's cloak in his face. 'Without your magical garment, eh, Urusso? The nightwatchman found it on the back of a blind beggar. Am I not right in thinking that you are no true *Rishi*, nor even a Dubchen, but a dishonest Urusso who supplies me with useless weapons so that I might not even fight again the Urusso who would turn on us, you who prey upon my goodwill like the *Tisas* who feed off burnt flesh? Very well, you will deceive me no more, you will take the Britisher's place . . . ' He unsheathed his broadsword and in that instant Kirsten was

312

on his feet, his monkey-skull staff in his left hand while his right hand twirled his cape as a matador would to defend himself against a raging bull. Loving every moment, Kirsten, with a hearty laugh, parried Kuma's heavy sword with the staff, for if there was one thing he was good at it was sword-fighting, learned the hard way at the Kutuzov Barracks. With a blood-curdling yell he leapt for the open door, flinging back the guards with the monkey-staff and making off along the stinking dark corridors underneath the fort, his whoops and shrieks echoing back like Tibetan war-cries.

They pursued him on Kuma's encouragement and example, broadswords unsheathed. Up and down, along walkways, corridors, up steps, along crenellated walls, into turrets, down again, up onto the embattlements and parapets, and finally caught up with him on the ramparts where they held back, hardly daring to believe what they saw, let alone go any nearer.

Kirsten stood on the very edge of the embattlements, his magnificent cape caught by the wind billowing around him so that he resembled a huge bird. 'I am the great *Rishi-Kudak*, a *Tulku*, magic sage of Ozymandias soon to be reincarnated yet again as a *Towo*, a wrathful deity who will bring destruction on all of us. Watch me as I fly away to become Lu, snake-god of immense wealth who will live in the waters of the Nyang Chu . . . *Lha Gyalo! The gods win* . . .' And with that last triumphant cry he turned and launched himself off the stone parapet.

They watched him fly, floating gracefully like a splendid bird with scarlet and gold wings. They saw him come to rest far below, just a small broken bird, golden wings outstretched in a crimson pool.

Chapter Twenty-Three

The Tibetans made their stand for Gyantse at Red Idol Gorge. Ochre and red carvings of Buddha hacked out of the sheer cliff sides smiled down on the heads of the Britishers. The monks busily distributed weapons to the soldier-peasants, a few Russian breech-loaders and a great many out-moded matchlocks which took too long to prime and fire. With effort and energy, ancient blunder-buss cannons known as jingles were drawn up to a high rocky spur overlooking the defile dropping to a depth of three thousand feet in which the Gyantse road followed the banks of the River Nyang Chu. The British had to capture this difficult position before they could march forward to the stronghold of Gyantse itself. The Gurkhas, numbingly hampered by snow and sleet, were ordered to take the heights above Red Idol Gorge. Lee Metfords, Maxim machine-guns and the ten-pounders of the 7th Mountain Battery, in a constant barrage of fire, poured a relentless torrent of destruction into the Tibetan position.

Blood-curdling war cries, cumbersome and inaccurate jingles and the bravery of their stance, were no match for the superiority of British arms or the fierce experienced hand-to-hand fighting of the Gurkhas. Hopelessly routed, the Tibetans finally turned tail and fled, losing two hundred men against three Sepoys wounded.

Kuma Sidheong, fatally wounded, was propped against one of his jingles. He couldn't breathe with bullets in his chest: he gasped for air and blood frothed from his mouth. The British Army doctor had wanted him to lie down on a medical-stretcher so that he could be taken to the British Field Hospital to receive treatment, but Kuma had refused. He knew he had not long to live; nothing mattered any more, not even the disgrace of losing a British spy, a valuable prisoner whisked out of the very bowels of Gyantse *Jong* by a mad Russian who had imagined he was a powerful Tulku able to practise *Lungom*, the art of flying. But, the Dalai Lama could not behead him now, he, the great Lamaist warlord, Kuma Sidheong, even though he'd lost the battle for Gyantse – more powerful gods had won this time . . .

Kuma's eyes glazed. He had no desire to look upon his men turning to the side of the Britishers, helping them to clear the battlefield, gather firewood, making them feel welcome after what they had done . . . slowly his head dropped forward upon his yellow and green tunic patterned brilliantly with blood.

The following day, 11 April, the British Mission encamped on the banks of the Nyang Chu river at a hamlet called Chang Lo, adjoining Kuma Sidheong's estate at Thug-Phul. From there, they could see the great *Jong*, an unassailable fortress on its rocky height. Colonel Young-husband sent for the fort's Commander. The sturdy dignified old *Jongpen* rode into Chang Lo accompanied by the Chinese Amban and other dignitaries of the town.

'I cannot surrender the *Jong*,' he maintained stubbornly. 'The Dalai Lama will behead me. Go back where you came from.'

'Then we will bombard the *Jong* with our big guns,' he was briskly informed by the British Colonel.

The *Jongpen* chewed his slack lip. After a while he unwillingly confessed. 'We cannot defend ourselves against such attack. My soldiers have fled. There is no one left.'

Colonel Younghusband and his Staff officers rode triumphantly into the *Jong*, hoisted the Union Jack, examined the place thoroughly, took all the stored barley, and rode out again. The British Mission would stay at Chang Lo as the fort was a terrible place with no running

315

water except that which dripped down its green walls.

A few days later the Escort Commander, having changed his mind about abandoning the Mission after events at Guru, took a company of men to reconnoitre and clear the road to Lhasa of any Tibetan aggression, leaving the garrison at Chang Lo seriously depleted.

ii

Sonya was making a layette for her baby. Disturbed by a commotion in the garden, she put aside her needlework and got up to investigate. She was most perturbed to see Indian soldiers chasing squawking poultry, rounding up goats and pigs and anything else they could lay their hands on. Peasants, serfs and most of the household servants had fled after news of their warlord's death, and she and Dolma were left in the house unprotected.

'What are you doing?' she demanded in Tibetan.

The men stopped their foraging activities. Unable to understand her, they regarded her with surly defiance until an officer appeared from one of the sheds. Noticing she was not like other Tibetan women he had so far encountered, he said automatically in English (without believing for one minute she would understand him), 'Sorry ma'am, orders.'

'What rank are you?' she replied in English and a broad grin spread across his ruddy and perspiring face. 'Sergeant Dilks, ma'am. It's a relief to find someone around here who speaks the lingo. Many apologies, ma'am, we know this is a nobleman's residence, but since he's dead, we've been told to round up the hens and chickens, most of the men being partial to a nice fried egg for breakfast.' He looked uncomfortable. 'They never told us Kuma Sidheong had a wife, ma'am.'

'Tibetans have husbands and wives like the rest of the world, Sergeant. But, yes, Kuma's wife is dead. His daughter owns this house and land, and I'll thank you to get off it at once.'

'Then can we speak to her, ma'am?'

Sonya hesitated. 'No. She doesn't speak English, neither is she very well. The combined deaths of her father and her

316

husband have been too much for her. She must not be disturbed. But I'm her sister-in-law, so I'll thank you to leave us alone.'

'Orders is orders, ma'am, sorry. And our men need feeding.'

'Then go somewhere else.'

'Well, if you can just let us have a couple of chicks and a sack of barley, ma'am, we'll be getting along.'

'Very well, but that's all.' Sonya watched while they helped themselves to two of the plumpest hens, a sack of roasted barley and some vegetables, and was thankful the soldiers left without further trouble.

For the rest of the month Sonya noticed how livestock and grain gradually dwindled on the farm, the British now obviously doing their foraging by night. She and Dolma were powerless to prevent them and by May were having to tighten their own belts lest their stocks of food vanished altogether. Gyantse town was besieged by angry Tibetan forces gathering to prevent the British Mission from reaching Lhasa, adding to the shortages of food and escalating prices. Gyantse Fort, abandoned by the British as unsuitable for their garrison, was soon reoccupied and re-inforced by the Tibetans with weapons from Lhasa as well as Lamaist soldiers better trained than the troops previously occupying the *Jong*. Day after day Chang Lo and Thug-Phul were bombarded by jingles hammering lead and stone cannonballs into the British Mission camping close by. When those had run out, shining red copper ones like tiny meteors came plummetting out of the sky from the direction of the *Jong*, making small craters in the fields and flattening the tender growing barley and bean shoots.

The seige lasted seven weeks.

Sonya, during that time, was very tempted to go to the British Commander to ask about Lewis and what had become of him. She had heard nothing, received no secret messages, no news. She did not even know if he had succeeded in reaching Lhasa since the awful day Kirsten had sacrificed his own life. Sonya tried hard not to dwell too often or too long on Kirsten's tragic death, her own private agony of guilt and remorse unbearable. She blamed herself for having been instrumental in placing his life in such grave danger. Kuma Sidheong had never paid any attention to her sudden appearance in Dolma's household, only too glad that Dolma had found herself a suitable friend and companion. So, while she herself had remained unsuspected by Kuma, Kirsten, through her, had had to die. After his death Dolma had remained unforgiving, withdrawn and difficult. She had even threatened to tell her father the truth about Sonya's identity and her relationship with the English spy. It had taken all Sonya's ingenuity to keep Dolma's tongue quiet, frightening her with all manner of curses and magic so that Dolma did not know what to do. In the end Dolma took to wandering down to the River Nyang Chu to talk to Lu, the snake-god who lived in rivers and oceans. She was always much more amicable and happy when she came home so Sonya encouraged Dolma's simple belief in Kirsten's new reincarnation. Then, after her father's death at the battle of Red Idol Gorge, Dolma became even more introvert and strange, sitting for long hours staring at Sonya with a strange cunning and assessing look in her dark eyes. Unnerved by her behaviour Sonya tried hard to ignore it, sensing Dolma's underlying insecurity and necessity to have someone to blame for having been deprived so cruelly and so swiftly of the two people in the world she had most loved and respected. And so the days passed for both of them in a terrible lethargy and depletion of spirit, in suspicion, in hope and fear, while Sonya concentrated all her energies on just having her baby safely.

One thing Dolma and she did have, however, was plenty of news concerning what was happening as the British made a push towards clearing the Lhasa road and setting up a telegraph-line to keep them in touch with India. From Karo La came news of a big battle in the sixteen thousand foot pass which the Tibetans took as a deliberate act of provocation. They attacked Chang Lo while the garrison was under-strength, and were beaten back, but not without having given the British Mission a severe fright. The *Jongpen* was then taken as a hostage so that those occupying Gyantse Fort would not attack Chang Lo again.

While all this was taking place Sonya wondered how

much of a hand Lewis had in it, how much intelligence he was managing to send back to Chang Lo, how much he was risking his life all over again to map Tibet's unchartered terrain so that the British knew exactly where to go and how to hit hardest at the Tibetans.

Unable to bear the nerve-wracking suspense and indecision any longer Sonya went to the British camp at Chang Lo. She was politely and respectfully informed that the Commanding Officer was elsewhere, engaged in peace talks with the Tibetans. If she wished to see him on an important matter then she had better come back the following week.

Disappointed, Sonya left it a fortnight, nervousness getting the better of her. Without knowing whether she was doing the right thing or not by enquiring after Lewis's whereabouts, bravely she set off once more to Chang Lo, dodging Tibetan cannonballs which fortunately gave ample and noisy warning of their approach. They usually dropped just out of range of Thug-Phul and Chang Lo and caused very little harm apart from crop damage. When she heard the whistling hum of a cannonball in mid-air, and the excited muted war-cries and blood-curdling yells from the Tibetans three-quarters of a mile away launching their missiles from Gyantse *Jong*, she had time to take cover, crouched in a ditch or behind a stout tree. For her stalwart efforts in ignoring Tibetan cannonballs, she was again told at Chang Lo that Colonel Younghusband was elsewhere and she had better come back another time. She turned away, her dismay showing in her face.

'Is it something I can help you with, ma'am?' asked the Duty officer kindly. 'It would save bothering the Colonel at this busy time.'

Sonya hesitated and the Duty officer, to put her at her ease, said, 'You speak remarkably good English, ma'am, where did you learn it?'

'Er . . . from an Englishwoman, an Anglican missionary who used to work in Gyantse. My father paid her to teach me good English, but I have forgotten much and can only speak a very little.' She smiled, and crossed her fingers for the white lie.

319

'I see, ma'am.'

'Perhaps you can help me . . . ' and before she could change her mind Sonya took a deep breath and said, 'Lewis Joyden . . . I am looking for a British officer named Lewis Joyden.'

The Duty officer screwed up his face thoughtfully. 'Can't say I've heard the name, ma'am. An officer you say?'

'Yes.'

'Well, begging your pardon, ma'am, I know all the officers around here and there's no one by that name. You sure he isn't O.R.'

'O.R.?' She looked baffled.

'Other Ranks,' he said.

'Oh, oh I see . . . no, he was in the Pioneers . . . ' She was confused and embarrassed and added hastily, 'It doesn't matter. I'll speak to the Colonel when he returns.'

'You do that, Miss . . . er, why don't you go on up to the big house? The clerics usually know more about anyone than anyone else.'

'Thank you.'

At Kuma's house, requisitioned by the Mission, Sonya's way was barred by a burly Indian Jemadar. His rifle in two hands he resolutely prevented entry. Before Sonya could speak to him a British officer in khaki rode up on a pony, dismounted, and said in English to the Jemadar; 'Not another Tibetan woman complaining about her dashed barley rations! Right-ho Jemadar, take my horse, she's sweating like a sow. I'll deal with this one since you won't be able to understand a word she's babbling. Here . . . you can give this brace of pintails to cook – dinner for the officers' mess tonight instead of that rubbish we've been getting lately.' Red-faced and perspiring, he took the birds from his saddlebag. 'By George, no one told me Tibet could get as warm as this in May! Now then, woman, follow me,' he said brusquely in Tibetan over his shoulder to Sonya as he entered Kuma Sidheong's house. She would have turned tail and fled there and then but the exit was barred by the jemadar and the officer's pony.

The Captain ushered her inside his office and from behind his desk barked at her again, still speaking Tibetan,

320

'What can I do for you? Be brief, my time is short and we've had enough whining Tibetans today.'

'Colonel Younghusband . . . '

'I'm not Colonel Younghusband, I'm Captain Rice-Smythe, one of his Staff officers. If it's about your barley ration . . . '

'It's nothing to do with barley!' Sonya interrupted forcefully in Tibetan. She drew herself up stiffly and regarded the arrogant Captain with an equal amount of hauteur. 'I'm here to talk to Colonel Younghusband only.'

'Then you'll have a long wait. He's not here and not expected back for some time.' A bachelor, Rice-Smythe's dealings with women had always been at an impersonal level. His brusqueness with Sonya, therefore, stemmed from an embarrassed nervousness towards the opposite sex, rather than calculated rudeness.

'Very well. My information will keep,' Sonya turned away.

'What information?' Rice-Smythe looked suddenly suspicious, and interested, eyes narrowed, his blonde moustache quivering expectantly.

'About a certain Englishman who hid on this farm before he was captured and imprisoned in the *Jong* Good day, Captain.'

'Just a moment . . . don't go, take a seat and I'll be with you shortly.' He left the room abruptly and Sonya sat down.

Through the half-open door adjoining another office, the low hum of voices carried to her, the Captain and two clerks in deep discussion. At first Sonya took no notice of what they were saying in English. After a while she could not help eavesdropping on a conversation they had no idea she could understand.

'Blighme sir . . . I reckon we're in the wrong department. These intelligence chaps seem to have it all their way. First the Russian woman and now this one, though it's carrying things a bit far to want to sleep with a Tibetan for what she can tell you – looks like she's in the pudding-club, too, begging your pardon, sir. Ah . . . here we are, the gist of their conversation at Guru . . . '

Then the sound of pages being rifled in a notebook, 'Agent; are you calling me a traitor, sir? Younghusband; I'm calling you a fool . . . I don't tolerate fools gladly. Agent; then let me remind you, sir, I am a civilian attached to the Survey of India and all knowledge of my activities with the Tibet Frontier Commission, the Foreign Office and any other official department concerned in the affairs of Tibet will be hotly denied, right up to the King himself . . . it goes on a bit, Captain. Then Agent says; a court-martial in my case will not be applicable. And as far as fraternizing goes, how the devil else do I screw information from the enemy? Younghusband; then Princess Sonya Dubrovka means nothing at all to you except that? Agent; exactly that. Younghusband; you would make that official? Agent; certainly . . . blah, blah, blah . . .Lord Curzon already has my feelings upon the subject and . . . if he wasn't happy with the situation, I doubt he'd have given me this assignment. I have been acting on orders from the Viceroy himself . . . though he left the actual methods of gaining intelligence up to me. Then the Colonel goes on to tell him; I admit I was greatly put out when pundit-reports reached me about your affair with the Princess since I felt it would jeopardize our own position. If the woman really means nothing at all to you except a means of gaining vital information concerning her brother's and husband's activities, I'm prepared to accept your word and the matter is closed . . . that's more or less it, Captain, the reason why the agent – identity unrevealed – was recalled from Gyantse to explain his movements. This Tibetan woman, what does she want, money for her information?'

'I'm not sure . . . he seems to go only for the rich and titled ones, so I don't suppose this one's motives are entirely mercenary. She's probably got no information other than issuing him with a paternity writ. However, I'll get the C.O. to deal with her when he returns, it's not my problem. All I know is, someone is going to be damn angry because someone else has become mindlessly reckless just lately. I doubt – whoever this Agent is – will get another opportunity to put thumbscrews on anyone, white or black. Let's hope he can redeem himself by recce-ing things a lot better between here and Lhasa instead of wrecking our chances because he fancies a bit of skirt more than doing his duty.'

When Captain Rice-Smythe returned to his office, she was still there, sitting poker-backed with her hands tightly clenched in her lap, her face shadowed by her elaborate headdress and veil. At first she did not seem to hear him when he spoke to her. 'When Colonel Younghusband returns, madam, I'll mention your visit. He'll probably call on you himself.'

Without a word Sonya got up and left the room with a glazed expression, though the Captain did not see her face. She felt as if she had just been badly injured, the shock of Lewis's betrayal and his use of her appalling her, numbing her to such an extent she felt she did not care one way or another whether or not he had managed to reach Lhasa safely.

A few days later Colonel Younghusband sent her a message, written in Tibetan, asking her to come to Chang Lo. She refused. 'But ma'am,' said the exasperated aide-de-camp who had come with an escorting Jemadar, the same Indian who had barred her entry into Kuma Sidheong's house, 'Captain Rice-Smythe said you had some information for us concerning an Englishman who was imprisoned in Gyantse Fort.'

'I do not speak English,' she said in Tibetan, looking at neither of them but staring straight ahead in prim disdain of their rank, status or nationality.

The Colonel's aide looked put out and shrugged helplessly at the Jemadar, then turned to leave. Sonya thrust two pieces of paper at him. The aide took them. One was written in Tibetan, one in English. The Tibetan message was addressed to Colonel Younghusband. He did not understand what the note contained, only that it was signed, Dorjee. The Colonel would know when Rice-Smythe explained.

Sonya had written; '*The information I have is contained in this other note I enclose from the Englishman who hid here before his capture . . . he asked me to give it to you; he spoke Tibetan.*' The note written on a torn scrap of paper in English, in Lewis's handwriting copied painstakingly by her from one of his letters, read briefly, '*The Dubrovka woman has returned to Russia, and the other Russians in the Gyantse area impose no further threat. All has gone according to plan.*'

Colonel Younghusband snorted in disgust. 'Is this all?'

'Yes sir,' replied the aide. 'She can't speak English, and only passed on that scrap of paper in English from the person who gave it to her.'

'Well, since this is all the out-dated information in her possession, I don't think we've lost out on anything, and there's not much point in my wasting time interviewing her personally.' Colonel Younghusband had a very shrewd notion as to the identity of the Tibetan woman's informer as well as the noblewoman herself. The Duty officer and Sergeant Dilks had come to him about an English-speaking noblewoman living in the house of Kuma Sidheong's daughter who had been name-dropping. She had mentioned the name, Lewis Joyden, did the Colonel know anything about the matter? Oh yes, the Colonel did! He would also bet his life on it that the noblewoman in the Sidheong household was none other than Princess Sonya Dubrovka in disguise. But he was powerless to act at the moment – one could not imprison a pregnant woman, neither could she be packed off to India or Russia in her condition. So, he would bide his time. She would soon have her baby and, in Lhasa, he was bound to catch up again not only with Lewis Joyden but also Sonya Dubrovka! And, when the Viceroy and the Foreign Office got to hear how careless and irresponsible one of their supposedly best agents in the business had become on account of a love-sick liaison with a foreign enemy, plus issuing forged and dangerous information to mislead his own side, plus not maintaining his dignity or his disguise, Lewis Joyden would vanish off the face of the earth together with all Blue Book reports concerning his activities.

Younghusband was bone weary, his thin yet aesthetically attractive features taut with a sense of overpowering devotion to his work, for he was nothing if not a perfectionist. With a heavy sigh, he turned back to his paper work, that was not always confined to military matters. Why should he, the

Commander and hinge-pin of an important mission like this, be saddled with domestic affairs, he asked himself wearily. Two sackloads of Army pay had gone missing and the thief or thieves had yet to be apprehended. His men were running out of footwear and warm clothing and Lewis Joyden, a British Agent he was relying on so much for his intelligence work in the van of their entry into Lhasa, had fathered a child on the Russian enemy, ye gods! The Colonel sighed again, the vicissitudes of this task assigned to him by the Viceroy of India galling to say the least, especially since he, even as a soldier, preferred peace to war. His wife had written him another forlorn letter telling him how much she and his little daughter missed him and asked when he would be home. He, too, missed his family dreadfully, and would go back to Calcutta tomorrow given the chance – how he wished it was possible! Now peace negotiations with the Tibetans had broken down, the Nepalese, Bhutanese and Chinese were powerless to intervene and talk sense to the Tibetans. Well, it looked as though the only place to talk was not here in Gyantse with a lot of second-hand officials but at Lhasa, face-to-face with the God-King sitting on his Potala! 'Get this telegram off to London at once! I want an answer one way or another by the end of the month without all this prevarication,' Younghusband snapped at his aide as a cannonball from Gyantse *jong* smacked into the outside wall and frayed his nerves to an even greater degree. 'And inform the Escort Commander I'm leaving for Kangma tomorrow morning. The sooner we get to Lhasa, the better for all of us!'

325

Chapter Twenty-Four

In the city square shadowed by the mighty golden-roofed
Potala, a dirty ragged pedlar, his face a cracked mask of
mud and yak-fat, got off his dusty tired pony. Only his eyes
and disposition were visibly alive as he whistled a catchy
ditty whilst unloading and displaying his wares.

Women, some young, some old and most of them housewives, ran out of hovels with their children to greet the
pedlar and eye as well as handle his shiny copper pots and pans,
colourful silk threads, sharp steel needles, brooms, feather
dusters, wooden spoons and bowls, and wonder of
wonders, sweet-smelling spices from India and the heady
sensuous perfumes from Arabia and the Orient which the
cheerful pedlar assured the ladies would make their
husbands love them more. Most couldn't afford his basic
wares let alone love-scents; they were too poor to buy even
the meanest quality barley-flour or rancid yak-butter in
order to survive. So, without envy or malice, but with
plenty of interest and curiosity, they sat in the filthy pot-
holed square and waited for something else the itinerant
vendor had which they could afford – a good gossip and
news of the outside world.

All around, pigs and curs fought off fat black ravens as
well as the children, tiny under-nourished scraps of
humanity, many of them blind and all with ghastly sores on
their mouths because they drank the same water and ate the
same food as the scavenging animals. The heat and smell

was sickening as the hot June sun smote the city, and, several times, the pedlar from Amdo Province sniffed the sweet aromatic odour of a clove-stuck orange dangling from a piece of string around his neck. It was the only way to get the smell of Lhasa out of his nose . . .

A disturbance at one corner of the square drew away the attention he was receiving. All heads turned to what seemed to be an execution procession. It looked like a grand one and the pedlar was as curious as everyone else. He stopped talking to watch the parade emerging from one of the narrow dark alleys that led onto the square. A sturdy Tibetan, naked apart from a loincloth, stood in a wicker cart, his hands and feet bound with chains. The watchmen of the city beat him relentlessly with yak-tail whips. His wounds gaped, his body smeared all over with his own blood. The wicker cart drew into the square, just a few yards away from the pedlar's pitch. The pedlar noticed that, despite the man's obvious pain and humiliation, he did not flinch but retained a defiant look in his dark eyes.

'Who is he? . . . what's he done?' the housewives around the pedlar shouted to those following the wicker cart, men, women and children hurling stones, refuse and abuse at the prisoner while the city's watchmen continued to exercise their whips. Riding beside the prisoner were Yellow Hat Lamas and Chinese officials, there to oversee the execution.

'He is one of those who ran away from Gyantse *Jong* when the *philangs* made their final attack,' the pedlar and other curious people gathering in the square were informed by those who had followed the cart through the city and knew what all this was about. 'The *philangs* climbed it with ropes . . . they managed to get their guns in a different position and bombarded the *Jong* from the Shigatse valley . . . the *philangs* should have been stopped. Boiling oil could have been poured on them while they hung from their ropes . . . but no, this one ran away like the others. Now the way is open for the *philangs* to come to Lhasa. The Shap-és and the Dalai Lama have ordered all cowards to be made a public spectacle like this one who is going to be beheaded.'

The confusion increased. Terrified women gathered up

327

their children, crying, wailing, screaming; 'We have heard the *philangs* are terrible men . . . they rule all the world because they despoil the women and vandalize like no other warriors. What shall we do, where shall we go?'

The Lamas told the people not to be stupid, the holy city would be adequately protected against the *philang*-invader, for nobody would assault the abode of the God-King, including the *philangs* from beyond the Himalayan mountains!

In the square the warrior was dragged from his cart by the watchmen. The crowd stopped stoning him in expectation of what was to come. Forced to his knees at the feet of a *ro-gyapa*, a butcher of animals as well as humans, for the first time the man seemed to become aware of what was about to happen, and with a wild inhuman cry struggled with his captors. His eyes rolled whitely, he foamed at the mouth soundlessly, strangled by terror. He kicked out like a madman. Muscled and strong, it took some time to curb him, the watchmen bringing their whips and legs into greater play. Pinned to the ground by ropes and staves pegged into the earth, he lay panting like an animal while his feet and hands were hacked from his body and finally, the jerking bloodied man, not yet dead, was placed back on his knees. A watchmen pulled on the victim's plaited topknot to straighten the neck. The *ro-gyapa* with several haphazard attempts managed to sever the head from the body. The butcher held up the head by its rope of hair, displaying it for the roaring, excited crowd's full and final approval.

A Chinese officer stopped beside the pedlar, who had been the only one to take no notice of the gruesome ritual. 'You have no stomach for such things, eh, pedlar?' He grinned, his slit eyes disappearing into his flat white face.

'I have seen it all many times before, master,' replied the pedlar, vigorously polishing the base of one of his shining copper pans. 'After a while it becomes nothing. It is rather like making love to a beautiful woman many times in one day, the excitement wears off after a while and is never the same as the first conquest.'

'Then you choose your women wrong, pedlar,' replied

the Chinaman grinning more widely, before adding, 'His Holiness, the Yellow Hat over there, wishes to know from where you stole such a fine-looking pony. Scum like you does not possess thoroughbred stock without stealing it.'

'Tell his Holiness I make humble apology for possessing such an animal when he does not. But I did not steal it. It was a gift to me from one higher than he.' The pedlar spat on the base of the saucepan and re-polished it.

The Chinaman went back to the Yellow Hat seated in all his ecclesiastical glory on a mule, and repeated what the pedlar had said. The lama rode over scowling. 'You have too much sauce in your mouth for such an idle pedlar, so watch your tongue fellow lest it be cut out for insolence. There is no one higher than a Yellow Hat apart from the God-King himself. Who gave you such a fine beast, if you are to be believed?'

'Kuma Sidheong,' the great warlord of Gyantse who, alas, I believe is dead now, peppered with holes on the slopes above Red Idol Gorge about two months ago. I got the pony as a reward, my lord, because I did him a great favour.'

'What favour, liar?'

'I put into his hands a *philang*-spy with much to give away in secrets, and the fool let him go because he listened to a madman, an Urusso with many tricks up his sleeve.'

'Yes, I heard the story,' said the Yellow Hat, staring hard at the pedlar. 'But you fellow, are you willing to hand your pony over so that I may ride on a comfortable pilgrimage while you, too, can be amply rewarded by dwelling on the Gyalwa Pal Ri, where not many ascend from this life?'

'For a price, *Rimpoche.* It would be fine to dwell on the Victorious Lotus Mountain, but first I have to dwell here. It's no living selling pins to poor women.'

'What is your price, vagabond?'

'That you might place this sweet-smelling holy orange in Buddha's lap at the Lamasery of your next pilgrimage.' The pedlar took the clove-stuck orange from around his neck and handed it to the Yellow Hat along with the sturdy Timor.

'It is a simple matter, pedlar,' said the Yellow Hat

sniffing the orange appreciatively, and then patting the pony, 'let us hope it wards off the evil odours that are coming to us lately from many directions.'

'Let us hope so, *Rimpoche*,' murmured the pedlar.

ii

Sonya's baby was born in the first week of July, two weeks premature. Dolma had summoned the Mother-Nun of Gyantse Convent to deliver the child which was born easily and without any tearing to the mother.

Sponging away the cheese-curd substances of birth protecting the baby as it lay for months in womb-water, the Mother-Nun noticed a birth-mark on the inside of the baby's left wrist, and drew the attention of the lady of the house to it. Dolma was equally startled.

'What is it? What's the matter with it? Is he deformed?' Sonya asked weakly from the bed, seeing Dolma and the Mother-Nun bent over the infant in close scrutiny and secretly whispering. Perturbed, she struggled to sit up straight. 'Bring him here . . . give him to me at once!'

Dolma wrapped the baby in its swaddling clothes and unwillingly handed him to Sonya.

'What were you two whispering about?' Sonya asked angrily.

'See . . . see here, Reverend Lady,' said the excited Mother-Nun as she bounced over to the bedside and exposed the baby's arm. 'You truly have given birth to a holy child, for here is the mark of Chenrezig! Jetsunma, look, this is the conch-shell on the wrist which is the sign of the incarnation of a future God-King!'

'Poof!' said Sonya, scathingly, not at all struck by the Mother-Nun's theory, 'it's only a birth-mark. My mother used to call them strawberry marks. My family have a hereditary tendency for these marks – only an accumulation of damaged blood vessels.' She remembered that from Pratikayit days – he always had a medical explanation for everything. 'Now go away and leave me to nurse my son in peace.'

When they had gone, Sonya could not resist another peek

330

at the angry red mark on her son's left wrist. It did look shell-shaped. What did a conch look like? Hollow, domed, half-moon? Like a shell-fish, like an ear? It resembled all those depending which way one looked at it. But it was only a birth-mark and would fade in time, she was sure of it. She dismissed the theory of Chenrezig's incarnation, the only incarnation this baby was likely to be was that of Lewis Joyden!

While Sonya nursed the baby she could not help thinking about the father. She had got over the first shock of listening to something she ought not to have – and eaves-droppers, she reminded herself, never did hear anything good of themselves. Whatever had possessed her to seek out the British Colonel in the first place? She must have been a little unbalanced at the time to let her feelings run away with her before the stony-faced British. Maybe the shock of Kirsten's death and her anxiety over Lewis's fate plus the fact that she was pregnant had made her more than a little unhinged. Now that she had had time to ponder the situation, of course Lewis would have had to show his Janus-face, say all those things to Colonel Younghusband when he had been summoned back to the camp at Guru. He could hardly have admitted a romantic attachment to someone the British regarded as the enemy! Now that she had had time to get over the embarrassment and humili-ation of what some people might be thinking of her on the strength of Lewis's hot denial at Guru concerning a love affair with her, she could look at things in perspective. She had known all along he was engaged in a dangerous game – if espionage could be called a game. He would have to deny his liaison with her, for her sake as well as his. Now she would have to be all the more careful as it would be doubly dangerous for him if it became common knowledge he had fathered a Russian woman's child. But he still loved her – didn't he? Even if he had never said so – he had always used the word 'want' not 'love'. She had tackled him once about it. Maybe he was just naturally reticent upon a subject that embarrassed him. Englishmen were notoriously cold characters when it came to a great many things, including wild displays of affection – unlike the passionate men she had been surrounded by in Russia, men like her father, Pratikayit, Sasha her mother's hot-blooded, hot-headed cousin, Ivansky and of course Kirsten. But actions spoke louder than words. She was just being neurotic, she must not let herself become carried away on mere supposition. Lewis knew she was having his child, he loved her without having to say it, and he would send word or come for her himself when the time was right.

Then why didn't he get in touch with her? Why didn't he prove his love by putting her out of her lonely misery? If he could do it for others, why not for her, the one he was supposed to love? The little devil of doubt persistently nagged in her heart . . .

The new baby did wonders for Dolma. She acquired a new lease of life, became the perfect nursemaid and guardian to the infant Sonya had unofficially named Lewis Haga Joonu, names discussed by Lewis and she in the barn the day Lewis had found out about her pregnancy, the day he had been captured and taken to Gyantse *Jong*. The baby became known as Luey. Dolma cossetted and crooned over the dark haired infant all day long. 'Lu is losing his hair,' she remarked one day as she smoothed Luey's head. 'His hair is all falling out and leaves only a soft down like a baby duck.'

'Let me see.' Sonya examined Luey's head. 'It looks perfectly all right to me. Perhaps all babies lose their hair soon after they're born. I don't think, though, he'll be bald for the rest of his life . . . at least I hope he won't be.'

'Many incarnations of Chenrezig have no hair,' Dolma said, hugging the child closely and possessively to her breast, tickling its cheek and lips to make it smile in sleep. 'If he has no hair, then he is a noble being. Only *philangs* who are like animals have much hair on the face and body. I have seen them exposing their white flesh to the sun on the banks of the Nyang Chu river when I have been there to talk to Lu, snake-god of all the waters.'

Sonya wished now she had not encouraged the diminution of her son's name. 'Dolma, please call him Lewis, not Lu or Luey! And you don't have to go to the Nyang Chu, either!'

'Lu has spoken to me and so has the Mother-Nun,' Dolma said, and Sonya did not quite understand her at first. Then Dolma looked at her with the same burning expression in her eyes and agitated excitement of manner she had displayed at the time of Kirsten's death. 'This child should be taken to the Monastery so that the Lamas can tell truly what kind of incarnation he is. The seal of Chenrezig does not fade.' She held out the baby's arm, exposing the birth-mark on the inside of its left wrist. 'It grows brighter and brighter, like a sign from Chenrezig to instruct us what to do. It is a sin to keep him here when he is born a holy child. The High Lamas will be glad of him. They will bring him up as the new Dalai Lama and we will receive many blessings for sacrificing him to the service of the holy ones.'

'Dolma, stop it at once! He is my son and I want to hear no more of this nonsense,' Sonya warned, snatching back her baby. Sonya felt Dolma was beginning to entertain an unhealthy notion that the baby belonged to her. In view of her childlessness, Sonya was perturbed by these strange mental fantasies of hers, imagining Kirsten to be Lu, snake-god of all waters, and now baby Lewis to be an incarnation of the Dalai Lama; whatever next! 'Leave him with me now and go away, it's time for him to be fed,' Sonya said, brusquely dismissing Dolma from the bedroom. Sonya was on her guard after that, and never for one moment left the baby alone with Dolma.

iii

The despatch Colonel Younghusband had been waiting for from the India Government had at last arrived; 'On any account do not commit yourself to abandonment of advance to Lhasa.'

On the 14 July, the British Mission left Gyantse for Lhasa, less than a hundred and fifty miles away, leaving behind a small garrison in Gyantse. They took the old caravan trail, heading for Karo La, fifteen thousand feet above sea-level. Brilliant yellow mustard fields like patches of sunlight through the rain were trampled underfoot, rippling green barley-fields waiting to be harvested were ravaged under the relentless tread of pack-animals and soldiers. The Gurkhas assaulted a Tibetan stronghold, scaling the heights as at Red Idol Gorge, and the Tibetans fled. The way was clear again and below them lay the picturesque Yamdok Tso, the Turquoise Lake. Held in the rugged embrace of the pristine mountains, brilliant alpine flowers covered the lower green slopes, water birds teemed, geese, teal, mallard, and the sandpiper echoed a dreary lament in the wide open sandy spaces of such austere beauty. The fort and monastery were held by the British, and here the Ta Lama and the Yutok Shap-é met again to talk with Colonel Younghusband as they had at Gyantse – but all to no avail.

After seven hours of mindless haranguing between the Chinese Amban, the Grand Secretary and the State Councillor of the Tibetan Government, Colonel Younghusband was again faced with the same deadlock as at Gyantse. The Tibetans would not budge from their decision. The British could not enter Lhasa to talk to the Dalai Lama. They would be met by great resistance and all future negotiations regarding peace and trading agreements would be placed in jeopardy.

That night, in the officers' mess at Nagartse on the shores of the Turquoise Lake, Colonel Younghusband, unspeakably weary, faced a barrage of questions from his Staff officers. 'Sir, what on earth's the point of coming all this way if it's not for the purpose of establishing a permanent British Representative in Lhasa?'

'Captain,' said Younghusband addressing Rice-Smythe, 'my sentiments exactly. But it's all to do with the Cavagnari affair back in '79. If you remember, Major Cavagnari was Britain's Political Agent to Afghanistan and shortly after arriving in Kabul he and his escort were massacred by the Afghans even though they had welcomed the Russians the year before. We had to fight a very bloody and expensive war over that affair, and the British and Indian Governments do not want to repeat the same mistake again. That's why we shall be establishing no Political Agent in Lhasa . . . what's this?' Younghusband asked the Jemadar who had thrust a basket of fruit under his nose. 'Is this all we're getting from India nowadays?' In disgust he took up a shrivelled, clove-stuck orange from the top of the basket.

The officers, gathered around the mess table laughed, and Captain Rice-Smythe said; 'It is a, *je ne sais quoi*, sir!'

'It is a very special one, Colonel,' said the Jemadar seriously. 'It has come all the way from Lhasa.'

'Excuse me, Gentlemen,' said the Colonel taking up the orange and departing from the mess.

'I smell a pundit here,' said Captain Rice-Smythe with a wink at the others. 'Is he monk or is he monkey? Is he fool or is he flunkey?' And in the wake of the Colonel's departure he immediately began organizing a shooting-party for the following day, hundreds of water-birds just waiting to be shot on the shores of the first non-salt lake they had encountered, Tibetan Buddhists abstaining from any such killing sport.

In the light of a hurricane lantern, Colonel Young-husband looked at the dehydrated orange with an expression of resignation while making allowance for ingenuity. If it was from whom he thought, this time Lewis Joyden had better tell him something he did not already know. The Colonel began to pick the cloves from the orange, and felt all the time he was de-fleaing a dog. After the last clove had been removed, the orange-peel came away easily and lay on the table in one piece. The white pith inside was rather too thick for a dehydrated orange like this one, and after screwing up his eyes in an attempt to find where the thin layer of pith had been stuck back to the inside skin, he carefully managed to separate the pith as well as a thin paper-layer sandwiched between peel and pith. Bringing the lantern closer, the Colonel began to wonder how long it had taken the fellow to skin an orange in this way. The flimsy piece of paper was blank. But schoolboys had their own tricks and, remembering one of them, the Colonel held the paper to the hot glass of the hurricane lamp. Invisible ink, ascorbic acid such as lemon-juice; simple, unoriginal, yet effective. The heat from the lantern made the writing appear, faint scratchy marks that had hugged the orange. It was hard on the eyes but well worth the effort of deciphering:

'Kamba La, last pass to Lhasa, more accurate height, four hundred feet higher than previously recorded – adjust weaponry sights accordingly. Tsangpo River, Lhasa's natural barrier is upper reaches of Brahmaputra. Not as wide as previous pundit estimates – one hundred and fifty yards, not one thousand! Difficult to cross, running at seven knots, swift, turbulent, thickly yellow with silt deposits. Valley of Tsangpo lush, ample grazing ground and fodder for animals. Village of Chaksam provides ferry service – don't rely on it. Suspension bridge (four chains) rusty and falling apart (four hundred years old!) yak-skin coracles hidden further up the shore, make use of them – safer than other kinds of river-craft. Lhasa arsenal run by Dorjiev and Prince ND – nothing to worry about, hardly any Russian guns – they're minting silver coins not jingles! All machinery wooden and hand-operated, English-manufactured lathes. City strongly defended by Tibetans from other Provinces. German and French objections to British interference in Tibet filtering through to Lhasa – Dalai Lama, a worried man. Will keep in touch. Samsâra!'

So, he had reached the Forbidden City first!

The Colonel could not contain an acute sense of disappointment . . . on the other hand, no one need ever know . . .

Wasting no time, Colonel Younghusband wrote a letter to the Dalai Lama.

Chapter Twenty-Five

The baby was now three weeks old. A thriving healthy infant, Sonya's son gained a pound a week, his birth-weight soaring from six pounds to nine. Sonya felt the time had come to start thinking about leaving Dolma's home, she and the baby could not remain hidden at Thug-Phul any longer. She had waited in the vain hope that Lewis might send word of his whereabouts, but since he had chosen to ignore her existence, Sonya felt she had to take matters into her own hands. The more she thought about it, the more she felt Lewis had let her down very badly, dismayed, too, at her own foolishness in being beguiled by a man whom she had imagined cared for her. Memories of Geyog's and Joonu's 'expendable lives' as far as Lewis was concerned, his utter ruthlessness and cold callousness in pursuit of some vain and selfish glory, questions and doubts pushed to the back of her mind since he had made love to her; all these conflicts reasserted themselves. Was she, too, another of his expendable lives? If so, how he must be laughing over the light relief she had provided during their travels together!

Sonya tried not to think about it, realizing it was now up to her to pick up the pieces of her life and start again with her son. And the place to do that was Lhasa where she would find her husband, Prince Nikolay Dubrovka. Sonya realized, too, that once the British gained a firm foothold in the Tibetan capital, her own safety would be at risk. At present, they could do very little about suspect foreigners since the country was not yet theirs, but if history was anything to go by, and it came to a showdown in Lhasa and the British won, then Russians like her would be the first to come under their scrutiny and internment. Like everyone else around Thug-Phul and Gyantse, she had not thought that the British would actually push ahead to the Forbidden City in view of all the foreign criticism and Tibetan resistance they had encountered. But when rumours circulated that the Mission had been authorized by the India Government to go ahead and enter Lhasa despite all opposition and the main body of their army left Chang Lo, Sonya began to realize she would either have to reach Lhasa before Colonel Younghusband or leave it until the fighting died down. Since there was no possibility she would arrive before an invading army, she had no choice but to bide her time, watch events, and plan her action accordingly. Perhaps, too, she might hear from Lewis as soon as he knew which way things were going for his country; she still lived in hope.

But while Sonya continued to toss things over mentally, chafing at having to cool her heels at Thug-Phul, matters were swiftly and cruelly taken out of her hands and she was precipitated head first into a drama that left her weak and shaken.

Dolma and the baby disappeared from Thug-Phul.

Sonya, who had never let the child out of her sight since Dolma's strange mental aberrations concerning the baby, and even slept at night with her son secure in her arms, woke up very late one morning, heavy-headed and slightly nauseated. The baby was missing from the bed, and in that dreadful moment of discovering her loss, Sonya remembered the milk Dolma had given her the night before – and its slightly bitter taste. Dolma, in her gentle thoughtful capacity as the perfect hostess of her noble household, had been bringing her a bed-time drink of yak-milk from the time she knew Sonya was to have a child, right up to this nursing-period, and so Sonya had never doubted Dolma'a motives were anything but sincere. But now! The bowl was still there on the table beside her, a blue-white residue in the bottom. Sonya sniffed the almondy dregs and was in no doubt Dolma had drugged her

338

with a strong sleeping-draught. Panic-stricken, Sonya shakily dressed herself and took what was left in the stables, a feeble old mule, half-blind and cantankerous – but better than nothing.

Sonya, guessing where Dolma was likely to take the baby, headed straight for the Monastery at Gyantse. But the monks could tell her nothing. No noblewoman with a newborn baby had come near them. They were sorry, but they could not help.

Sonya did not know what to do. Were the monks lying? She would not put it past them. If it turned out they, too, believed in the bizarre notion that the baby could be an incarnation of a future Dalai Lama, they would hardly be likely to tell her.

Beside herself with anxiety, Sonya went to the Convent, hoping the Mother-Nun would know something the monks did not. Here again she drew a blank. The Mother-Nun was kind and solicitous but knew absolutely nothing about the lady Dolma and the baby. She did offer to send nuns into the town to seek information, and Sonya was grateful for this small consideration. By nightfall the nuns returned. They had learned nothing in Gyantse town. No one had seen the lady Dolma or the baby. Two of them had even braved the British soldiers left behind at Chang Lo and had searched along the banks of the Nyang Chu River in case the Nemo Dolma had gone to talk to Lu, the snake-god, as was her custom.

The baby would be hungry and Dolma would be unable to feed it: her breasts painful and heavy, a mother-clock timing exactly the hour of her child's need, Sonya returned to Thug-Phul, feeling she would go out of her mind if she were to spend the night not knowing what had become of her son. She had of course questioned all the servants remaining at Thug-Phul, a mere half-dozen who managed the household tasks as well as the ploughing and tilling of the fields, but not one knew of the mistress's whereabouts. Sonya, together with one of the field-hands, a sturdy boy of ten who had been Kuma Sidheong's yak-herd, returned to Gyantse to ask the night-watchmen if they had seen or heard anything about Dolma, 'noble Nemo of Thug-Phul'.

If Dolma had left Gyantse the night before – as was very likely, thought Sonya – then one of the night-watchmen might have seen her.

Her perseverence was rewarded.

An old man guarding the iron-bridge had allowed a pilgrim-woman to cross it in the early hours of the morning. 'The Neskorma took the Shigatse road,' he told Sonya.

A weight lifted from her shoulders. At least Dolma wasn't taking the baby to Lhasa. Sonya prayed the watchman wasn't mistaken, and asked; 'Did the woman have a baby?'

The old man shrugged. 'She might have had a child tucked into her *amphag*, I don't know. It was dark, I couldn't see.'

'Was anyone else with her?'

'No one else. She went alone.'

'Walking or riding?'

'Walking, m'lady. She was a poor and humble Neskorma without even the customary pack on her back.'

'Thank you for your help.' Sonya gave him a silver tranka.

If Dolma was taking the baby to the Monastery at Shigatse, on foot, then it would be an easy matter to catch up with her. Sonya only wished she had a swifter and more reliable animal than the mule. She asked the boy with her; 'Yul, where can I get a good fast pony?'

'Nowhere, m'lady. Even if you had enough money – they are very expensive – you would not be able to find one in Gyantse because all the soldiers want them.'

'But I need one.'

The boy was silent. Sonya could see he was mulling something over in his head. Then he asked; 'You will be returning to Thug-Phul now, or carrying on to Shigatse?'

'Oh, carrying on at once,' Sonya said emphatically. 'I must get my baby back before Madam Dolma reaches Shigatse.'

The boy shook his head. 'Then it cannot be. In two hours time yes, but not right away. It is also dangerous to travel to Shigatse alone at this time of night. If you set off as soon as it begins to get light, you will still catch up with the

Nemo long before she reaches Shigatse, and I, by sunrise, will have got you your pony.

'For how much, Yul?'

'It will be a small price, nothing like you would normally pay. I know someone who has a pony for a pair of silver shoes.'

Fifty taels could not be argued with since Sonya had no idea what a good pony would fetch. 'All right,' she agreed reluctantly. 'You'll get the money when you bring me the pony.'

The boy ran off, and Sonya went back to Thug-Phul to wait for him.

ii

Four hours later Yul appeared at the house, leading a sleek rowan. The thoroughbred pony looked capable of any distance and Sonya, delighted, paid Yul his fifty taels and counted it money well spent. She had packed some food for herself, plus extra warm clothes for the baby, wondering if a newborn baby could live off its own fat for twenty-four hours or more. She certainly hoped so, otherwise Dolma would have a very unhappy bundle in her *amphag* all the way to Shigatse.

Sonya rode hard and long, and discovered half-way to Shigatse that the pony's leather bridle, saddle and reins were stamped with the insignia of an Irish Regiment. So, Yul had stolen the pony from Chang Lo – probably the British despatch rider's own mount, in which case the artful boy might even have helped the Tibetan cause! Sonya decided to get rid of the pony as soon as she was able.

Despite the swiftness of the pony, she did not catch up with Dolma. It was well past midnight when Sonya entered Shigatse, dishevelled, dispirited and wishing Lewis was with her – he would know what to do. She sat down by the roadside, swamped by feelings of total isolation and loss. Glad to be alone, she indulged in the luxury of tears, and afterwards, her mind and emotions cleared of self-pity, she took her courage once more in her hands, determined Dolma would not get the better of her. Sonya rode directly

to the gates of the Gompa. Built high on a rock like the vast
Gyantse Monastery, it was shrouded in darkness reinforced
by the mysterious odour of overcrowded sanctity. Several
thousand holy men dwelling together in flat serried
buildings, row upon row carved into the mountainside, day
after day in prayer and meditation, it was an eerie
frightening place, like every holy place in Tibet.

As it was night, Sonya was not allowed to enter the
Monastery. She had taken care to preserve her holy status,
having decided it was easier to get what she wanted from
everyone, including monks, if they realized she had prestige
and the wherewithal to pay – and in that last respect, too,
she decided to hang on to the pony. The monk who came to
her tut-tutting under his breath at her loud and imperious
summons on the Monastery bell, stood at the gates with a
lantern in his hand, and denied all knowledge of a baby boy
having been brought to them that day. He advised her to
return in the morning when the High Lama would speak to
her personally.

'I come from Gyantse, I'm a stranger in this town,'
Sonya emphasized. 'Can't you possibly help me now? Wake
the High Lama, tell him I must see him immediately.'

The monk shook his head emphatically. 'I cannot do it.
We are a strict religious order. Go to the Convent, lady, if
you require a bed for the night.'

With no option to comply, Sonya set off for the
Convent. She would just have to be patient until morning.

The following morning, however, the High Lama of the
Monastery knew nothing more than the lowly monk the
night before. No baby had been brought to him, he could
not help her. If she was perturbed about the fate of the
baby, then she should go to the Ponpo who would exercise
his magisterial influence on her behalf. Thanking him for
his time, Sonya left empty-handed. Hope was beginning to
die. What on earth had happened to Dolma and the baby?
Surely someone would have seen or heard something of her
by now? Had something happened to them on the way to
Shigatse? No, she must not think like that! She could not
afford to think in such a way, she warned herself . . .

Sonya returned to the Shigatse Convent to collect her

belongings. The Mother-Nun sent for her immediately. Unlike the Mother of Gyantse, this one was a noblewoman from a highly regarded Lhasa family, educated, sensitive and sympathetic about Sonya's plight. 'Madam,' she addressed Sonya as courteously as she herself liked to be addressed, 'two nuns arrived in the Convent while you were talking to the Abbot of the Shigatse Gompa. The nuns have come from the direction of Lhasa. At the Karo La Pass, they met a woman with a baby on her back. The woman said she was a poor Neskorma on a pilgrimage to Lhasa, but the nuns saw that she was of good breeding by the state of her soft white hands. The woman was plumpish and not so very young – perhaps about thirty. Her companion was much younger, the infant's wet-nurse according to the Neskorma. Could this so-called Neskorma possibly be your sister-in-law?'

'It might well be . . . ' Sonya was puzzled. 'The Karo La Pass, you say?'

'Yes, madam.'

Sonya was confused and dismayed. Perhaps the watchman on the Gyantse bridge had misunderstood. Perhaps the pilgrim taking the Shigatse road had not been Dolma, after all. Perhaps Dolma had taken the Lhasa road out of Gyantse and was even now heading via the Karo La Pass to Lhasa, surely the quickest route to the city rather than via Shigatse? And Lhasa was the most obvious place to take a potential Dalai Lama, wasn't it? Perhaps, perhaps, perhaps! It was all supposition. 'I think I've wasted your time, and mine, Mother,' Sonya said wearily, the lead-weight settling more firmly inside her chest.

'Nothing has been wasted, madam,' the Mother-Nun reassured her. 'The Karo La is a difficult and tortuous route, so if you follow the straighter road following the Tsangpo River from Shigatse, you might catch up at the Chaksam crossroads with this woman who has stolen your child.'

'Thank you,' said Sonya. 'I think I'll probably do that. It's the only thing I can do in the circumstances.'

'Would you like a couple of my pilgrim-nuns to accompany you?'

343

'No . . . I don't think so. They would never be able to keep up with me. I shall be all right on my own.'

'As you wish,' said the Nun, respecting Sonya's judgement.

iii

The retreating Tibetan army had looted and sacked the village of Chaksam on the banks of the swift-flowing Tsangpo River, but they forgot to scupper the village's two ferry-boats. The British arriving at Chaksam made full use of the boats, twelve feet wide and forty feet long, each prow carved with a weird and wonderful horse's head. Together with the army's own Berthon boats and the yak-skin coracles they found beached higher up the river bank, the British Mission and their army of animals and big guns were hauled magnificently across from one bank to the other in five and a half days, with only three men drowned.

The main contingent of the British Mission forging ahead towards Lhasa, Captain Rice-Smythe and a handful of Sappers and Royal Irish Riflemen were left behind to unhitch the steel-hawser that had been slung across the river to facilitate a safer crossing as well as haul back barges that had been swept downstream during transportation. Chaksam had been made secure, so there was no likelihood of any more trouble from the Tibetans. As Rice-Smythe and his men weren't following the main body of the Mission until the following day, they decided to celebrate at the village inn on the local unfermented beer called *chang*, ignorant of its abrasive and potent qualities. Tied to one of the iron hitching-rings embedded in the wall of the inn, they noticed instead of the usual mule, yak, camel or donkey, a fine-looking rowan.

'By George!' exclaimed the Captain who was a little short-sighted, only vanity preventing him from wearing glasses, 'Someone's managed to ride down that dashed vertical mountain which was such a confounded hazard to our animals.' He circled the pony, a connoisseur in horse-flesh, but this one gave him a funny feeling for another reason.

''Tis just like the one sneaked from under our noses a

344

week ago,' said Rifleman Mullen, voicing the Captain's feeling. 'I'll be thinking, too, sir, 'tis one called Phineas's Fairing, pride o' the Chang Lo polo-field.'

Phineas's Fairing, alias Fanny, her glossy coat dulled with dust and sweat, whinnied in delight at being recognized. It could not be disputed, the rowan was definitely one belonging to Captain Rice-Smythe of the Royal Irish Rifles, brought all the way from India at great cost to provide him with an escape from camp-boredom, and since stolen from Chang Lo a hundred miles away.

'Lame 'an all, sir!' said Rifleman O'Neal, getting up off his haunches after examining the pony's fetlocks.

'Lame, lame!' bellowed Rice-Smythe, brandishing his baton in the air. 'I'll give the dirty little thieving rascal who lamed my Fanny a sound thrashing! I shall lambast him from here to Hindustan!' His wonderful golden moustache twitching violently, he entered the inn, shouting, in the nearest Tibetan translation Sonya could ascertain; 'Who's the black-faced little bugger who stole my Fanny from Chang Lo? Come on, own up you ignorant Buddhist peasant, whoever you are! Otherwise I'll arrest every one of you blaggards!' He glowered at the occupants of the smoke-filled room, and his tempestuous blue eyes alighted on a lady sitting regally amid the black-faced thieving rabble. 'You!' he stormed, coming up to her as though he would lambast her, too; 'I recognize you in that outfit! What the deuce are you doing here? Weren't you the one complaining about her barley-rations at Thug-Phul?'

Sonya replied in Tibetan from behind her veil; 'Captain Rice-Smythe, I'll thank you not to spit in my face.'

Taken aback, he withdrew a pace, then came forward again, bent over her to peer at her more closely and turning purple blustered; 'By George, madam, I think *you* stole Fanny!'

'I did not steal your pony, Captain. It was sold to me for fifty taels. If you can give me fifty taels, you can have your pony back as I shan't be needing it to cross the Tsangpo.'

'Fifty taels . . . fif . . . madam, you have lamed my best polo-pony!' He seemed to lose control of his temper and vocabulary, and bumblingly turned to the grinning men behind him, who did not understand the gist of the conversation between the Tibetan woman and their Captain, but could see it was a highly entertaining confrontation; 'What are all you jackanapes grinning at?' Captain Rice-Smythe barked, and added a *coup de grace*, which gave him the uttermost satisfaction; 'Arrest this woman! I want to know exactly who and what she is and why she stole a valuable pony . . . search her bag!'

The Riflemen hesitated.

'Do it, I say!' Rice-Smythe ground out from between his teeth. Slowly the Irishmen cocked their rifles, uncertain who to aim at.

The atmosphere in the inn, having changed from one of light-hearted carefree revelry to a noticeably uncomfortable tension the moment the British soldiers had crossed the threshold, now became volatile, charged with undercurrents of hostility and as dangerous as a lion's den in which adult male lions patiently tolerated sparrows on their heads. In the weighted silence, the Tibetans eyed the soldiers, watching every move they made, and dark Tibetan faces betrayed nothing.

Sonya kept her head. In a remarkably cool and clear voice she said in English; 'Tell your men to put away their guns, Captain Rice-Smythe. Every Tibetan watching can throw a knife quicker than a gun firing a bullet.'

The small group of soldiers were startled by the attractive voice speaking perfect English with only a trace of a foreign accent, and Captain Rice-Smythe conveyed his astonishment most. Obviously relieved by a lady's less hot-headed approach than their Captain's in defusing a delicate situation, the Riflemen obediently lowered their weapons while Captain Rice-Smythe said accusingly; 'You speak English! Who are you? What are you?'

'Only an ill-educated Tibetan woman, Captain – but from a noble household, nonetheless. I speak a little English which is sometimes useful – as on this occasion when I don't wish these peasant-farmers to know what we're talking about. You wish to arrest me, very well, but do it outside if you don't want to be hacked to pieces by them.' Sonya got up without haste, and paid the inn-keeper for her

346

bowl of milk. Leaving her bag where it was on the floor beside her chair, she walked out of the inn with her head held high.

She had been fully aware that those Tibetan men drinking and laughing inside the inn would not have harmed her in any way out of respect for her sex and status since most of them were Buddhists. Captain Rice-Smythe's chances of survival she could not guarantee.

Coolly she turned to face him. 'I have no other place to sleep tonight apart from the inn, sharing the floor, I dare say, with a lot of lice-ridden unwashed female pilgrims. If I'm under arrest, then one of your soldiers – or perhaps even two if you think one will be powerless against me – will have to share the same accommodation. I don't think you're going to get any volunteers, Captain. So please let me explain my presence here. My baby has been stolen – kidnapped I think is your English word for it. I know the woman who has done this thing . . . at least, I'm almost sure who she is. I believe she's taking my infant son to Lhasa. You haven't by any chance encountered her crossing the Tsangpo while you've been here?' She met the Captain's eye unflinchingly.

'No, madam, I have not!'

'Thank you, Captain, I'm sure you would have told me if you had. I think, by now, she must be well ahead on the road to Lhasa – so Lhasa will have to be my destination, too. Let me suggest, Captain, that if you still want to arrest me for being an anxious overwrought mother searching desperately for her missing child, you post a guard outside the inn tonight, and I'll give you my word I shall not try to escape. As far as your pony's concerned, I bought it from a rogue for fifty taels to make my journey swifter and safer. I don't want to be recompensed, you may have Fanny back, and the fifty taels is my loss.'

'Hurruph!' Captain Rice-Smythe snorted and twiddled his moustache in embarrassment. The dashed woman had come forward of her own volition to tell her sad tale – if it could be believed! Yet, bound by chivalry to give her the benefit of the doubt, he said grudgingly; 'Madam, I, er, may have been a little hasty . . . I was not fully cognizant of

347

the situation. I'm sorry your child has been stolen, kidnapping is a serious offence. If I find out who it is, I'll mention you're looking for the baby.'

Someone behind him sniggered and Rice-Smythe turned to the soldiers with a chilling look designed to silence all upstarts. He turned back to Sonya apologetically. 'Very well, ma'am, stay in the inn tonight, and we'll say no nore upon the subject of Fanny.'

'Thank you, Captain, that's very generous of you. I . . . er . . . I wonder if I might make the river crossing with you in the morning? I'm terribly afraid of water – I almost drowned once, and it had rather a traumatic effect on me.'

'By all means, ma'am, by all means.' Considerably mellowed by her tender approach and woeful circumstances, Captain Rice-Smythe was never so happy as when playing the dominant protective male in the face of feminine helplessness. He was utterly taken in by Princess Sonya Dubrovka, without realizing, for one moment, her real identity.

'Fitzpatrick to a blarney stone,' said Rifleman Lismoyle, 'I thought she couldn't speak much English! Is the man thick to be so beguiled, I ask meself!'

Chapter Twenty-Six

The pedlar from Amdo settled himself in everyone's way at the foot of the steep stone ramp that led up into the very eyes, ears and mouth of the Potala; the Dalai Lama's Audience Chamber. It was amusing to sit and watch pedestrians struggling up and down the ramp worn to the slippery treachery of a glacis by centuries of devout feet. The abode of the God-King claimed the mountain and the land below, overshadowing it, subduing it. Golden roofs burned the eye. White walls gashed by sacred scarlet behind which lay the private apartments of Chenrezig's incarnation. Draped down the outside walls like vertical eyelashes yak-hair curtains screened the monks and lamas from the gaze of the curious, while statesmen and officials dwelt side by side with the holy ones, and the most Holy One of all, the God-King. The Potala was a city within a city, and beneath the city hid the scorpions . . .

The pedlar scratched his face and felt nothing, so thickly encrusted was it with dirt. But he was not unusual, Tibetans never washed. Normally pale-skinned, it was unusual to find a Tibetan in Lhasa who was anything but black, dirt ingrained so deeply into the skin, nothing short of acid would remove it. The pedlar scratched his armpit and watched the mangy animals biting the undernourished children even he avoided, since he had no wish to contract their scrofulous sores and ulcers. He moved aside fastidiously as a bedraggled woman with a shawl over her head, clutching a bundle to her breast, almost knocked him and his tray over. He only knew she was carrying a baby in her arms by the feeble bleating that came from the rags and he hoped she would find some food from the monks' kitchens for the baby and herself. Idly he observed her progress up the steep walled ramp and got the feeling there was something familiar about her. He told himself not to be so jumpy, he was always running into vagrants. He had probably seen her somewhere along the road, and, with more pressing matters to attend to, he dismissed the woman from his mind.

Presently his patience was rewarded.

A servant of the Potala skidded at breakneck speed down the ramp. Hunch-backed and ugly in his shabby brown robe, his arms tucked into his wide sleeves, he was nevertheless remarkably nimble on his feet and came to a graceful ballerinic halt in front of the pedlar. His front teeth missing, he lisped; 'My masters allow you permission to sell your wares to the inhabitants of the Potala, as long as you do not trespass into the apartments of the God-King. What's this?' From the pedlar's tray, the inquisitive servant picked up a round glass instrument with a handle, and the pedlar smacked his hand.

'Don't touch if you don't intend to buy! It's a magnifying-glass that will burn your nose, it's been lying so long in the sun. Now lead me to my customers, I've been waiting here a long time like a dog without a tail while your masters and their wives have been making up their minds whether or not they wish to darn the holes in their clothes . . . you look as if you, too, Geyok, could do with a few stitches to keep the tears on your back together.'

Over his shoulder the servant poked out his tongue at the pedlar trying to keep his tray steady and articles together as he struggled clumsily up the ramp in wooden clogs. 'Amdoman,' he said, 'your goods had better not be paltry, otherwise I shall be your guide to the scorpions' den instead.'

The pedlar groaned. 'Are you to follow me everywhere, knave?'

'I am not a Geyok for nothing! I have to earn a living,

350

too, since my parents could think of no other way to make me a holy man other than by giving me as a servant to those more holy than me. In the hope, I fear, that some of their holiness might brush off on me – hence my holey garments, pedlar.'

'The only thing to brush off on you, Geyok, appears to be slippery feet and a slippery tongue,' the pedlar remarked as he followed the Geyok through endless dark bare corridors, right into the very heart of the incense-clouded Potala where Buddha-shrines illuminated the darkness.

Religious grandeur painted in sacred colours, scarlet and gold, combined with the more ascetic blues, yellows and whites of idols, incense-candles and iconographs, was the rather disappointing aura of the places he was allowed to enter, and the pedlar was unimpressed. During the afternoon, the servant showed him to another part of the great building, the pedlar's triple-stacked tray practically empty by now. Custom had been brisk that morning, everyone residing within the Potala in need of something from the outside world.

'These are the apartments of the privileged foreigners,' said the Geyok. 'They are from all over, ambassadors, envoys, emissaries – even scientists, musicians and doctors, so I doubt you can sell them anything they haven't already got.'

'Which is just as well as I haven't much left to amuse them except a tale or two,' the pedlar remarked, squinting closely at a brass name-plate clumsily tacked to a red-lacquered door. 'Why don't you get me something to eat?' He turned to the servant contentiously, 'I can't be expected to traipse around all day for the benefit of these people while my stomach is shrinking. I could do with a drink, too . . . and while you're about it, have something to eat yourself, your rumbling stomach annoys me. You know where to find me, I shan't be tempted to run off anywhere.'

The Geyok looked dubious. 'You promise me you won't attempt to find the apartments of his Holiness, the God-King?'

'What do you take me for, a fool?' asked the pedlar irritably. 'If you're worried about me wandering off alone,

351

I'll wait in here and hope this Russian Prince will oblige me by buying my magnifying-glass since no one else has.'

The servant, hungry and thirsty himself, needed no further persuading. The pedlar knocked on Prince Nikolay Dubrovka's door. A thin reed-like voice, wavering plaintively, told him to enter, the door was open.

A shrivelled, bald-headed man, his yellow brocade three-quarter-length coat extremely dirty, sprawled on a dais of cushions reading a book. His thin legs in tight black pantaloons were planted out stick-like in front of him so that his feet looked like swollen red bulbs in his Chinese felt boots. He took off his gold-rimmed half-moon spectacles and observed the pedlar curiously.

So this was Prince Nikolay Dubrovka, the pedlar thought, laughing to himself.

He need not have worried, the buffoon was eighty if he was a day, and grotesque! Whatever had possessed her to marry him?

Before the Prince was aware of it, the pedlar had shot-fast the bolts on the inside of the door and set down his cumbersome tray.

'What . . . what?' Prince Nikolay struggled to get up off his cushions but found he had made himself too comfortable. He sank back again helplessly, suddenly afraid. 'Hey . . . hey, fellow! What do you think you're doing? Who are you? What do you want of me? I have diplomatic immunity . . . I am protected by the Tibetans and Chinese, they will knock down the door if I strike this gong . . . ' He leaned over for the wooden striker to hit the silver gong beside him, but it was just out of reach and the pedlar got there before him.

'Don't strike anything, Prince, not before we talk. I'm a British Agent, so I think you'll know why I'm here.'

The Prince's Adam's apple bobbed up and down in the folds of his thin scraggy neck. He eyed the pedlar cautiously. 'You don't look like a British Agent. How did you get in here?' He cast nervous glances at the door, hoping someone would interrupt – but no one ever did, not these days. 'I have a bad heart.' He put his hand over it. 'I mustn't receive any severe shocks otherwise the doctors have warned it will be very bad for me.'

Lewis read the man's thoughts, and was sorry for him. Tapping the carved wooden gong-strike against his right palm, Lewis said, 'I got in here very easily and I hope to get out the same way. But first, I want you to be aware of several things. Your wife is in Tibet, at a place called Thug-Phul . . .'

'Thug-Phul? That's where that foolish boy Kirsten is. He's taken up with a Tibetan woman, a war-lord's daughter, and so now he imagines he's some sort of magician. Count Kirsten always was a card . . . and a cad!' The Prince chuckled.

'Kirsten Vremya's dead,' Lewis said curtly.

The Prince looked at the pedlar with rheumy eyes, then blew his nose loudly on the hem of his yellow coat. 'You're a bold fellow, coming here like this. If they catch you, they'll put you in the scorpions' cave, or worse.'

'They won't catch me. Don't you want to know about your wife?' Lewis, in exasperation, gazed helplessly at the Prince. This was going to be far harder than expected, the fellow was such a senile old fool.

'Which wife? I've had several. My memory is getting a bit sketchy these days – especially in view of all the fasting I've been doing lately. I find that sitting in a dark cupboard, drinking only water, is very good for the bowels. It clears the system. These Tibetans are no fools, you know. Ah . . . I think you mean Sonya! Yes, she was my last wife. A pretty little thing but a bit of a puritan. I don't care that much for truly chaste women.'

'She's going to have a child.'

'Mine?'

'No, mine.'

'Good heavens!' said the Prince incredulously, staring long and hard at the filthy Tibetan pedlar. 'What is this, some kind of joke at my expense? Have you seduced her against her will? Oh, I know, ha, ha, ha, it's my birthday and I've forgotten, but my friends the Yellow Hats haven't. They and the Dalai Lama have arranged this joke, yes? No! Well then, Dorjiev . . . no that can't be right either. He and the Dalai Lama aren't here any more. They've left Lhasa together and are probably half way across Mongolia by now. The British are coming, you see, and they didn't want the Dalai Lama to be captured by them. Dorjiev doesn't want to be captured by them, either, in case they slit his throat. When they get here, they'll only find the Regent . . . and me of course. But I'll be unable to tell them anything. I've done nothing wrong. I've only served my country to the best of my ability, and if the Tibetans and Chinese didn't mind, why should the British, hey fellow?'

Lewis turned his back on the old man. God, Sonya! How could they have done this to you? He looked up at the high elaborate ceiling burnished with gold-leaf and vermilion lacquer and, with a sigh, wondered what to do now. 'Sonya wants a divorce,' said Lewis turning back to the Prince. 'She has come all the way to Tibet to ask you to divorce her.'

'What a foolish child! She and I both know it cannot be; the Church would not allow it.' The Prince bit his thumbnail, unable to take his watery opaque eyes narrowed in distrust off the pedlar whom he still could not reconcile as being a British Agent. 'Is that why you're here, to kill me, so you may marry her and legitimize your bastard-child after I'm dead?'

'No. I'm here to kill you because my Government wish you out of the way.'

'Why, what have I done?'

'Nothing – I'm beginning to realize.' How could he tell this man, no, not even a man, that he was nothing but a misguided puppet dangling pathetically from Dorjiev's powerful strings. He and the Dalai Lama had even left him behind to face the British alone because they knew full well the Prince had no worthwhile secrets stored up in his doddering old head. All he had been guilty of was running an archaic arsenal that minted money instead of weapons, while suffering from bowel-trouble! What was he going to tell Curzon, Younghusband, the Foreign Office? That he had failed to eliminate the enemy because he had lost his nerve? And what was to become of Sonya, still married to a hairless living-corpse like this one? God forbid he could still father her with children. Lewis picked up his pedlar's tray from the floor and eased the straps around his neck. 'I should get out of Lhasa if I were you,' he told the Prince wearily. 'The British Mission is only a few miles from here.'

'Then why aren't you going to bump me off if that's what your Government wants?' asked Prince Nikolay, retaining a pathetic yet dignified composure.

'I ought to, but I can't,' Lewis said gruffly, realizing foolishly that this whole bogey of Prince Nikolay Dubrovka being a dangerous Russian spy was nothing short of farcical. The man he should really be after was Dorjiev, but that big bird had flown off too swiftly. He had arrived just a little too late.

'Aren't you afraid I might bang this gong and alert the whole Potala to your little game?' asked the Prince curiously.

'Go ahead, it doesn't matter any more.' Lewis retrieved the gong-stick and tossed it to him. 'My capture won't prevent the British Commissioner from entering Lhasa. It's not a little game anymore, Prince, and I doubt it ever has been. You and I are mere individuals up against war-machines desirous of ruling the whole world. Great Britain, Russia, Prussia, France, Germany, they will go on rolling over the earth, regardlessly crushing little people who get in the way. I've done what I was asked to do by my Government and so, I think, have you. Let's leave it at that, shall we?' He drew back the lower bolt on the elaborately carved red door as Prince Nikolay struggled to get up off his cushions and this time succeeded.

Breathlessly and wheezily he came up to Lewis, who could not help thinking in that instant, why do very old men look and behave like children? Hardly reaching his shoulder, Prince Nikolay gazed up at him trustingly, and with much clicking of ill-fitting false teeth, asked mildly and without malice; 'Do you love my wife, Englishman?'

'Yes.'

The Prince placed a finger on his lips and whispered; 'Then I won't say anything if you don't, pedlar.' He put out his shrivelled yellow hand. 'I am an old man with a bad heart. I cannot return to Russia because my heart would not be able to stand the journey. As you can see, I am a prisoner of my own body. Take Sonya and make her happy if that is what you both want. She always was much too headstrong and serious for me to cope with . . . ' again he chuckled, 'but she can handle a troika and a pair of horses magnificently! Disappear now before they start getting suspicious . . . oh, and give me that magnifying-glass,' he added, peering into the tray and fingering the few articles left. 'My eyesight went years ago and I can't get proper spectacles in this place. My old ones are useless, and I do so like reading.'

He went back to his cushions and his book, delighted with the magnifying-glass he had got for nothing.

ii

Colonel Younghusband could not believe his ears. 'You did what? You let her go! Didn't you know who she was?'

'How could I, sir?' Captain Rice-Smythe defended himself.

'Don't you read any reports, Captain?'

'Yes, sir, but with all due respect, I don't have access to confidential information.'

'The whole of this camp, Captain Rice-Smythe, is aware of the fact that Princess Sonya Dubrovka, is a Russian spy!'

'Yes, sir. But I wasn't to know that the Tibetan noble-woman from Thug-Phul and the Russian Princess were one and the same person.'

'Then why didn't you make it your duty to find out? Why didn't you telegraph me you had apprehended a woman behaving suspiciously at Chaksam?'

'I wasn't aware she was behaving suspiciously at Chaksam, Colonel. And, begging your pardon, you were moving too rapidly for the telegraph-line to keep up with you,' Captain Rice-Smythe reminded the Colonel.

'Captain Rice-Smythe, you have jeopardized the whole mission! We are seven miles from Lhasa. I daresay that princess Dubrovka is now well within the protecting walls of the Potala, feeding information to her husband who will in turn inform the Tibetans and Chinese of our incompetence! I will probably be faced now with all eight thousand of the

Drepung monks in whose shadow, may I remind you, we are camping, while the whole of the Tibetan army and Russian arsenal awaits us inside Lhasa itself! They will try to prevent us from signing a peace-treaty with the Dalai Lama, because this Russian woman has imparted the wrong sort of information! We are not an army about to wage war on the Tibetans, but a peaceable delegation here to negotiate terms. Tibetan losses in the skirmishes we've had with them have been their fault, not ours, since they refused to talk and act rationally and peaceably. We don't want a full-scale battle on our hands at this critical stage of the negotiations . . . ' He broke off his diatribe when his aide appeared in the tent.

'What is it?' he snapped irritably.

'There's a pedlar out here, Colonel, wanting to speak to you rather urgently.'

'A pedlar? What the devil does he want? All right . . . it might be important.'

He turned back to Captain Rice-Smythe, standing red-faced to attention, and abruptly dismissed him. 'But make no mistake, Captain, I will file a Blue Book report on the incident at Chaksam.'

Captain Rice-Smythe went out unhappily as the Tibetan was shown in.

Colonel Younghusband looked up into the face of the pedlar who had managed to straighten his bent back after setting down his tray of goods on the soggy ground. He had no doubt as to the pedlar's identity. Without preamble, and before the pedlar could do anything, the Colonel took his pistol from the holster of his Sam-Browne belt; 'Joyden, you're under arrest.'

'What?'

'Jemadar . . . fetch the guard! Tell them to present arms outside this tent!'

Lewis stared stupidly at the Colonel. 'Are you out of your mind?'

'No, Joyden, but you are. Before you are taken back to India under an armed escort, I have been instructed to divest you of your status as a British Agent in the Samsâra affair.'

357

'On whose authority?'

'The King of England, the Viceroy of India, and the Foreign Office.'

'Go to hell . . . for what reason?' Lewis sat down suddenly in the nearest canvas chair. He flung up a hand in defeat and resignation. 'All right, but before I'm to be carted off in disgrace, don't you want to know why I'm here?'

'I know why you're here. But Princess Sonya Dubrovka, your mistress, is not.'

'God in heaven, Colonel,' Lewis said, jumping up again and ignoring the pistol wavering about in the Colonel's hand, 'you're not going to shoot me, so don't let's carried away by heroics – it's more than your career is worth and we both know it. I came here to tell you the bird has flown . . . both birds, and all you can do is insult me with false acc . . . ' He broke off when the Jemadar and two soldiers appeared at the flap of the tent with bayonets, but Colonel Younghusband curtly dismissed them again and told them to wait outside.

'What birds?' he demanded, wheeling hawk-eyed on Lewis.

'The Dalai Lama and Dorjiev are half-way to Mongolia. The Tibetans weren't taking any risks where they were concerned.'

'How do you know?'

'That's what I'm paid to do when you so kindly pass on my pay-drafts from the Survey of India . . . however! I have been right inside the Potala, I have spoken to Prince Nikolay Dubrovka, and a great many more influential people besides. The Dalai Lama is not there, neither is Dorjiev. The only one to meet you will be the Chinese Amban, the Tashi Lama or the Regent. Take your pick whose seal you wish to place on your peace treaty that won't be worth the paper it's written on!'

In silence, Colonel Younghusband placed his pistol heavily on his camp-table.

'Passive resistance is all they're offering you, Colonel,' Lewis continued. 'There is no great Tibetan army facing you, only a pathetic conglomeration of monks, peasants

358

and bewildered people. There is no Russian bogey hiding in the Potala apart from Prince Nikolay Dubrovka who's on his last legs anyway. His wife . . . my mistress, as you took such pains to remind me, is not a Russian spy, but a harmless woman searching for her husband to ask him for a divorce, that's all.'

Colonel Younghusband's little laugh was mirthless. 'Am I to believe she has come all the way from Russia merely to ask her husband for a divorce? Do you think I was born yesterday?'

'Believe what you like, Colonel, but it's the truth.'

'Then why did you pass on false information to me when you were at Thug-Phul?'

Lewis looked mystified. 'What false information?'

'You sent me a message . . . here it is.' From a report book the Colonel snatched the scrap of paper Sonya Dubrovka had passed on to him via his aide.

Lewis read it; 'The Dubrovka woman has returned to Russia, and the other Russians in the Gyantse area impose no further threat. All has gone according to plan.' Lewis looked up. 'I did not write this.'

'That's your hand-writing isn't it?'

'No, it is not! Cleverly copied though, I grant you. But I never commit messages like that to paper, Colonel. The only recordings I ever make are to do with my calculations and area-surveys, and they're always secreted in my prayer-wheel. Anything else is passed on via verbal pundit reports so that nothing is ever committed to paper . . . nothing as blatant as that . . . that message, anyway.' Lewis flicked a derisive finger at it.

'Then Princess Dubrovka falsified this information and your hand-writing, why?'

Lewis shrugged. 'Why didn't you ask her yourself? She was right on your doorstep at Chang Lo, wasn't she?'

'You might well ask, Joyden!'

'I am asking!' he replied snappily as he, too, began to lose his temper.

'You're absolutely obsessed by the idiotic notion she's a Russian spy and my mistress, so why don't you interrogate her yourself?'

359

'Isn't she . . . your mistress, and the mother of your child? How will that sound in the upper echelons of the Foreign Office?'

The two men glared at one another, and Colonel Young-husband was the first to break the silence charged with so much enmity. 'Make no mistake, Joyden, I will question her personally the moment I arrive in Lhasa.'

'In Lhasa, what the devil are you talking about? She's at Thug-Phul.'

'She is in Lhasa. I was powerless to do anything about her at Thug-Phul on account of her . . . er, condition. But she has had her child . . . your child, let me remind you, which is no light matter in view of the enormity of your assignment and the number of lives depending on your successful handling of it. You're here to get rid of hostile elements hindering our progress towards implementing a favourable treaty for the British, but instead, you choose to make love under a Tibetan haystack! Sonya Dubrovka has come to Lhasa on the pretext that her baby was kidnapped by a deranged woman from the Sidheong household – like you, I think she thinks I was born yesterday!'

Lewis, shaking his head, tried to get a grip on reality and the facts presented by the Colonel's garbled and angry accusations. 'Kidnapped?'

'Yes, kidnapped!' the Colonel said, biting like a dog at a bone it did not want to relinquish. 'I don't believe one word of her gross fabrication concerning why she wanted to come to Lhasa . . . apart, I dare say, from contacting you again. Ask Captain Rice-Smythe. He spoke to her at Chaksam, although he had no idea who she was at the time, dressed up as she was in her Tibetan garb. She was escorted by him to the edge of this very camp, where he left her to continue alone into Lhasa . . . '

'When?' asked Lewis, suddenly as brittle as glass. He stood not two paces away from the Colonel.

'This morning . . . ' The Colonel made a little choking noise when he saw the knife taken from the pedlar's sleeve.

'Not a word Colonel,' Lewis whispered, the knife pressed to the Colonel's chin, 'otherwise you will jeopardize the whole of this Mission, and the course of British and Tibetan history will be ingloriously altered. No Blue Book Reports now, sir, but a gentle steady pace through the camp until I'm outside it. And keep smiling as at Guru.'

'Joyden, don't do it . . . she's not worth it . . . '

'How do you know what she's worth?'

'There are guards and sentries posted all over this place.'

'I never doubted it. But you won't get hurt if I don't get arrested. The Chinese Amban is waiting for you to make your great Durbar-entrance into Lhasa, don't let him down, Colonel.'

'You are insane!' hissed Colonel Younghusband. 'This is a treasonable offence.'

'Perhaps . . . now, keep smiling and walk out of here, otherwise the swamp of Lhasa will be the first and last you see of the Forbidden City?'

'Damn you, Joyden . . . the Tibetans should have finished you off at Gyantse! You've been nothing but a pain in the neck to me ever since I got here.'

'And you wouldn't have got here if it wasn't for me . . . eh, Colonel?'

'You'll never get away with it . . . '

'Then it won't be for want of trying.' Lewis, close behind him, pressed the point of the blade against the Colonel's khaki-clad spine.

The guards could not quite make out why the Tibetan pedlar was walking so close behind their Commanding Officer, but since he was smiling and wished them a good day cheerily enough, thought he must be in an excellent mood due to the Potala shining on the horizon, and saluted him accordingly.

Captain Rice-Smythe in his shirt-sleeves, a curry-brush in his hand while he personally supervised the grooming of Phineas's Fairing, brought into camp that morning, kept his back turned to Colonel Younghusband as he approached.

'Captain Rice-Smythe,' said the Colonel smiling as if there was something wrong with his face, 'could you lend this fellow a pony to get him to Lhasa.' It was not so much a question as an order. 'The one you're grooming will do.'

'Begging your pardon, Colonel, Fanny will not do! She has been ridden hard and is lame!' His vanity wounded

361

through a gross misunderstanding, the Captain turned to view the vacuously grinning Colonel who had verbally reduced him to the ranks just a short while ago, and the Captain's memory not being as fickle as the Colonel's, he felt justified in glowering.

'It's an order, Captain! Give the fellow the pony!' Younghusband seemed to lose control of himself.

'Then he'll have to ride bareback!' Captain Rice-Smythe almost snarled, wasting time in argument and Lewis, who had no intention of riding bareback, whirled as a Sikh soldier rode past. The knife in his hand now visible, swiftly Lewis dragged the astonished Sikh from the saddle and grabbed the reins before the soldier was aware of what was happening. He would have got away with it had not his unwieldly tray presented an incumberance, or Captain Rice-Smythe's revolver in his exposed hip-holster been so readily available to Colonel Younghusband's hand. The Colonel whipped the gun away from a still-bemused Rice-Smythe and pointed it between Lewis's shoulder-blades.

'Nice try, pedlar, but I told you you'd never get away with it.' The Colonel shook his head sorrowfully. 'What a pity you did not allow the Samsâra affair to be laid to rest with dignity five minutes ago, but had to blot your copy-book still further. Now I cannot guarantee what your future might be in Chumbi gaol.'

Lewis, his foot imprisoned awkwardly in one stirrup, turned around. He relinquished the Sikh's pony into Rice-Smythe's hand and directed the blade of the knife he had been staking his life and career on in an arc of shining steel to the soft grass at the feet of the bruised Sikh. Open hands displayed in a gesture of defeat and regret, with a rueful grin he murmured; 'If wishes were horses, Colonel, even pedlars might ride!'

Chapter Twenty-Seven

Sonya congratulated herself on her skilful handling of the British Officer she had unfortunately encountered at Chaksam. In the end, however, it had all turned out in her best interests. She had travelled the forty miles from Chaksam with Captain Rice-Smythe and his escort, riding nothing as illustrious as Phineas's Fairing, but a docile and obliging mule whose leisurely pace during the rest of the journey she had much preferred. Saddle-sore and weary by the time she had arrived on the outskirts of Lhasa, she was allowed to continue into the city, while the Captain and his men joined their camp at Drepung.

Her entrance into the Forbidden City was not filled with as much accomplishment and joy as she had once imagined. The Potala might wink and scintillate like a brilliant jewel hung on the neckline of snowy ridges rising to the higher mountains beyond, but her thoughts were only on her missing baby and Lewis. Inside the city gates, all was chaos and confusion as hundreds of people from the outlying villages and towns converged on Lhasa, either for personal protection, or to protect their God-King from the *philang* invader. Apart from those closest to the Dalai Lama, no one had any idea that he was not inside the Potala anymore, but had been secretly whisked away at night before the British could take him prisoner. Faithful Tibetans had brought out the only defence they had, ancient Chinese cannons which they lined up like a row of battered toys at the foot of the God-King's palace to prevent the British from entering the Potala. The crowds were dense, the stench overpowering. Open gutters were choked with the most unimaginable filth, the people were dirty and ragged and children stared at Sonya with dull eyes, faces covered in running sores. Dogs snapped and snarled for the refuse, mangy, lame, beaten and dangerous. Sonya was frantic for the safety of her baby. She imagined she saw Dolma on every street corner, she imagined every pedlar doing a brisk trade in Lhasa was Lewis in disguise. She stopped every time, bought some cheap bauble and inevitably started to question him, but she did not find the man she was looking for. Throughout that first day she searched and questioned, until, exhausted, she fell asleep at last, her head on her knees, couched on one of the darkened steps of the Potala along with hundreds of others like her who could find no accommodation.

The following morning – she remembered the date so vividly, an unforgettable day, recorded long afterwards, 4th August, 1904, her son just one month old today – she lifted her head painfully, her eyes sticky with dust and tiredness and saw the sun creeping over the edge of the eastern mountains, tinting the whole world in a misty pink glow. Golden-red flames leapt from the burnished roofs of the Potala, merging with the sunrise to engulf Lhasa in a golden bubble of glory. She had never seen anything so brilliant or so beautiful.

And then the beautiful illusion burst and the pus-filled bubble disgorged the beggars and animals. They converged on the gutters with the women and children, picking and sifting the filthy refuse to eat or to sell. A woman with a shawl over her head fought a child for a piece of stale bread, it might have been a bone, Sonya was too appalled to care.

The woman's shawl slipped off, revealing her grimy face. '*Dolma*!' Sonya screamed, leaping off the steps and falling over sleeping bundles of desperate humanity clinging to the golden Potala. '*Dolma! Dolma!*'

The woman dropped the food she was clutching and turned and fled. Sonya pursued her through the backstreets and alleys. 'Wait, Dolma, wait.' Sobbing and stumbling she ran after the woman, convinced she was not wrong in thinking she had at last found Dolma.

Drawn away from the city, Sonya had only one purpose in mind, to catch her before she lost sight of her. She was not aware of where she was being taken, only that it was out into open land beyond the city gates. The smell made Sonya retch. The air was unbreathable, like an abbatoir . . . it was the abbatoir. Oh God . . . don't let her have brought my baby here, he will have died . . . Sonya, desperate to keep the awful woman in sight, prayed she was mistaken, prayed, on the other hand, that she was not . . .

Through narrow walled alleys, caves of bones, animal and human, offal and skin and blood in the gutters. Hard faces looked crazily from their bone houses. A mixture of races, not Buddhists but butchers, here were the outcast dwellings of the *ro-gyapas*, the butchers of Lhasa who did not bury the dead, but hacked them to pieces, men, women, children and babies, for the vultures. Sonya all but collapsed in the realization of where Dolma had brought little Luey.

The frenzied woman flung herself into one of the bone-caves and Sonya crawled in after her. On hands and knees, her veil over her nose and mouth to stop her from vomiting in the foetid air, in that moment Sonya could have killed Dolma for bringing a newborn baby to such a grave-yard . . .

She crouched back in a dark corner, barely visible, terribly afraid, her hands raised to shield her face, her eyes sore from the bright light filtering through the entrance. She mewed like an animal in pain. Sonya caught her by the shoulders and shook her. 'Dolma . . . I knew it was you! Oh God . . . what are you doing here? What have you done with my baby, tell me! Please tell me, Dolma . . . please . . .' Dolma wouldn't answer. Sonya looked around her frantically but there was no baby, dead or alive. She shook Dolma again, this time so savagely, Dolma's head rocked on her shoulders. 'What have you done with my baby!'

Dolma whimpered.

'What . . . ?' Sonya pressed her ear to Dolma's mouth. Her lips moved but no sound came. Staring into Dolma's bright mad eyes, Sonya was dismayed and overwhelmed by what she read there – nothing, not a trace of recognition whatsoever. 'Oh, Dolma, what has happened to you?' Sonya's whisper was a groan of anguish. She released her and rocked back on her heels to look helplessly at her. After a while Sonya said more gently, 'You must come with me. You cannot stay here. We'll go back to Thug-Phul together. You'll be looked after there by your servants. But first you must tell me what has happened to little Luey. Is he dead, Dolma, is that why you won't tell me?'

Still Dolma did not say anything and in that dreadful moment Sonya realized Dolma had lost the power of speech. There was nothing at all to be gained from her except Dolma's own inward misery personified in her blank accusative stare.

A shadow darkened the entrance. A man's figure, squatting on his haunches, wearing a turban, he thrust his head into the cave. Pock-marked and dirty, his hands and clothes covered in fresh blood, Sonya realized he was a Mohammedan. But he spoke Tibetan. 'Who are you? What are you doing with this woman? She is mine.'

Sonya turned to him in desperation. 'No . . . no she's not,' Sonya said, 'she's a noblewoman from Thug-Phul who has no business with you people. She is sick, very sick in the head. She stole my baby and I've come to ask her what has happened to it. Would you know anything of its whereabouts, please?'

He shook his head. 'Nothing. I don't know about a baby. This woman came here of her own accord. She brought nothing, she had nothing, certainly no baby. I can't help you, so go away.'

'Look . . . I have money . . . ' Sonya fumbled for the purse tied to her waist. She thrust the leather pouch of silver *trankas* at the man. 'It's all I have left. Take it, take it all. Buy her food . . . and food for yourself. Look after her, I'll be back.'

She eased herself out of the cave and left Dolma and the Mohammedan together. There was just a chance Dolma had taken the baby straight to the Drepung Monastery or even to the Potala before she had become lost among the *ro-*

gyapas. Sonya decided to go to the Potala first, and the Drepung later if she could find out nothing inside the Potala. She would ask for an audience with the Dalai Lama. After all, her husband, Prince Nikolay Dubrovka, was working for the Tibetans, and so she had every right to know what was happening with him. Then she could find out if a baby had been brought to the Potala. They would know all about a potential Chenrezig reincarnation.

She fumbled inside her reticule for her letter of introduction from Tsar Nicholas to a Governor of Authority, which Lewis, the Red Cap, had returned after the incident at Rika's farmhouse. It was still there at the bottom, a little worse for wear, but quite safe. She put it away again and went to find the mule she had tied up by the city gates the night before. It was not there any more. Well, if it came to it, she would just have to walk six or seven miles to the Drepung.

Sonya wondered what was going on in the city. The masses were pressed so tightly, she found it difficult to get anywhere near the Potala. The stench and heat was unbearable. Lamas in yellow silk robes, on foot, on horseback, were everywhere waving Tibetan flags, rallying the people. Chinese soldiers with pikes, watchmen trying vainly to control the seething crowds with yak-hair whips. 'What's going on?' Sonya asked one of them.

'The British are coming. The Chinese Amban has made a public announcement from the Potala that the British intend to enter the city today. There will be a big battle for the city, the Chinese are already manning the cannons.'

Sonya, on tip-toe, could not see above the heads of the crowd. She squeezed her way breathlessly through the unwashed bodies all eager to get near the Potala steps. She was lucky enough to get close to the ramp leading directly to the Dalai Lama's Audience Chamber but her way was barred by monks and soldiers. 'You cannot come nearer, the place is closed today. There is to be a special parade.'

'What special parade?'

'The Chinese Amban will be officially welcoming the British Commissioner who will be riding into the city presently to sign a peace treaty.'

Relieved that there was not going to be any fighting after all, Sonya perched herself on the wall with others who also wanted to obtain a good view of the parade. She might even catch a glimpse of Lewis in the uniform he had been wearing the day he had come to Thug-Phul after having ridden so hard from Guru. Surely now, there would be no reason for him to remain in disguise if his countrymen were claiming Lhasa for themselves? The day before, Sonya had seen British machine-guns directed at the Potala. They had been in great evidence on the marshy plain surrounding the city, and looking now at the small rusty cannons the Chinese had brought out, it really looked as if the British had won the day without firing a shot. The sun was hot on her head and she threw off her gauze veil, her huge silver earrings absorbing the heat of the sun as they dangled hotly against her neck. Overwhelmed by the heat and crowds, Sonya was about to move from her place, when a distant cheer proclaimed something was happening by the city gates.

Tibetan hautboys at the top of the ramp endeavoured to sound a fanfare of welcome but died sadly in treble-pitched plaintiveness; shouting, voices raised in welcome, in protest, in indignation, in abuse, it was all a cacophony of confused exchanges and then, with bayonets fixed, marching along the main thoroughfare encircling the Potala came the British Mission protected by Chinese soldiers with pikes. In front, curiously small and insignificant, a lone figure in khaki rode a sleek pony, a ceremonial sword at his waist. Sonya realized this must be the famous Colonel Young-husband. A small detachment of men in khaki rode behind him, the Union Jack fluttering in the warm breeze. The British Mission looked anything but invulnerable to her. A few machine-guns, however, were trundled far back in the rear of the delegation should the Tibetans choose to become violent, no doubt, Sonya surmised, there as a small gesture underlining a far greater threat out on the plains where the main body of the British army encamped.

The Chinese Amban had climbed out of his sedan-chair, and stood regally on the ramp with the rest of the Tibetan welcoming committee. In his yellow quilted coat, embroidered shoes, scarlet beret with trailing ribbons, his hands tucked into his wide sleeves, his face and personality were curiously colourless. Swollen slitted eyes unfathomable in their pouches of skin, only the Amban's grey moustache displayed any expression, a drooping weariness asking the question, how has all this come about?

Despite her dreadful experience with Dolma and the *rogyapas*, her anxiety over her baby and Lewis, her fatigue and hunger and the intolerable heat and stench of hotpressed bodies, Sonya was imbued with a sense of anticipation and wonderment, of the spirit of the moment surrounding history in the making. Sitting on the Potala walls and steps, *shape-és*, lamas, monks, officials, servants, all there to witness the British with their Union Jack laying claim to being the first official representatives of any nation to enter Lhasa, Sonya's heart lurched. She clasped her hands tighter in her lap, her neck craned forward in eager scrutiny, tense with the kind of excitement and anticipation only one particular person in the whole world could bring about; was he here? Yes, please God, let him be here . . .

Titters of amusement, hearty laughs, bellows of something greater, British soldiers looked infinitely comical to the Tibetans as they struggled up the smooth ramp in their hobnailed boots while trying to maintain their dignity. Only the Chinese Amban did not smile. Beside him stood the Tongspa Penlop of Bhutan wearing his golden crown, Captain Jit Bahadur representing the State of Nepal, and the High Lamas of all the important monasteries. Only a long time afterwards, in reading the account of that fateful day in *The St Petersburg Gazette*, did Sonya know the identities of the key figures waiting outside the Potala to greet the British soldiers. Sitting on the ramp wall, squashed by smiling flag-waving Tibetans, she had thought at the time the man wearing the crown was the God-King, beside him, his Regent.

The thin khaki line of British Officers were helped along by laughing Tibetans, and then she saw the only one she wanted to see. 'Lewis . . . Lewis . . . ' Sonya struggled to extricate herself from over-excited Tibetans waving prayer-flags and banners, holding her back because they wanted a better view, too. 'Lewis . . . ' She jumped off the high wall, but had not anticipated the slope of the ramp. Her weak ankle, damaged by her fall down the mountainside at Gartok, gave out, she fell awkwardly. In the wake of the khaki figures disappearing inside the Potala, a riot broke out, Chinese and Tibetan soldiers arguing over who should fire the cannons in a ceremonial salute to the British. Sonya, lying helpless on the ramp, was surrounded by fighting men, kicking and shoving, the Chinese laying into the Tibetans, the Tibetans hurling stones, sticks and abuse. Women and children happily joined in the fight. Monks, soldiers and watchmen tried to quell the rioting.

Gasping with pain and effort, Sonya clawed and beat her way desperately back to her feet. She limped, agonizing over Lewis and her wretched infirmity preventing her reaching him. She was sure she had not been mistaken. She would know Lewis anywhere – as certain as she had been of the identity of Dolma picking in the gutters that morning. At the top of the ramp the officer in Pioneer's uniform turned and looked down at her as though he, too, recognized her. He was tall, he was dark . . . he was Lewis. 'Lewis . . . oh, Lewis!' she cried out wildly, fighting her way back to him, heedless of the bamboo staves and yak-whips trying to keep the peace in the wake of the British delegation. Sonya flung up her hands to shield her face, sobbing, 'It's me . . . Sonya . . . Lewis, it's Sonya . . . '

Flung back against the sloping wall, a hunch-backed figure in a brown robe grabbed her, pinned her against the stone, put his hand over her mouth, 'Princess,' hissed the black-faced, gap-toothed servant-monk, 'that man is not Lewis. Please do not cry any more. Lewis is not here. I will explain.' He took his hand away.

'Explain, explain what?' She struggled to be free of the ugly Geyok.

He held her tightly, both arms wrapped around her. And then she noticed the stump of his left arm, the sleeve dangling empty below the wrist. She stopped struggling. 'It can't be . . . this is absurd . . . ' She shook her head dis-believingly and then peered closer at the unfamiliar face. 'Joonu?'

His right hand stamped across her mouth again. 'Shhh! Do not tell the whole world, Princess. Of course it is I, Joonu, who else would it be?'

She felt in the grip of some irreconcilable nightmare. Everything combined to knock her down flat. A gush of some internal fluid told her she was haemorrhaging – but she wasn't surprised. Riding for long hours after only recently being delivered of her child, anxiety, fatigue, long periods of starvation, coupled with the terrible events of this morning among the *ro-gyapas*, Sonya suddenly saw everything in hazy wavy lines and felt the terrors of the world catching up with her . . .

'Princess . . . hey, Princess!' Joonu smacked her face anxiously, 'you're not going to faint, are you?'

'No . . . of course . . . not . . . I just feel a bit peculiar, that's all . . .'

'Take a deep breath.'

She took several deep breaths.

'I . . . I'm all right now . . . truly.' She opened her eyes and stared at him. 'Joonu,' she said, not knowing whether to laugh or cry, and then did both. 'I . . . thought you were dead.'

'Princess, to think anything is always dangerous. It is always best not to think about anything, only take life as it comes so as never to feel let down by it.' They looked at one another solemnly, and then burst out laughing, hugging each other in pleasure and friendship.

'Tell me . . . tell me I'm not dreaming or imagining things. Tell me what happened after I left Rika's farmhouse. Tell me what you're doing here. Do you know anything about Lewis?'

'One question at a time please, Princess. But not here, it is too public . . .'

'Joonu,' she gripped the front of his robe, 'Joonu, I'm looking for a baby . . . a very special baby, mine and Lewis's. It was born a month ago and was brought to Lhasa by a mad woman who wanted to give my son to the monks because she thought it was an incarnation of the Dalai Lama . . .'

'Whoa, whoa, Princess!' Joonu gently unfastened her

371

grip on him, his hand clasping hers. 'Come with me, we will talk this thing through. There is much to say, I think, so let us get away from this unruly mob.'

Joonu led her through the mass of people, pushing and shoving as violently as the crowd, abusive as only he knew how, threatening to get his masters, the Yellow Hats, to beat every one for disorderliness.

'Where are you taking me?'

'Where else but where I live, Princess . . . for the moment, anyway.'

'Right inside the Potala itself?' Sonya asked in amazement.

'Only temporarily, Princess. I managed to find employment as a Geyok, a servant-monk, with a Yellow Hat. He is a kindly old fellow, not the usual run of the mill type. He is well educated, well bred, wealthy and above all, humble enough to see good in others. He took me into his service when I escaped from Rika's farmhouse . . . '

'You escaped?'

'Naturally. That is why I live to tell the tale.'

'How?'

'That, Princess, is the story I have to tell in my master's apartments. Come, he will not be here for the moment as he's in the Audience Chamber witnessing all kinds of pledges between two nations who do not care a fig about each other.'

Sonya looked at Joonu twice – the odd feeling that she was once more being manipulated by a certain person creeping up on her. 'You sounded remarkably like someone else then.'

'Who, Princess?'

'Lewis Joyden . . . the Red Cap who wasn't a Red Cap at all but an Englishman operating here in Tibet on behalf of the British Government.'

Joonu laughed. 'I think the sun has touched your head a little, Princess. I do not know what you are talking about!'

ii

In the Yellow Hat's apartments, Sonya listened to Joonu's

extraordinary story. 'After I was beaten by the muleteer, I passed out. When I woke up . . . '

Sonya interrupted; 'That must have been after the Red Cap . . . Lewis, dragged me off with him to the mountains.'

'Yes, Princess, it was. But do not worry, it was all pre-arranged.'

'Prearranged, what do you mean?'

'It is like this, Princess, my master the Yellow Hat, is not my real master. But he is . . . er, sympathetic to my side . . . '

'Whose side, Joonu?'

'We British of course. It is the best side to be on for the next fifty years. After that, I do not gauge much on her chances because I think the great game will be played by other nations . . . yours and perhaps, who knows, America.'

Sonya put her hand to her head. 'Joonu, please slow down, I'm lost. So much has happened to me recently, I just don't know where I am. Who and what are you, besides being a master of disguise just like the Red Cap?'

'I am a student of history, Princess. I am also an opportunist. I go to the side that pays me the most. I told you once, I aim to be a rich man some day.'

'Joonu, I don't believe you any more. If you wanted to be a rich man, you wouldn't be doing what you're doing – I don't know what you *are* doing, but I know it's something you enjoy. And anything one enjoys is never lucrative.'

'Those are truly words of wisdom, Princess. So let me tell you why I am still not a rich man, and hope you are still the woman I trust and respect – even though you are a Russian. I am a Hunza man. I am also a pundit . . . '

'A pundit . . . like Lewis . . . like the Red Cap, I mean?'

'Do not worry, Princess, I know who the Red Cap is. We work for the same side.'

Sonya's huge grey eyes registered comprehension. So many things all of a sudden began to click into place, and she wasn't happy about what she was slowly discovering. So this was what they called the 'great game', a network of spies encircling the world. 'You mean . . . Lewis allowed

373

you to take the beating you did at Rika's farmhouse, all because you are on the same side? I don't . . . I can't believe this sort of thing happens.'

'It happens, Princess,' said Joonu sadly, 'because other people want it to happen. Because men like Lewis and me want it to happen for the excitement, the release from ordinary boring mortal lives. For goals that are far greater than ordinary boring mortal lives can even dream of. For the sheer hell of living life to the fullest. For a great many other reasons.'

'That sounds shallow. I don't believe you and Lewis are shallow men. I believe you're both very dedicated men, dedicated to the country that made you what you are. Tell me, Joonu, how did you escape from the Ponpo after your beating?'

'The Ponpo was bribed. Anyone can be bought for the right price . . . that is something the Red Cap taught me. I was to be given only seven lashes – two for you and five for me. Lewis threatened the Ponpo with legal action if he carried out the flogging too severely, or the sentence of mutilation. Mutilation, you see, Princess, was abolished by the Dalai Lama five years ago. It was all Geyog's fault. If he had not decided to kill Lewis that night, none of it would have happened. But it did, and we still had to play our respective roles despite everything. The sad thing was, you could not be told anything and so you thought the worst of my master. But he, too, took a severe thrashing at Geyog's hands, and had a knife wound across his stomach . . .'

'He never said anything about it. He behaved quite normally – normal that is for the Red Cap.'

'It was nothing, a scratch he told me afterwards, covered up by the gum-skin he uses to disguise his face. After my beating, the Ponpo did not return the following morning to carry out the rest of the sentence, so Rika's daughters looked after me for a few days until I was well enough to travel to Lhasa where I was to meet up again with Lewis . . . Princess . . . I only call him Lewis in front of you, but that is not what I am supposed to call him.'

'What are you supposed to call him?'

'That is classified information, Princess. When we are on an assignment together, like this one, we call each other only by our code names.'

'You have worked with him before?'

'Many times.'

'I suppose, to tell me where, is also classified information?'

'Yes Princess.'

'How did you lose your hand, Joonu. Was it on one of these "assignments"? Did you allow your hand to be cut off because Lewis wanted you as a back-up system to his espionage activities? Tell me Joonu.'

He looked away. 'I told you how I lost it, Princess.'

'Very well, Joonu, I don't wish to pry into matters that concern only you and Lewis. You are both very clever in what you do, but I can't begin to understand why you enjoy it so much. I know you are a pundit. I also know Lewis is a highly trained British spy. I know now you both work together and I know, too, that you and I did not bump into each other accidentally in Samarkand. You were ordered to tail me, weren't you Joonu?'

'Yes, Princess.'

'By whom? Lewis or your precious British Government?'

'They are one and the same to me, Princess.'

'Joonu, look at me!'

Reluctantly he turned to face her, his dark eyes intent and serious. 'Princess,' he said unhappily, 'you are not my enemy. You never were my enemy. I love you. I love you as my friend and a woman who is above all others. Whether or not your husband is the Russian enemy inside the Potala makes no difference to me. I did what I was asked to do, that is all. You see, Lewis knew you were on your way to Samarkand because of something you wrote in one of your letters to him. He knew then you were heading for Tibet – whether to spy for your Russian Government, or to genuinely look for your husband and brother, he could not be certain at the time. So I was detailed to hang about Samarkand until you arrived, and to go wherever you went. Then Lewis was drawn into things because of this British Mission to Lhasa – you know the rest. But you won,

Princess. You won because you loved, you did not hate. You vanquished my master and me as surely as if you held a sword in your hand. We are the enemy laid at your feet through love, not war.'

She smiled. 'Only because I'm a woman, Joonu. If I were a man, I don't think you and Lewis would be lying at my feet now. I think I would be the one to be vanquished, just like those Tibetans out there draping your Union Jack everywhere. It's a silly world, Joonu,' she sighed. 'And I still have to find my child . . . and Lewis.' She looked at Joonu suspiciously. 'I don't suppose you have any idea where he is?'

'He was here three days ago.'

'A pedlar?'

Joonu nodded. 'He spoke with your husband for a long time.'

'My husband? Lewis and he met?'

'Princess . . . ' Joonu got up off the floor where he had been sitting cross-legged. He took a deep breath. 'Princess, I ought not to be telling you these things, but I know you and my master are deeply in love, yet pomp and circumstance are getting in the way of your happiness. That is why I feel free to speak to you as a friend and advisor. Because I love my master and I love you – I serve you both. I am here to spy . . . just as your husband the Russian Prince was planted in the Potala by your people to do the self same job while pretending to work for the Tibetan cause. He is past it now, and does not care which side he is on. Your people do not need him any more and the Tibetans do not want him any more. He only constitutes a burden to them because he is old and sick. That is one aspect of things. The second is, I have not heard from Lewis for three days now and I am worried. He always keeps in touch. I feel in my bones something has happened to him . . . but I don't want to alarm you, perhaps it is nothing. Perhaps I am growing too old for this game and cannot stand the strain any longer. Lewis was here three days ago for one very valid reason, his orders were to get rid of Prince Nikolay Dubrovka, one way or another . . . '

'You mean, he was to kill my husband, in cold blood?'

376

'To kill, to send away, to pack off back to Russia, to bury in the deepest Chang-Tang ice, to get rid of the opposition, Princess.' Joonu shrugged, 'Somehow, he was supposed to remove Prince Nikolay Dubrovka and Dorjiev from the Potala.'

'What happened?'

'He failed to carry out his instructions. That, Princess, is not good from Lewis's point of view.'

'Then . . . then he really wasn't the man I saw . . . standing on the ramp next to Colonel Younghusband?'

'I don't know who you saw, Princess, but my master does not wear khaki.'

'He did once, Joonu.'

'Then it was a disguise, Princess. He is not an army man, he is his own man. But we are drawing away from the point. I think, if he failed to do what he was supposed to do, that is serious.'

'How serious, Joonu?'

'I cannot say, Princess. We are all expendable in this game.'

Sonya stood up. 'Is a man expendable because he happens to fall in love?'

'In this game, the answer is yes,' Joonu replied sadly.

'*Game*? He also called it a *game*!' It doesn't appear to be a game to me, Joonu. We are talking about the lives and deaths of human beings! Can that be a game? Because he loves me, because he could not kill an old man who happens to be married to me, is Lewis expendable?'

'No . . . not because he might love you, Princess. But because he might have been in too much of a hurry to get back to you and forgot to look behind him.'

'In other words, Joonu, you're saying Lewis might be dead.'

Joonu did not answer.

Sonya made a little impatient sound, clicking her tongue in exasperation, refusing to believe Lewis was dead. 'Oh, I'm tired of talking in circles, going round and round with all this spy-talk! You would have made a good politician for the Hunza, Joonu. I'm sure there's a very simple explanation for Lewis's sudden disappearance. Now, is it possible you could arrange a meeting between Colonel Younghusband and me?'

'It is impossible, Princess. The Colonel does not know of my existence. He only knows about . . . Lewis. They knew each other in England and in India. The Viceroy of India would have told the Colonel all about this assignment, since Lewis was here to smooth the path of Colonel Younghusband and his Mission to Lhasa. As far as I, and other pundits go, we are a bunch of faceless nonentities. We do not exist except in the annals of the Survey of India. But I will tell you what I can do, Princess. The Yellow Hat who employs me is sympathetic to everyone, he takes no sides. I can arrange for you to meet him. You can tell him about your missing child . . . I have heard nothing about a child having been brought here. He might be able to help you more than I, by introducing you to the Regent. At the same time, he will arrange for you to see your husband.'

'Thank you, Joonu. That is more than I expected. Meanwhile, please will you do all you can to find out about Lewis?'

'Princess, you never have to ask me such a thing. I would lay down my life for him as many times as he has for me.'

Chapter Twenty-Eight

The Yellow Hat Lama, at first glance, appeared to be an intimidating figure, though Sonya would not have let that worry her. He was tall and regal, with a clear tanned complexion and very light eyes. He did not look Tibetan, and in the course of his polite conversation with her, she learned he was a Kashmiri by birth, and that beneath his rather austere and haughty demeanour he possessed a sensitive and intelligent nature. He listened to her sympathetically, but was reticent in committing himself about a boy-child brought to the Potala as a potential inmate to be tutored for the future office of Dalai Lama. He got off the subject abruptly by offering her China tea from an ornately chased silver-gilt tea-pot, and that little diversion by design, nourished the hope in Sonya's heart that this man did know more about a certain baby than he was prepared to admit. The Yellow Hat, however, obtained an introduction for her to talk to the Regent as the Dalai Lama was not in Lhasa. Disappointed that she would be unable to meet with the God-King after coming all this way, she had no choice but to be content with his deputy.

'But,' said the Yellow Hat, 'today will not be possible. The Regent is officially engaged with the British Mission stationed in Lhasa, so it will either have to be tomorrow or the day after. I will send word to you when the meeting can be arranged. Where are you staying?'

Sonya hesitated, and then decided to take the bull by the

horns. 'There is no accommodation left in Lhasa.' She gave him one of her dazzling smiles. 'Last night I slept on the Potala steps. I had hoped, you see, to rejoin my husband who has a grace and favour apartment here.'

'It can be arranged. Steps are no place for a lady to sleep.' His transparent fish eyes stared at her unblinkingly. 'You will find him looking well and spirited – he is a remarkable man for his age.'

Sonya held out her hand. 'Thank you so much for your help. I'd like to see my husband now.'

He bowed his head. 'I will send my servant to you at once. He will take you to the Prince's apartments. I hope all goes well in the search for your missing child. Goodbye, Princess Dubrovka.'

Sonya found her husband extremely chirpy and animated. 'Look, my dear,' he said, holding up a magnifying-glass while Joonu poured them tea, 'isn't it a fine glass? It's made the world of difference to my eyesight. It's very powerful and even has a silver handle. The pedlar must have known my eyes were bad, the crafty devil – though I would have thought he'd have wanted payment for it. But I think the poor fellow was in too much of a hurry to get out of here, although I can't think why!' Prince Nikolay chuckled gleefully. He squeezed Sonya's hand tightly and she flinched. 'You look pale and sad, dear child. You're not saying much, either. You ought not to have come looking for me, it was too strenuous a journey for you all the way from Russia. But now you're here, I'm very pleased to see you, very!' His ill-fitting false teeth clicked together horribly. He crushed her hand again. 'I feel so well, I've decided, after all, I will go back to Russia with you as the Tibetans have no need of my services any more. We will go home to Dubrovka-Dvaryets together, and I will buy you a pretty new frock for the journey because I don't much care for the one you're wearing. Smile, child, smile!'

ii

Sonya met the Regent two days later. The room into which she was shown was so much more opulent than the spartan

380

cell surroundings of the Yellow Hat's sanctuary. Thick Chinese carpets, exquisite handwoven tapestries and hangings, silver and brass lamps, huge sandlewood chests overlaid in silver-gilt filigree, lacquered furniture both durable and delicate; it was altogether more the kind of room she had expected to see in a palace.

The Tri Rimpoche of Ganden, Regent appointed by the Dalai Lama when he had fled Lhasa, turned out to be an elderly scholarly monk, determined, strong-minded and with a no-nonsense air about him. He had successfully dealt with the obdurate British the previous day, and had got them to promise to leave Lhasa within two months in exchange for trading-rights in Tibet. What he wasn't too happy about was the £50,000 indemnity the British wanted from the Tibetans! He had a lot on his mind, and so came straight to the point.

'I'm unable to spare you a great deal of time, Princess Dubrovka, in the light of the British camping on my door-step – they are such a determined and unimaginative race, I've discovered. I have already made some enquiries concerning your baby son. A child was brought here a few days ago and the mother was told to take it to the Drepung. The High Lama of Drepung has since notified me the boy is still with them as it is indeed born with the mark of Chen-rezig. They are at present carrying out tests on him . . . '

'What tests?' asked Sonya, interrupting the Regent in alarm.

'Nothing drastic, I assure you. In order to establish that this child is truly a reincarnation of Thupten Gyatso the Thirteenth Dalai Lama, objects and clothing belonging to him will be placed around the child. If he shows a marked affinity towards any of these items, say a cup, a spoon, a book or even a toy the Dalai Lama had as a child, then it will be taken that this particular child is his reincarnation.'

'What will happen if my son does pick up, say a spoon, a rattle or a piece of cloth belonging to Thupten Gyatso the Thirteenth?' Sonya asked. 'Babies often do cling onto things like that. It's just a normal instinctive reaction, surely?'

The Regent shrugged. 'That is why the baby is kept under

381

constant observation in the Monastery. As he grows, the lamas can see what other signs there are about him to prove he is an incarnation of Chenrezig, the first Dalai Lama. They are never wrong in their choice, Princess, I assure you.'

'That is all very well, Rimpoche, and might well be applicable to Tibetan baby boys. The woman who stole my son from Thug-Phul is unable to have children of her own. She is Dolma, the only daughter of Kuma Sidheong, the warlord killed at Gyantse. Anyone at Thug-Phul and Gyantse will tell you she is a barren woman – especially the Mother-Nun of the Gyantse Convent who delivered my child. I am a Russian. The father of my child is . . . not a Tibetan. That must surely count against my baby being an incarnation, reincarnation or anything else of the present Dalai Lama.'

'That is true. But the High Lama of the Drepung will be able to tell. Go to him with your story . . . '

'It is not a story! It is a fact! Now I want my baby back and I want him soon. Prince Nikolay Dubrovka and I will be leaving Tibet shortly, and we want to take the child home to Russia with us. We cannot afford to wait until my son is older to see whether he is a true likeness of Chenrezig or not. Rimpoche, my son is not a Tibetan! If you truly must know the facts – my child's father is British.' It was the shock required to make the Regent think twice about Chenrezig's incarnation. Sonya flicked her hand in the air derisively. 'Let's just say I was seduced by a Britisher while I was travelling through Tibet to meet my husband in Lhasa. My child was born at Thug-Phul where the British were camping at that time at Chango Lo – you know what kind of men they are, Rimpoche, desirous of ruling not only the world, but every woman, too. But that's neither here nor there. I can either go back to Russia and tell the world my son was taken away to be brought up as a future Dalai Lama, and the world will laugh mockingly when it's established that a Tibetan God-King is the illegitimate offspring of a Russian woman and an Englishman with no morals, or, I have my child returned to me here and now, and the matter will be closed.'

The Regent scratched his chin. 'I will send word to the High Lama of the Drepung immediately. Naturally, there is no possibility of any nationality other than a true Tibetan Buddhist becoming Dalai Lama. But, it is curious he is born with this special mark upon him.' He scratched his chin again.

'It's only a birthmark,' Sonya said, losing patience very quickly, 'a hereditary mark that will no doubt fade in time, as mine has . . . look . . . please see for yourself and don't be embarrassed, I'm not.' She rolled down her stocking and showed the astonished Regent the faint pink sickle-shaped birthmark just above her left knee. 'That is exactly the kind of mark my father had on the back of his left hand, and my son has inherited, but on the inside of his left wrist. It is a family trait, nothing more.'

'Of course, the woman who brought this child to us may not necessarily have been the lady Dolma of Thug-Phul. I only assume this child is yours, but it could easily belong to a poor Tibetan woman whose son was also born with the mark of Chenrezig upon him,' said the Regent, as stubborn, it appeared, as the British.

'In which case, Rimpoche, the mother will still be with her baby in the Drepung. I doubt if she would wish to give up the glory of sharing her son's god-like status within the Potala. Infants of a month also require to be nourished by breast-milk, something the monks can't do. The lady Dolma, I believe, hired a wet-nurse for my child. If the girl is still with him, then ask her the true story. I'm sure she will be too humble to tell you anything but the truth.'

A slow wide smile spread across the Regent's lined Mongoloid features. 'What a pity, Princess Dubrovka, you weren't with me yesterday to argue with the Britishers. I think you would have won our case. You would not consider staying on in Tibet as Russian advisor to the Kashag?'

Sonya returned his wise old smile. 'I'm flattered, Rimpoche, but no thank you. I've done what I had to do here in Tibet, and that was to find my husband. We will be leaving Lhasa shortly – with the child.'

'Then I will say good-bye now. I have to stop the British

from looting any more images and paintings and other priceless objects from our holy places. They are as bad as the Chinese – but they will deny it, I'm sure.'

Later that day a Tibetan nun was shown to Prince Nikolay Dubrovka's apartments. In her arms was a baby boy with a birthmark on the inside of his left wrist. His complexion was milky-peach, his eyes a misty grey-blue, he had a dimple beside his rosebud mouth and fair fuzz on his head had replaced his darker birth-hair. His bunched pink fists with dimples on the knuckles beat the air hungrily. Sonya gazed on him lovingly. She had no doubt, whatsoever, this was her child, he belonged to no other. With him had come a letter from the High Lama of the Drepung Monastery, written in a scratchy Tibetan hand; 'This child is thought not to be a true incarnation of his Holiness, Thupten Gyatso, Thirteenth Dalai Lama. He has rejected all paraphernalia belonging to the God-King and has established no bond with him. Neither does he show the early temperament and behaviour of the young Thupten Gyatso who was a subdued and intelligent infant.'

Sonya laughed in delight. 'So!' she told her son, placed regally on Kolya's cushions while they both played with the baby, 'You were rejected by the highest in Tibet for being a stupid cry-baby, how glad I am!'

'Hey . . . hey fellow,' Kolya said in alarm. 'Sonya . . . he has taken my magnifying-glass, would you believe! Don't let him put it in his mouth, you don't know where that wretched pedlar got it from.'

The bond between father and child firmly established, Sonya smiled to herself as she took the glass from the baby and handed it back to Prince Nikolay.

'Who's a clever baby then?' she crooned while she tickled infant toes.

A knock on the door distracted their attention from the baby. It was Joonu.

'May I talk to you alone, Princess?'

'Kolya, please watch Luey for me.' She drew the door all but shut and stood with her back to the opening. Kolya would be unable to hear what they were saying, though Sonya supposed he wouldn't have cared anyway. He seemed to have forgotten all about meeting her lover in the guise of a pedlar and had never mentioned anything of their encounter. She had played along with his subtle game of cater-cousin, and was only grateful for Kolya's unpredictable acceptance of a newborn baby emerging from nowhere to disrupt his peace and quiet in surrogate fatherhood at the age of seventy-five!

'Joonu, have you found out anything?' she whispered in the dark bare corridor, echoing and cheerless.

'Nothing, Princess, nothing! I have scouted around for hours. I have asked all sorts of questions, nobody can tell me anything. They do not know, and if they do, are not saying. Lewis would have contacted me by now, I know it. The last thing I heard was that he was going to the British camp at Drepung to pass on to the Colonel what he had picked up when he was here in the Potala – the day he met your husband. They have since said no pedlar ever came to the camp that day, nobody knows anything about it. It is most strange. It is as though they're covering up something, and I am not happy.'

'Could he have returned to India now that his assignment in Lhasa is finished?'

'Not without letting me know first, Princess. We work in unison, I back him up, he backs me up. We cannot do that if we do not know what the other is doing or where he intends to go. It is too dangerous any other way.'

'You know that Prince Nikolay and I are returning to Russia in a few days' time?'

Joonu nodded sadly. 'I will miss you, Princess.'

'Me, too, Joonu . . . I will miss you. But please, you might hear something in the next couple of days, so let's not say our good-byes just yet . . . oh, Joonu, there is one more thing I'd like you to do for me. Go to the *ro-gyapas* . . . no, please don't look so alarmed, listen to me first. There's a woman called Dolma living with them and she ought not to be. She's a noblewoman from Thug-Phul, the one who stole my son. I promised to return for her, but I don't think I could go into that place again. Please could you see that she gets back to Thug-Phul where her own people can look after her. She's sick and has no money, but I'll see to her expenses if only you can get her away. Hire anybody you like. Will you do it for me?'

He nodded again, and sounded briefly like the ebullient Joonu she once knew in Samarkand. 'For you, Princess, I will cut off my left hand. But how will I know this woman?'

'She is living in some sort of a bone-cave with a Mohammedan. He's pock-marked and wears a turban.'

'They are all pock-marked and wear turbans, Princess. But I will find her and make sure she goes back to her home, so do not worry.'

iii

The Tibetans arranged an escort for them. Their luggage packed and ready to be loaded onto yaks, mules and pack-ponies, Kolya and the baby were made comfortable inside the palanquin which would convey them, carried by four sturdy Tibetan porters. In Kolya's bare dingy rooms, which had been his home for five years, now that all his possessions had been packed up or sold, the strange starkness of the place brought home to Sonya more than anything, her final link with Tibet and with Lewis Joyden. He, too, had been inside this very room, touched the door-handle, trodden the same floor, breathed the same musty dank air smelling of an old man and all his ailments . . .

That was where Joonu found her alone.

Before Joonu could say anything, Sonya knew by his face he had bad news and wondered how she could take it. She leaned against the wall, her body suddenly lifeless beneath her heavy travelling cloak. 'You've come to tell me he's dead.'

'Princess, I have been recalled.'

She opened her eyes, and slowly the blood started flowing again. 'By whom, Lewis?'

Joonu shook his shaven head. 'No. By my department. I will be returning to India. I have fresh orders. I am pleased, because there is nothing for me to do here. Lhasa is an open city now, and I don't like its smell. Your woman-friend Dolma, by the way, is safely on her way home, too.' He smiled wanly, sensing the end of the road had been reached and there was only the inevitable parting of the ways left.

'And Lewis? Have you heard from him?' Sonya asked, determined still to stave off that final moment.

'I still have heard nothing. But I will know when I get back. I will send you news, Princess, I promise. One way or another, I will send you news of him.'

'Oh Joonu . . . ' She clung to him. 'Joonu, promise me, promise me! You know exactly the route we're taking. Just . . . just forward your news to me, anything, everything. We will be stopping at every main posting-station and I'll look out for something from you. You also have my address in St Petersburg. But where can I contact you?' she asked in further agitation. 'I must be able to contact you.'

'At Baltit. I go whenever I am near the Hunza to see my great-grandmother. If you over-winter there, you must get her to weave you another shawl.'

'Oh, Joonu . . . I love you, my dear dear friend. But please find Lewis for me, please. I can't live without knowing what has become of him.'

'I will do my best, Princess. You must send my great-grandmother and me pictures of your son. Please go now, Princess, otherwise I will start to cry.'

She hugged him one more time and then dashed her hand across her eyes and sniffed. 'Joonu, what happened to your front teeth?'

'Oh, I am a man of many parts, Princess. When I do not wish to look like my great-grandmother anymore, I put them back.'

'And your hand, you rogue?'

'That I lost forever in Samarkand along with my heart. Safe journey, Princess.'

He ran off quickly, a slim brown shadow vanishing into the greater mysteries of the Potala.

Chapter Twenty-Nine

CONSTANTINOPLE
1905

Summoning Islam to prayer for the fifth time that day, the muezzin's call from his high golden minaret, echoed across the divided city. In the Bayazid quarter of Stamboul a Moslem *hojo* and his Armenian landlord sat in desultory conversation over small glasses of thick black Turkish coffee, a ritual they had indulged in every evening since the *hojo*'s arrival in Stamboul to teach small boys the message of the Koran. The house of the Armenian was narrow, dark and ramshackled, and for the rooms he let out to lodgers, he charged an exorbitant rent.

'I do not know what they do every night, but it is like living with the whole Turkish Army above my head,' whined the Armenian as he raised disparaging black eyes to the ceiling.

The Moslem helped himself to more coffee from the jug on the rickety table, using his left hand to pour. He liked his coffee hot and sweet, the same with tea. The teacher murmured his mutual agreement about the Turkish Army encamping above their heads. He had a nervous tic in his eye and blinked rapidly as he took off his thick gold-rimmed spectacles purchased in Pera. He recalled in that moment that the Christians across the Galata Bridge were not above charging him an exorbitant fee for the spectacles. He wiped them carefully. 'It is a strange thing when they live in a perfectly nice house next door, to want to take rooms here . . . who are these rich young men?'

'Who else but the elite of the Military,' replied the Armenian. He picked his nose with the long nail of his little finger and leaned closer, his expression sly, his thick lips wet and rubbery. 'I have listened outside the door to their political talk. They tear the Sultan to pieces, and wish only to establish their own state, a military state! They should be careful they are not found out and denounced to the Secret Police for what they are, for then the Sultan behind twenty-foot thick walls of the Yildiz will pull them limb from limb. Abdul Hamid is not a man to be trifled with, he is a despot!'

Presently the *hojo* announced his intention of seeking his bed. 'I have an early start in the morning and must keep a clear head for my pupils who ask me the most puerile things! They think I am an ignoramus, that my brain is weak like my eyes so they think they will trap me with their idiotic questions. Therefore, I must always be one step ahead of the little brats. Goodnight, landlord.'

Before he left, the Moslem put some money on the table. The Armenian took it greedily and shoved it into a money pouch tied securely to the waist-cord of his grubby kaftan. 'Goodnight, *hojo* – you at least are a good tenant and pay up on time – unlike the young Turks!'

In the dark narrow corridor outside, the *hojo* bumped into the young men from upstairs. They were making their way out to the street and the teacher could smell raki on their breath. Newly gazetted Staff Officers from the Military College at Harbiye, they were full of their own importance. 'Ho there, *hojo*!' one of them said, jostling the teacher playfully. 'What now, fellow, not another early night?'

'I am tired, young sir. I have had a busy day teaching the joys of the Koran to others.'

'Then you, too, must take time off to share the joys of the Koran . . . why don't you accompany us to the café down the street where a friend keeps a rendezvous with us?' The young man who now spoke to the teacher, stood apart from the rest. Quite unlike his fellow Turks, his dignity, blond handsomeness and quiet authority singled him out as their leader. His extraordinary blue eyes, vivid and piercing, assessed the portly Moslem behind the gold-rimmed spectacles, his stiff white tunic and shalwar, and the young Turk smiled lazily.

The Moslem looked shocked. 'No, no, indeed! Excuse me young sirs, I am too old for that kind of gallivanting.'

'But not above prowling around in the dark after us, eh *hojo*?' said the unusual blond Turkish officer.

The Moslem blinked nervously. 'I do not know what you mean, young sir. I go to bed early every night.'

The fair one laughed loudly. 'You hear that, Ali? He is a rogue, is he not? Come, come *hojo*, we all know what you are after – as we are all after the Armenian and Christian girls who show themselves like stars at night to drive a man mad. And since we all need to satisfy our masculine urges, you have nothing to be ashamed of. Bring him, Ali, maybe he can give us a few lessons.' The fair-haired young man, laughing like the rest, turned on his heel and marched off while Ali Fuad, bolder than the others, together with another Staff Captain lifted the *hojo* bodily. Supported by his elbows the Moslem wiggled his feet that did not touch the ground and vociferously protested their boisterous fun and games.

'We will give him raki to loosen his tongue further,' said Ali Fuad. 'Maybe he can then remember where he goes to at night.'

'I do not touch alcohol – it is against my religion,' said the Moslem.

Kemal, the fair one, laughed again. 'Religion, my friend, is the curse of civilization.'

ii

The café where the *hojo* was taken was insalubrious. He felt very conspicuous in his Moslem dress in the midst of all these bright young Staff Officers in their smart uniforms. After a while the rowdy soldiers forgot all about him as they engaged in conversation with others while awaiting their friend, host of the evening who had instigated such a rendezvous. The *hojo* looked around him nervously, and had just made up his mind to disappear quietly, when their table was surrounded by other Turks of a more hostile nature. A gun appeared, thrust shockingly at Kemal's breast. 'You and your cronies are under arrest, Kapitan!' said the swarthy gendarme confronting the fair Kemal.

The *hojo* had no doubt in his mind these were the Sultan's black-faced Secret Police and without a second's hesitation, dived for the open door. A pistol shot reverberated around the small café and the Moslem dropped to the floor with a bullet in his right knee. Kemal and his fellow officers gave themselves up without a word; it would be suicide to resist in the face of the Sultan's men surrounding them and they knew it.

'Betrayed!' Ali Fuad spat in disgust, 'by that shitbag cadet expelled from Harbiye . . . you should never have allowed him to lodge with us, Kemal . . . it is he who has betrayed us to the Sultan while pretending to be our friend – that is why he is not here! He lured us to this place on purpose . . . I will kill him if I get my hands on him.'

It was unfortunate that the Moslem teacher was with the young Turks when they were arrested. He was thrown into prison with them. Only a few more days and he would have got all the intelligence he required and would have left Stamboul as inconspicuously as he had entered it via Afghanistan. Singly, they were all interrogated, the methods of interrogation used by Sultan Ahmed Hamid's Secret Police very brutal. Only Ali Fuad was returned to the communal cell without a mark on him.

Kemal, his handsome face battered, bruised and bleeding, opened a swollen eye to say to Ali Fuad, 'Why are you still in one piece?'

Ali Fuad grinned slyly. 'I told them that as I wore the Sultan's uniform, no man below the rank of the Sultan himself was allowed to dishonour this uniform by striking me.'

'Now why didn't I think of that,' murmured Kemal with a wry smile, adding, 'They are keeping the Moslem a long time . . . I wonder why.'

391

Abdul Hamid's Secret Police at last established the fact that
the Moslem *hojo* was a British Agent operating in Stamboul
against the Sultan. His spying activities centered around the
discovery of the Sultan's westernization programme for his
backward country, where and to whom he was going for
outside aid, and above all, secrets concerning the extension
and modernization of the Turkish military machine . . .
Lewis Joyden had come full circle.

He was unconscious when he was flung into solitary
confinement. His blood loss had been severe from the bullet
still embedded in his knee-cap, added to which, the Turkish
police had not spared him elsewhere. He was not given
medical attention.

'I think, Kemal,' said Ali Fuad to his friend while
shaking his head sadly, 'you were right about the Moslem.
He is not all he appears to be. I think that when the four of
us left here together are separated, it will be time for us to
die too.'

Lewis Joyden, however, was made of sterner stuff – as
the Turkish officers were soon to discover. When he
regained a hazy consciousness the first thing he did, despite
his weakness, was tear his baggy *shalwar* pantaloons into
strips to act as a tourniquet. The filthy straw pallet on which
he lay was soaked with his own blood as well as the vomit,
urine and excreta residues from previous prisoners. He
realized he had been manoeuvered into this inexorable situation by those in high places. Chumbi gaol and thereafter
Calcutta only the beginning of his long downward spiral from
the pinnacle of his career – all on account of what had
happened between himself and Princess Sonya Dubrovka
over the Samsâra affair. So, instead of having him shot for
disobedience and traitorous activities – according to Younghusband in his odious Blue Book no doubt! – the Viceroy
had assigned him to Turkey so that others might do the
dirty deed– diplomacy at its highest and most devious level,
the washing of the hands! But he was not going to die,
he was yet going to beat them at their own 'great game'.
Then he once more passed out.

A few days later he was again interrogated. When he next woke up, he discovered that Kemal and Ali Fuad flanked him, one either side of him in their tiny foetid cells.

iv

They were kept in the Stamboul prison for many months awaiting the Sultan's final decree as to the manner in which they were to be put to death. During that time, when it was discovered the Britisher could take anything and everything the Turkish police could give him, and that he had made up his mind to live and that was that, they left him alone for longer and longer periods.

One day, Lewis, hanging weakly to the bars of his cell door, said to Kemal, 'Kemal, what about lending me one of your forbidden books?'

Kemal's educated voice evinced surprise. 'How do you know about my forbidden books, Englishman?'

'I'm a spy, aren't I?' Lewis growled.

Kemal and Ali Fuad laughed lustily when they heard the Englishman in his fluent Turkish growl at Kemal, the guards not caring one way or another what the three men discussed at the bars of their cells as long as they were firmly under lock and key. 'I like your poetry, Lewis Joyden, so I will lend you my forbidden books – on condition you write me an English poem next time, and not a Turkish one! One day, I should like to visit England that has reared so many *civilized* men, and see your Oxford. One day, too, I shall abolish the fez in this country, for it is a heathen and barbaric custom. I shall introduce hats with brims, for then it will be more difficult for a man to abase himself with his forehead on the ground while he prays to Allah! I shall introduce *many* such reforms in our religion, education and government. I shall do it, Englishman, I have made up my mind.' He spoke with a quiet steely conviction, and Lewis had no doubt in his mind that one day, this twenty-four year old Kemal, if he was not put to death here and now by the cruel Sultan would rise to be a great leader of the Turkish people.

The pattern of their days was thus established, discussions

on poetry, philosophy, literature and religion whiling away the painfully tedious hours. Until one day Kemal, Ali Fuad and the other two Staff Officers who had been with them in the café at the time of their arrest, were taken out of their cells to hear the Sultan's verdict concerning their prohibited political activities.

When they were next returned underground by the Turkish guards, the soldiers were exuberant while they collected up their few belongings. 'The Sultan is not going to have us put to death; we have been reprieved as he has a use for us after all!' Kemal said with controlled passion that belied his joy. 'Ali Fuad and I are to join the Fifth Army stationed at Damascus – I am willing to go to the desert to found a new state there!'

Lewis considered his own fate, his mood grim and sad. After a while he said; 'Kemal . . . '

'I am still here Englishman, but not for long.'

'Will you do something for me please?'

'Anything for a man after my own heart.'

'I have certain . . . er, things, I would like you to put into the hands of one whose address I shall give you.'

Kemal asked no questions. Lewis, behind the stout door of his cell drew down what was left of his tattered pantaloons and did something which would have made Kemal and Ali Fuad roar with laughter had they been able to observe him. Lewis peeled away patches of 'gumskin' that had stood him in such good stead in Tibet, and uncovered scraps of paper adhering secretly to his body.

'Addresses . . . and verses I've written while I've been here,' he explained to Kemal through the bars. 'The gendarmes did not find them . . . and I don't want them to be found now, when there is hope, too, for me. Especially as one is a Russian address.'

'I understand, Englishman,' said Kemal, 'no need to go into details. I shall always be indebted to you for having enlivened my stay in this heathen place. I have enjoyed our civilized talks together amongst all these barbarians. As soon as I am in Damascus, I will work for your release. There is a way I know. The Sultan wishes for the return of a very important Turkish diplomat who is at present in British hands. Maybe we can get together around the bargaining table. Lewis Joyden from Oxford, I am, at your service, Mustafa Kemal Atatürk!'

EPILOGUE

ST PETERSBURG
Winter 1907

A golden flying-angel was held in an icy embrace, frozen in time and space and destined to hang from the golden cross of St Peter-and-Paul Cathedral until the icicles melted in the spring. The River Neva crystal-hard, the Baltic Fleet anchored in warmer waters. The harbour was once again the ice-rink for the city's inhabitants to glide, bridge to bridge, from November to April.

Nothing seemed to have changed at all in five years, and yet, everything had changed . . .

In the Rastrelli Room in the Winter Palace, Princess Sonya Dubrovka, looking expensively chic in a blue-grey embroidered afternoon coat with a silver fox fur collar designed by Worth, over a stunning navy and grey costume accentuating her tiny waist, a dark grey astrakhan hat with ostrich feather complementing the heavy glossy chignon on the nape of her neck, delivered an account of her amazing travels through Tibet. Her audience consisted of the Tsarina, Alix, the Grand Duchesses and ladies of the Court of St Petersburg.

'And so, to sum up, I want to impress upon you all, that out there in the vast untamed world beyond our comfortable drawing-rooms, there is so much we can do. We are the new generation of women who must change to fit the times

397

in which we live. We are the women of the twentieth century! This new exciting era dawns, an era of advanced science, technology, medicine, exploration, and so we must not be left behind, second-status females in a man's world. We must share that world, too. We must become individuals in our own right, demand what the new Suffragette Movement for women of England are demanding, a voice, and a right to express our own opinions. Not those of our husbands, our fathers, and grandfathers. Yes, we are wives, mothers, grandmothers, first and foremost, and we will always remain so – but we can also be the power behind the throne . . . the Tsarina, I know, will not mind if I say that prerogative does not belong to her entirely, since every woman is the queen of her own castle.'

The Tsarina smiled, and dipped her head in agreement when she caught the Princess's eye.

'In Tibet,' Sonya continued, 'a land of truly incredible beauty and potential, I saw such appalling poverty and wretchedness simply crying out for something to be done. But, not only in Tibet, in India, Africa, Europe . . . right here in Russia, too, our charity, our time, our influence are required to help the under-privileged classes. But, above all, we need the inclination! So, while our menfolk might fight their wars of power and do not see the blood and the tears of those who are powerless, we, too, can fight our own very special wars, against poverty, famine, disease and social injustices. We can wipe up the blood and the tears by caring about the needs of others, not just here at home, but wherever we are needed. We can start today by proving we have that inclination, and the resolve, to improve the lot of others less fortunate than ourselves by giving generously to the Lhasa Foundation set up by the Tsarina.'

The applause was loud and generous. The Tsarina rose to her feet. 'Thank you Princess Dubrovka, for a most enlightening and interesting talk, not only about your travels in Tibet, but also on the changing role of twentieth century women. I can truthfully say, not one of us here this afternoon has been bored by the subject. Ladies,' she turned and addressed the glittering audience behind her, 'the Lhása Foundation has been set up not only to provide funds for a children's hospital to be built in the city, but we also require clothing of good quality, picture-books, toys and gifts. Volunteers, too, are needed to help in the organization of this project. Willing helpers give their names please to my daughter, the Grand Duchess Olga, the first of three other volunteers,' she smiled at the rest of the Grand Duchesses, 'to help Princess Dubrovka and myself get the Lhasa Foundation off the ground – or I should say, to lay its foundation stone! Now let us all have some tea.'

In an ante-room adjoining the Rastrelli, at a small round table impeccably set for afternoon tea, the linen snowy white, silver and china gleaming, fresh hot-house blooms of gardenias and tea-roses heartening the sullen afternoon, the Tsarina and Sonya chatted intimately for a little while. 'I was so sorry to hear of your husband's death last month,' the Tsarina began on a consolatory note.

Sonya, still far away in the mountains of Tibet, marshalled her thoughts. 'It was a merciful release, really. Kolya had been ill for a long time. It amazes me how he withstood the journey home. It took us over a year because of the frequent stops we had to make on account of his failing health. But an inner strength seemed to buoy him up, and the baby helped marvellously well – he became very fond of his adop . . . of his Luey.'

'But at least he died in his own bed at Dubrovka-Dvaryets! How brave you were, Sonya, to do what you did. Managing to bring him all that distance by yourself. I don't think I could have done it.'

'I think any woman could have done what I did – if she had put her mind to it firmly enough by refusing to be intimidated by the world and men in general, or allowing herself to become a prisoner of her own biological limitations. So, your Majesty, you could have done it.'

The Tsarina smiled. 'How is your son?'

'Luey is very well, a growing bundle of mischief all the time.'

'How long will you be away? Not too long I hope, we shall all miss you greatly.'

'Thank you. But I've really no idea how long I'll stay in

England. Grandmother Lizaveta left me her home in Abingdon, and I have much of her affairs to sort out – which, I'm sure, are in appalling disarray! I have so much I want to do.' She returned the Tsarina's smile. 'I haven't even the time to look for a new home. Dubrovka-Dvaryets, as you know, goes to Kolya's eldest son, Prince Paul, by his first marriage, so I'm house-hunting among other things.'

'What about Kirovsky Ploshad? Count Mikail would be delighted to have his daughter and grandson live with him, surely?'

She was fishing, Sonya was sure of it. She smiled, to herself this time, as she picked up her cup again and made the Tsarina happy with a little gossip over everyday affairs. 'Yes, he has offered to have us live with him, but really, I don't like my father's new wife. I'm certain life would be very difficult for Luey and me living with them. Besides, Kirovsky Ploshad would only remind me of mama's death while I was away in Tibet. Her presence is everywhere in the house – even though my father's new wife had everything belonging to my mother disposed of without consulting me. No, I prefer my own residence. I'm sure I'll find something soon.'

The Tsarina put down her cup, and instead of using the monogrammed table-napkin beside her, wiped her lips with a lace handkerchief taken from the sleeve of her cream velvet and Honiton lace frock. 'But enjoy your holiday in England first, my dear, and don't work too hard over your grandmother's appalling disarray! Now I must go to Nikky. He works so hard these days, the poor darling – what with workers' strikes, the new Duma demanding greater powers, and the revolutionary factions threatening Nikky's life. But we must not be down-hearted, despite everything!' She sighed heavily and evinced a false smile. 'That man, Stolypin, is doing an excellent job in crushing the inflammatory elements of our country. Good-bye, Sonya dear.' She brush-kissed Sonya on both cheeks before rushing away to an Empress's duties.

Sonya went over to the Grand Duchess Olga to help scribble down the names of all the willing ladies eager to be associated with the Lhasa Foundation. She wondered how long this Tibetan euphoria would last when there was so much seething unrest right here on the very doorstep of the Winter Palace in this, the first anniversary year of free elections and the second reminder of St Petersburg's bloody Sunday.

ii

ST ANNE'S RECTORY, ENGLAND
Summer 1907

A soft summer breeze rustled the ox-eye daisies growing wild and tall in the ditch by the pathway, stirring Sonya's black tulle veil as she clung tightly to her three-year-old son's soft cherubic hand. She did not want to see who lay in the grass, but a terrible yearning to know the truth compelled her to read the names on the tombstones.

MARGARET JANE JOYDEN
Dearly beloved wife of
Desmond Lewis Haga Joyden
Rector of St Anne's Church, Nuneham
Born 1848 – Died 1887

AND

JENNIFER JANE JOYDEN
Beloved daughter of
Margaret and Desmond Joyden
Born 1870 – Died 1887

THE LORD GIVETH
AND THE LORD TAKETH AWAY

A yearning apprehension buffeted her, haunted eyes warily seeking the one name that meant anything at all to her in the sunlit grasses of this sad little plot . . .

The last two letters Sonya had received from Joonu had been devastating in their effect on her morale. He had told

401

her that Lewis, after having been acquitted of negligence and treason over his handling of the Samsâra affair, had been given an assignment in Turkey. Without revealing details, Joonu had later informed her that Lewis had been captured, and all that the Survey of India was aware of afterwards was that 'in the absence of conclusive proof, Lewis Joyden was believed to have died under interrogation and torture in Stamboul.' With Joonu's second letter had come a scrap of blood-stained paper, purported by the Turks to have been found hidden on Lewis's person at the time of his capture. That piece of paper and a few other sundry items belonging to Lewis had been despatched back to India by the hand of a man who signed himself Mustafa Kemal Atatürk. Joonu had sent the blood-stained scrap of paper to her rather than Lewis's father because he thought it concerned her more than Reverend Joyden. It had contained her name and address in St Petersburg, written in a large girlish scrawl. Sonya remembered it had been torn from a corner of an old exercise book, given to Lewis the day he had visited her grandmother in Abingdon, the day after he had rescued her from the Thames; so long ago now, everything that had happened to her since, seemed like a dream . . .

'I'm so glad you could come.' A pleasant deep voice behind her startled Sonya.

She turned to see a tall spare man with thin greying hair, smoking a pipe, his eyes twinkling genially. He wore a shabby maroon cardigan patched and pinched at random, grey flannels earth and grass stained from the potting he had been doing in his greenhouse, and carpet slippers. He took his gardening hand from his sagging pocket and came forward to greet her. 'I was so afraid you wouldn't accept my invitation to have supper with me tonight. So this is the rejected Thupten Gyatso!' Reverend Joyden took the pipe from his mouth and dropped to his knees to examine his grandson. 'Well, young fellow, you're not a bit like your photograph . . . much better looking. It's about time we put you down for Aedes Christi – unless of course you'd rather be a train driver.'

'I'm afraid he hasn't picked up many English words so

far,' Sonya explained apologetically as her bewildered son thrust his face into her black silk skirts.

'No, of course not.' Reverend Joyden rose creakingly to his knees, wincing as his hand instinctively clasped his back, and then with a smile added, 'It's so nice of you, Sonya, to want to take supper with me on your first evening in Abingdon. Maud, my housekeeper, has prepared a game pie for us. I've even managed to discover a very special bottle of wine in the cellars. But first, let's look around the garden. I want to show you my pergola.'

Sonya followed him across an artistic log-back bridge over a small stream, brooklime rife on mossy banks reflecting the sky in tiny azure-blue flowers. Then along sweet-scented thyme paths in a less sad garden separated from the churchyard by a rose-covered brick wall. He was not at all the terrifying man she had expected. She did not know what kind of man she had expected to meet, confused in her own mind about what characteristics Lewis's father ought to possess, passed on in the son and grandson. In her imagination and nervousness surrounding this long-awaited moment of meeting him, he had immediately banished her fears by his relaxed informal reception. And in that alone she was grateful to him for vanquishing the bleak moment she had experienced beside the tombstones of his family.

He hesitated by the pergola, thick with honeysuckle, dog-roses and clematis, a shady place to linger on a warm summer's evening. 'Sonya,' he said, 'I have another guest for supper.'

'Joonu? Has he arrived in England? I wrote and told him I was coming here.'

Her expression suddenly alive, she searched the Rector's face for clues, still unreconciled to the fact Lewis might be dead. It was all to do with that one revealing and very heartening sentence in Joonu's letter, 'in the absence of conclusive proof,' that had kept hope burning eternally within her – and, having been introduced by Lewis himself to an English writer's words concerning a woman's hope, Sonya preferred to let her 'hopes remain woven with sunbeams without a shadow to annihilate them'. 'Has Joonu brought news of Lewis?'

'Go and ask him yourself, my dear.'

Tricks of light from another time, another place, fed her imagination, and the shadows on the fields of Thug-Phul beneath the poplars made her heart leap, her breath stop right here in an English garden filled with a timeless essence, filled with wonder, and Sonya cried; 'Lewis! No . . . it can't be . . . *it is* . . . !' The shadows merged, she was lifted off her feet and then they both took root beneath the pergola arch while the Rector clasped the little boy's hand and led him away to show him a snail underneath a flowerpot.

Her mourning veil for her husband lifted so that Lewis could kiss her and wipe away her tears, Lewis's own eyes filled with the moistness of a foolish treachery. Laughter and tears spilling over on the whims of governments, of time and circumstance, of so many things that had kept them apart, so that, in gazing at her now, he was only filled with a silent futile anger against a system that had made him, and almost destroyed him. But, he was a wiser man now, thankful he had seen the light before it was too late. 'Why are you crying?' he asked, his voice husky with a deep emotion. 'I thought you were happy to see me.'

'Lewis . . . why, oh why? Why couldn't you have written?' His presence, his charisma, his effect on her, all that had filled her dreams, her waking and sleeping hours for three torturous years was confounded now by the way she gave vent to what she considered to be his terrible betrayal of her. She could only find it in her heart to accuse him in the moment when she had imagined reconciliation would bring forgiveness. 'Why couldn't you have told me? Why didn't you let me know what has been happening to you these past three years? Why did you stop loving me so that you couldn't even confide in me any more?'

'Sonya . . . I've never stopped loving you . . . come here and sit down. Let me explain . . . ' His arm around her waist, he led her to a rustic bench in the shade of the Pergola. 'I got into a lot of hot water, just like H20 . . . ' He rambled, as she had done a moment ago, making no sense to her as, wildly and stormily, he punctuated his narrative with laughing kisses while he held her tightly and looked at her as though he still couldn't believe his eyes.

She could only return the loving wholeheartedly until the headiness of their reunion had subsided a little and they could speak again. Then he told her as much as could be contained in that short space of time before duties of a domestic nature intruded. 'I was supposed to get rid of your husband, one way or another, out of the Potala and the reach of the Tibetans. Everyone, you see, was afraid he would stir up more trouble for us if he was allowed to remain in Lhasa after the British Mission arrived. It wasn't much use signing a treaty with the Tibetans, who, the moment British backs were turned, would go back to the Russians. But I couldn't do it. I went afterwards to the British camp at Drepung to tell the British Commissioner, Younghusband, why I couldn't. He told me about you, how he was going to arrest and interrogate you in Lhasa and I'm afraid I saw red . . . sorry, I didn't mean to sound flippant about your revolutionary countrymen.' He grinned and stroked the back of her hand. 'You're such a brave lady in so many ways, but I'm glad you're here now, not in Russia where they're bent on doing away with people like you . . . Sonya, I didn't know you had had the baby and then travelled to Lhasa so soon afterwards. I'm afraid I did what I ought not to have, I threatened Younghusband with a knife in his back if he didn't allow me to return to Lhasa to find you . . . he had me placed under arrest, you see. Anyway, I got as far as putting a foot in a stirrup and that's about all before all hell was let loose.' He grinned sheepishly. 'But then, hell is paved with good intentions, I believe, although at the time I couldn't forgive Younghusband for being the architect of my own private hell in Chumbi gaol, and afterwards, in being banished to Constantinople. I gnashed my teeth, wept tears of blood and devised ways and means of getting even with him the moment I set foot again in the Geographical Society's hallowed halls. I'll do it, too, believe me!'

She smiled and squeezed his hand tighter. 'Is that what happened to you when you and Geyog fought in the river? Did you gnash your teeth, and weep tears of blood, then wash it all away along with your sins before you returned to Rika's farmhouse looking like a drowned Red Cap rat with a bad scratch on its stomach? Did you cover it all up with your magic skin so I wouldn't notice your injury when you practised Thumo Reskiang on a glacis and when we lay in your bedroll together?' Sonya, a light in her eye teased him. 'Speak, you red-faced Englishman who never confesses to any weakness, including the commitment of love. How well I know you, Lewis Joyden!'

He laughed heartily. 'They were good days in Tibet, weren't they? Well now, you can see for yourself any time you like how battle-scarred I've become even since then. Stamboul was a hell-hole from which everyone thought I'd never emerge again, but I beat the system – anyway, I'd rather not talk about it. As for Joonu, I'll tan his hide a deeper shade of brown when I next get hold of him.'

'Where is Joonu, Lewis? Didn't he come to England with you? I was half-expecting him to visit your father and me.'

'So, the soft spot for Joonu still lingers in your heart, and I'm jealous.' He brushed back a spiral of chestnut curl caught by the light evening breeze and tucked it carefully behind her ear. 'He's with his wife and children and great-grandmother somewhere in the mountains, or if he isn't, then he's pundit-ing somewhere . . . classified information.'

'Joonu's married?'

'Why not? He's old enough. Joonu's an old married man of twenty-six though, to give him his due, he looks and behaves like a juvenile. In fact, he's gone one better than me by having two children . . . which reminds me, where's father taken my son?' He peered around the edge of the pergola.

'He'll be back . . . Lewis, I want to know what happened to you after you left me at Thug-Phul? Why were you sent off to your death in Stamboul? Joonu never told me anything specific.'

'Darling Sonya, he couldn't. After Younghusband had me arrested at Drepung and packed me off to Chumbi prison to prevent me from being a greater flea in his ear, I was next shunted off to Calcutta where I had to explain myself before the Viceroy and the rest of governmental hierarchy. I had to tell them all about you, the purity of our relationship . . . and why I wasn't a traitor to my country.

It took some hard and fast explaining, I can tell you. It was simply ages before they were satisfied I wasn't about to become a British Dorjiev, having fathered a half-Russian child and all that. Joonu and I were then watched closer than bugs under a microscope. Soon after, I was packed off to Turkey and into a situation in which, I believe now, everyone at the Foreign Office hoped was the last of me.' He pulled a wry face. 'What is known in the business as "expendable". However, those are only my feelings about what happened there – but it's also another story. I'm not going into details right now as we've better things to do with our time. Suffice it to say, if it wasn't for an up and coming young Turkish military leader by the name of Kemal Atatürk, I'd never have lived to get out of Stamboul ever again. He at least was more civilized than the rest of those Turks, having some regard to decency and the code of human behaviour. He worked very hard to secure my release on an exchange of prisoner deal – the Sultan's desire to regain an important Turkish diplomat far greater than his desire to behead me – I'm glad to say!'

'Were you tortured? Joonu told me you were.'

He shrugged carelessly. 'Mentally yes, physically not as bad as being buried up to one's ears in ice as I was at Gyantse.' He changed the subject quickly, 'Sonya, I've died a thousand worse deaths over you these last three years. I only longed to be free of commitments to people who couldn't give a damn about my welfare. After I managed to get out of Stamboul, I was sent back to India. I wanted to come to St Petersburg to see you, but I couldn't because no one would let me. You belong to the Russian nobility – more dangerous than a Plehve-bomb. I am British, and in certain people's eyes, never the twain shall meet. The Okhrana know more about espionage tactics than the British, and I wouldn't have stood a snowball's chance in hell between the Bolsheviks and Rasputin if I'd shown up in St Petersburg after just emerging from a hot-bed of Turkish intrigue – not to mention Tibet. Someone in Russia would have loved to get their hands on a potential turncoat like me who might have furthered their revolutionary cause – thus putting an end to our relationship once and for all. The

407

worst I got from my side over the Samsâra affair, was being thrown in at the deep end of the Sultan of Turkey's little military schemes that ended up with the Ottoman Empire wanting to bury me like the Tibetans – and incidentally my side, too, for falling in love with you – so much back-biting and intrigue, you wouldn't believe the half. So, I decided I didn't want to be a general dog's body and whipping boy any more, and since I'm getting a little too old for the great game, I've resigned from the Survey of India and the Foreign Office who, incidentally, were glad to see the back of me. Even though I managed, by the skin of my teeth, to redeem myself in Stamboul, I don't think anybody fully trusted me after what happened between us in Tibet.' He took up her hand and examined her neatly filed pink finger-nails. 'I've come back to England for good. I only arrived back in May.'

'May! You might have written to me, told me what had happened to you!' she accused him again.

'Yes, I know, my love, but I had a very good reason not to contact you in Russia. Wait a minute and I'll tell you! Firstly, I was de-briefed and then hospitalized for a time in Simla while they sorted out a Turkish bullet left behind in my knee and secondly Joonu told me all about you returning to Russia with your husband. I realized then, that, while he lived, there was no future for us because your conscience wouldn't permit it . . . I know you by now, Sonya. You made your choice in Lhasa, to stay with your husband, and I could not blame you for that – neither could I bear to be on the outside watching you wasting your life and our love on a sick old man. The only consolation was knowing he couldn't live much longer and then we would have the rest of our lives together – if you still wished it of course. And that was my own private agony – that he might live forever or you might have thought twice about me when you were back in your own home with your own people. Your letter to my father telling him about your husband's death, and that you would be coming to England to sort out your grandmother's affairs, arrived the week after I got home. So I bided my time. With you here, on neutral ground, we were safe . . . we are safe. Don't you see, Sonya, so often I

408

was ready to throw out the scruples and contact you – Joonu has never forgiven me to this day for doing what I thought best for both of us, by keeping away from you until I knew Kolya was dead and you were on your way to England with our son. Ask father, these past few weeks have been agony for me – and for father, too. Wondering if you really would show up here or something would crop up to keep you in Russia. Yes, there is still one more thing keeping us apart, Sonya, and I have to say it.'

'What?' she asked impatiently.

'Your grand title, your privileged place in Russian society . . . don't deny it!'

She had made a small clicking sound of denial, and he had ignored it because he had to be certain. 'Sonya, it's still something that has to be thought about carefully. You are a Russian Princess, what can I give you?'

'If you have to ask that, you don't deserve me! I never thought you were a stupid man, Lewis Joyden, but I'm beginning to change my opinion. Listen, I don't need a hero, I want a husband – *you*, you fool! I love you, Lewis, I love you, isn't that enough? Isn't our son enough for you?'

'It's too much . . . '

'I would give up my country, my nationality, my title, everything, if you asked me. That's why I wrote to your father so often, hoping some day I would hear from you. Did you persuade him, too, not to tell me you were alive and well and released from your assignment in Turkey?'

'Yes.'

'You're a horrible man.'

'I know. I asked him to bribe you over here tonight with one of Maud's terrible pies and a bottle of elderberry wine looking as if a storm had brewed in the bottle.' He fisted her chin tenderly and pulled a face. 'But I'd have come to your grandmother's house anyway to beg you to marry me before you returned to Russia, hoping against hope you wouldn't return. It's not safe there anymore, Sonya. I keep in touch with current worldwide events. I read the *St Petersburg Gazette*, and realize Russia is on the brink of revolution. I know, too, what a fine job you're doing in setting up this Lhasa Foundation and how you've been made an Honorary member of the Russian Geographical Society. I've hesitated in asking you to marry me because the best I can offer you is a plain Mrs married to a Mr Joyden, geography and language teacher at some rotten English school for delinquent boys.'

'I accept.'

'I haven't even a house to offer you.'

'There is always grandmother Lizaveta's.'

'God forbid! No, we'll find another. We'll build a pergola of willow boughs, grow roses and honeysuckle over it, call it Samsâra and live under it for the rest of our lives. My Reverend father will first have to make you an honest woman, though.'

She smiled, and the scent of honeysuckle was intoxicating. 'If that's a proposal of marriage, thank you, Mr Joyden. I'm honoured to accept. Tell me what Samsâra really means, Lewis.'

'It means,' he murmured, tracing her lips with his thumb and looking at her with an expression of profound wisdom – and something else she recognized from his intense little quixotic smile – "a jewel in the lotus of the world". I think I've found mine . . . shall we ask H20 to the wedding, just to keep him happy?'

'H20?'

'My man who constantly gets himself into hot water with pretty women . . . only my name for him of course. His official name is . . . '

'Classified information! I know,' Sonya said, feigning exasperation. 'Lewis, won't you miss it all? The excitement of this . . . this "game" you and Joonu enjoyed so much together?'

'Not if you keep me happy and excited.'

She could not cope, in these few moments of reunion, with the promise and the expectation, the fulfilment of all her hopes after the desperate yearning that had tormented her for so long. She had a lifetime to savour all, in the freedom of a new country, a new life, and the renewal of his pledges of love laid before her – yet still she hesitated even while she kept to herself the knowledge of a blood-stained scrap of paper from an old exercise book, taken with him right into the heart of Constantinople. 'Lewis, are you sure you'll be happy with me . . . a Russian woman, the enemy?'

'No!' He shook his head emphatically, utterly serious. His dark hair, the lean tanned lines of his face, the glints in his hazel eyes absorbing the greens, golds and yellows of the bower under which they sat. She stared at him nonplussed, the living icon she had cherished in her heart since the day he had picked her out of the river. Was it, after all, to be the great game versus domesticity? He suddenly grinned the impish smile that had endeared him to her when he had first looked up at her from the rhododendron bushes in her grandmother's garden, and she just in time stopped herself from getting angry and smacking the knee that had sustained a Turkish bullet.

'Don't be a goose, Sonya, I want to marry you. I want you beside me always. Listen, even the Viceroy couldn't pin the label of traitor on me for getting carried away for, er . . . ' he scratched his ear, 'an *affaire de coeur* . . . oh, and that's another thing, your forged little billet-doux to Younghusband at Chang Lo, with my name on, is something we have to talk about later – I look forward to your explanation. Ah! here comes father. I think it's about time my son and I got to know each other if we're to live together amicably for the rest of our lives.' Lewis got up and, limping slightly, went to meet his father and son coming along the path. He lifted the boy in his arms. 'Hello, old fellow, so nice to meet you at last. My, you're a hefty weight! It's about time, I think, we put you down for . . . the office of Dalai Lama. Let's take a look at that birth mark . . . good heavens! It's not often one gets to meet one of the heaven-born.'

Luey smiled into the eyes of the man he did not know and shyly thrust a small fist fully into his mouth, extending his other sticky hand in his mother's direction. Sonya took him, and he nestled his head contentedly in the curve of her neck. 'He's very tired, I think I ought to put him down somewhere to sleep while we have supper.'

'Mama . . . ctop-mi . . . '

'What's he saying?' asked the Rector, proud and suitably astonished that his grandson had a tongue, after all, even if it was a strange one.

'He wants a bedtime-story . . . come along then, let's go.' Lewis retrieved his Turkish walking stick from the pergola and stiffly followed Sonya and his father down the garden path to the house.

'While you two do what has to be done, I'd better warm up Maud's game pie again,' said Reverend Joyden, gaining a new lease on life as he dashed off to the kitchen, while Sonya laid her child on the couch to sleep.

'You tell him a story in Russian, Lewis, you've got to make a start somewhere.' Sonya smiled, her dimples deep with love and the release, at last, from the past three years' emptiness – she would tackle him about that later, she promised herself, and drew the curtains.

'Well now,' said Lewis, settling himself at his son's feet, 'I don't know about anything in Russian that might be of interest to you, but I have something in Tibetan your mother didn't want to know about when I wrote it. I wrote it especially for her, you see. Sonya, I always knew we'd have good-looking intelligent children, some day. Close your eyes, Luey, and we'll blow out the yak-butter lamps. Your mother can close hers too, if she promises to hold my hand while I tell you both a true story.'

Samsâra

Give me your hand through meadows sweet, on a College
    path let's wander.
Stand with me by honeyed stone, and join me in
    surrender.
But ask me not when youthful dreams, in a quill of
    golden ink,
I, in squanderlust, had lost that final tender link.
Nor, when I, beyond oriels searched, the jewel of the
    world,
To satisfy this burning thirst, before the lotus burst.
Only share with me one evensong, by a brook through
    a garden bubbling,

And shadows have rung a lonely bell to a lych-gate
   slowly crumbling.
Then come again to another glade, beneath mountains
   overwhelming:
And ask me where a nightingale's prayer
From the throat of the *djolmo* is tumbling:
And ask me why, with a nightingale's sigh,
Samsâra, the lotus, is trembling.

                  To Sonya, from Lewis, Tibet, 1903.

Glossary

Amphag	Breast pocket formed by wide dress tied by belt.
Arjopas	Pilgrims on foot, often begging for food.
Bardo	Emptiness, next world where dead go.
Chang	Beer or barley spirits.
Chorten	Tibetan monument erected to hold religious objects or remains of great departed lamas.
Dokpa	Inhabitants of solitudes/cowmen without husbandry.
Dolma	Hymn of praise to goddess *Dolma*, in Sanskrit *Tara*.
Dorjee	Bell.
Doubtob	Sage and wonder worker.
Dragpoi-Dubthab	Magic rite to bring about death or injury.
Dubchen	Great and successful one/magician.
Gelong	Lama/monk who keeps the vow of celibacy.
Geyog	Servant of Virtue.
Geyok	Novice of poor parentage whose family cannot maintain him and who does menial work at a lama's house for a living.

Gompa	Monastery/lamasery.
Gomthag	Sash used as binding and support of mystic sects who spend long hours in seated meditation. When travelling, it is worn across shoulders.
Jetsunma	Reverend Lady.
Jowa	Lord/master.
Kale Pheb	'Go slowly', polite farewell.
Kashag	Tibetan Council of government.
Khang	House.
Kudak	Nobleman.
Kyapdo	Repeated prostrations on ground during recitation of Mantra.
Lha Gyalo!	'The gods win!' An exclamation of triumph Tibetans make especially on top of passes and other summits.
Lus	Snake-gods who live in rivers and oceans, said to be owners of fabulous wealth.
Lungom	The art of flying.
Mani Padme	'A jewel in a lotus'; *Aum Mani Padme hum!*
Mi-deussa	Resting place. Stones that have been arranged by travellers with/fire for cauldron/where water can be got/ wayfarers are able to camp.
Mig kar	'White eyes'. Abusive term for foreigner.
Nagspa	Most dreaded kind of sorceror, expert in magic formulae, able to command demons and kill from afar.
Naljorma (Fem) } Naljorpa (Masc) }	One who has embraced religious life and follows mystic path and has gained serenity.
Neskorpas	Pilgrims.

415

Nemo (fem) }	Mistress of house/hostess.
Nepo (Masc) }	Master of house/host.
Pamo	Female medium thought to be possessed of demons who speak through her mouth.
Philang	Foreign devil.
Phurba	Magic dagger.
Ponpo	Chief.
Rimpoche	'Precious One'. Polite term to address lama.
Rishi	Sage possessed of supernatural powers.
Ro-gyapa	Butcher of human and animal corpses.
Rolang	Corpse that stands.
Sangar	Small stone block houses.
Shamtab	Pleated large skirt worn by lamas/monks.
Shap-és (lotus foot)	Councillors.
Siddha	Man possessed of supernatural powers.
Thumo Reskiang	Tibetan art of 'self-heating'.
Tisas	Demi-gods who feed upon odours, good or bad.
Towo	Wrathful deity.
Trapas	Real name of Lamaist monks.
Tsampa	Flour made of roasted barley. Staple food of Tibetans.
Tsawai Lama	Spiritual Father.
Tulku	An illusionary body created by magic. According to popular belief, the reincarnation of a powerful being, man or god.
Urusso	Tibetan name for Russians.
Yak	Long-haired ox of Tibet.
Yangku	Wealth and prosperity.
Yul	Country.